Wolves at Our Door

Wolves at Our Door

—w—

J. P. S. Brown

UNIVERSITY OF NEW MEXICO PRESS —w— ALBUQUERQUE

LIBRARY OF CONGRESS CATALOGING-IN-PUBLICATION DATA
Brown, J. P. S.
Wolves at our door / J.P.S. Brown.
p. cm.
ISBN 978-0-8263-4387-1 (ALK. PAPER)
1. Ranchers—Fiction.
2. Arizona—Fiction.
3. Mexico—Fiction.
I. Title.
PS3552.R6856W65 2008
813'.54—dc22

2007048257

Book and jacket design and type composition by Kathleen Sparkes
This book was composed using Palatino STD OTF 10.5/13.5, 27P
Display type is ITC Ozwald STD OTF

FOR MY WIFE PATSY

THE SONGBIRD WHO SINGS IN MY TREE

EVEN WHEN IT GETS CHOPPED DOWN

Acknowledgments

The author is grateful to former Special Forces and China Foreign Area Officer Lieutenant Colonel Greg Long (ret) and ATF officer Adam Ging whose experience and expertise in weaponry and tactics lent truth and plausibility to the raid on La Culebra. Lifelong friend Jack Ging also gave the fictitious movie actor Jack Brennan school on how to graciously charm an enemy.

One

—〰— Jim Kane did not pilot the Cessna 172 airplane he called Little Buck, he wore it like a suit of clothes. He wore it anyplace he wanted to go in the sky, and he was confident that he could set it down anywhere he wanted on the ground.

Now, he throttled down and trimmed to fly slow up the wide, dry Arroyo de los Mezcales in the Sierra Madre Occidental of Mexico to look for his partner Juan Vogel. He followed the centuries-old horseshoe thoroughfare toward the foot of the Sierra. At the head of the arroyo, the trail led into the thick brush of the foothills. He throttled up, trimmed for slow climb, and skimmed tall leafy trees along the trail. As he approached the first mountain called Las Parvas, the Flocks, he saw Juan Vogel on a switchback near the top. The man and his mule stopped and turned their faces toward him. Kane veered away at full power and climbed until he was above Vogel and out of his sight around the side of the mountain. He banked against the mountain, flushed a flock of parrots out of a thick stand of oak trees, doubled back toward Vogel, leveled his wings and hugged the mountain, cut his power to descend in a whistling glide, burst into Vogel's sight from around the shoulder of the mountain, smiled as he passed eye to eye with Vogel on his wingtip, and saw his partner's face go serious as the mule danced on the edge of the high trail with surprise. He waved and powered on and flew through Puerto de las Parvas, Pass of the Flocks, a saddle below the crest of the mountain.

Kane smiled because he was comfortable in his machine and having fun. Vogel had not smiled because he and his mule had seriously pounded each other's butts for the past four hours. Vogel needed to climb the rest of the mountain, ride another two hours over high, rocky trails, and cross a deep gorge before he caught up to Kane.

Jim Kane was seventy-five years old and Juan Vogel was eighty, and they had been partners fifty-five years. Vogel provided their partnership with Rancho el Trigo, five other ranches in the Sierra Madre of Chihuahua, and a farm at Cibolibampo on the coastal desert of Sonora. He and Kane bought cattle from other ranchers in the Sierra for export to the United States and raised native Mexican Corriente cattle. Kane provided the partnership with a ranch on the Arizona-Sonora border near Nogales where the partners also raised Corrientes.

El Trigo airstrip came in sight as Kane flew through the saddle of the Pass of the Flocks. The airstrip was at almost the same altitude as the saddle. No one who ever flew with Kane believed that the slash in the timber that could barely be seen on the horizon was an airstrip when he first showed it to them from the saddle. The four-thousand-feet-deep Arroyo Hondo gorge lay four minutes away between Las Parvas and the airstrip. The strip's top end and sides were hugged by tall ponderosa pines. The first foot of the runway lay on the very brink of a sheer cliff that fell away to the bottom of Arroyo Hondo. A dip in the middle of the strip made it look shorter than its nine-hundred-meter length. Beyond the dip, the runway sloped upward drastically to the feet of the pine trees at the end of the runway. Once a pilot committed and cut his power, he had to land because he would never be able to power on and clear the trees to go around and try again. With the tall pines on its sides and on its end, the dip, the steep climb, and its measly length, the strip looked more like a quarter-acre cornfield in dense forest than a place on which to land an airplane.

At 6:00 a.m. in that month of May 2006, Jim Kane saw that everything looked good for a landing at El Trigo. The air was calm—the only chance advantage any pilot ever enjoyed at that strip. In another hour a tailwind from the southwest would whip up and make a landing perilous for any airplane, let alone one with as little power as Little Buck. Once that tailwind began to blow, nobody landed at El Trigo, not the good pilots who had landed there before, and certainly not the ones who found themselves gazing at it with disbelief for the first time.

As Kane lined up on the strip, he looked down at the bottom of Arroyo Hondo more than forty-five hundred feet below. This was the Sierra Madre. A man could stand on the brink of the cliff on the end of the airstrip at five thousand feet and spit to the bottom of the arroyo. The spit would not touch anything but the bottom of the gorge.

Thank God, the closer I get to the strip, the bigger it looks, Kane thought. He lowered his flaps and powered off for descent. *Thank God for the stillness of the morning. Coolness goes with stillness for good landings.* He wore Little Buck to the first foot of runway on the edge of the cliff, cut all power and floated to the ground, fell into the dip on his wheels, then rolled up the hill and stopped fifty feet from the end of the strip without having to brake.

Adan Martinillo and his grandson Marco Antonio sat on top of a *trinchera*, a rock wall at the end of the runway, watched the airplane, and softly poked the wall with the spurs on their naked heels. The huaraches they wore on their bare feet were only tire-tread soles tied on with leather thongs. They held the reins of two saddled mules and one saddled horse that bugged their eyes, arched their necks, and stiffened their legs at the sight of the machine until Kane shut off the engine and the propeller fell still. The Martinillos did not move or change expression until Kane climbed out of the airplane.

Kane had not seen them for a year and a half. He embraced them in turn with pats on the back and murmured his greeting with theirs. Kane saw that Martinillo had not taken on any weight or gray hair. Inside Kane's embrace, the sixty-five-year-old was stout and strong as a green oak stump. Marco Antonio had grown longer legged, broader shouldered, and more muscular. He was only seventeen and would keep growing. His face still belonged to the little boy Kane had known since birth. He looked more like the men of his mother's family than Martinillo. He was lighter complexioned and taller than his grandfather, a handsome youngster who knew his trails in that Sierra the way Kane's grandchildren knew the streets of their cities. Kane had already done something about that. Two of his grandchildren knew the Sierra well, because they often visited it with him.

Eighteen months before, a saddle horse had fallen off a mountain with the seventy-three-year-old Kane and rolled over him several times on the way to the bottom. Kane's brain, liver, lung, kidney, and spleen had been bruised, a shoulder broken, his knee and tailbone shattered. When he and the horse stopped rolling, he found that his foot was caught underneath the horse in a broken stirrup, so he held the horse down on top of himself until his friend Andres "the Lion" Cañez found him a day later. The effort he made to save himself from being dragged to death by the horse nearly finished him. He lay close to death in the hospital for two weeks.

The *abrazos* and pats on the back that the Martinillos gave him when he arrived at the airstrip showed that they were plenty glad to have him back. The feat of landing an airplane again at El Trigo also made him feel good, made him feel that he was on his way to make a hand as a horseman and a cowman again.

To get around the sentiment that he and the Martinillos felt at his return, Kane walked up to the three-year-old chestnut stud named Gato that carried his saddle. The colt was the best of a band of good lookers that Kane and Vogel raised at El Trigo and would be their next herd sire.

The band of horses into which Gato had been foaled had never walked on a level pasture or a soft trail. They knew how to make their living in heat, brush, and jungle at sea level, and they knew the high, cold, pine forests. They had never seen a painted wooden fence or a field carpeted only with sweet green grass, never drunk anywhere but in a running stream or a stagnant tank, never sheltered themselves anywhere but in the lee of a hill or under the branches of a tree or in a shady canyon. They knew to protect themselves from barbwire, cactus, and thickets with spines like scimitars. They knew all the *voladeros* of their *querencias*, their haunts, the high, deadly places on the trails where cattle and horses, deer and javelina lost their footing and flew to their deaths into the canyons. They knew how to pick their way like goats to feed on steep, rocky aprons on the sides of mountains. They knew to watch and listen for *el tigre*, the jaguar, and *el león pardo*, the tawny lion, when they dipped their heads to drink, to graze, to browse, or to rest.

So Kane and the Martinillos considered it a sort of miracle that day when he finally was able to walk up and admire Gato the stud. Kane did not have a scar on him to show that a horse had fallen off a fifty-foot cliff with him, and Gato did not have a scar or a blemish on his sleek hide to show for the three years that he had run free in the Sierra Madre. Two miracles.

"*Bueno*, the horse came through his bronco youth in fine condition, didn't he?" Kane said.

"Yes, Jim, like you," Martinillo said, and he and his grandson laughed softly.

"You've put my saddle on him, so I guess I'm the one who will have to ride him away from here."

"*Seguro*. Of course. Who else could be the horseman for El Gato?"

"His *jinete* who broke and trained him, I suppose," Kane said.

"Trained him, that's all. He has only been dominated to the extent that he's gentle to the touch of a man of proper temperament. He has been trained to the extent that your touch on the rein will cause him to turn and stick his ears into his own tail, if you want him to. Who knows how a lesser man would get along with him?"

"And who has broken him gentle as a dog with such a rein on him? You, Adan?"

"No, my duties with El Trigo cattle kept me from it. I don't have the touch that this horse required and deserved in his training. Marco Antonio is the horseman in our family. His touch can cool a fever. His heel only bends the hair without touching the skin of a saddle horse."

"You, Marco Antonio?" Kane asked. "Did he buck?"

"No, thank God, for he is the Cat," Marco Antonio said. "If he ever decided to buck, no man could ride him. I could have cheated him by riding him in the corral, but I rode him outside from the first day. Nothing but my hand has ever turned him."

"Ahhh, that's a good way to start a horse. He's had the best, then."

"Juan Vogel told us about your fall. He told us that he gave you his half interest in the horse while you were in and out of consciousness in the hospital, to prove his faith in your recovery. I knew he would have to be gentle when you came for him. When the horse saw how much I wanted him to surrender his wildness, I swear, he taught himself to be gentle. He made himself my friend. He's also the friend of my sister Luci.

My grandmother has ridden him and loves him. Sometimes all three of us get on him. You might hurt your sore and broken places in a thousand ways again in this Sierra, but this horse will not be the cause."

Adan Martinillo's Las Animas ranch lay at the bottom end of Arroyo Hondo where it joined Arroyo de los Mezcales. Martinillo also worked as the mayordomo of El Trigo cattle. He was one of the few decent men who had stayed in the Sierra when drug traffickers invaded the region.

He was a good vaquero and cowman, afraid of no man, and famous as a hunter of predators. People who knew him swore that he could follow a track by scent as well as any hound. Although he did not claim to be that good, he could explain his tenacity and success as a tracker and hunter no other way. He could track a lion, jaguar, or wolf across a league of smooth rock. When a predator invaded his region and threatened livestock and human life, Martinillo suspended his other duties and went after him.

When he first met Jim Kane, he owned only a single-shot .22 rifle. With that rifle and only four rounds of ammunition, he tracked down and killed El Yoco, a full-grown jaguar that had come into the country to kill livestock and had killed at least one person.

When the drug growers arrived in the country with Uzi machine guns that they called *cuernos de chivo*, the horns of a goat, an army cavalry troop had confiscated all the firearms on the ranches. Martinillo's .22 single-shot had been taken. A week later Kane smuggled in three new Winchester .22 magnum lever action carbines with five hundred cartridges apiece. Kane, Vogel, and Martinillo each had one. In that same load he brought three Remington 12-gauge pump shotguns with two hundred shells of oo buckshot for each gun. Those arms were kept hidden but always at hand.

The ranch families of the Sierra had been at war against the drug traffickers of Sinaloa for thirty years. Most of the decent people had moved to the cities and abandoned their ranches to the intruders, although some youngsters and men stayed to fight. Martinillo had not been a youngster when the war began, but he stayed. His wife Lucrecia, oldest grandson Marco Antonio, and youngest granddaughter Luci also stayed, but his three sons had migrated with their families to the coastal desert of Sonora.

The intruders from Sinaloa came heavily armed and began to till any land they could find beside active, hidden watercourses for marijuana and opium poppy crops, regardless of who owned the land. Owners the intruders did not kill were officially denounced to the government in Chihuahua City as drug growers. The intruders used the drug crops that they planted on the ranches as evidence against the owners. The crooked officials put the owners in the penitentiary and the invaders went on and raised the crops unmolested. One hundred and seventy-five ranch owners and young men native to the region had been killed in the war since it began in 1975. Adan Martinillo's son Robe, the father of Marco Antonio and Luci, had been murdered on the trail as he returned to Las Animas one night with a pack string of provisions. At present, native sons had driven away most of the intruders, but this lull in the war was not expected to continue.

While Kane and the Martinillos waited for Juan Vogel, Martinillo told Kane that recently a man named Arturo Mendez, a well-known liar and thief and errand boy for the Lupinos, had visited Martinillo to talk about harvesting timber after he had patrolled the region in a helicopter. He said that trees were being cut on the neighboring La Golondrina ranch that belonged to the Lupino family.

"How did Arturo Mendez say the logs would be transported to a mill?" Kane asked. "The nearest mills are at Creel and Madera. Creel lies four hundred kilometers across trackless Sierra from here. La Golondrina is five hundred kilometers from Madera or Creel. Roads could not be built to access those mills in less than fifteen years."

"Arturo said a helicopter will transport the logs off the mountain to the nearest road where trucks can pick them up," Martinillo said.

"I don't think so," Kane said. "It would cost more to skid one log off any of these mountains with a helicopter than it would to build ten big, comfortable houses on El Trigo or Las Animas."

Martinillo kept a straight face and spoke in a soft voice, no matter how passionate he might feel about the stories he told, but Kane could see he did not care one dirty damn about helicopters or logs. "Anyway, I don't think Arturo Mendez was here to talk about logs," he said.

"What did he really want?" Kane asked.

"To do an evil thing."

"What was that?"

"To release wolves in our country."

"No. What do you mean?"

Marco Antonio laughed. "My grandfather tracked the helicopter."

Martinillo smiled. "No, but when it flew over my house from the direction of Guasisaco at the same hour for three straight days, I decided to see if I could find where it came from. I marked the spot I first caught sight of it each day, then waited for it at that spot the next day. I finally saw that it came from the direction of La Golondrina every day, hovered over the high ridge of Guasisaco awhile, then flew on past my house. I searched the ridge and found that it had landed on the *devisadero* of Guasisaco, the place everybody uses as a lookout point."

"What did you read in the tracks?" Kane asked.

"Men in the helicopter released five wolves. They linger there. They don't want to leave."

"They've probably been raised in a cage and don't know how to make a living here."

"That's what I think. I went back to watch them twice. Four females and a male, all young. I saw them again day before yesterday. They were gaunt and shrunken as though they had not found water."

"They'll find water soon enough. Then they'll find cattle to eat."

"That's what I think."

"Sure, they've been raised in cages, so they've been fed beef. The first animal they kill will be a cow. They'll tear off her udder on the run, then devour her alive from tail to throat."

"Why would anyone visit us with that kind of evil?"

"I can't give you a good reason, only that some people don't have enough real work to do, so they entertain themselves with the idea that the world needs wolves to prowl cow country again."

"That's the reason they release wolves here?"

"Probably. What were the markings on the helicopter? Did it show a number?"

Martinillo opened the palm of his hand and handed Kane a slip of paper. "I memorized the numbers and wrote them down when I got home," he said.

Kane took it. "With this I might find out who it belongs to," he said.

"I think it belongs to the Lupinos."

"What makes you think so?"

"It came from that direction every day to keep track of the animals. It flew back toward La Golondrina. I've seen helicopters fly out of La Golondrina before, although I never thought to write down their numbers."

"They're from La Golondrina," Marco Antonio said. "I was riding circle on the cattle at Guazaremos on those days that my grandfather tracked the helicopter. It flew over me from the direction of La Golondrina every day, and later it flew back and the sound of its motor stopped at La Golondrina."

"Why would the Lupinos set wolves on us?" Kane asked.

"You will have a chance to ask the old man. His grandson Ibrahim came to Guazaremos last week to tell me that they have gathered the three hundred yearlings you and my compadre Juan have come to get. There's another thing," Martinillo said.

"What?" Kane asked.

"They're not wolves."

"What do you mean?"

"They don't look like wolves to me. They're more like dogs. My compadre Vogel might know what they are by now. He said he would try to find out more about them."

"If they're not wolves, what do you think they are?"

"Some animal somebody thinks are wolves. They don't look like the ancient savage that I know as a wolf."

Juan Vogel appeared at the end of the airstrip on his mule, single footed on to the wall where his friends waited, stopped, lit a cigarette with a kitchen match that he struck alive on his saddle horn, and said, "What *chingado* kinds of destruction have you three plotted while you waited here for me? You, Marco Antonio, tell me what my compadres have cooked up."

"Nothing, Godfather. They've been good."

"I told Jim about the wolves," Martinillo said. "Did you find out where they came from, compadre?"

"Maybe," Vogel said. "The secretary of the Unión Ganadera de Chihuahua told me that somebody raises them in Parral and sells most of them to somebody in the U.S. They're a mix of wolf and some other animal. The animals you saw might come from Parral. Anybody can buy them.

"And you, Jim. What did you do, track me in that airplane to Las Parvas Mountain? Do you think you could have come any closer to me with the buzz saw on that machine? Did you have to look right down into the bottom of my tracks?"

"I only wanted to see if you still had cigarettes."

"If I hadn't, would you have circled back and given me a package?"

"I gave it some thought."

"*Malhaya*. You blew hot air into my mule Negrito's ear."

"Didn't you notice how considerate I was? I cut all sound before I passed you by so as not to bother your mule. Quiet as a snake, I was."

"Except for the quiet little scream you made . . . the little wind that screamed as you slipped by. That was not good."

"I had to see if you were all right."

"Next time, I'll wave to you from a league away. *¿Qué tal?* What's going on? What do you want to do now? Shall we ride to Lupino's tonight, or wait until tomorrow?"

"You've been on that mule, how long, six hours?"

"I started early so we could go on to La Golondrina today. Lupino expects us, but it's up to you. It's eight hours from here. You and I have ridden farther than that hung over, but that was before the horse landed on you. Can you ride that far, or don't you plan to go with me?"

"I can ride and I'm going."

"Then you've been on a horse since your accident and you're in shape for an eight-hour ride? What will you ride?"

Kane pointed to Gato.

"I saw him there, but can you ride a bronco after that other bronco rearranged your gizzards for you?"

"Of course."

"Gato's gentle," Marco Antonio said.

"But he's a three-year-old and he's never carried a man eight hours, has he?"

"He can do it," Marco Antonio said. "He won't tire. He won't even draw a long breath."

"Nesib Lupino wants to buy the horse, so you might as well ride him to La Golondrina if you can, Jim," Martinillo said.

"What's this I hear from Martinillo?" Kane asked Juan Vogel. "You gave me your half interest in Gato when I was in the hospital?"

"I gave him to you the first time I went to see you. Don't you remember?"

"I'm sorry, I don't."

"Lupino wants to buy him, so if you want to sell him, you can get a lot of money. Lupino is desperate to have him. He expects you to bring him the horse, so I told Martinillo to have him here for you to ride. When Lupino wants something he does not worry about the price. After all, he has more money than the treasury department."

"He wants everything he sees. I bet he saw Gato once, then heard Marco Antonio was breaking him, so he wants him now. The minute he sees something good of ours, he wants it. He wants my horse? I'll have some fun and dangle him under his nose, but I'll never sell him."

"Adan brought your mule Paseador, if you'd rather ride him. It's up to you. He's a lot more gentle."

"No, I can ride the horse."

"Well, if you're in shape to ride, Jim, let's go."

Kane had not said that he was in shape. He only said that he could do it. Eight hours on a green horse would hurt, but he wanted to do it. He had to start making a hand again, or have a look at the end of his life. He tightened the cinches on his saddle and led Gato in a circle. He led him to the rock wall, climbed clumsily on the wall, and mounted him. "Pardon the way I get on," he said. "I can either embarrass myself by getting on the horse the easiest way, or I can embarrass myself more by reaching for the stirrup from the ground on weak legs and hauling myself into the saddle with weak arms, grunts, and gasps."

"*No hay cuidado*, no problem, Jim," Vogel said. "You're with the three people who worried most that you would never mount another horse."

"Maybe I'll do it better in another week," Kane said.

"No, how can you say a week?" Martinillo said as he fussed with Gato's bridle. "A chore that would take someone else a week to do will take Jim Kane only a day or two."

"Ay, Jim," Vogel said. "Are you sure you want to do this? Your joints must creak like an old wagon."

"It's only because they're rusty," Kane said. "How can that be a problem? I'll have three hundred leagues of rock wall between here and La Golondrina to stand on when I want to mount my horse. It's only the getting on that's hard. Once I'm on, I'm good. Don't you want to get off Negrito and rest awhile before we go, compadre?"

"Not necessary," Vogel said.

"Let's go, then."

Two

Martinillo and Marco Antonio said they would ride along with Kane and Vogel as far as Vogel's headquarters at El Trigo. Vogel had scraped a jeep road from the airstrip to his hacienda with oxen and a Fresno, so the trail was wide enough for riders two abreast. Kane and Marco Antonio rode side by side behind Martinillo and Vogel.

Kane knew that Marco Antonio probably wanted to ask him about his granddaughter Dolly Ann Kane, who was about his age. He might start by asking about her brother Cody Joe.

"Nino Jim, I guess you noticed that I'm riding your mule Paseador," Marco Antonio said. He called Kane "Nino" because Kane had sponsored him when he received the sacrament of confirmation in the Catholic Church.

"I'm glad you are," Kane said.

"We needed to bring him in case we found that you were still too damaged to ride Gato. My grandfather said that you would want to ride Gato, so I put your saddle on him. Paseador was the only other animal in the corral for me to ride. I told my grandfather I would rather walk than presume to ride your mule. I never ride him. My grandfather does."

"Ride him. He has to earn his keep. The best way to ruin a mule is to make a *consentido* of him, a pet. A mule that isn't worked regularly will spoil on his own juices, and the man who goes sweet on him deserves the kick in the slats a juicy mule will give him."

"I've saved some money and would like to buy Paseador, if you would consider selling him, Nino."

"I ought to give him to you, Marco Antonio, but he was a gift from don Nesib Lupino. As much as I would like you to have him, I wouldn't want don Nesib to hear that I would rather have money than his gift."

"I understand. I thought you and Nino Juan bought these mules from don Nesib."

"No, he gave me Paseador and gave Negrito to your nino Juan at the same time. He said he wanted to make sure we would have a way to visit him at La Golondrina."

"I understand."

"But ride him all you want when I'm not here. I'll tell your grandfather that he's yours to ride from now on."

Kane thought, *Now the young button will have worked up the courage to ask about Cody Joe. By doing that he hopes he might find out if he will get to see Dolly Ann this summer. How well I remember the way a boy thinks. How he must long to find out about the girl of his dreams. All of a sudden he finds himself side by side with the one person who can tell him everything about the girl. He thinks I'm ignorant of his awful desire for news of her, that I don't realize how blessed I am to know everything about her. He's sure he'll have to trick me into giving him information about her because I need to protect her from young men. He wants news of her so much, his heart is about to wring itself out of his chest, so let's see how long he can stand it before he comes right out and asks for all the real news of her. She's been gone from the Sierra a year and a half, so he's probably dedicated all his bedtime thoughts to her for at least the past five hundred nights.*

"And . . . will Cody Joe come to the Sierra this summer?" Marco Antonio asked. The flush on the kid's cheeks was shot through with bloodless streaks, as though the question had pinched the pink out of his face.

"Cody Joe has joined the military service, but he's been given a month's leave. He'll come home to the 7X ranch in a few days to help brand the calves. After that I'll bring him here. Today is the fifteenth of May?"

"*¿Sepa la fregada?* How the heck would I know?" Marco Antonio growled softly, then smiled. Nobody in the Sierra kept track of the days of the week, or the dates. Kane liked the boy's answer. So what if he did not know the day, or the date? He knew the work he had to do and how to do it. Kane relented. "I'll bring Dolly Ann too. She wants to come and visit your sister Luci. Do you think that would be all right? I guess they exchanged letters all this time."

"Do you speak of La Muñeca?" Marco Antonio asked, as though Dolly Ann had not been in his thoughts at all.

"Yes, when I say Dolly Ann, I mean La Muñeca. Don't you think the name fits the girl?"

"*¿Sepa la fregada?* That person's been gone from here so long that I probably don't know her anymore. She might have grown hair on her face by now, for all I know."

"Ah, believe me, she has not grown hair on her face. Didn't Luci read you her letters?"

"No, hombre. I saw only the outside of the letters, was only privileged to carry them to Luci from time to time. Luci and La Muñeca together are strangers to the rest of the world. What has La Muñeca done with herself, besides write letters to my sister and exclude me from her life?"

"She wants to be a professional boxer. She's good at it, but I hope she doesn't make a career of it."

"A boxer? Did you say *boxeadora*? How can she be a boxer? She's a girl."

"It's my fault. I've taught Dolly Ann and Cody Joe how to box since they could make fists."

"I know you were a boxer, Jim. My grandfather saw you fight in Navojoa. He said you knocked out all your opponents except the Buffalo."

"A long time ago."

"But why teach a girl to box?"

"Girls' boxing is popular as a sport in the United these days, but I didn't teach La Muñeca so she could compete. I taught her so she could defend herself from cowards who attack girls." People in Mexico commonly referred to the United States simply as "United," so that is what Kane said too.

Marco Antonio smiled. "I don't know boxing, but it's hard to believe

La Muñeca could stop any man from hurting her if he really wanted to. The last time I saw her she was only a skinny, long-legged little girl with arms like sticks."

"Well, she's filled out, and make no mistake, she's learned to wing punches from every angle. She can hit a man five times with all her weight behind it before he can even blink an eye."

"Imagine that," Marco Antonio said, still smiling. "I might believe it of some of the mud hens I know, but never of the blonde doll."

Kane realized that the boy knew only a little more about boxing than Kane knew about medieval sorcery. In that part of the Sierra Madre children only had their lariats to play with and knew little about organized sports like baseball, boxing, soccer, or basketball. Most had never even seen a sporting contest.

"Where will La Muñeca go to fight, if she becomes a boxer?" Marco Antonio asked. "Will you and Cody Joe help her do that? I would think you would try to prevent it."

"What can I say? She wants to be a champion in the sport, and I think she's good enough. If she makes it a career, I guess her brother and I will have to help her."

"Where are her parents? What do they think about it?"

"I thought you knew. They died in a plane wreck twelve years ago. I guess you were too little to remember. I've been her father and mother these last five years since my wife Adelita died."

"No wonder she's a boxer. I wonder what my Nina, my godmother, Adelita would have thought of La Muñeca becoming a boxer."

"Don't get the wrong idea. The doll can cook, look beautiful, and be a lady too."

"Won't she have to get tough as a javelina to be a boxer?"

"I won't let that happen."

"What if something happens to you and Cody Joe? Who will protect her, look out for her?"

Kane thought about it. Where would the girl be safe, here in the Sierra with Kane, the wolves, and the drug growers; at the 7X ranch on the border with Kane and the drug and human traffickers; or as a boxer alone in a big city? How safe was a girl boxer in New York, Los Angeles, or Las Vegas? "That's a good question, boy," he said.

After Adelita died and left him alone to raise their grandchildren, Kane had found that he was not good at it. They were too smart and quick for him. He was too soft and vulnerable to their little cruelties to be their taskmaster. He discovered that they needed a taskmaster of the kind that Adelita had been. He could not make them do his bidding as he had his own son, their father. They kept him on a tether and worked him like an old, gentle mule.

One day they had discovered his boxing scrapbook and after that wanted him to watch and explain boxing on TV and kept after him to coach them. He knew it would be a way for him to control them on the kind of gentle rein that he needed to hold if he was to raise them the way he wanted, so he put them in training. He had boxed twenty-two years, in grammar school, high school, university, the Marine Corps, and as a professional. Boxing had always been a refuge for him, a discipline that kept him ready to meet any kind of travail, not only opponents in the ring. He had gained and kept full control of his two hoodlums after that, and they did not even realize how he did it, did not seem to know that he had become the maestro of their fates. He loved that, but so did they.

With Kane's help and boxing, his grandchildren learned self-respect and respect for everyone else who deserved it. They had learned self-confidence and the real value of courage. They had learned that life is full of everyday contests that can bloody and often defeat a person, unless he or she could find the strength to throw one more bucketful of effort into the fray to gain a victory, or at least to survive. They also learned that they could get up and try again when their last bucketful had been thrown in and they had been felled. They learned that they had to get a bloody nose to learn boxing. They learned that everyone had the option to stay in a conflict until it was over, whether or not they remained standing at the end. To stay in until the end of the contest was always preferable to being a quitter. Boxing had been Kane's way of showing them how to do right, and they loved the training. It helped his lot as a grandfather even more when they proved themselves to have talent and developed into first-class fighters with verve, class, and style.

The only trouble that Dolly Ann faced in becoming a champion boxer was the dearth of opponents available to her while she developed her talent. Cody Joe was her only sparring partner. He had found plenty of opponents in grade school and high school and would find more in the Marine Corps. He had already won several amateur championships and outstanding boxer awards.

Dolly would bloody his nose if he did not watch it. He had to be careful not to bloody hers, and that put his nose in more danger. She could always outpoint him, not only because she was a better boxer, but because he held back and did not use his power on her. He knew his range and was in command of it. He could unleash a straight right hand or a jab with power and speed that would only tap his sister way out on the tip of her nose. He did not find it as easy to hook her without hurting her when she was in range of bent-arm blows, and he could not keep her at arm's length forever. She was extremely canny about slipping inside his straight-arm blows and peppering him with combinations of hooks and uppercuts, and she never held back. He told her not to hold back, and then she made him sorry.

Kane had only been able to find four lady opponents for Dolly in Arizona and New Mexico, but he and she had run them down and put on exhibitions with them for Elks Clubs, Veterans Clubs, and church fund-raisers so she could have the necessary ring experience in front of crowds of people. To put on exhibitions was a good way for her to stand up and show her stuff the way all boxers have to do, because it was the final discipline for her display of poise, patience, and pace. Exhibitions forced her to control her power. Nobody won an exhibition and no one should try to use it to do anything but put on a good show of the "Sweet Science." Participants should come away from an exhibition feeling equally victorious for the show they put on.

Now that Kane found himself horseback in the Sierra again, he remembered how far away in another world his grandchildren were and how lonesome he could be without them. Their increasing ambitions, activities, sweethearts, and institutions kept them away from him. Kane counted himself lucky that he would have them for the next month. Since his wife Adelita had died, his days were good only when he was with his friends and animals or his grandchildren. Kane counted far too much on keeping them close.

Adelita would know how he felt, would stand in the way of her granddaughter becoming a professional boxer, all right, but she would probably tell him that for now he should try to make a hand again with this man Vogel. He would have to stop crippling along in his thoughts. Put all that boo hoo lonesome and worry about little girls becoming boxers behind. Pay attention to the fine animal he rode today after a year and a half of lying on his back. Think and act healthy as a horse again.

He looked up and his daydream had carried him past Rancho El Trigo and the Martinillos had already turned back. He began to think like a cowboy again and appreciate where he was. He sat aboard the best animal in the region, maybe in the whole Republic of Mexico. He rode in the company of the best man and the best friend of his life. He was lucky to find himself again inside the heartbeat of the mountains he loved best and knew well, even though they were unknown to almost all other men. He knew how to be a man, have some style and a lot of fun, and that had got him here. The big hole in him from the horse fall would heal shut. He would perform his duties one by one, as they came. First, sit up on the horse and pay attention to him.

He looked down at Gato's thick, graceful neck and the lights in his coat and realized how well the horse filled his legs. The horse moved as though the two-hundred-pound man he carried was not even there. Kane would have to ride a week before he found his old seat on the horse. This colt owned the power and the action to unseat him with one breath, but he stayed under the man, careful of every step. He made no quick moves and gave Kane his every consideration, as a gentle veteran would.

A three-year-old could be expected to panic, lunge, and fall when his foot slipped on smooth rock, but Gato did not. At the slick places he shifted into lower gear and crawled like a tractor until he left them behind. He knew what happened when feet skidded on high trails, and he did not like it. Kane's top horse Pajaro had been like that. Pajaro was the only other horse that Kane ever knew that learned it on his own. He had been so surefooted that he negotiated every *laja*, smooth rock slab, of every trail of his entire life, in the dark, in rainstorms, in snowstorms, on downhill runs, on steep uphill pulls, without a slide or a fall.

The horse that had fallen off the cliff with Kane had skidded on a slab of smooth, steep bedrock that Pajaro would have stepped over and not even touched. The horse had slipped a little, then panicked, then lunged, then fallen. Those four predictable steps that could befall an ordinary horse on a high trail had been realized, to Kane's misfortune.

Kane had been positive that he would never see another mountain and rock horse like Pajaro. If Gato turned out to be as good, he would be another miraculous gift from God to Jim Kane. Gato was from the same stock as Pajaro. Pajaro's sire was Gato's great-grandfather, the great chestnut stud called Tiger that had belonged to Kane's father.

Kane and Vogel paused on the ridge of Guasisaco and looked down into the canyons, ravines, and cordons of mountains below. Their horses stood on the high spine that marked the border between Chihuahua on their right and Sonora on their left. They sat their horses in pine forest at five thousand feet and could see the Mayo River at only five hundred feet above sea level at least twenty miles away. A flock of green parrots skimmed the canopy of trees below them at Rancho El Limón, where the buildings of the Vogel family's first hacienda had been erected in 1870.

Kane and Vogel rode down the steep slope past El Limón to the trail above Arroyo de Teguaraco, on through verdant tunnels that had been slashed by machete through *vainoro* thickets to Gilaremos, then made a detour over long stretches of smooth rock in the canyon below Guazaremos to see if their cattle had salt. They rode back out and stopped at Guazaremos to visit with the branding crew that was glad to see Kane horseback again. They forded the blue water of the Mayo River at midafternoon and followed it upstream into the Sierra de la Golondrina. An hour after sundown, they reached Puerto la Golondrina, the gateway to the ranch, and rode down into the bowl where the Lupino hacienda lay.

They waved to a one-armed watchman who sat on the porch of his house high on a promontory below the pass. The hacienda was surrounded on three sides by a five-hundred-foot escarpment of sheer cliffs. The sentry waved back and called them by name. His wife and small children came out and waved too.

"He's got Toribio up there now," Kane said. "Since when?"

"I guess the old watchman Balbanedo got too blind to watch," Vogel said. "Toribio only has one arm from the horse fall, so he's a watchman now. See, Jim, you could have lost your arm like Toribio."

"The nosedive that horse and I took off the trail could have been worse, no? Maybe then you could have retained me at El Trigo."

"We'll never see that day, compadre."

The swallows of La Golondrina that nested in the escarpment were at work and play in the sky above the bowl. The trail widened and the men rode side by side. They passed an acre of a newly sprouted *verano*, vegetable garden, and a large field of young corn.

Lupino hailed them from the veranda of his house in the bottom of the bowl. *"Hua. Aaaahuuuaaa,"* he howled. The partners could see his smile a quarter mile away.

"Why does the old thing act so glad to see us?" Kane asked.

"Because nobody else ever visits him," Vogel said. "He hasn't got another friend in the world."

"I've always wondered, how come we're his only friends?"

"Because after all the years that he has entrusted us with his cattle, he considers us part of his family, as he considers his horses and cattle to be close family. I think he loves his Arabian horses more than he does his daughter and four grandsons."

"He does love his Arabians. I'm sure we'll be given another tour of the stable."

"How many times have we driven his young bulls away from here without paying for them, Jim?"

"Not for a long time, but in the beginning, many times."

"We always come ready to pay, but to help us he always tells us to first find out what we can get for them, then to pay him what they are worth. Right?"

"He's tried to be good about that, even though we only took his cattle on the credit a time or two when we were young. We always take the cattle on faith, but send him his money within a day or two."

"That's right. He's wanted to keep the transaction a kind one between friends. He's wanted to trust us. You ever wonder why?"

"Of course. His livestock has to be sold every year, but he hates to see it leave home. It eases his heart to put it in our hands."

"Exactly. He trusts us, and every year he makes sure of us by offering to let us take his cattle on faith. It eases his betrayal of his darlings, his consentidos. He feels like a traitor for sending them away to market. He likes us for doing it for him, but he has to like us, or it would hurt too much."

"Well, we've always known that we weren't the only ones who hated to see our livestock sold and driven away."

"No, Jim. You and Nesib Lupino are the only ones I know who almost cry when your calves and colts leave the ranch."

"Don't tell me that, Juan. You're more sentimental about the livestock than any of us. You think I haven't watched you gentle down more every day as you drive them closer to market? You're gentler to your calves on market day than a mother cow with an udder full of milk. You practically snuggle up to them when it's time to say good-bye."

"You're old and sentimental, Jim. Are you sure that horse didn't fall on your heart? Is it sore and oh-so-very sensitive now from that fall?" Vogel chuckled at his own wit.

At that moment, Kane saw something very different in the landscape ahead. "Ay, look," he said. "Stop here and light a cigarette, and I'll show you something."

"Why? What for?"

"Just stop to light a cigarette, and I'll show you something the old Lupino would never want us to see."

Vogel stopped. While he took cigarettes and matches out of his pocket, Kane said, "Now, while you light your cigarette, look ahead from under your hat and tell me what you see ten meters from here on your side of the trail."

Vogel lit his cigarette and looked over his cupped hands. "Ahhh," he said. "It's already so tall? I thought the old man planted his poppies later. That is a sprig of an *amapola*, is it not?"

"That's what I see. It might be too early in the season for his crop to be that size, but he didn't plant that sprout. Somebody accidentally dropped a seed there."

"You're right, but why hasn't the old villain cut it down, or transplanted it inside the rest of his crop?"

"Why would he have to? Nobody visits him."

"I guess you're right. See, he trusts us not to tell anyone what we see when we come to get his cattle, as he has trusted us for twenty years to help sell his horses."

Twenty years ago, Lupino had sent his grandson Ibrahim with a crew to the El Trigo hacienda to build a row of stables and paddocks. At that time he was ready to sell his first crop of Arabian colts but did not want buyers to come on his ranch. Without asking Kane and Vogel, he decided to use El Trigo as a site to show his colts to the buyers. That way he did not have to see the buyers take his beloved horses away, and they did not come on his ranch where they might see stray poppy sprouts, or anything else he did not want them to see.

Nesib Lupino had grown poppies on La Golondrina and harvested their opium gum for sixty years. Everyone in the Sierra knew it. Juan Vogel and Jim Kane were the only people he treated as friends. He communicated only with them when he wanted to buy or sell livestock. However, nobody, not even Vogel and Kane, ever visited La Golondrina uninvited. Government and state policemen had disappeared when they visited the ranch uninvited. Some reappeared, but in highly agitated states. The *serranos*, people of the Sierra, knew to stay away from the Lupino empire.

Nesib Lupino's father had emigrated to Mexico and the Sierra Madre from the Middle East. No one knew why one Arab horseman had fled so far into one of the most obscure regions of the continent before he came to ground. Nesib had only been out of the Sierra Madre six times in the past fifty years. He did not like for his ranch and livestock, especially his Arabian horses, to be out of his sight. He had traveled to the Middle East twice and to Rio Alamos on the coast of the Sea of Cortez in Sonora four times in those fifty years. In the Middle East he bought pure Arabian stallions and mares that he brought home. He had visited Rio Alamos more recently because two of his grandsons lived and ran the family produce, trucking, fishing, aviation, shipping, agriculture, and hardware businesses there.

His grandsons did business all over the world but flew back to La Golondrina every month to report to him. They were millionaires, but they had to land at the El Trigo airstrip in a single engine airplane with their hearts in their throats and then ride eight hours on mules to La Golondrina every week.

The terrain in the bowl of La Golondrina was plenty big and level enough for a two-thousand-meter airstrip, but Lupino vowed that no airplane would ever land there as long as he lived. Horseshoe trails would be the only access to La Golondrina. Horses and mules would always be the prime movers for all Lupinos, no matter how many fishing boats, ocean liners, and flying boxcars they owned.

Lupino's oldest grandson Ibrahim, who was married, worked as mayordomo of the ranch and was as devoted to it as his grandfather. He had everything in common with Kane and Vogel. He was younger, but had known them all his life, but he remained reserved and formal when he dealt with them.

Lupino had always been hospitable and chivalrous in a way that reminded Kane of Bedouins he read about. He was 100 percent serrano, steeped in the lore of that country, but also well versed in his Arab heritage. He liked to discuss horsemanship and Arab horse traditions that cowboys, vaqueros, and the Moors of Spain and Africa shared.

As the partners rode into the yard at the main house, the old man made people scramble to prepare for his guests. Young servant girls and old men and women retainers hurried back and forth on the veranda at his orders.

Softly, Kane said, "I'd like to know where he grows his poppies. In all the years we've come here, I've never even seen a flower."

"Shhh, he'll hear you," Vogel said. "I don't think he lets them flower. He harvests the gum from the bulbs before they bloom."

Then they were too close for Kane to say more. An old retainer held Gato and Negrito as the partners dismounted. "Take their mounts to the stable and fill them with corn and hay, Filomeno," Lupino ordered the old servant softly. He did not look away from the faces of his guests. He opened his arms and embraced them both and patted their backs, then stood back and beamed at them as though they might be the last sunrise he would ever see. They enjoyed the sight of him too, even though they knew the hardness of his heart. He had always been open and hospitable as though he considered himself to be their good friend, and they liked it, especially because they knew that people who met with his disfavor flat disappeared. Nobody could say he murdered them, because none of the *desaparecidos* ever even left a shoestring behind as evidence to link their corpses to La Golondrina.

A troop of army cavalry usually made an appointment and rode in to inquire at La Golondrina for folk that disappeared in the region. After Lupino made sure that the ordinary soldiers were comfortable and contained in the front yard, he would invite the commander into his home, give him a drink, and offer to give his troop a half of a beef. After the commander stated the reason for his visit, that a visitor to the region had disappeared, Lupino would say solicitously, "I will make inquiries and watch for the unfortunate myself." With that, the commander knew it was time to mount his troop, leave, and not look back. To whom would Lupino make inquiries? His nearest neighbors were the Vogels and their crew at El Trigo, thirty miles of horseshoe trail away.

Each small village of the Sierra owned a constable who almost never left the village, but held police authority over thousands of square miles of wilderness. Mounted soldiery patrolled the mountains periodically. News by word of mouth passed through the Sierra quicker than it had when Kane and Vogel maintained a telephone network that covered almost every ranch in their municipality of Chinipas, Chihuahua. The Sinaloa intruders had torn down the telephone line and the partners got used to communicating without it again and did not rebuild it. They were able to receive and send messages to the coast by radio fast enough for their needs. The only discipline of law or behavior that was constant in the Sierra came from the goodness taught the children by their families. This was the discipline that had always existed, before the telephone line, before constables, and before army patrols. People of that municipality were even too isolated to have a church. Priests' visits to the Sierra were as rare as tours by old ladies from Ohio. The people did not even know the function of a Catholic priest. Maybe once every five years one might visit to tell them that he could legalize their baptisms and marriages, if they wanted it. The grace of the sacraments administered by the Catholic Church would probably visit Saturn before they came to be known and appreciated by the serranos of the municipality of Chinipas.

As Filomeno, Lupino's servant, started to lead the partners' mounts toward the stables, Lupino looked at them again and said, "Whoa, what *bestia*, saddle horse, is that?"

"That's Jim's horse Gato," Juan Vogel said proudly. As far as he knew, no other horse of Gato's good looks, except Jim Kane's Pajaro, had ever walked on the soil of La Golondrina. That included every horse that had come from Arabia and every single one ever foaled and raised at La Golondrina.

"Stop, Filomeno. Bring those animals back," Lupino ordered. The stooped old man patiently turned Gato and Negrito back to face him. "What a fine head and eye. What a color. What do you call that color?"

"*Alazán tostado*. Toasted sorrel. Or, you could call him a *castaño*, a chestnut sorrel."

"So, that's a castaño. You know, that goes to show, we can never know everything about a horse. I have never seen a horse of that dark sorrel color. He looks burnt on the edges. And look at that, only a small and perfect diamond in his *frente*, in the very center of his forehead. And that, one white sock on his near side, the side on which he is mounted. You know the saying, *albo al lado de montar* . . . , white hind foot on the near side . . ."

"*Ni hablar*," Vogel said to complete the saying. "Is a good horse, without saying."

"What a fine animal you brought me, Vogel."

"He belongs to Jim."

"Where did you get him, Jim? I have never seen such an animal, such a beauty."

"You mean, other than an Arabian?" Kane said.

"Oh . . . yes, of course," Lupino said. "But I need this horse. This must be the horse I sent for, the one my grandson Ibrahim saw being ridden at El Trigo by Martinillo's grandson. They told you, and you brought him to me."

"We brought him, but he's not for sale," Kane said.

Lupino turned to address Kane, but his eyes were still full of the horse. "You want to give him to me? Oh, no. He must be the best of his crop. I couldn't take him as a gift. I'll pay for him."

"He's not for sale, and I hate to disillusion you, but he hasn't been brought as a gift to you either."

"But he's the one I want. I sent word to Martinillo that I wanted this horse. Isn't that the reason you brought him?"

"No, I had no idea you wanted him."

Lupino would not come down off his cloud. "Then why did you bring him?"

"Martinillo had him saddled and ready for me to ride when I landed at the airstrip."

"But you two know a good business transaction when you see one, do you not? Get together with your partner Vogel a moment and think. Deliberate, then name your price. What better transaction could you make? Aren't you business partners? Doesn't each of you own half the horse?"

"No, Vogel relinquished his half to me. I couldn't sell him if I wanted to. He's a gift from my compadre."

With that, Lupino shut up and Kane thought he would weep. He asked a woman to show the partners to their room so they could wash for supper, but he did not accompany them to the room, as he usually did. He was so distracted he stumbled on his way into the house. Kane figured he had thought that the Gato that Ibrahim told him about was only an ordinary horse, not one that would make him stumble and weep when he could not have him.

The woman led them through the cool hallways of the house to a corner room with a view of the cornfields, the granite cliffs of the escarpment, and the swallows. Kane turned to thank her at the door before she left. Her head was swathed in a black rebozo, a shawl. She had wrapped it across her mouth like a mask, but he recognized the eyes of Fatima, Lupino's only child and mother of his four dynamic grandsons.

"Fatima, it's you?" Kane asked.

"You have water to drink in the pitcher on the stand, soap and towels and the basin in which to wash," the woman announced. "Warm water will be brought in a moment."

She started out the door. "Fatima," Kane said again. She turned and her eyes flashed at him with such a malevolent look, he wondered if he was mistaken. She said, "As soon as you're ready, come to the dining room where my father waits with your supper." She went out and shut the door.

"That's cold," Kane said.

"I thought so too," Vogel said. "What have you done to the woman? What *could* you have done? You've been on your back in another world far away for a year and a half. Oh, *no*. You did something to her, didn't you? I know you did. My God. Only you could make an enemy of a woman five hundred miles and four complete mountain ranges away at the end of fifteen horseshoe trails while you were flat on your back, helpless, and one half a breath from death. What did you do?"

"Nothing."

"Don't tell me that. I don't know how, but you did something."

"I did nothing. She sent me a beautiful letter when Adelita died and another when the horse fell on me, and I sent nothing back. That's the story."

"Why not? You could have written in care of her sons in Rio Alamos. You must have known how much she would appreciate some word in return."

"I guess I forgot."

"I don't believe that. You and she were close. She told me she saved all your letters."

"I wrote to her long ago when she was only sixteen and I was twenty-eight, before I married. I wrote to a lot of girls in those days."

"How come you wrote so many letters?"

"I wrote letters to the ranch girls who didn't have telephones. I wrote them from the ranches where I worked because I didn't have a telephone. I wrote to Fatima when I was with you at Gilaremos, or El Limón, or Guazaremos, or when I prospected by myself at Tepochici, or on the Mulatos River. It was a way to keep a journal, a record of what I did every day. The letters weren't poetic, and I didn't try to kiss anybody on the ear with them. I sent more news about myself to Fatima than anyone else, because she always answered."

"Well, I know she looked forward to them and felt close to you because of them. Didn't you ever think that yours might have been the only correspondence she had from a man her whole life?"

"No, she wasn't backward. From her letters I knew she was plenty smart and capable enough to make a good life for herself. I didn't know she wanted me to marry her away from La Golondrina. She did all right for herself, didn't she?"

Fatima had married Juan's cousin Eliazer and birthed and educated four sons who had known nothing but success. She also acquired Eliazer's ranches when he died.

"You were the one she loved. My cousin was a drunk when they married, and he managed to drink himself to death as soon as he had sired her sons," Vogel said.

"I can't be blamed for that. She was only sixteen when I sent those letters. She told me she wanted to practice writing in English. I wrote to her more as a mentor than a suitor. What she thought is not my fault. I thought we both married well and would always be friends. I did not expect her ever to come into a room as a masked woman with hate in her eyes for me because of some letters I sent, or didn't send."

"Well, there you are. You were wrong. How has she treated you in other years?"

"I haven't seen her in five years, since before Adelita died. You haven't noticed? She's always been gone to Rio Alamos or Huatabampo when we came for the old man's cattle these past few years."

At supper, Lupino no longer acted friendly and open with Kane and Vogel. He put on his formal face, the one they imagined he used with strangers who wandered onto his ranch uninvited. Kane could not imagine who else he used that face on, because he never left his ranch, except to take a packhorse and sleep at campfires by his trails like an old wolf. He had used that face on the partners a time or two before when they would not give in to outlandish stipulations he tried to make when he bought livestock from them, so it did not bother them. They knew he would get over it.

The partners were not prepared to see all four of Lupino's grandsons at the supper table. Ibrahim lived there, so he was no surprise, but

Rafa, the middle grandson, Jacobo, and Ali, the youngest, were there too. Kane and Vogel were interested in observing the new city ways of the three younger ones. They had known the boys all their lives, known them since their toys were rocks.

At first, Kane thought that the high spirits that Rafa showed were only due to the cordiality he felt at seeing his father's guests. After a while, the man's flushed, sweaty face and slurred speech so bordered on the foolish that Kane figured it must be due to some chemical he swallowed.

Lupino began to ask his grandsons questions about the family enterprises in Rio Alamos. For an uneducated mountain man who never went to town, he seemed to know those businesses in detail. When the grandsons finished their reports, he addressed Kane.

"You . . . er . . . Kane, I want you to go back and look over the colts that you have of the same age as this . . . er . . . red horse that you rode here today and pick out a stud that I can breed to my *burras*, mare donkeys." He put disdain into the word *burras*. "Any one of the eight or ten studs you have should be adequate for my use."

"Common studs," Rafa interjected.

"All our stud colts except Gato were gelded last winter," Vogel said. "Even if we might have had one that would breed an ass, it's too late. They've all been cut."

"A pity," Lupino said. "It seems that I can't buy any kind of horse at all from you."

"Why bother with them, Grandfather?" Rafa said. Lupino gave him a sidelong look, but said nothing.

"You must prefer the hinny mules, the ones sired by a stud horse rather than sired by a jackass," Kane said.

"I do, and I can't think of a good reason for it, except that *burreros* act and look more like a horse and less like a jackass."

"Some people are also less acceptable to you, because they act as though they have been sired by a jackass, aren't they, Grandfather?" Rafa smirked.

"I guess a lot of people prefer the hinny," Kane said, ignoring Rafa. "The trouble is, it's hard to find a stud horse that will breed an ass. It seems that most stallions have too much self-respect."

Rafa laughed like a fool at that, but Lupino raised his hand and shut him up.

"That's a new one," Lupino scoffed. "What quarter horse, that mongrel combination of Percheron draft horse and *corriente*, common native stock, ever rejected any animal or any thing when it came in heat. I bet you your red horse would mount a mesquite tree if I painted it with the right scent."

Kane and Vogel looked at each other. The old musk hog had never been meek about expressing his opinions, but he had always been too hospitable to insult the bloodlines of El Trigo livestock at his supper table. In fact, he had always seemed to admire the stock.

Vogel gave the old man a chance to soften the insult. "Don't tell me that you never owned a stud that would breed an ass, don Nesib," he said. "How else have you produced your good hinnys?"

The old man looked down his nose at Vogel. "I've never owned an Arabian stallion that would dirty himself with a burra," he said.

"Well, then, you must have used corriente. You know it's not easy to find a stallion that will breed donkey females."

"I have never owned a corriente stud or mare, not for the past fifty years since I brought my Arabians home."

"My, my. Imagine that," Vogel said as he glanced at Kane. They both knew Lupino kept a harem of common mares that he bred to jackasses. They wondered that he thought he could make them believe that he had no room for any kind of horse on La Golondrina except his precious Arabians. They knew his Arabians would never have to perform any menial task at all. He needed corrientes for those tasks.

The partners were not offended by Lupino's derision of the corriente stock that had helped him make a living all his life. They were past trying to explain why old mountain men like themselves owned odd opinions about livestock, or were angered when they could not have their way with their neighbors' livestock. The discussion did not harm Kane's appetite, and he could see it did not keep Vogel away from the steak platter and the rice bowl either. Broiled flank steak and rice was not the best fare a man could find in the Sierra Madre, but the table was piled with it, it tasted good, the beef was not too tough to chew, the rice was plain old rice, and the coffee was strong and hot.

Even though Kane knew he had vexed the old man, he felt at home at his table. Tomorrow he and Vogel would look at the cattle, take their annual tour of the stables, start the cattle on the drive home, turn back to say good-bye, and everybody would cheer up enough to wish each other well.

Ibrahim's young wife came in with her oldest child, a boy of nine or ten. Ibrahim sat at the foot of the table, opposite his grandfather. His face softened when he looked down at his son. The boy climbed into his lap and stared at Kane.

"My great-grandson Abdullah," Lupino said. "Now, here is a horseman. He has his own mount, he saddles him every day, and he rides with his namesake don Abdullah. He has wonderful intuition about horses."

Ibrahim looked from his son Abdullah's face to Kane's and said, "Do you have great-grandchildren?"

"No, not yet," Kane said. "None of my grandchildren are married."

"And how many grandchildren do you have?"

"Three boys and a girl."

"Do you have pictures?"

Kane produced a picture of eighteen-year-old Cody Joe in Marine Corps blues and a glamorous picture of sixteen-year-old Dolly Ann. He handed them to Ibrahim and thought to himself, *Now, eat your heart out*. He was proud of the good looks and abilities of his grandchildren and proud of the stock they came from. No Lupino had ever looked as good or ever stood up to them in conformation, disposition, or performance, and none ever would.

Ibrahim looked at the pictures and passed them on to Rafa, who handed the picture of Cody Joe to Jacobo but grinned into the full-length picture of Dolly Ann. The picture showed off a lot of long, bare, pretty leg and a face that resembled the girl's grandmother and Kane's mother too. To Kane, two more beautiful faces had never existed in the history of Sonora, and the women of Sonora, since Emperor Maximilian of Mexico had praised them all over Europe, enjoyed the reputation of being among the most beautiful in the world.

Jacobo handed the picture of Cody Joe to his grandfather. "Ah, a soldier," Lupino said, and he finally seemed to relent and forget his vexation. "How old is your grandson, Jim?"

"He's eighteen, don Nesib, and he's a marine."

"A handsome boy, so young and already in uniform. Will he go to Iraq?"

"Probably. He's an infantryman, and he finished most of his training yesterday."

"Ah, God help him."

Lupino looked down the table at Rafa, and Kane followed his gaze. Rafa was still grinning broadly into Dolly Ann's picture. He must have been aware that everybody at the table stared at him, but he did not look up from the picture for a long moment.

Finally, he smacked his lips lasciviously, turned to Kane, and held the grin. "I have to give American females credit," he said. "They are good at what they know best how to do. What will you take for the granddaughter? I can get a lot of money for a female like that."

Kane did not answer him, because he did not answer insults with words.

"I held that picture for only one minute and I'm hot. Just that picture of a common, ordinary American female made me lustful. That's proof that what they do is done better by them than by any other females in the world. And only by their example, they have begun to teach every other female in the world how to do it."

Fatima came in from the kitchen and stopped at the door, for a dead stillness had fallen on the room.

"Practically from their birth, they are truly and naturally the best whores in the world," Rafa said.

"Rafa!" his mother cried.

"No mistake. Every single one of them dresses and makes herself up like a whore, acts like a whore in public everywhere she goes, is the easiest and cheapest to get naked for the whole world to see, and then into bed. The very pictures of them arouse the lust of men. Theirs is the most vigorous and popular campaign in the world. *Meestair* Kane, how does it feel to have a child of Satan call herself your grandchild?"

None too steadily, because of the long ride he had made to get there, Kane stood up, stepped away from his chair, and walked toward the grinning man.

Rafa's grin disappeared. "I don't know how to fight," he said. He got out of his chair in such haste that he tangled in it and sprawled on his hands and knees on the floor.

Kane shoved the chair aside so he could put the boots to him while he had him down. Rafa scrambled backward on his butt and kicked wildly at Kane's legs. Kane started around the feet to get at his head, but Fatima planted herself in his way with both hands on his breast.

"Please don't hurt my son, Jim," she said.

Kane went around her. Ibrahim, with his child still on his lap, and without turning his head toward Fatima, said, "He really needs his mouth smashed, Mother."

Kane pursued Rafa but could not catch him. He thought, *The man can move faster with his butt on the floor than I can move on foot. What is this? I can't catch a man on his ass? I can't even kick a man when he's down? I'm already out of breath.*

Jacobo stepped in front of him and put his hands on his shoulders. "Please, don't hurt my brother, Jim. He didn't mean anything. He lacks dignity and he makes a bad clown, but he meant it as a joke. You don't believe he meant to insult your granddaughter, do you?"

Kane did not shake, or feel weak, but his mind cleared enough so that he realized he was not strong enough to move this young man out of his way so he could stomp his brother. All he could do now was look this one in the eye, pretend to listen, and wait for another chance to stomp the little coward.

Three

Kane's angry trance began to clear away. With Jacobo planted in his face, he realized he would not be able to stomp Rafa that day. He was forced to see into the young man's eyes. The brothers had their mother's hypnotic, black, glittering eyes, eyes so black the pupils could not be seen. Black eyes, black hair, black brows, dark skin.

Nesib and Ibrahim wore only mustaches like Vogel's and Kane's. Rafa and Jacobo were handsome men, but their elaborately trimmed beards bothered Kane. The pattern, the arrangement of the black hair on their faces, the slender lines of hair sculpted down from the drooping ends of their mustaches to their chin whiskers, the beard lines that scored their jaws from sideburns to chin accentuated the wolfishness of their faces. The trimmed stripes of their mustaches and beards made them look more unmistakably feral, seemed to define them more as beasts than men.

Wolves wear distinct feral black lines on their faces and jaws, their noses and throats, and the corners of their eyes, lines that help their camouflage and add to the wildness and fierceness of their demeanor. Now, with Jacobo's face two inches from his, Kane clearly saw the reason he had never liked the Lupinos. He saw the evidence of their black hearts in their meticulous beards.

Rafa and Jacobo needed to use great effort and much time every day to trim those beards. Kane thought the labor of it must have taken hours and made them look like Faust's Mephistopheles. They must have wanted to look Satanic, because they took enough care to trim the feral lines of the Beast into their own faces.

Old Nesib, Ibrahim, and Ali used heavy mustaches that almost hid their wolfishness. Their upper front teeth were long and thick. Their lips did not keep their teeth covered. The men were always reaching up and masking them, hiding them with their hands.

As Kane looked into Jacobo's black eyes, he realized that the faces of all the Lupino men were lupine, wolflike, and not only because they intentionally made them that way, but because they had been born that way. Had the family acquired the name Lupino because of its wolfishness? Or had it become wolfish after it assumed the name? He decided if he could stop and wonder about them so much, he must not need to stomp Rafa anymore.

Rafa had scrambled backward only as far as the nearest wall. He still sat on the floor, probably because he figured Kane would not hit him when he was down. Old Lupino stood over him. "Get up, boy," he said.

"I'm sorry, Grandfather," Rafa said and stood up.

Lupino turned to Kane. "Thank you, Jim, for not killing my grandson . . . or do you still entertain the idea?"

"I don't know," Kane said. "I wanted to kill him, but didn't even come close."

"Listen. You know how to kill. I'm only glad that you pulled up before you took hold of him." He turned back to his grandson. "Now, apologize to our guest, Rafa."

"I apologize, Mister Kane," Rafa said. Eyes downcast, he seemed innocent as a child. The sweat on his brow had cooled. He rubbed his face with both hands and did not look at Kane. He did not fool Kane either. Mexicans called an American *meestair* when they wanted to insult him. Now he was Mister? Wait until the gorge rose in the wolf again.

"It's the white powder," Lupino said. "You dipped your nose in the baby powder again?"

"No, Grandfather. I don't do that."

"Oh, I think so. I know it. But who am I to tell you what to do? You're a grown man and you think you can afford it. However, can you afford to have the foot of a big man like Jim Kane stuffed into your mouth? What do you think, Jacobo? What caused your brother to act like such a fool?"

"I don't know, Grandfather," Jacobo said.

"If the white powder is not to blame, what is? If a chemical is not the reason he becomes a fool and insults his grandfather's guests, then God help us, for he must be a born fool and there is no remedy for that."

"Father, he's only stupid," Fatima cried. "He doesn't know the difference between a joke and an insult, never has."

"That's right, Grandfather," Rafa said. "I'm not a good clown. I make people angry when I try to make them laugh."

"What do you think, Kane?" Lupino asked. "Do you want more apology, or do you think he might only be an awkward fool you can forgive?"

Rafa made the mistake of looking up at Kane with glowering eyes. "Get out of my sight," Kane said to him. "You are not my friend."

Rafa looked away and left the room.

"We're still friends, here, are we not?" Lupino asked.

Vogel still sat at the table with Ibrahim and the little boy. Kane said, "Compadre Juan, I think I'll rest now so we can start early tomorrow."

"Rest seems to be indicated for us both," Vogel said.

Lupino followed the partners to their room. "I expected to have a longer visit with you this evening," he said. "Don't let my grandson's foolish mouth chase you to bed."

"Nobody is chasing us away, don Nesib," Vogel said. "We need to start the *toretes* on their way early tomorrow so we can get them sold and pay you for them. The sooner we get them to market, the sooner you'll get your money."

"No, no, no, don't go because of that. You know I don't require immediate payment. Take them. Keep them. Pay me when you like. Pay me next year when you come for the new crop. Or don't pay me. I don't care. I don't need money."

Kane sat on his comfortable bed and wished Lupino would shut up and leave. The old man was still miffed. He did not want Kane to go to bed until he had prodded him about the spat with his grandson, and he still probably felt spurned about not being able to acquire Gato.

Lupino ensconced himself in a chair by the door. The partners saw that he would stay, so they resigned themselves to wait him out.

"I've been wanting to talk to you about something," Lupino said. "It's too bad that the kind of mares you prefer don't produce better colts, but the stock you have will never get better. Why don't you let me help you? At least let me give you some advice." Kane and Vogel only looked at Lupino.

"I want you to think about your Gato horse, Kane, and listen to me for one minute. Don't you think that those huge hams he uses for hind-quarters would be better as steak to be eaten than used to travel the high trails? Don't you know that the heavier a horse's muscles are, the more he is apt to cramp when he makes a hot climb?"

Kane just stared at the man. Every single person in the world who had ever ridden a horseshoe trail knew that. However, skinny little horses with no muscle had a whole lot more trouble of several other kinds on hot climbs. To Kane and Vogel, who were big men who used their horses hard, Lupino's Arabs were only skinny little dinks. They were not fit to carry a two-hundred-pound man in those mountains, not even in a level corral, even if a level corral could be found in the Sierra.

"Didn't you tell me that your horse Pajaro, who was heavier and more powerful than this Gato horse, was prone to cramp and tie up on a long, hot, uphill climb?"

"Pajaro tied up on me once in his life," Kane said. "That was on the Guasisaco climb, probably the longest and steepest in this whole country."

"There you are. My Arabians never have trouble on the *cuesta* of Guasisaco."

"It depends on what a horse has to carry on the climb and how much he had to carry before he started the climb. What besides a skinny, bony, wormy little serrano have your Arabians ever had to carry on a climb? Rafa and Ibrahim are the biggest men your horses have ever had to carry, and they seldom do any work on a horse except ride on the trail from one camp to another. Pajaro had worked a solid week on and off steep trails and in corrals dragging heavy cattle without a rest. The day he tied up I had ridden him since before sunup, and I had roped and dragged cattle on him all day. Evening had fallen when we started up the grade. Pajaro cramped half way up in the dark. I got off and led him for half an hour, then remounted and rode him on to El Trigo hacienda. You have never owned one Arabian that could have done half the work Pajaro did that week. The best horse that ever walked on this ranch would have fallen over in a swoon from overwork halfway through it."

"There isn't any way you will ever prove that to me, unless we have a contest of some kind between your best horse and mine."

"That's right, I guess there isn't, and there won't ever be any contest, as far as I'm concerned. My horse doesn't need to prove anything to you. El Trigo horses have long proven themselves as cow horses and mountain trail horses. They have more cow sense, more strength, and more speed than any Arabians you will ever raise if you live another hundred years. Ask any vaquero of this region."

"All right, you won't sell me the horse, but why won't you open your mind to the good qualities of my Arabians? I'll tell you what I think we ought to do. I'll trade you one of my horses for your horse only for a time. I'll breed six of my burras to your horse, and you breed six of your mares to my horse. Let's at least see if your horse can breed me a better mule and if my horse can breed you a better horse."

"I'm sure my horse would be of great service to you, don Nesib, if he would breed your donkeys, but why in the world would I want to breed our mares to one of your horses? Yours may be well educated, but I don't think you have even one that could pull a sick whore off a piss-pot."

"Nooo, Jim, man. My horses don't pull anything, not a plow, not a calf on the end of a rope, and I certainly would not demean them by giving them chores to do in a whorehouse. My saddle horses fly. My *mules* pull the plow, rope the calves, and do the other work that requires them to grunt, sweat, and get filthy. A twenty-league ride across the Sierra does not even draw the sweat from my horses."

"Fly? I haven't seen them even come close to that. A horse has to be fast on his feet to fly. I never saw a horse of yours that could outrun a fat woman."

"You insult me, Jim."

"That wasn't my intention, but you don't have one horse that can outrun a fat woman. That's sad but true, and no insult to anybody."

"There's a simple way for you to prove your claim and we both know what it is."

"I'm not going to match you a horse race, don Nesib."

"We'll turn our horses loose and let them play on a racetrack, then. Let's see which horse is faster for half a mile."

"My horse is not a play pretty. It would not make me happy to see my horse run away with his rider in front of a crowd of people. Forget it."

"A half mile is too far for your horse? Bueno, he's a quarter horse, isn't he? That means he is fastest at a quarter mile. I'll match my horse Auda against your Gato for a quarter mile and a purse of ten thousand pesos. You ride your horse, I ride mine."

"No, I don't want your money."

"You don't like my choice of jockeys? I'm many years older than you, Jim, but I still ride as well as any man. When I'm on my horse, I'm not old anymore."

"Now, how in the world could I allow you to jockey a race? Just take it that I'm the one who thinks he's too old to jockey and leave it at that."

"All right, we each pick our own jockey. Let's run horse against horse. I get your horse if I win, you get mine if you win."

"That's sure not fair."

"What do you mean, not fair?"

"I absolutely do not have any use for the horse you call *Ah-oo-tha*. You admit that you have drastic need of mine."

"All right, your horse against my horse and ten thousand pesos. You win, you get my horse and ten thousand pesos."

"I don't want your horse, I told you."

"All right. You're so high on your horse? How high? Put a price on your horse. Put him up against any amount of money you want me to put up."

Kane thought, *Now I've finally got him. I'll name a price so high the son of a gun will have to shut up and leave me alone.* "I'll put up my horse against no less than a hundred thousand dollars in cash and your horse, don Nesib."

"*Hecho*, Jim."

"What do you mean, 'done'?"

"I mean I call your bet. The race is on."

"I won't hold you to it, don Nesib. People will think you're crazy. You don't want to put up a hundred thousand dollars and your top stallion against my horse. Gato will make a fool of your horse and a fool of you for betting so much money on a losing proposition."

"Nevertheless, the race is on. Name the time and place."

Kane still did not want to run his horse. He thought he had made that clear enough. He would give the man a way out of it. "All right, don Nesib. On the darkest night of next year, let's turn out all the lights and run the race in front of the Hotel Santa Isabela in Mexico City."

"No, Jim. Name a reasonable time and place, or risk being called a big-mouthed, big-talking, backing-out coward for the rest of your life."

"I don't want your money, don Nesib. I came here for the *partida* of young bulls that Vogel and I buy from you every year. I don't want to run my horse, and I don't like being prodded into doing it at all costs. Why don't we forget this talk about a horse race and go on with the business that brought us together again in friendship?"

"The money means nothing to me. I have millions more than I need. Now, name the time and place for the race, or leave my house and don't ever come back. You will run this race, or you are not my friend."

"All right, then. I thought I could treat you as a friend, regardless of whether or not we ran a horse race against each other. Since you won't allow that, we'll race six weeks from now, August first at the Rio Alamos Charro Arena. The horses will come to the starting line at five p.m. Lap and tap and no fooling around. You name the starter."

"Juan Vogel is good."

"Very well."

"I ask for only one favor."

"Name it, don Nesib."

"I ask that no one spy on the training of my horse Auda. I don't want to see your horse until the race, and I don't want you to see my horse. I want to train my horse in secret, if you will. Give me your word that you won't spy on him."

"Of course. That goes without saying."

Lupino smiled and offered his hand to seal the agreement. Kane shook it, turned away, and started to unbutton his shirt. He still did not want to run his horse, and he did not want to listen to another word from Lupino. His feelings were hurt. How could Lupino suspect that he would spy on his horse? Besides that, he knew he could not have backed out after he set the wager at $100,000 and his top stallion, but he had wanted to give the man a chance to reconsider, not because he was a coward, but because he did not want to take the money of somebody he had always tried to befriend.

⌣

Kane and Vogel were in the barn preparing to leave the next morning when Jacobo and Rafa came in and drew Vogel aside. Kane sat on a bench with his back to Gato's stall and listened.

The Lupinos wanted to "expand their ranching enterprise" and buy Vogel's El Trigo ranch, including the El Limón, Gilaremos, Guazaremos, and Canela divisions that covered more than one hundred thousand hectares.

Vogel laughed at the idea and told them he would not sell, because he and Jim Kane wanted to "expand their cattle enterprise."

"Forgive us," Jacobo persisted. "We took a liberty that we hope you won't resent. We consulted your brothers and sisters about this and they are agreeable to a sale. They deferred to you, but indicated that they hoped you would keep an open mind about it. We came away with the belief that your family is *anxious* to sell. You are the only one in your family who wants to keep El Trigo. Why don't you name a price and make your family happy?"

Kane began to worry. He and Vogel were not partners in their ranches, only in the cattle they handled. Who could tell how much the Lupinos would pay for El Trigo? Kane had just been introduced to a Lupino method of getting what they wanted. Most people worked only for money. Kane and Vogel worked ranches and cattle for values other than money, but everybody is said to have his price, and that might be true about Vogel. The Lupinos had enough money to buy anything and Vogel was eighty years old. He could not take El Trigo with him when he died, so he might bow to the wishes of his family who would have to deal with the ranch when he was gone. None of them loved El Trigo. His family would want the money, not the work.

"Listen, let's not go any further with this," Vogel said. "I won't let you persist until you offer two times more money than the ranches are worth. I watched your father do that to Jim, but I won't let you do it to me. I know you'll pay any amount of money I ask, but I won't sell, so go away and think about something else, or stay here and visit, but change the subject."

"Nevertheless, keep us in mind. Who knows, tomorrow you might wake up and want to sell," Jacobo said.

"Not while I'm alive and still wake up every morning," Vogel said.

Rafa laughed and said, "How soon do you plan to die? We hope soon, because we have uses for your place."

From his seat a few feet away, Kane said, "You don't learn, do you, Rafa? Do you think that your brothers will continue to protect you if you keep insulting us?"

"I don't mean to insult you, *meestair*. I only say what comes into my mind and sometimes people don't like it."

"That's the *pinchi* truth. I just heard from you that you want my best friend dead, because it seems to be the only way you can get his property."

"I didn't mean that. I meant that we have use for the property and we wish we could acquire it sooner rather than later."

"Oh, and how do you explain what you said about my grand-daughter?"

"What did I say about her? I don't remember saying anything about your granddaughter. I think I said American women make me hot."

"We both know what you said, but if you want to apologize, I'll listen. I'm not satisfied with your other apology, and I still might bash your head in."

"I only meant that American women always seem ready to give themselves as playthings to any common lout. They boldly advertise themselves as whores. Their tattoos are their playbills. I have to admit that Mexican women also have become more and more like them and so have European women, so they are not the only ones who want the world to see them as whores."

"Oh, and you're an expert? How is that? You've cruised around Europe and taken a poll?"

"We Lupinos do business all over the world. Yes, I watch television in Europe and the United States. Anyone who does that can see that the Western world is hypocritical. It professes to be god-fearing, but practices godlessness."

"God-fearing? Who are the people you believe are god-fearing?"

"All right, I don't think anybody doubts that Muslims are god-fearing. The Muslims haven't become whores of Satan. They don't flaunt sex throughout the world in open parade, don't wage war against a people and kill them for their own good in the name of freedom and democracy."

"No, they only cut off the heads of innocent hostages, slaughter whole blocks of their own innocent people with bombs, blow up whole cities with hijacked airplanes in the name of Allah. In Muslim countries, any rotten old man can beat a woman on the street with a stick only because he thought she looked at him wrong, or her veil dropped too low."

"You blame the Muslim religion for September eleventh?"

"I blame Muslims. Not every Muslim is a terrorist, but every anti-Christian, anti-American terrorist these days seems to be a Muslim. Good Muslims could stop them a whole lot sooner than anybody else could."

"Look, *meestair*. Your President Bush believes that he has taken the initiative by starting a Judeo-Christian crusade against all non-Christian nations, especially the Muslim nations. Name one non-Christian nation that is not considered an enemy by the Americans."

"Any nation that is not against us is our friend, Christian or non-Christian."

"Yes, and name one non-Christian nation that does not harbor your enemies."

"Jordan, a Muslim nation. Kuwait, South Korea, Japan."

"Don't kid yourself, *meestair*. The U.S. has as many enemies in those countries as they do in Iraq. How do you think the Arab princes will like it when the U.S. decides to make democracies of their countries? You think those other Middle Eastern countries want to see Iraq become a democracy? You think those princes don't take your oil money, then pay it to terrorists to kill your young soldiers? There's a world war on, *meestair*. The whole world is inflamed against your country and your democracy, and Muslims will be the winners. Your country long ago embraced Satan, *meestair* Kane. How can you win?"

"Well, Rafa, the old goat has got us East and West, then, doesn't he? The western devil parades naked and flaunts sex and free love. The Middle Eastern devil flaunts hate and wears thick robes and a mask and kills people in the name of Allah."

"But you know what I said is true, don't you? Maybe not about your granddaughter, but what's a man to think? Even supposedly decent women like your granddaughter go out of their way to look like whores. Come on, *meestair* Kane."

"Yes, and how can anybody in the whole world know a good Muslim from a bad one by the way they look? Should we call all Muslims murderers and terrorists by the way they dress and mask their faces against the wind and sun as you called my granddaughter a whore by the way she looks in a photograph? Should we wage war against all Muslims because we can't tell terrorists from the God-fearing?"

Vogel took Kane away from the Lupinos by saying they should go find Fatima and say good-bye. They found her in the orchard. Her youngest son Ali, a clean-cut, bareheaded young man, followed her around with a shovel to control irrigation water on the trees. Kane was astounded at Fatima's beauty. He knew that she was sixty-two years old, but she looked half that age. Her hair was as black and shiny as it had been when she was sixteen, her eyes as clear and expressive. Her lips were still full and unmarked by the ordinary notches and whiskers of old age.

This time when she looked at Kane her eyes were not malevolent, but she acted impersonal and made Kane keep his distance. He decided, *What the hell? Why should I want to get personal with her? I probably only imagined that we were friends. After all, my supposed intimacy with her would have had to be achieved by letters that took a month to reach her and eventually petered out.*

He sat under a tree to visit with her. He thought, *Now that I'm back from the dead, all I want to do is search for feelings and examine them. I'm getting to be the kind of fool my grandfather talked about. He once said, "My, my, such a fuss as people make over the way they feel." That's me since my gizzards got mashed, a fool who makes a fuss over a friendship that's been dead for decades.*

Ali interned as a doctor in a Tucson hospital. Kane had been around him only a few times since he had grown into a man but had him figured as a little softy. His hands looked tender and did not fit the shovel handle. He could barely lift it. He could not bury its steel where he needed to and seemed threatened by it. It could hurt him. The looks he gave Kane and Vogel as he tried to stick the shovel in the ground and change the water from one row to another were soulful as a girl's. *Help me, I know you can do this better,* they said.

Vogel suffered a little cough. He smoked three packages of cigarettes a day, but had never been bothered by a bad cough as other smokers were, only this little one, and only lately.

In the orchard, Vogel took a drag of a cigarette down the wrong pipe, had a coughing fit, and woke up Ali's doctor's office. The young man put his ear to Vogel's chest and asked him to cough again, then tapped on it with his forefinger, then did the same with his ear against Vogel's back. He came back in front of Vogel and his eyes were not soulful anymore. They were speculative as a wolf's who had just heard the sound of a soft, juicy rabbit close by.

"How long have you had that cough?" Ali asked.

"About eight months. It's nothing," Vogel said.

"It doesn't sound like anything serious. Does it hurt?"

"Not at all."

"Still, it seems chronic."

"I had bronchitis with a bad cough last fall. It left me with this little thing that doesn't even bother me."

"Still, to relieve all doubts and fears, you should have an examination. You're a smoker and I bet not a moderate one. Why don't you let me arrange for you to have an examination at my hospital?"

"You mean in Tucson?"

"Yes. Let me arrange it."

"I don't know when I can do it. I don't want to go all the way to Tucson only to have a little pinchi cough listened to."

"Well, don't wait too long."

"Look, Juan, you're going to Nogales with me when we cross the Lupino toretes," Kane said. "I'll take you to the hospital then."

"We'll see," Vogel said.

Kane and Vogel led their animals out of the stalls to saddle them, and Abdullah, Lupino's chief horse wrangler, came out to greet them. A desert Bedouin from Arabia, this *caballerango* had come to La Golondrina with Lupino's first Arabian horses more than fifty years ago. Kane and Vogel were Abdullah's friends, and they often talked about him. As far as they knew, he had not made friends with anyone else except Ibrahim and his little namesake Abdullah in all his years in the Sierra.

Kane and Vogel felt an affinity with Abdullah because of his dedication to the husbandry of the Lupino livestock. Nothing in the world mattered more to him than La Golondrina horses, and Kane believed the horses felt real affection for him. Kane had always suspected that no horse could love a man, because no man could be equal to the matchless horse. However, even though Abdullah did not solicit the affection of any person or animal, Kane could see his horses loved him. No matter how much other people claimed their horses loved them, Kane believed that a real bond of love between a man and a horse was only rarely seen.

Abdullah gave Kane and Vogel abrazos at arm's length, one very light pat on the back apiece, and the trace of a smile. His hawk face remained severe, but the trace of the smile unmistakably showed, even in the predatory eyes. "God be praised," he said to them.

"Thank you for the care you gave our animals, friend," Vogel said. His saddle lay by the door to the stall in which Negrito the mule had been stabled. He unbuckled his saddlebags, took out two cartons of Lucky Strike cigarettes, and handed them to Abdullah.

Kane took two boxes of .30-.30 cartridges from his saddlebags and gave them to the man. "These are also for you," he said. Abdullah carefully accommodated the cigarettes in one hand so he could take the cartridges in the other. "Come," he said. They followed him into the stall that served as his quarters. The room was full of the vapor of strong coffee. The partners sat on a wide cot, and Abdullah handed each a small cup of thick, hot, heavily sugared coffee. A clean, worn carpet covered the dirt floor. Abdullah sat in a corner and folded his legs. The stall was uncluttered and furnished only with the carpet, the cot, a military surplus locker box, a washstand, ceramic washbowl, and an enamel water pitcher. His bedding lay rolled and tied with rope on the foot of the cot.

His bare and horny feet appeared never to have worn shoes. The blunt toes, brown nails, and calloused heels looked scuffed and worn with everyday use, but healthy and supple.

He carefully opened a new carton of cigarettes, opened a package and extracted a cigarette, and offered it to Kane, then offered it to Vogel, then wet the end with the tip of his tongue, put it in his mouth, and struck a match to it. His big toes caressed his second toes in a wiggle of delight.

"The Gato is much horse," he said as he drew on the cigarette. He exhaled slowly and noisily and watched the smoke leave his lips and flow into the room toward his friends. He looked at the cigarette in his right hand, passed it to his left, took hold carefully of his coffee cup on the locker box beside him, lifted it to his face and sucked at it noisily, swallowed with the strangle sound of a horse, and exhaled with a loud, satisfied gasp.

Abdullah seemed to feel that the sounds he made for his swallows of hot coffee were as good as conversation, because all he did for the next few minutes was sip his coffee, puff on the wet end of his cigarette, and watch its smoke. Once in a while he gazed into the eyes of the partners and nodded as if to say, "Yes, this is all right."

The partners often told their friends and loved ones about the sounds Abdullah made when he called his hot coffee to its consumption. At their breakfast tables, they imitated his routine. Kane's grandchildren and Vogel's wife and daughter knew exactly how Abdullah took his coffee. Now, with straight faces the partners called their own coffee and smacked their lips over each mouthful and swallow the way he did. They swallowed with the noise of horses and gasped with satisfaction afterward because they knew he thought it proper to give evidence of the pleasure of each sip, and that was all the communication they needed, for a while . . . except for a nod or two . . . and a look into the eyes . . . and a look at the smoke.

In his broken Spanish, Abdullah finally said, "Your young colt is already much horse, and with those stones, will be much of a sire."

The partners sipped their coffee and nodded. Abdullah nodded too.

Kane found something new about the man's face every time he looked at it. He was not sure how many years it had been since his birth in Araby, but he knew that he was not a youngster when he came to the Sierra with Lupino's horses. Lupino said that he had won fame as a master horseman in his own country before he left, so he must have been at least thirty, more likely forty. Kane had known him fifty years, yet he did not think his face had changed any more than the topography of any mountain in the Sierra had changed, or the desert of his Arab homeland. Old lines on his face had always been too deep to get deeper. The short, narrow hawk nose and hawk eyes in that face could seem a threat to other humans, as though the face was a weapon, as a hawk's eyes and beak are weapons. His movements were still supple. Kane had never heard him cough, never heard him groan under a weight. He did not walk, he glided. When he took hold of something his grip was sure and did not fumble. He did not "get on" a horse, he stepped into a stirrup and took his seat.

The only time he had ever said a word of praise to Kane, he said, "You sit a horse well." Kane knew he sat a horse well, but when that old horseman said it, he finally felt rewarded for his lifetime of horsemanship. When that old Arab wanted to have his way with a horse, he only conveyed the thought to him. When somebody else wanted to have their way with the same horse, a whole team of men might have to throw him down and sit on him.

The partners finished their coffee, and before they could set their cups down, Abdullah took them and made them disappear. He opened the locker box and brought out a heavy object wrapped in new, white felt, the cloth used in the Sierra as sweat pad under the saddle. He unwrapped the felt and uncovered a shiny blade. The handles had been fashioned from bull horn and looked old and smooth, except for the shiny brass ends of the pins that held them in place. The blade was two inches wide, eight inches long, curved from hilt to point on the cutting edge, and straight backed, except for the last three inches at the point, which dipped from the spine of the blade to the tip and had been honed to facilitate entry of the blade into flesh, with no effort on the part of the handler. A golden snake with ruby eyes twined around the length of the hilt. A hawk's head with yellow agate eyes graced the butt. Abdullah suddenly tossed the knife end over end into the air, caught it at the point of the blade with two fingers, and handed it to Kane. "Yours," he said.

The gift was too rich for Kane's eyes. The knife pricked an old nerve in him. He had admired knives like this that were works of art ever since his childhood when he first learned to appreciate the open blades of vaqueros who worked with his father and uncles. He had coveted them and wanted one of his own. When he read about the knives in *The Arabian Nights,* and about singing, jeweled swords of times when blades were man's storied weapons, he had wished for an ornate and finely crafted blade of his own. Now, he finally held it.

Everyone in the region knew that Abdullah was an artisan of knives, an art that he brought from Araby. Kane had seen many of the blades he made and sold. He could not imagine how much money they were worth. He looked down and saw the clear reflection of his own face mirrored in its surface, so clear that it seemed to look back at him from inside the blade, not from its surface.

"I'm honored," Kane said. "What could I give you to equal this gift? I have always wanted this knife. This is a perfect gift for me. Other than my horse Gato, no other gift could satisfy my wishes so well. This is something that I would never have given myself, because of its extravagance. In two days, I have been given the two most precious material gifts that I have ever known, the young horse Gato that my compadre Juan gave me, and this instrument of your making. What can I give you?"

"I prayed when you were hurt. We heard that you would die. When you recovered, I gave thanks to God and began to fashion this blade as a gift for your return. Now you are alive again with a blade in your hands. As your gift to me, use it well."

Kane cradled the knife in his open hands. Vogel looked down at it, but did not ask to hold it.

"Where are all the knives you've made, Abdullah?" Kane asked. "Your art has given much pleasure to people. Where are they? I've never seen one of your knives in the hands of the Lupinos. I've seen Lupino and his grandsons in almost every situation in which knives were needed since I first came to know them, and I've never seen one of your knives in their hands."

"Ibrahim has one," Abdullah said. He extracted another cigarette from his new package.

Kane did not ask if any other Lupino had been given a knife. He knew the reason Ibrahim carried one. He was a husbandman to the core like Abdullah. He knew why Nesib Lupino did not have one. He probably had never shown interest in Abdullah's artistry. He probably had never praised or thanked Abdullah for the decades of care and advice the old maestro had given the Lupinos either.

After a while Abdullah said, "The others believe their ticks are gazelles."

Four

With the help of Lupino's vaqueros, the partners drove the three hundred young bulls through La Golondrina Pass where Martinillo and a crew met them. The crew would brand, castrate, and vaccinate the herd at Guazaremos. After that, it would be driven out of the Sierra to San Bernardo in the foothills on the Sonora side where trucks would haul it to the U.S. border for export.

The hacienda buildings had been destroyed by fire early in the drug war and only now were being rebuilt. Che Che Salazar had been born and raised on the hacienda and was in charge of its reconstruction. The son of a former mayordomo of the ranch and a mother who had been a servant of the Vogels, he had been its caretaker since the age of seventeen when don Panchito Flores Valenzuela, its former caretaker, died after seventy-five years on the job.

When the drug wars began and young natives of the region joined the fight against the intruders from Sinaloa, Che Che had been overlooked because of his busy stewardship of the hacienda. However, he had been more active than any of his peers as a marijuana grower in competition with the Sinaloans. As a vaquero for Vogel and Kane, he had helped gather herds of livestock in the farthest corners of the region. He knew every fence, every canyon and mountainside, in the night as well as day. When he elected to grow his own crops of marijuana, he found very secret places for it.

Without a word to anyone, Che Che stole some seed and planted his first crop. He worked barefoot with a broken-handled shovel to divert a stream into his first rows of *mota*, marijuana. He watched the Sinaloans and taught himself how to care for his crop and how and when to harvest it. He watched them bale and package it, stole their materials, and did the same with his own harvest.

At the age of eighteen, when he needed to look for a buyer for his first crop, he had never been out of the Sierra Madre. The Vogels lived in Rio Alamos, Sonora, so he walked in his tire-soled huaraches to San Bernardo, caught a ride on a Montenegro truck to Rio Alamos, then showed up at Juan Vogel's door. Vogel's wife Alicia gave him a cot and meals on her patio while he searched for a buyer. He roamed the town as an illiterate young man from the Sierra whom no one suspected of owning a $20,000-dollar, five-burro pack string load of marijuana. He did not have to search long for a buyer, because when Alicia told Juan Vogel the reason he was in town, Vogel referred him back to the Montenegros.

So Che Che sold his first crop inside the family of El Trigo, because Manuelito Montenegro, his brother Pancho, and Juan Vogel were lifelong compadres. The Montenegro brothers' trucks hauled all of Kane's and Vogel's livestock. They owned mercantile stores in every village in the mountains of Chinipas and Loreto. They dealt in illicit crops as well as legal ones, and they were honest with Che Che.

That was the only time in his thirty years as a marijuana grower that Che Che's closed mouth caused a false start. He could have asked the Montenegros to buy his crop when he first arrived at their store in San Bernardo and asked for a ride to Vogel's house. He never again made a false move. The only people who knew that he grew the mota, even after he bought his first pickup truck, were the Montenegros, two of Adan Martinillo's sons who drove trucks for the Montenegros, Juan Vogel, and Jim Kane.

The new car dealer of his first pickup taught him how to drive it. He loaded it with new clothes and provisions and drove it as far into the Sierra as he could get it, then ditched it about three minutes before it fell completely apart. After that, he worked to repair an awful jeep road that Vogel and the Montenegros had once built from San Bernardo to El Trigo. It had fallen in disrepair after ten years of heavy rains and no maintenance. Che Che finally repaired it enough so he could jockey another new truck all the way to El Trigo and back down to San Bernardo again before it fell apart, but that was the last time he used a pickup in his business. He preferred to pack his crops out of the Sierra on burros, because he could hide burros better, use different trails, travel at night, and did not have to buy new ones after each trip.

Che Che did not mind negotiating his jeep road with a pickup in the day, but he needed to transport his crop off the mountain at night to escape detection. The headlights of a pickup hardly ever shined on that road. Its switchback turns were so numerous and tight that the beams of the headlights only shined uselessly over thousands of feet of space most of the time. Che Che told Jim Kane that his nerves had not proven to be cold enough to help him drive a pickup over that road even one more night.

As Kane, Vogel, and Martinillo neared El Trigo on their return from La Golondrina, Kane asked Martinillo about Che Che.

"Ah, he knows you're coming, and he'll be ready for you with a swallow of *soyate* mezcal," Martinillo said.

"He's a good boy," Kane said.

Vogel chuckled. "He's *listo* enough. Ready for anything."

"You should know something, Jim," Martinillo said. "When I found out that you'd been hurt, I made a special trip up here to tell him. You know what he did?"

"No."

"He sat on the ground, held his face in his hands, and cried for an hour."

"No, hombre."

"He loves you a lot."

"Well, he's been like a son to me and my compadre Vogel."

"Just so you know."

"I wonder where we're going to sleep," Vogel said. "He sent word that he could give us better accommodations this time."

"Who helps him rebuild the place?" Kane asked.

"Carpenter and bricklayer help in the Sierra is occupied too much with its own affairs," Vogel said. "Everybody makes more money doing other things, as you well know. He can't get help, but he seems to do well without it."

"It rained this winter and the streams are up," Martinillo said. "Che Che could do as his neighbors do and grow the mota, but he told me he wants to stay with this job until he restores the hacienda buildings."

That told Kane that Martinillo still might not know that Che Che grew his own crop of the stuff, or Martinillo thought that Kane did not know. At any rate, Martinillo gave no sign that he knew Che Che grew marijuana. The secret was being kept, and that was necessary for Che Che's protection.

"We pay him well, don't we, Juan?" Kane asked Vogel.

"Yes. He has other businesses, though. He packs provisions and foodstuffs up from San Bernardo with his burros, and he drags pine beams down to San Bernardo. He sells his harvests of beans and corn. You know that he runs fifty cows with us now. He makes and sells cheeses from the milk. He cut all the lumber for the new roof of the hacienda with an ax and dragged it here. Alone, he laid the cement of the floors, patio, and veranda. He made the adobe. We pay him for the materials and his work. He does well and never stops working."

The walls of the house had been rebuilt with new adobe but not stuccoed yet. A bundle of new ax-hewn ceiling and attic beams stood on end in a corner. The ends of the beams had been rounded when the burros dragged them through the mountains. Kane could smell the new pine fifty yards away.

Che Che appeared in a doorway, leaned against it, and smoked home-grown tobacco in a corn leaf. Kane thought, *Anyone would think he could afford tailor-made cigarettes, with his money. Pretty soon he'll be good for a loan.*

Che Che came forward and held Gato while Kane dismounted, then gave Kane an abrazo with tears in his eyes. He and Martinillo led Gato and the mules around to the stables to unsaddle and feed them.

The partners dragged their spurs across clean cement through the front door to see how much of the work had been finished. The kitchen and a big room beside it were completed. Two cots in the room were made up with sheets, pillows, and blankets. A washstand, washbowl, pitcher of water, and an old mirror were set up between the cots.

Che Che's wife Juanita came to the door to say hello and tell the partners their supper would be ready soon. While she prepared scrambled eggs and fried jerky, white ranch cheese, fried beans, flour tortillas, and coffee, Che Che brought glasses and poured them full of *lechuguilla*, the mezcal of the region, from a five-gallon demijohn.

Kane and Vogel recounted their visit to La Golondrina for Martinillo. They wanted him to know about the horse race, Lupino's stipulation that nobody spy on the training of his horse, and the fight between Kane and Rafa Lupino. Kane told Martinillo that he wanted Marco Antonio to train Gato for the race.

Juanita served their supper and Che Che brought the three men ice-cold bottles of Pacifico beer. "I tried to get Superior beer, because I know how much you like it," Che Che said. "But nobody in Rio Alamos has it anymore."

"This is fine," Juan Vogel said. "All our old-time friends and companions in adventure have begun to disappear, even the beer. We have to make new ones, or do without and miss them. It's the pain of survival that old geezers sooner or later are bound to feel."

"Yes," Che Che said. "The Superior beer disappeared after you two dammed it up and drank it all."

Vogel and Kane only grinned at him.

"When were you in Rio Alamos last?" Kane asked.

"Four months ago," Che Che said.

"And this beer has lasted you and your friends all this time?"

"I don't make friends of beer drinkers, except you three. I brought twelve cases, and these are the first eight bottles I've taken out of the cartons." He opened two bottles apiece for his friends, then opened two for himself.

Kane looked at melting grains of ice on the shoulders of his bottles. "How do you make ice, Che Che?"

"I bought a generator and an ice maker and packed them here on mules. Tonight, you'll have electric light when you read, Nino Jim."

"Where do you and Juanita and the children sleep? You have three children or four?"

"We have three. We sleep in the kitchen with the woodstove."

"Where are your cots?"

"We don't use them. When I lived here all those years with don Juanito, I learned to sleep on the floor. I like it better than a cot and Juanita and the children like it now."

"Why is that?" Kane said. "It's an awful way for a man to get his rest."

"Don Juanito said that nobody sneaks up on a man who sleeps on the ground."

"Yes, and I've heard that only men of guilty conscience sleep alone on beds of rocks," Vogel said to Kane.

"That's right. Do you still sleep on a bed of rocks, Nino?" Che Che asked.

They referred to Kane's habit of sprinkling the sheets of his camp bed with gravel before he crawled in between them. He also always slept alone. He had slept very few entire nights with Adelita in their forty years together.

"Will you put gravel in your bed tonight?" Vogel asked.

"No, I didn't last night at the Lupinos and not tonight."

"Why not?"

"I need to sleep sound. I don't think anything will try to slip up on me in the night with you people on every side of me. I'm too weak and lazy to jump up and fight if anything tries get me anyway. I might as well lie still and let them cut my throat."

Kane's three friends laughed.

Vogel rode with Kane to the airstrip the next morning to see him off and to lead Gato back to the hacienda. As always, he looked at Kane as though he thought it might be for the last time. He watched Kane from the time they left the hacienda until Kane rolled away from him in the airplane. When Little Buck lifted off the end of the runway and Kane turned down Arroyo Hondo, he looked back and Vogel was still standing where he'd left him with their horses at the head of the runway. The sentimental old thing always stayed for a last look at Kane until he flew out of sight, but he never waved.

An hour later, Kane landed at the airport on the edge of Rio Alamos. He had learned to pilot an airplane at that airport and at the same time learned to dodge buzzards. The first slaughterhouse of Rio Alamos had been on the edge of that airport, and its scraps of meat, bones, and offal were piled outside. Flocks of black, naked-headed vultures had feasted there, then taken flight to digest their cargo high on stoops of cool breeze. Kane had never chopped one up in his prop, but he still could not help but watch for them.

A haze of dust hung close over the town, as it had for the fifty years that Kane had known it. Most of the streets were paved now too. Its people called it Polvojoa, Dustywater. Most of the buildings had been painted in bright colors but had begun to take on thick layers of dust every hour since the paint dried. Its universal color was adobe that did not wash off anymore when it rained. When Kane first settled in the region, it enjoyed a hundred inches of rain a year, but no rain of the quantity the region needed to thrive had visited it for twenty years.

Vogel's wife Alicia picked Kane up in her sedan, and after he left orders with the airport attendant to top off Little Buck's tanks with gasoline, she took him home. Alicia was Adelita's sister. Kane wanted to visit for only an hour, then go on to Nogales, but she would not have it. She and her daughter Mari had prepared a feast for him.

"How come you're so glad to see me this time?" Kane asked Alicia. "You've never been nice to me and my compadre Juan before when we came down from the Sierra."

"You're both old now. I have Juan to myself. You almost got away from me when you fell off that horse, so I'm glad to have you back—this time."

"I didn't fall off; he fell on me."

"Well, whatever happened when you tried to die. When you two were young, nobody wanted you. When you came down from the Sierra together I paid men to keep you away. Now that you are old, I don't mind having you around. My Juan comes straight home and goes to bed early now. I waited him out, and he's finally all mine."

She winked at Kane. In their youth Kane and Vogel had celebrated their return to town from the Sierra for a week or two before they went home. From the time they were in their twenties until their sixties, they had never understood why all their wives could think about was having them home, why they spent all their time trying to make them come home. Kane guessed he ought to be happy that Alicia could finally have her husband home. That would make it so his compadre would probably go to heaven. He wished Adelita was here to see the change in Vogel. Kane still did not care about being home all the time, although he knew he would if Adelita was still there.

"I wasn't in the Sierra long enough to celebrate my return to this town this time," Kane said. "Only two days. I have to get on to the 7X as soon as I can anyway."

"Yes, but I have much to thank you for. You were gone from here for a year and a half and my *marido*, my spouse, finally discovered that he had a house. He likes his house now."

"I can't understand that."

"So, you have to stay with us awhile. I'll find you another wife. You need rest and food. You are thin as a ghost, Jim."

"No, we have a horse race to run in six weeks. I'm going home to get Cody Joe and Dolly Ann so they can come back with me and help get the horse ready."

"Ay, *carajo*, here we go again. Ali Lupino was here yesterday and told us about the race. With you and Juan, if it's not whorehouses, it's a horse wreck, or a horse race. When will you learn to live in quietude and stop taking risks? Don't you know that horse races only lose money and make enemies?"

"My horse Gato is going to win Vogel and Kane a hundred thousand *dolares grandes*," Kane said. He explained the terms of the matched race.

"That reminds me. When will my husband do something about his cough?"

"He says it will cure itself."

"Ali Lupino is worried about it. He stopped here on his way to

Tucson especially to tell me that my husband's lungs need to be examined and a biopsy taken."

"Oh, now Ali comes to blab to Juan's family? Who the chingado does he think he is, the Red Cross?"

"Yes, he's the Red Cross, and Juan's having a physical examination. He can just go to the United States with you the next time you go."

Alicia, Mari, and other Vogel family women were waiting for him at the house and would have liked to harangue Kane about Vogel all evening, but after supper he went away and took a shower, climbed into clean sheets in his room, and listened to them from there. He liked the sound of their voices after they lowered them so he could rest, and he slept well.

He rose early and left Alicia's house to have coffee in the kitchen of the Restaurant Teresita. Kane's and Vogel's old friend Teresita Rojo, the owner, had been the mistress of a famous revolutionary general. She gave Kane an embrace and looked into his eyes to see if he might have gone daft since she last saw him but said nothing about the horse fall.

He took off in Little Buck to Nogales before sunup.

As Kane flew the three and a half hours to his 7X ranch on the border, he wondered what new catastrophe might have befallen it in only two days. Lately, all anyone could expect on a border ranch was conflict. Criminals used his trails to smuggle people and narcotics in and out of the country. The Mexican government seemed to want the whole business to escalate so that Americans would learn a lesson about being too rich and generous. What other lesson they might want Americans to learn he did not know, but the Mexican president said that the border problem was all the fault of the Americans.

Border patrol, customs, and immigration services worked honorably and hard to stop illegal traffic, but a bunch of impatient citizens who had never lived near the border had formed a private militia to show them how America should be defended. Theirs was an ordinary people's fear of snakes. For every hundred snakes, perhaps ninety-nine are good, and one is poisonous or can swallow somebody. The ninety-nine good snakes take the rap for the bad one and get their heads stomped on because of this ordinary, common fear. For every hundred illegal immigrants that cross, one is a killer, or smuggles hard drugs, or preys on his poor fellows who cross the border in search of jobs. One in a hundred is a viper, so the militia straps pistols on its hips and comes to the border to play John Wayne and see who it can shoot.

The militia was the outfit that most caused Kane concern about his position on the border. If one of them ever used a popgun on some poor immigrant, Kane's home and livestock could become the bull's-eye in a border shooting war.

Illegal border traffic had undoubtedly become a dangerous flood. No longer did it consist only of honest people in search of work. Criminals from all parts of the world came hidden inside the hordes of honest workers. A gang of organized criminals that called itself Los Lobos had begun to guide high-paying illegals into the United States. They also preyed on the border crossers, smuggled hard dope, and trafficked in kidnapped women and children.

Thirty minutes from the Nogales border in Little Buck, Kane radioed the international airport so he could have a customs inspector on hand when he landed, then he began his descent. He would do some work in his office in Nogales and buy groceries before he flew on to the 7X.

As Kane prepared to land in Nogales, Cody Joe and Dolly Ann Kane drove into the yard of the 7X ranch in Cody Joe's pickup, a day sooner than expected.

"Pappy'll be surprised," Dolly Ann said as she unloaded a sack of groceries and carried it to the house. The youngsters called their grandfather Jim Kane "Pappy."

"He'd have to be here to be surprised," Cody Joe said. "He told me on the phone that he would not start back from Rio Alamos until today."

"I want to ride today. I've waited more than a month to ride."

"Well, Pappy doesn't want us to ride unless he or the Lion goes with us," Cody Joe said. "Too much new stuff going on."

"What new stuff?"

"When I told him we were coming, he said that he'd found a woman's knapsack by Aliso Springs. Inside he found a pair of lady's shoes, a dress, underwear, other personal stuff, and a plane ticket from Tucson to Baltimore."

"What happened to the woman?"

"No woman. No sign of her. She'd been taken, or something. Neither Pappy or the Lion could tell from the tracks what happened to her, because she left the backpack by the trail that is most used by those people."

"I think it will be all right if you and I ride together. He only meant that he doesn't want us to ride alone."

"His orders are for us not to ride if he or the Lion aren't here."

"Now, what's the good of you being a marine with combat training if you aren't bodyguard enough for your own little sister? I'm telling you, as proud as Pappy is of you being a marine, he won't get mad if you take me out for a two-hour ride."

Eighteen-year-old Cody Joe was on thirty-day leave after months of Fleet Marine Force combat infantry training. Sixteen-year-old Dolly Ann was in her senior year at a Tucson high school. Dolly Ann steered her brother to the corrals. Her horse, a mare named Quarter Moon, and Cody's horse Chance were in the main corral with a pile of hay. "See, they've even caught our horses up," she said.

"I see they're up. I don't see anything that says Pappy will like it if he flies in and finds that we've disobeyed his orders."

"Look, let's do this: I'll make sandwiches and fill a couple of water jugs. We'll ride out and help illegals who need food and water. I feel sorry for those people. They get turned loose by their coyote guides and told that Tucson is just over the next hill. Then they wander two or three days without food or water. They could die here, Cody. It's happened on other border outfits. How would you like that? We both want to ride, so let's see if we can be a little help to those poor people."

"Yes, and the next thing you'll do is give them a ride to Tucson, get caught, thrown in the brig, and you won't get out until you're an old hag."

"No, I won't. Pappy'd kill me."

They went in the house and Dolly Ann made ham and cheese and peanut butter and honey sandwiches and filled two plastic jugs with water. They carried it all to the corral and caught and saddled their horses.

Cody Joe did not try to dissuade her. She had made up her mind to ride, so he had to go with her. If he let her go alone, he would be in a lot more trouble. He never said much. He did not like to talk, and he sure did not like to repeat himself to his sister. He mounted his horse and carried the water jugs in a gunnysack that he hung on his saddle horn. Dolly Ann carried the sandwiches the same way and they rode south toward Manzanita Mountain and the border.

Kane landed on the 7X's dirt strip an hour before sundown. He saw Cody Joe's pickup in the yard. He taxied into the wire corral that kept the livestock off his airplane, parked it, and tied it down, then walked up to the yard.

He knew his grandchildren had gone somewhere or they would have driven the quarter mile to pick him up at the strip. He saw that their saddles and bridles were gone. He picked up their tracks at the corral gate. He saw that the Lion had ridden north alone. The youngsters had gone south. His worry made him get his old bones moving. His bones did not care about his worry, because they dragged at him and tried to hold him back.

He saddled his horse Mike, led him out and mounted, and his carcass became young enough again. He saw that his grandchildren had taken the Manzanita trail along a high ridge, so he took an easier trail that paralleled it to make better time. He caught up to them as they stopped for five people on the trail, a half mile away.

Dolly Ann's yellow hair was tied in a ponytail under the brim of an old, sweaty Stetson hat. In the lead, she had ridden around a bend and come face to face with three men and two women on foot. She stopped Quarter Moon in the narrow trail and greeted them. The women and two of the men only gave her blank looks, as though she might only be a tree in their way. The man in the lead grinned and took hold of Quarter Moon's rein.

"Are any of you hungry or thirsty?" Dolly Ann asked in Spanish.

The people only stared at her.

The man who held Quarter Moon answered in English. "You've

brought us something to eat?" he asked. "Do you live here? What's your name?"

"I have sandwiches for you, and my brother has water," Dolly Ann said. The leader handed the sandwiches to the next man, ignored Cody Joe, and did not release Dolly Ann's horse. The man behind the leader held the gunnysack with the sandwiches, but did not look inside.

"Let me ride your horse, while my friends eat," the leader said.

Cody Joe studied the people. The wiry leader wore a mustache trimmed to a thin line along his upper lip. He wore camouflaged U.S. Army utilities with the trousers bloused at the tops of the boots. His watch looked expensive. His shirt lay open to the second button and gold chains adorned his chest. Cody Joe figured him to be the coyote guide of the other four people.

The four people were not dressed for a long hike. One of the women only wore thin-soled loafers.

"Mister, let go of my horse," Dolly Ann said.

"Where's the water?" the guide asked without looking away from Dolly Ann's face. "Tell your brother to come up here."

Dolly Ann turned to look at Cody Joe. The guide took hold of the bottom of her stirrup, held her foot in it, and tried to lift her out of her seat to dump her off the other side of the horse.

Cody Joe spurred Chance and rode up beside Quarter Moon, broadsided the man with Chance's shoulder, and knocked him away from Dolly Ann's stirrup. He offered the gunnysack that contained two full gallons of water to the man as he stumbled backward. The man caught himself, straightened, and reached for it. Cody Joe gave the gunnysack an overhand swing and brought its contents down on the man's head, ran Chance over the top of him, turned Chance and Quarter Moon around, and led Dolly Ann back down the trail at a gallop.

Kane watched the whole event and thought he recognized the man under Cody Joe's horse as Güero Rodriguez, a bastard son of Eliazer Vogel, Fatima's deceased husband. Güero was a special friend of Rafa Lupino's and had gone to the same schools as his four Lupino half brothers. Kane had known for a long time that Rodriguez used the 7X's trails to guide illegals into the United States. Kane met him on the trails from time to time. Because he was the son of a Vogel, Kane allowed it.

Kane caught a movement in the corner of his eye and saw Andres "the Lion" Cañez wave to him from his same side of the ravine. They rode to meet one another.

"Did you see what happened over there?" Kane asked the Lion.

"I did," the Lion said.

"Who is that holding his head, the one Cody Joe ran over with his horse?"

"Did you see that too? It looked like Cody Joe smeared him all over the trail after he knocked him down. What did he knock him down with?"

"I think the boy is carrying water in a gunnysack. I didn't think the man he ran over would get up. Who is he? Is that Güero Rodriguez?"

"That's who it is. He uses this trail sometimes."

"Well, he just shit in his mess kit with us," Kane said. "I've looked the other way and let him alone, because he's related to Vogel and the Lupinos, but that's all over now. Let's ride over there and have a talk with that gentleman."

Kane and the Lion were sure Güero had not seen them, absorbed as he had been with the youngsters. They crossed the ravine and waited for him. They could hear him talk for a long time before they saw him. Just before he came in sight, he said in English, "I'll see young Miss Kane again. I can get a lot of money for a long-legged blonde like that." Then he looked up into the eyes of Kane and the Lion as they rode out in front of him and blocked the trail.

"Güero, what kind of idiot are you to fool with my grandchildren?" Kane asked.

"Señor Jim Kane, my heart feels good to see you," Güero said.

"What heart, Güero? You mean your chicken heart? Who are these foolish people who depend on it for guidance? Do they know how cowardly you are?"

"I only guide a poor family of Mexicans on their way to a new life in the United, with your permission."

"You can take them where they're going . . ."

"I'm grateful to you, Señor Kane."

". . . this time. However, this is the last hike you make across this ranch. The next time I meet you on one of my trails, you'll have to limp home on one foot, because I'm going to shoot you in the other one."

Güero grinned at Kane to see if he was joking.

"I saw your encounter with my grandchildren. I won't call the *migra*, immigration, but I will take away the use of one of your feet the next time I see you on this ranch."

"I've intended to stop by and thank you before this for allowing me safe passage, Señor Kane, but you've been away from home a lot. You know. I often stop by your home to make sure nobody does it damage when you are gone."

"So, I give you a friendly warning and you answer me with a threat to damage my home? You are only here because you are the bastard son of a Vogel. A lot of people have helped you because of that, but from now on, you're only another bastard to me, so stay off my trails."

"Look at his clients, Jim," the Lion said. "Who have you brought us this time, Güero?"

"These are only poor Mexicans looking for work, like all the rest," Güero said.

"You are not Mexicans, are you?" the Lion asked the followers in Spanish. "Speak to me. Where in Mexico are you from? Do you even speak Spanish?"

The people's eyes went blank, and they looked away.

"They're Arabs," Kane said, and one of the men looked him in the eye. "Where are you from?" Kane asked him in English.

The Arab turned away and sat on a rock.

"What kind of Arabs are you? Are you Hottentots? Philistines? Babylonians? Egyptians? Dervishes, or Bedouins?" Kane asked.

They all sat down.

"I know you speak English," Kane said. "I heard Güero talking to you. Don't come through this ranch again. You appear to be well-to-do people, maybe even good people, but you aren't Mexicans." He pointed to the Lion. "*That's* a Mexican."

"You look prosperous and that means you're not here to do honest work," Kane said. "If you are Arabs, you have a tradition of hospitality, and I've been shown wonderful hospitality by my Arab friends, so I'll let you go on. But don't come back. Don't think you can use this ranch until a time comes when you can import camels.

"Güero, I've never reported anyone who made his way across this ranch to look for work, and I never will. But now get your 'Mexicans' out of my sight as chingado quick as you can."

Kane and the Lion backed their horses off the trail and let Güero and his people go by. "Follow them, Lion, so we'll know where they meet their transportation," Kane said.

"You think he'll come again?"

"Sure he will. He's enjoyed special status as a Vogel all his life. I'm sure he believes that I've only given him his first little bawling out. I'm sure he thinks he has at least two more coming before I say anything I really mean. That's the way a bastard thinks."

Kane's grandchildren came out of the house to meet him when he rode into the yard. They followed him into the corral, and Cody Joe quickly unsaddled his horse. Kane walked out to the middle of the corral and made a show of inspecting the dried sweat on Quarter Moon and Chance.

"What could possibly have put you two in such a breeze that you ran your horses all the way home and put them away wet like that?" he said.

"We went out riding and had a little trouble," Dolly Ann said.

"I see that. Did you have some awful emergency?"

"We went out to see if we could find people who needed food and water, Pappy."

The girl's mouth and chin became hard to control with the truth, but she managed it.

Kane looked at Cody Joe. "You think that was a good idea, Marine?"

"We both wanted to ride, Pappy."

"Cody didn't want to do it," Dolly Ann said. "He went because I said I would go no matter what. He didn't think you would want him to let me go alone, Pappy."

"Do you know who that cannibal is that you ran into and then had to run over to get away?"

"No, Pappy," they said.

"That's the greediest bastard in Sonora. He would sell you to some other greedy bastard piece by piece and start with one finger, if he could get more money for you that way. Do you now have an idea why I don't want you kids to ride out alone?"

"Yes, Pappy," they said.

"The only people on this outfit who ride alone are the Lion and me. It's not smart for us to do it, but we've done it so long, we can't break ourselves of it. You don't ride alone because you don't have to. If you ever do it again, I'll ground you forever. Is that understood?"

"Yes, Pappy."

"Let's go get dinner. You two have to cook because you're in the dog-house. And hurry before the Lion gets back and wants to cook. All he knows how to make is spoilt tortilla."

The Lion returned in time for supper and took Kane aside. Güero and his clients had met someone at the abandoned Vincent mine and driven away to the north in a brand-new Hummer.

The youngsters made hands of themselves and cooked supper. The next day the three Kanes and the Lion started the spring roundup.

Five

Martinillo returned home to Las Animas and found his wife Lucrecia in a bad mood. Her bad humor did not extend to her grandchildren, only to him. He heard her laugh with Marco Antonio's sister Luci when he rode into the yard, but he stopped the fun right quick when he called to her. She came out of the house with a smile and a hug for Marco Antonio, but none for him. He knew something had gone wrong and she blamed it on him because he had been gone too long. She did not like to deal with crisis without her husband, and the very elements seemed to turn against the Martinillo family every time he left the house.

Martinillo sent Marco Antonio to the corrals to unsaddle the mules while he sat on the veranda to listen to his wife. Luci brought him a glass of mezcal, and he relaxed on the floor with his legs sprawled out and his back against the wall.

"Adan, you can't leave us here alone anymore," Lucrecia said. "You or Marco Antonio have to stay home, or move me and Luci to Rio Alamos."

"What happened?"

"Luci and I went to wash clothes in the stream and found wolf tracks. Wolves watered within fifty yards of this house night before last."

"How many?"

"Five. They have to be the five you saw at Guasisaco."

"Four females and a male."

"Yes. Luci and I tracked them to Puerto de las Parvas and caught them lying down sunning themselves yesterday morning. Only two of them got to their feet when they saw us. They acted as though they knew us. The male circled us, no more afraid than he would have been if he had us in a cage."

"Juan Vogel found out from the Chihuahua Cattleman's Union that fake wolves like these are being raised and sold out of cages in Parral."

"I was more afraid when they showed no fear of us than I would have been if they had growled and threatened. They only lay there and stared, as if to say, 'Give us food, or it's you we'll eat.' I think they came down to the stream to size us up, discovered our penned animals, found a woman and girl alone, and decided that we would be their food supply from now on."

"That's probably right."

"I know it. They only wait for the right phase of the moon to fall on us."

"That's probably true. Now, will you kiss me hello, or do I have to fall on you and take it?"

"No, the children."

"I am a man who has traveled long and far over trackless wilderness, as Jim Kane describes it, to arrive finally at my haven, and have been desperate for my woman's love. Now, come and sit on my lap and kiss me woman, or I will fall on you like a beast."

Lucrecia smiled at him, raised her head, and called out, "Luci, do you have the stew ready? Your grandfather needs to eat." She rose, took his glass, wiggled her butt at him, and went in the kitchen. He washed his face and hands at a stand on the porch. He went to the end of the porch and looked up toward Las Parvas.

A four-legged predator had not bothered Las Animas since El Yoco the jaguar had terrorized the Martinillo women, children, and livestock thirty years ago, since the night their Toro Buey, their work bull, took on El Yoco in their front yard and put him in the breeze.

Martinillo knew the wolves would come. The best time to kill them would be when they gave their full attention to the prey in his yard and pens. The best way to kill these cur ones that were used to having their meat carried to them by handymen was to catch them with their heads in the blood of their prey, or when they thought they were about to take their first bite.

Right now, before they learned to kill, before they learned how much fun it could be, his family was not in danger, only his penned animals were. Martinillo remembered his childhood when he and his brothers and sisters trembled at the mention of the black lobo. That savage hunted alone and snatched babies out of their yards and grown men and women off the trails and did not leave a track. That lobo feared nothing. He killed as though he hated his victims, because he did not eat them, did not even play with them. He savaged his victims for the viciousness in him because he was evil.

These fake wolves had chosen Las Animas as a store of meat. Their meat fattened at Las Animas and awaited their pleasure. They could come and get it anytime, no hunting, no tracking, no need for wile.

Martinillo ate his supper, then took his new .22 Winchester lever action, magnum carbine from its felt bed under a board in the kitchen floor and loaded its magazine. He took a Remington pump magnum shotgun and loaded it with oo buckshot. He stood both weapons beside the kitchen door, helped Marco Antonio feed the livestock and milk the cows, stepped naked into the #10 washtub in the kitchen, took a bath, and went to bed.

In the night, he heard the fair facsimile of the moan of a hungry wolf. The moan summoned the primordial beast, resonated with its loneliness, but did not ring true enough for Martinillo. He remembered the black wolf that ran alone in the Sierra Madre of his childhood, the phantom of the night that not even the American government trappers could kill with cyanide plugs. The American trappers eliminated the Mexican wolf, the gray one, the one everyone knew, but they did not get the primordial one, the legendary black one, the great-grandfather that ran alone. When that one moaned, a man's blood lost its color, he sat up in bed and blessed himself, and he became an animal until that sound ceased to resonate in his memory.

The Martinillo family ate their breakfast at four in the morning and sat and waited for first light so they could care for the animals. The chickens had not dropped from their roosts. Martinillo and Lucrecia spoke softly and said little. The grandchildren did not speak. The family drank sweet coffee and milk together while the fiber of their bodies came alive for a fight, and they listened for the arrival of the wolf pack. This was the way it would be every morning until the wolves came.

Martinillo had penned El Toro Buey, his work bull, with his two milk cows. Their calves, a newborn and an eight-month-old, were in the milk pen. A direct descendent of the Toro Buey that had whipped El Yoco the jaguar, this toro had grown up to be every bit as strong and brave. Gentle as he was with his people and other cattle, he also served as the family's first line of defense. Martinillo did not doubt that he would teach the wolves to fly if they got in the pen with him before Martinillo arrived with the shotgun.

Martinillo expected the chickens to sound the first warning. These wolves would start their careers as *corsarios*, pirates. They probably expected to raid the family's corral in a gang to kill and bloody themselves, then feast until they were full and did not think the people could do anything about it. People were only the handymen who carried their meat and water to them.

The Martinillos heard their hens grumble uncomfortably. Then a rooster cackled loudly, incensed. El Toro Buey bugled one shocked grunt, and the family knew the raid was on. On their way out the door, Martinillo grabbed the shotgun, Lucrecia, the rifle, Marco Antonio, the ax. Luci switched on a powerful battery lantern and ran to the top of the corral to illumine the battleground and blind the wolves with the spotlight.

The family saw a wolf tossed into the air by El Toro Buey. He flew end over end above the *retaque*, the main corral's wall of mesquite, and fell back into the corral. As Martinillo went over the corral wall, he saw the bull pin the same snarling male wolf into a corner of the corral. The wolf slashed at the bull's muzzle and eyes, but the bull hooked him left and right with his horns like a boxer, then pinned him against the ground.

The bawl of the cattle and the screeches and screams of the other animals became a bedlam. A bitch wolf took the yearling heifer's muzzle in her front teeth and held her. One of the heifer's ears had already been torn off. Another bitch held her by the tail and another had begun to feed under the tail. Martinillo's shotgun blast blew the heart out of the wolf on her muzzle. The heifer whirled and stood spraddle legged between Martinillo and the two wolves on her rear end. El Toro Buey's wolf scrambled out from under him and ran straight at Martinillo. Intent on the bull, he did not see Martinillo, who put the next wad of oo buckshot into his ear.

Marco Antonio hurried to the bawling of the calves and went over the wall into the milk pen. Another bitch wolf had already killed the newborn calf and taken the hindquarters of the other calf in her jaws. Marco Antonio brought the butt of the ax down on the wolf's back but did not dislodge her. The wolf shook and tore at the bawling calf's hams and paid no attention to the boy. The boy fell on her with the sharp edge of the ax and sliced through the root of her tail. The wolf rolled away from the ax and scrambled through the gate poles into the main corral but left her tail behind.

Lucrecia's magnum bullet exploded through the heart of the wolf that tore at the yearling's hindquarters. The other wolf bit through the heifer's tail and she ran free. The bobtailed wolf and the wolf with the heifer's tail in her mouth scrambled through the gate poles and streaked across the yard toward the timbered mountain behind the house. Luci held them in the beam of the spotlight. Lucrecia ran into the open yard, stopped still, sighted her rifle with Luci's beam of light behind her shoulder, held her breath, and killed the wolf with the tail in her mouth as she was about to gain cover in the timber. The bobtailed bitch, now all alone, made it into the timber and used its protection expertly to flee up the side of the mountain.

"Grandmother, kill the other one," Luci shrieked.

"She's gone." Lucrecia turned back toward the main corral and levered another cartridge into the Winchester's chamber.

Martinillo raised up over the top of the corral wall. "We killed four and bloodied the last one," he said. "Not too bad."

Marco Antonio climbed up and squatted on top of the wall with his ax and grinned. Luci shined her light on him. He had blood on his face, blood and manure on his breast.

"Are you hurt, boy?" Lucrecia asked in her low voice.

"No, Grandmother. I slipped and fell in the runny calf manure when I swung the ax at the wolf that killed our calf."

"I thought you cut her, son," Martinillo said.

"I did, but I only got this." The boy held up the tail.

The family dragged the four wolves to the yard and skinned them, then hitched them to El Toro Buey and dragged them down the canyon for the coyotes. They skinned and quartered the calf to save the meat. The wolf that had fed on the hind end of the heifer had opened a hole into her insides, so Martinillo butchered her too. The family spent the day slicing her meat into sheets. They salted and peppered the sheets and hung them on a wire to dry. They went inside for supper at sundown.

"Which one did I let get away?" Lucrecia asked after the youngsters had gone to bed.

"A female," Martinillo said. "I killed the only male. El Toro Buey had already hooked him on a horn and tossed him, then broke him up against the rock wall of the milk pen. He couldn't run very well when he broke away from El Toro Buey, and he was more worried about him than he was about me when I killed him. Another three jumps and he would have run me down."

"Too bad. The one who got away will have little ones."

"I don't doubt that."

"Too bad we didn't get them all. I'm scared for the children and for my old grandmother self. I'm tired of this fang and claw life that's always only one little mistake, or one little step from hurt, or death."

"I know, my love."

"Remember a long time ago, when we could count on our neighbors? We were never safe, but we knew how to save ourselves and make a living. In a crisis, we could at least reach out to a neighbor for comfort and help. Now, our neighbor releases wolves to plague us. Our other neighbors carry machine guns. How long before new enemies come to plant the seed for the big cash crop anywhere they want to, as they have for the past thirty years?"

"My compadres Kane and Vogel think the Lupinos have caused the trouble."

"Their wolves cost us a calf and a heifer today. Why did they release them on us? If they want wolves, why don't they release them on La Golondrina?"

"If what my compadres suspect is true, the Lupinos want to do away with all their neighbors, have wanted to for thirty years. They probably thought the wolves would help them do it. Look at you. The wolves made you sick of your own home."

"Bueno, if you know who to fight to make our home safe again, get after them. You know who to stop, *stop* them. I don't think you should wait and talk about it. Look, Adan, we're the only family in the region who even grows our own corn and beans anymore. Everyone else buys their corn and beans. Everyone else raises the big cash crop instead of corn and beans. That business will bring us another war. I don't want this family to go through another one. I don't want to lose another of my children."

"No natural predator has bothered us as El Yoco did, until now," Martinillo said. "The Sinaloans are the only predators who bother us. Nobody ever thought to wonder where the Sinaloans got the money to come and camp on our streams with machine guns. If they had the money to buy the seed, why didn't they plant it in Sinaloa? They have the Sierra Madre there too. Why did they come all the way over here, where they had to kill people to do it? It has to be because, as my compadres say, someone in this region financed them. Who was already established here in the drug business thirty years ago and has harvested opium gum successfully for sixty years?"

"Don Nesib Lupino."

"Well, of course."

"I don't think that old man wants to do away with us. That's hard for me to believe, husband. My parents said that his opium crop was legal, that he sold it directly to the government. Doesn't the government need it in every hospital? Aren't hospital drugs made from opium?"

"All right, if that's true, why didn't the Sinaloans camp on his watercourses to raise their mota? Why didn't they get their crops started on La Golondrina and then run to the officials in Chihuahua and denounce the Lupinos as marijuana growers? They tried it with every other big rancher in the Sierra: Vogel and Kane, the Guevaras, the Willys, the Breaches, the Floreses, the Parras, the Almadas, and many more. Vogel and Kane are the only ones who did not give up and sell their ranches to the Lupinos. Think of that. Who else has bought ranches in this region for the past thirty years when every other decent person gathered his belongings and hit for town?"

"Only the Lupinos."

"Nesib Lupino is the one against whom we should have warred all this time. When he and Jim Kane matched their horse race, he made Jim promise that he would not spy on the training of his horse Auda. Kane and Vogel wonder about that. Everyone knows they would never spy on an opponent's training, because they don't have to. They can win regardless of the way their opponent trains his racehorse.

"Jim may have promised not to spy on Auda's training, but *I* did not. I'm going to find out why don Nesib is so secretive about his horse. Does he want to hide something new about the training? Is it some person he hides? Or is it some place or camp that he wants to keep secret? He hides *something*. He must be senile to call attention to it, but he has done that. I've never seen his high country. I bet I find the answer to the wolves up there."

Martinillo rested a week and did the work he needed to do so his family would not need him for a while. He rode Kane's mule Paseador to Guazaremos. At Guazaremos he packed Vogel's mule El Negrito with his provisions and led him eight leagues southeast into the mountains to Vogel's Canela camp on the border of the high Sierra of La Golondrina.

The Canela camp had a generator for electricity, but Martinillo did not fire it up because he wanted quiet. He had to know when any man or beast came near, and he did not want anyone to know he camped there. After he unsaddled the mules, he turned them loose to return to Guazaremos so he would not have to worry about them.

He unlocked the house and went inside. Kane and Vogel had been the last ones to stay there. They had left a lot of canned provisions, so he would be able to stay longer than anticipated. He had brought fresh jerky. He found a box of .22 magnum cartridges, but he had left the rifle with Lucrecia. He found a bookcase full of cowboy novels that Kane had left there, but all in English. He picked one up to see what he could understand about it. "*Sepa la chingada*, who the fornication could know what it says?" he said, and put it carefully back into the bookcase.

Martinillo knew that Kane loved that place because it was in the deep middle of a separate world. He often made himself comfortable there with his work, his generator, his cowboy novels, and his beer. He sent Che Che Salazar with beer and novels to that remote camp even when he did not expect to be there for months. When he camped at Canela, he did not care if the rest of the world came apart, and he never left any beer.

Martinillo lit a coal oil lamp and cooked a supper of fried potatoes, onions, eggs, and jerky. After supper he sat on a veranda that faced north and the high Sierra of La Golondrina. From Canela, the high Sierra did not seem so far away and obscure. The high, quiet mountain peaks were at eye level. He commanded the high ground from a comfortable camp.

Six

 On the first day of spring roundup, Kane, his grandchildren, and Andres "the Lion" Cañez led five mules packed with their beds and provisions and drove a remuda of eight horses to Buster camp on the west side of the 7X. The seven-square-mile division that they planned to round up first was called the Ruby pasture. The north end of a range of mountains called the Sierra de San Juan cut it off from the other forty-seven square miles of the 7X.

The Ruby pasture was an open, high plateau with a good stand of native grass. Even people who had been Kane's neighbors for twenty years knew little about it. Its only access was by horseback, and not many of Kane's neighbors ventured off their ranches horseback. He could use it any way he wanted, because he owned it, and it was not the business of any government agency.

The only eastern access to Ruby pasture was through Buster Pass on the Sierra de San Juan, where Kane's grandfather had built a cabin. When Kane was a youngster, all the neighbors knew about the Ruby, but through the years the Kanes had stopped talking about it, and now only bears, wolves, lions, Kanes, and an occasional illegal immigrant found their way through the pass. A trail that ran north and south crossed the border there and followed the spine of the Sierra de San Juan. Illegal immigrants were guaranteed unopposed entry into the United States if they used that trail. They were also guaranteed a place to rest and water, for natural springs welled up all along the trail. The vehicles of the migra, American border patrol, could be seen miles away from the vantage of that trail.

After the crew of the 7X corralled the remuda at Buster cabin, they unpacked the mules, remounted their horses, split up, and rode away again. The youngsters rode around their horse pasture fence to check for holes before the remuda was turned out. Kane and the Lion rode the high trail along the spine of the mountains to reconnoiter the pasture for cattle. They could see every inch of the 7X from various lookout points on the trail. They could watch the progress of the youngsters as they rode around the horse pasture.

Kane and the Lion stopped to look for cattle and enjoy a light breeze on a cliff beside the trail. They dismounted and took off their hats so the breeze would cool their sweaty heads. The brink of the cliff at their feet was more than a thousand feet above the pasture.

This spot was Kane's favorite place on the ranch. A clear spring flowed out of the ground beside their horses' feet. During wet times of the year, it became a waterfall that could be seen many miles away. This was the place that made him feel most that he owned the 7X. Seventy percent of the rest of it was owned by the U.S. government, and he only owned the grazing rights to it. Environmentalists and nature conservationists were suing the government for the abolition of grazing rights. Many of Kane's fellow Arizona ranchers' rights had been taken away, or drastically reduced. The reasons given were that cattle threatened a certain minnow in a ranch's streams, or a certain woodpecker or owl in its trees. Cabins and corrals were being leveled because they had been ruled an eyesore to the natural order.

Kane was the fifth generation of his family to own the 7X and its government grazing rights. At the end of his life he would turn out his last bunch of cows on the Ruby pasture and live there by himself until he died. He would turn the rest of the outfit, or what was left of it after his grazing rights had been reduced on the government-owned part of it, over to his grandchildren. He would let them visit him when they needed him, but he would stay clear of the rest of the world during his final years.

Kane and the Lion had built a dam below the waterfall that held a large pool. They stepped to the edge of the cliff and looked down into its blue depths. Native trout already lived and multiplied there. Only he and the Lion knew that he had stocked the pool with the fish. They planned to go to that pool after they had located the cattle for tomorrow's drive. They would catch the first dozen trout ever caught there and surprise the youngsters with them.

Kane was about to put his hat on and find a good, solid stepping-stone on which to lift his bones into the saddle when he saw movement in the grassy center of the Ruby pasture. The Lion had already seen it.

"What's that? It looks like a pack of people have surrounded something," Kane said.

"People," the Lion said. "One, two, three, four big people have two little people surrounded."

"Damn my old eyes. Are they playing or fighting?"

"The little ones throw rocks at the big ones."

"It's not coyotes after our calves, is it?"

"No, Jim. It looks like four men after some children."

"I'll never come up here again without my spyglass," Kane said.

"We better get down there."

They stayed on the high trail north for another five minutes, then dropped off through a steep chute to a game trail that wound to the bottom of the mountain. Kane was riding his tough fourteen-year-old sorrel horse called Mike that was about half cold-blooded, but plenty big-hearted.

The eighty-five-year-old Lion rode a five-year-old bronc named Trago. Kane was in the lead, but when they reached a scree slope at the bottom, Trago bucked and lunged past him. The Lion grinned at Kane as he went by. The horsemen hit the grass at the bottom running, but they pulled up and slowed down to a steady lope so they would have plenty of horse under them when they reached the people.

They were not seen because when they reached the level plateau, a low ridge hid them. They pulled up behind the ridge about a hundred yards from the people and let their horses blow. Kane took down his forty feet of nylon, hard-twist rope and laughed when he saw that the Lion did the same. He said, "At least we're well armed," and over the ridge they charged.

Four men with shaved heads dodged back and forth in a thick stand of sacaton grass. A boy and a girl had backed up to the ridge to throw rocks at them. The necks, faces, and heads of the men were tattooed. The two tall cowboys on twelve-hundred-pound horses must have looked big to them, because they stopped dodging rocks and stared.

Kane picked the two on the left and the Lion picked the two on the right and they proceeded to run them down. Kane's first thug was too surprised to move and save himself. All he did was say "Hey" when Kane's horse ran over the top of him. When the second one saw that, he turned and ran for his life. Without looking back, he drew a tiny pistol and threw shots back at Kane. Kane caught up to him, rated him at the same pace, and bounced a loop of his rope off the shaved head, neck, and shoulders for ten good jumps before he let Mike's hooves drag the man down.

Kane held Mike while he danced a Schottische on the tattoos. It bothered Mike to tromp on what he thought was a person, so Kane rode him off, dismounted, and stomped another tattoo on the thug's head. He left him for dead and looked back to see how the Lion was doing. The Lion had caught one of his by both feet and was dragging him through the sacaton. The man's head bounced like a volleyball across the open ground and flew high every time his carcass struck a clump of grass.

Kane found the .25-caliber popgun the thug had fired at him, removed the clip, and threw pistol and clip away in different directions. He rode back to see how much damage Mike had done to the first thug but could not find him. He went on to look for the two youngsters the thugs had tried to take.

He found the Lion's other thug in high grass. His carcass lay in a heap on top of his head. Kane prodded him with Mike's front feet and he rolled on his side. He seemed well on his way to the next world, if not already there. His neck looked broken.

The sacaton grass was so thick and high that Kane could not see the two youngsters. He rode in a wide circle, found their tracks, and followed them to a half-acre tank stocked with rainwater. He surprised them when he rode over its clay dam.

A girl about twenty and a boy about fourteen stared up at him with big eyes. They were small brown people from way down south and too tired to run. They were drinking the muddy tank water from a plastic cup. Kane saw in their faces that they believed he had come to gather them up and ship them home.

He stopped ten yards away. "Don't be afraid of me. Where are you from?"

"From Michoacan," the girl said.

"Brother and sister?"

"Yes."

"Your names?"

"Concepción Bojorquez," the girl said.

"Luis Bojorquez," the boy said.

"Where are you going?"

"Taos, New Mexico."

"Good place. Do you know how to get there?"

"Oh, yes," the girl said.

"You've been there before?"

"I've worked there four years."

The Lion rode up leading three thugs with his rope around their necks. He had collared them with clove hitches. The thug who had fired his pistol at Kane was the burliest of the three.

"One of mine and your two can walk, but my other one is down with his *pelón* head under him," the Lion said.

"Man, are you trying to choke us to death, or break our necks?" the burly thug said.

"You don't like it?" the Lion said

"No, we don't like it, old man. Turn us loose, if you want to live." He reached up and tried to loosen the rope collar.

The Lion dallied the end of his rope on his saddle horn, spurred Trago into a run, jerked the thugs down in the dirt, and dragged them about ten yards before he pulled up and gave them slack. They sat up choking and clawing at their collars with their mouths full of dirt.

"You like that better?" Kane asked.

Their mouths were too full of dirt and they were too choked to talk.

"We're taking you back to Mexico. You can walk, or we can drag you by your necks. You decide which it will be while I talk to these children you tried to hurt, but keep your mouths shut except to spit out my dirt. Spit out all my dirt, because it's not yours to keep."

Kane turned back to the children. "How will you make it to Taos?" Kane asked the girl.

She looked away. "Who knows?" she said.

"She doesn't want to say," the Lion said.

"You don't have to tell us," Kane said. "I only want to know if you can make it on your own from here."

"If someone doesn't catch us," the girl said.

"How far do you have to go before someone picks you up?" the Lion asked.

". . . *saaabe*," the girl said and looked at the ground.

"It doesn't look like you have far to go," Kane said. "You didn't bring food or water, did you?"

"In here," she said and pointed to her small backpack.

"You can't carry much in that."

She pointed to her brother's pack.

"Have you come this way before and watered at this tank?"

"Yes."

"Why did you go to your home in Michoacan? Why risk being caught by the migra if you have a job in Taos? You were safe there."

"Our mother died."

"I'm sorry. Your father lives?"

"Yes."

"Take my advice and stay in Taos if he dies. He won't know if you don't go home. If he's like me, he wants you to be safe."

Neither child said anything about that. They looked at the ground.

"How did you know about this route? Did your coyote bring you this way, then leave you?"

"We had no coyote guide. My father brought me the first time. This is my brother's first time."

"I just wonder when this place is going to turn into a *camino real*, royal highway, like the trail that passes by our headquarters," Kane said to the Lion.

"We ought to attend to these *pelones* before it gets dark," the Lion said.

"All right. That everything goes well for you," he said to the youngsters.

They looked at the ground while Kane and the Lion rode away with the thugs in tow.

"They don't have far to go. They brought no food or blankets," the Lion said. "Somebody's waiting for them close by."

"I hope so. I don't want to be the one who finds their dead little bodies," Kane said.

Kane and the Lion stopped the thugs beside the one who was down and still comatose.

"Is he dead?" Kane said.

"See if your filth is dead," the Lion ordered the burly thug.

All three thugs had to kneel so the burly one could feel for a pulse. He looked up at the Lion and said, "I can't feel a heartbeat."

The Lion dismounted and touched the fallen thug's jugular. "It's beating enough. Let's go."

The three thugs stood and headed toward the border.

"No, no, no," Kane said. "Pick up your filth. You'll leave no garbage here."

"How?" The burly one asked.

"Carry him," Kane said.

"How can we do that?"

"Show them, Lion," Kane said.

The Lion told the burly thug to grab the prone one under the arms and the other two to pick up the legs. The two who carried the legs started walking toward Mexico, but the burly thug saw that he had to carry a whole lot more weight and dropped his colleague's head on the ground.

"I can't do this," the burly thug said. He knelt and stuck his fingers inside his collar to ease the strain. "I can't and I won't."

Kane got off his horse, hitched another length of the Lion's rope around the burly thug's ankles, threw the loop of his own rope around the prone thug's ankles, remounted, and he and the Lion began to drag the pile of thugs toward the border in a tangle of rope, dust, brush, and cactus. After about ten yards the burly thug was the only one who could make a sound and he began to squeak, "I can do it, I'll pick him up. Stop, stop, stop."

Kane and the Lion dragged the pile another ten yards before they stopped. The burly thug took the ropes off his and the prone thug's legs and picked him up so he and his partners could carry him.

This was not the first time that Kane and the Lion had caught members of this gang doing violence on the American side of the line. They had been at war with the Lobos gang for two years. The war started when the partners caught four Lobos on the run carrying the quarters and loin strip of a 7X beef they had killed. After the thugs had fired the barn at the 7X headquarters, Kane and the Lion had tracked them back to the carcass of the beef. The hoodlums had evidently fired the barn as a diversion so they could kill the beef and escape with the meat.

The Lobos gang was now a fixture on border ranches. They robbed, raped, and beat everyone they could catch and vandalized any property left unguarded. They had built a reputation as predators. Newspapers on both sides of the line gave them publicity. That made it so Kane and the Lion knew exactly with whom they waged war. The thugs even wore uniforms: shaved and tattooed heads and bodies, sleeveless T-shirts, high priced athletic shoes, and trousers that hung down on their hips and bagged over their shoes.

Now, Kane and the Lion were being given the undivided attention of the three conscious and bruised Lobos. "We better shoot them," the Lion said, and he drew his Winchester from a holster under his leg. "What if they come back when we're not around and hurt somebody?"

"They might come back," Kane said. "But it will be a while. The first one I hit still looks woozy and will probably not wake completely up until the middle of next month. I whipped the second so bad he'll pee every time he thinks about it. One thing about reata, and hard-twist whippings, they linger unpleasantly in the minds of thugs."

"Let's shoot them and drag them back across to the line," the Lion said. "Nobody lives on the ranch on the other side since the Roldan family went broke in the drought. The Mexican bank that owns it now doesn't look after it. We won't even have to dig their graves. We'll just lay their carcasses in a wash and cave the bank over them. Their corpses will rot in peace and not even their bones will be found. Nobody will miss these maggots anyway."

"Well, if you want to do that, Andres, let's drive them over there and shoot them after we've got them in the wash. Why tire our horses by dragging them?"

"Fine with me," the Lion said. "Get going pelones," he ordered.

The three sound thugs shuffled toward Mexico.

"Wait a minute," Kane said. "Pick up your partner, or drag him, but he goes with you."

Kane whacked the burly thug on the head with the double of his rope. "What's your name, Snake Eyes?" he said.

The burly thug could only see Kane from the corner of his eye because the Lion's rope was too tight on his throat. "Now you want to know my name, man?" he squeaked.

"Give me a name and tell me the truth, or I'll look in your pocket and find out for myself, or I'll make one of your friends say it. You don't want to tell me your name? How would you like us to drag you again?"

"Armando. It's Armando, here or anywhere."

"Well, Armando Here or Anywhere, you and your friends are going to lose your lives when we get you across the line, so if you know any prayers, say them."

Kane drew a .22 magnum pistol from his chaps pocket and fired a round between Armando's feet without aiming. "I'm not a good shot, but I won't have to shoot you from far away, collared as you are. You're lucky that bullet didn't take off your knee, or your balls, because I didn't take aim, but I'll pull the trigger on the next one with the barrel in your ear."

The thug who Kane had run over with his horse, the smallest in the pack, had been making gasping, sobbing sounds. *"Ay que la chingada,"* the Lion said. "The little one's about to bawl. No, he *is* bawling."

"Are you *weeping*, you miserable little shit?" Kane said. "It won't save your life, so save your breath. Shut up and walk."

Kane and the Lion herded the thugs across the border and up a dry wash to a place by a stretch of loamy bank and ordered them to lie on the ground head to toe. The partners dismounted and tied the thugs' hands and feet behind their backs with piggin' string. Kane then unsheathed the knife that Abdullah had given him and earmarked each thug the way he did his 7X calves by notching out a swallow fork in the top of their ears.

As the partners rode away and left the thugs tied, bleeding, and bawling, the Lion said, "Good idea, Jim. Now we'll know who they are. It would have been a shame to turn them loose without earmarking them. Even their mothers probably disowned them long ago."

"Yeah, some shaved-headed, tattooed people who dress that way must be good people," Kane said. "This way, we start a new brotherhood of the failed thugs we've captured. Now at least they carry the kind of disfigurement that will do some good. The disfigurement of a tattoo doesn't do any good for them, or for us. Now we can tell the good ones from the bad ones."

The partners intercepted Dolly Ann and Cody Joe as they rode out the gate of the horse pasture to look for their grandfather.

"What happened, Pappy?" Dolly asked.

"We caught four Lobos threatening two young illegals," Kane said.

"What did you do to them?"

"Nothing. They scattered and ran too fast."

"You didn't chase them?"

"What for? What would we do if we caught them?"

"We thought we heard shots."

"One of them had a popgun that he shot at us while he ran away."

"He missed?"

"He didn't think he had time to stop and take aim."

"We saw you driving some people. What was that for?"

"Oh, those were some Lobos who got lost."

"Where did you take them?"

"Back across the line."

"Why did you do that?"

"They got lost over here, but they knew their way home."

"Just so you don't get in trouble, Pappy," Dolly Ann said.

"Don't worry, darling. We got no trouble. Those Lobos have the trouble. I think we scared them." Kane grinned at the Lion.

The 7X crew returned to the Buster camp and found it in shambles. Their beds had been shredded, their victuals and utensils stolen or scattered on the floor. The cast-iron woodstove lay in pieces, the victim of someone who had wielded the camp's sledgehammer. Kane did not tell anyone that his grandfather had packed that stove to the camp in pieces on mules. He did not show how much it bothered him, because he did not want to make a fuss over the way he felt.

The crew used the rest of the day to salvage what they could. The tatters that were left of their beds would serve them if they worked hard enough to be tired when they lay down to rest at night. They found canned food that was still good, and they found all the eggs intact. The Kanes always packed the eggs on the mules last and unloaded them first. Dolly Ann had laid them in the cool, dark bottom of a closet.

The next day, on their first drive, the crew found a yearling steer with a broken leg. They left him behind and went on with the herd. He wandered in later to be with his fellows. After they worked the herd, they caught him and butchered him and found a .25-caliber bullet in the leg. The crew discussed this and decided that the wound was fresh enough to have been caused by the thugs Kane and the Lion had escorted across the line.

The crew hung the yearling's carcass in a tree every night, then wrapped it in a tarp and stowed it on the floor inside the closet during the day. At six thousand feet, Buster camp was plenty cool at night. The crew also salvaged some coffee, flour, beans, potatoes, and most of the grain for the horses. They cooked over an open fire and got used to it.

The crew's precious coffeepot, cast-iron skillet, and Dutch oven had been hidden under the floor of the cabin, so the raiders missed them. Soon, all the signs of destruction disappeared. After they cooked one meal on the open fire the first night, they decided to sleep outside too. Their tarps would still turn water, and that was all the shelter Kane and the Lion had used for half their lives. The crew even moved its camp to the pool at the foot of the high mountains for a while and caught trout at suppertime.

The crew did not speculate on who had tried to destroy their camp.

They did not even discuss it until the last evening before they returned to headquarters. Dolly Ann worried about it more than any of them, and she finally brought it up.

"Who do you suppose tore up our camp, Pappy?" Dolly asked.

"It doesn't matter," Kane said. "We'll never catch them."

"What can we do about it?"

"We've always left this camp wide open, so people who needed shelter could use it, and we've never been sorry about that. Now, we'll pack up everything we can and take it back to headquarters, like other ranchers do."

"We'll have to get a lock for the door, Pappy."

"Won't do any good. Vandals would love an excuse to break down the door. No, we'll have to leave it open, but we won't be able to count on the cabin for shelter anymore. Somebody will probably burn it, before long. The government has been after us to tear it down anyway."

"Why, Pappy?"

"The environmentalists want the government to condemn our property here and restore it to its natural beauty. That means no cabin."

"Can they do that?"

"No . . . well, maybe and maybe not, but some darned tree hugger can come up here and burn it down and we can't stop him."

"Gosh, Pappy."

"Don't worry about it, darling. We're all right. From now on we'll make camp at a different place every time we come up here and keep an eye on the country better. We'll gather and brand out of a holdup at a different place every day and do a better job."

"What's a holdup, Pappy?" Cody Joe asked.

"You know what a holdup is, Button. We'll hold them up where we find them, rope them out of the holdup and brand them right there, then go on to the next bunch. We'll carry our outfit on the mules and camp anywhere we want. We might even break some workhorses and pull a wagon up here and live out of that. That'll be a lot more fun and a lot less worry than being dependent on a cabin for shelter. The great outdoors is a whole lot better place to live anyway."

"What about those hoodlums you and the Lion ran off the day we packed in, Pappy?" Dolly Ann asked. "What can we do about them? They're the ones who shot and crippled the yearling we butchered, aren't they? Them, or somebody like them."

"That's not hard to figure out. We'll go armed like our grandfathers did when they came to this country. We'll have to learn to defend ourselves against different kinds of bandits again, that's all. I'd call them Apaches just to give them a name, but that would be an insult to Apaches."

"You shoot somebody, you're in trouble, Pappy."

"They say a man can shoot in self-defense, or in defense of his property. Those hoodlums who got away the other day would shoot us in a Hong Kong minute, claim self-defense, and get away with it."

"Nobody's going to actually shoot anybody, are they, Pappy? Nobody in this whole country would try to hurt you that way, would they?"

"No, and I'm not going to carry a pistol, Dolly Ann. Too heavy, and it might get in the way of my roping arm."

"I don't know. It might not be a bad idea to go armed from now on, Pappy," Cody Joe said. "How can rustlers be stopped without a firearm? If we have to run and get the law, the rustlers'll get away before the sheriff can head them off. If they're going to be stopped, the rancher has to do it."

"We put the run on them a few times, they'll probably learn to stay off our place, won't they, Cody?" Kane said. "What do you think, Lion? How do we stop the cow thieves?" This he asked as though he and the Lion had not figured out how to deal with cow thieves years ago.

"Report them to the sheriff," the Lion said. "It's the only way. Any other way brings too much trouble."

"I say kill them where we catch them and lay them across the carcass of the beef they butchered, then call the sheriff, like ranchers used to do," Kane said.

"Don't kill anyone, Pappy," Dolly Ann said.

"I'm only kidding, girl," Kane said.

"I know it, Pappy. And I know you wouldn't want to hurt anybody, but you don't fool me. I know you have a pistol in your chaps pocket."

Güero Rodriguez had been using Kane's Buster trail along the spine of the San Juan mountains for two years. The day Kane caught him bothering his grandchildren on the Manzanita trail, Güero had been careless and in a hurry, or he would never have been caught out in the open by Kane. From now on, he would only use the Buster trail, and Kane would not catch him again.

He needed that Buster trail and had begun to think of it as his own. He did not mind being caught with his Arabs by Kane as much as he minded being terminated by the people who paid him to smuggle warm bodies and merchandise in and out of the United States. His backers had already warned him that he better learn to stand prosperity and not get careless about it, or he would be terminated. That meant that he would be left outdoors with a hole in his head and the coyotes would eat him and scatter his bones.

Güero had not authorized the destruction of Buster camp, because he used it often. The three men who had done it were angry at Kane and Cañez for running them down and dragging them with their horses.

Güero had been ordered by his superiors to harass the ranches along that border. That was why he sent the four Lobos to kill a steer in Ruby pasture. That was a good way to harass a rancher who was married to his cows, and it was also a good source of pocket money for the Lobos. Güero let them keep the money they received for meat they carried back across the line. As a training exercise, he sent them out afoot with knives and a small caliber pistol to steal meat and bring it back. To steal fresh meat afoot was a bloody, strenuous business and a good initiation for a young man into Los Lobos.

Güero had a more practical and profitable method of rustling beef for himself. He owned two pickups with campers. His men cruised remote pastures in those pickups, shot a beef for each pickup, winched them into the trucks, cut their throats and let them hang off the bumpers, and bled them out as they drove away. One minute *máximo* to shoot the beef in the forehead and hook on to him. One minute to winch him aboard and cut his throat. Five minutes to bleed him out, a few more seconds to winch the bloodless animal all the way into the truck and close the camper door, *y vámonos* back across the line with the meat.

From a peak only three miles away, he watched the 7X headquarters with his binoculars on the day the Kanes rode back from Buster camp. His peak was a few feet higher than eight thousand feet and Kane's house was at forty-five hundred, so he could look down on it with his $4,000 German binoculars and watch everything the Kanes did outside their buildings. After he decided that he would steal Dolly Ann Kane and retire from all this hiking in the woods, he had watched her at Buster camp and now he would watch her at headquarters every day. Now, a four-man crew would accompany him when he crossed the border onto the 7X for any reason. Now that the girl was at headquarters, he would leave the crew on the trail and go down for a better look at her. From another hiding place only a hundred yards from the house, he could see into her room and right into the shower in her bathroom.

That night the family of the 7X sat down to a supper of fried chicken, mashed potatoes and gravy, and corn on the cob. The men did not take their eyes off Dolly Ann. She was the only woman in their family. Cody Joe was too young to have formed an enduring attachment for a wife-like woman, and the two geezers had outlived all of theirs, so they loved to watch Dolly Ann, the only female they had left to attend to them.

Halfway through supper, a highway patrolman drove into the yard to tell them that some of their cattle were out on the I-19 freeway at Tubac. Only one of their pastures bordered I-19. The Lion had ridden around that fence only three weeks ago and found everything intact. The 7X crew saddled horses, loaded them in a gooseneck trailer, and hurried to the freeway.

At Tubac, the Kanes came upon their cattle dodging headlights of north- and southbound traffic and grazing on the grass of the median. Kane stopped and unloaded the Lion and Cody Joe and their horses on the north side of the cattle, then made a U-turn and took Dolly and their horses back toward Nogales and unloaded on the south side of the cattle.

The patrolman called his cronies to help him stop traffic while Kane's crew bunched the cattle in the median. The cattle were not easy to handle, because the headlights of the cars and trucks blinded them. Then, before the patrolman's help arrived to stop traffic, a pickup load of people roared up and unloaded on the highway between the cattle and their 7X pasture.

The crew tried to start them across the southbound lane of the freeway toward their pasture gate and the people turned them back. A tall, leggy blond in tight trousers that showed off her busy butt and sported a holstered revolver high on a hip gave the orders. When the cattle turned back, the crew gave them room so they would not spill over the northbound lane into the traffic and the town of Tubac.

"Now, everybody, keep your arms outstretched and advance on the cattle and we'll do these *cowboys'* job for them," the blonde ordered.

"Lady," Kane said, "what do you think you're doing?"

"What does it look like I'm doing?" the woman said. She stood in the headlights of the pickup, and Kane did not think she could see beyond her nose.

"Whatever it is, it's wrong," he said. "If you'll just please move yourself and your friends out of our way, we'll move these animals back across the highway and into their pasture in one minute."

"You idiot, we're here to keep them off the highway. Are you so stupid that you don't know you're about to cause an accident?"

"They need to cross the highway to get home. You're blocking the way. Get out of the way."

When two of the older militia saw that she did not understand "Get out of the way," they tried to interpret for Kane, but she paid them no attention.

"Stand your ground, Militiamen," the woman ordered. "We're in charge here now."

That was all Dolly Ann Kane could stand. "Militia my dying ass," she yelled at the woman. "Militia is it? Take your counterfeit militia asses out of our way, or we'll run these cattle right the hell over the top of you." She rode around the herd toward the line of Militiamen and shouted, "Pappy, stick these cattle right up my horse's butt and I'll lead 'em across."

As Dolly Ann's horse took his first steps across the payment, the cattle watched her go, Kane moved in on them from the south side, the Lion moved in from the north, and Cody Joe pushed them from behind. A cow took the lead and followed Dolly Ann's horse, two more tiptoed hesitantly after her, and that was all the rest of the herd needed to follow her through the militia and across the highway en masse.

The crew pushed the herd through the pasture gate and the Lion and Cody Joe went to find and repair the hole in the fence where the cattle had escaped. Kane and Dolly Ann rode back to get the pickup and trailer.

They dismounted behind the trailer. The Militiamen pulled up behind them and blinded them with their pickup's headlights. Kane did not want to try to load the horses with the headlights bathing the inside of the trailer.

He held his hand over his eyes and looked toward the pickup, to show the people their light was too bright. Nobody in the pickup moved or spoke. Kane could have led his horse back to the driver's window to speak softly and with much consideration for the feelings and sensibilities of the Militiamen, but that would have endangered his horse. The traffic had begun to run by and the trailer was parked on the edge of the highway.

Horses can be loaded at night into a trailer bathed in light, but only if they trust the person who leads them in. They don't like to go anywhere that is bathed in bright light, because of the way their eyes have been positioned in their heads by their creator. They have wonderful eyesight straight ahead, and they can see as well behind themselves. Because of that, a bright light from behind them does not show them anything in front of them, it blinds them.

At seventy-five years of age and no longer light of foot, Kane did not want to get in front of his horse, coax him over the high step into the trailer, and lead him inside on top of himself. From his position in front of the pickup, Kane asked the driver to shut off the headlights so he could load his horse.

"Goddammit, that's why we're here, to light up the trailer so your stupid animal can see where it's going. Load it so we can go," a woman's voice shouted.

"He can't see," Kane said.

"Dammit, you damned dumb cowboy, that's what we're here for, to furnish light so your damned horse can see. Load your damned horse. Are all cowboys as damned stupid as you?"

Dolly Ann stepped in front of the pickup and took Kane's horse's reins. "I guess you'll have to go back and give them some school on how to load a horse, Pappy, or we'll be here all night."

"No," Kane said. "We won't." He searched the ground until he found a rock the size of his fist, walked up to the right headlight, and put it out with the rock.

"What the . . . What in the world . . . ?" came from inside the pickup. Kane looked straight at the blank windshield, took two deliberate steps to the other headlight, and put that one out too. Then he raised the rock over his head as though he would let go at the windshield. "Back up, back up, back up," a man's voice shouted. The driver peeled rubber backward out of the mad cowboy's range. Kane and Dolly Ann loaded their horses and drove away while the Militiamen got out and wailed about the damage he had done to their peepers.

As Kane exited the southbound lane to go back and pick up the Lion and Cody Joe, Dolly Ann said, "Pappy, you scare me sometimes."

"How's that, darling?" He was trying to decide on the horse he would ride tomorrow.

"For one thing, didn't you see that those people had guns? What if they had decided to shoot you in self-defense when you attacked their pickup?"

"Don't you know, darling? Those people's guns don't shoot."

"They do too, Pappy, and those people thought you were crazy."

"I'm no crazier than my granddaughter who told everybody her ass was dying a while ago."

The Lion and Cody Joe were standing in the parking lot of the Tubac bar when Kane returned with the trailer. They loaded their horses and piled into the 7X's crew cab, and Kane headed for home. Cody Joe fell asleep immediately. He could not sit five minutes in a moving pickup without falling into a dead sleep. Then again, it had been a long day.

"Where was the hole in the fence, compadre?" Kane asked the Lion.

"In an arroyo. The hole was wide as the wash, and all the wire was gone."

"What are you telling me?"

"Whoever cut the fence took all the wire with them and left a hole they didn't think we could patch without making a trip to town for new wire."

"What did you do?"

"I stole the wire we needed from Jimmy Garrett's house fence."

"You had enough with that?"

"Oh, yes. His is an old five-wire fence, so we took the bottom strand off one side and closed our hole. Jimmy probably won't even know it's gone."

"Good."

"As soon as I can, I'll take back the wire I stole."

"I'll call Jimmy tomorrow."

"Who would cut a hole in a man's fence so his cattle could get out on the highway?"

"Edward Abbey." Kane laughed.

"Who is that, Pappy?" Dolly Ann piped in, wide-awake.

"I thought all you hard-twists were asleep."

"Who is Edward Abbey?"

"He's a guy who used to cut fences."

"Why would he do that?"

"He was looking after the world, like the Militiamen."

"Yeah, the great Militiamen."

"Ain't we lucky, granddaughter? We had Edward Abbey and a militia of true Americans looking after us tonight."

Seven

Adan Martinillo spied on La Golondrina for a week from a place in the escarpment above the hacienda. He realized the first day that he had arrived too late, because no racehorse was being trained there. He watched Ibrahim and the grooms bring all the horses out of their stalls every day and no racehorse was put to work. Martinillo realized he might not find where they had taken the horse. Abdullah was not at the hacienda either, so Martinillo was sure he had gone somewhere else to train Auda. The horse might even have been taken to the racetrack in Rio Alamos for his training.

Martinillo had about decided to give up and go home, but that night Abdullah returned horseback to La Golondrina, and the next morning he and Ibrahim appeared at 4:00 a.m., saddled horses, and rode east. Martinillo followed and at dawn he saw that they carried rifles slung over their backs. The muzzles jutted on the skyline. Martinillo followed them back toward Canela and into the High Sierra.

He kept his distance behind them. At sundown an armed sentry appeared and led Ibrahim and Abdulla into a deep ravine. Martinillo followed more carefully after that. If other sentries were posted on the way, they would be facing Adan and would have a good chance to see him before he saw them. He left the trail and stalked the ravine the way he would a cave full of lions.

Ibrahim and Abdullah were too taciturn. He wished they would at least carry on a conversation as other travelers did. They did not talk at all between themselves or with their guide as they descended into the ravine. They rode good, quiet rock horses too. The trail was well used and well maintained, so they did not roll loose rocks. After they descended into the ravine, Martinillo lost all sight and sound of them and thought he could not follow without being seen. He decided to watch the ravine from on top. If he had to go in, he would wait until full dark.

The canyon was a quarter mile wide and at least five hundred feet deep. A clear stream flowed along the bottom. A large field of uniform and neatly spaced poppies grew beside the stream.

Martinillo hid in a place that allowed him to see across the ravine and watched the bottom for Ibrahim and Abdullah. They appeared again directly beneath him, and he kept pace with them as they rode along the bottom. They dismounted in front of a group of adobe buildings at the head of the canyon.

He found a good lair in which to hide. He could see into the windows of the buildings and hear the conversations of the people. He heard horsemen patrolling the mountain behind him, but he knew he could not be seen. No one could see him unless they stopped directly above him.

Martinillo knew how to make himself comfortable in a hunting lair. This one was spacious enough so that he could change positions and sleep. He could lie on his stomach all day and study his prey. Now, at an age when everybody considered him old, he could be more comfortable in a lair than he had ever been. He could make a querencia, a haven of almost any measly place as long as he could see and hear what he wanted to and not be seen from any side. He enjoyed a feeling of *bienestar*, well-being, when he found himself in a good lair from which to hunt formidable prey. This lair on a vantage point above the ancient ravine called La Culebra, The Snake, was as fine as any he had known.

The helicopter that had unloaded the wolves at the lookout point of Guasisaco was parked at the end of a landing strip. Martinillo remembered the number on it. The people in the buildings sounded happy. The ones who served as sentries called often to one another, so Martinillo almost always knew where they were. Most of the people in the bottom had gone inside the buildings by the time he settled in his lair the first night. Counting the sentries, he estimated that about thirty people lived there, an unusual gathering in the Sierra. He had never seen a gathering of more than ten people this far away from a village. At roundup time on the ranches only five to ten people came together. Roundups were gatherings of men. Martinillo could hear women in the buildings. The people spoke softly and that meant they were content. He liked it when his prey was content, because that meant he had not been discovered. It disturbed them and made them anxious when they discovered him.

He liked it that he could put a name and location to this place. He had always heard of La Culebra ravine. The Lupinos had owned this part of the Sierra all his life, but he had never seen it. His father had once delivered some oxen to don Nesib Lupino here and had told Martinillo about it. Now, comfortable in his lair, at the successful end of eight days of patient stalking, he slept.

A tart odor awakened him early. He raised up and saw that a clean white smoke emerged from the chimney of the newest building. He did not know much about opium *goma*, gum, but he knew when it was cooked it became a heroin dope called Mexican Brown. Everybody in the Sierra knew that, and he had been told that it smelled like vinegar when it was cooked.

The denizens of La Culebra were early risers. They began to stir at the end of the second sleep, about 4:00 a.m. Martinillo's lair was above horse corrals. He had heard them move and blow softly in the night, heard a mare squeal none too softly. At first light, a man with a tattooed, shaved head walked to a place underneath Martinillo and talked to the horses while he fed them. Martinillo could not see him attend to the horses, but knew what he did. The sounds men and animals made at feeding time were known to any man who did it himself.

Martinillo watched the man head back to the lighted bunkhouse.

He dressed oddly. The people inside the bunkhouse coughed, sneezed, and spoke softly in the early morning. Martinillo heard the sound of their coffeepot when someone set it on a stove, heard it picked up and the hot stuff poured into a cup. Anybody knew that sound. He missed the warm vapor of a cup of coffee under his nose and the smell of the brew. He heard the people sip loudly, the way Kane and Vogel said that Abdullah sipped his coffee. They said all Arabs did that. Martinillo thought, *If that is true, there are a lot of Arabs in that bunkhouse.* They sounded as though they had a contest going to see who could sound most like a man who strangled when he sipped his coffee. Martinillo smiled to himself. He could smell and almost taste the coffee.

One building was used as a cook shack and the women slept and worked there. One of them carried food to the building where the men slept. A man met her at the door and took it from her.

Before sunup Martinillo heard an airplane approach. Then its sound filled the canyon. A twin-engined, red and white airship came into sight and passed him so close he could see that it carried three men. The pilot's sleeves were rolled halfway up his forearms. Martinillo watched the airplane bank over the buildings, double back, land on a strip along the poppy field, and taxi to the side of the helicopter. The airplane buzzed like an insect, then the engines ceased and the propellers clacked and stopped.

Ibrahim and Abdullah and three others came to the stables to saddle two horses with riding saddles and four mules with packsaddles. Martinillo saw plenty to study in the men who helped Ibrahim and Abdullah. He seldom left the Sierra, or read a newspaper, or came within a hundred miles of a television set, so he did not know what a city slum gangster looked like. He had never even heard of such a gangster. So it was that he had a chance for the first time in his life to marvel at the appearance of the three men who walked away with the pack string. He had never seen such outlandish dress. Two of them wore trousers cut off below the knees to show their hairy legs. One's trousers had slipped halfway down his hips, bagged on the legs, and dragged the ground. The trousers bunched over his shoes and hid them. The man never tried to hitch his trousers back up where they belonged, on top of his hips, but somehow they stayed on. The two men in short pants had shaved the hair completely off their heads, but the other had shaved lanes between thick, short borders of hair that appeared to have been lacquered and lay uniformly, like the rows of opium poppies in the ravine.

He had never seen anybody wear tattoos over every visible surface of their skin the way these men did. They wore tattoos on both cheeks, their chins and foreheads, and the tops and backs of their heads. The one in the long trousers wore a ring in his nose and the end of his nose was tattooed red. All of them wore dainty earrings and clumsy-looking, clodhopper rubber shoes that made tracks like a tractor.

As people emerged from the buildings, Martinillo saw that thirty of them wore the uniform of tattoos and shaved heads—they were what Mexicans called pelones.

Men emptied out of the buildings, formed in the center of the yard, and began to exercise in unison as a leader gave orders. The leader spoke good Spanish, but his accent was foreign to Martinillo. Martinillo knew only the accents of his countrymen in Chihuahua and Sonora. After he had listened to this group of pelones awhile, he knew that he had never heard their special brand of Spanish.

Only seven of the people wore full heads of hair. All of these people were dark-headed, olive-complexioned, and cultivated full beards. They wore sweatshirts with hoods and most of the time kept them pulled over their heads. The hoods were ample and loose, and when they were in place, the faces could only partially be seen.

The seven who wore the hoods were instructors who lectured the pelones in English. The hooded men did not care if the pelones saw their faces, but they seemed to care that somebody might be watching them from afar. Martinillo could not imagine that they suspected he was there, but it seemed that they wore the hoods to keep somebody like him from seeing them.

Three young women came out of the cookhouse and sat by the door to take the sun, but their heads and necks were covered with rebozos. They watched the airplane's two passengers cross the stream on stepping-stones and walk up to the cookhouse. The pilot went to the helicopter to perform some service to the cockpit.

One of the passengers was short and slight and wore khaki trousers, hiking boots, and a pilot's leather jacket. A red baseball cap and black sunglasses almost masked his small face completely. He carried a long, flat case by its handle.

The other passenger was Rafa Lupino. After the exercise session, Rafa introduced his companion as John Smith, the company's new weapons instructor. John Smith laid his case on a chair by the women and in English began to lecture the pelones on the value and absolute necessity of well-aimed small arms fire in combat.

Ibrahim and Abdullah and their helpers loaded the pack animals with cargo from the airplane and led them across the stream to the buildings. Rafa ordered the helpers to unpack and open the cargo. Four heavy canvas duffel bags were opened in the yard and Martinillo took out paper and pencil to draw what he saw. He drew two projectiles that looked like big bullets. He drew a hollow tube that an instructor held on top his shoulder and sighted while he gave instructions on how to use it. He drew rifles that used heavy, curved clips of ammunition. He drew Uzis and their clips. He drew grenades, and brown, square pack-ages that Adan knew must contain high explosives, because the faceless man demonstrated the application of detonator caps to the contents.

Each instructor separated four or five students from the rest to give them individual schooling. Weapons, ammunition, and explosives were spread on tarps on the ground and the hooded men instructed the pelones on their uses and capabilities.

Ibrahim and Abdullah brought the animals back to the stables. Abdullah then came out with Auda, the horse that Lupino would race against Gato, and led him down to the stream. The horse drank spar-ingly. Martinillo had seen the horse win two races in Rio Alamos. Abdullah talked softly to the horse. He brought him back and saddled him with a jockey saddle. He led him in a wide circle by the buildings and let him stop often to watch the men at their school. After an hour of this, he returned the horse to the stable, tightened his cinch, and helped a boy up on his back.

The boy rode Auda at a walk down the smooth path of the airstrip between the stream and the poppy crop, then around a bend in the canyon out of sight. After a while he came back to the airstrip, back to the stable, then turned around and repeated the sashay up the airstrip.

Auda watched everything, from the buzzards high on their invisible steps in the sky, to the glint of the sun on the skins of the airplane and helicopter. He listened to the voices. He looked back over his shoulder often at Abdullah. He walked and watched with healthy vigor and enthusiasm.

An hour later he was unsaddled and led into a pool in the stream. The boy stripped to his underwear and bathed him with a pan. He brought him back to the stable wet and dripping. Abdullah wiped the water off his coat with a slim board that had been whittled into a blade, then handed him back to the boy to be walked dry.

Martinillo's lair was directly above the spot where Abdullah wiped the water out of Auda's coat. Martinillo's face was concealed by meager brush on the edge of the lair. He was almost positive that once, while Abdullah stood on the other side of Auda and faced Martinillo's hiding place as he scraped the water off the horse's side and his eyes barely cleared the horse's back, he looked up suddenly and his gaze locked with Martinillo's.

Martinillo thought it improbable that their gaze met for that one instant, but he could not be sure. Abdullah looked and acted like a hawk, so he might have the eyes of a hawk. A hawk could have seen him, a hawk that felt his gaze and looked up into the true line of sight that Martinillo had established. This often happened between a hunter and his prey, especially when the prey was another predator.

Martinillo did not feel secure in his lair anymore. The longer the afternoon wore on, the more he felt that he had been discovered. He watched Abdullah and worried when he went away from the corral and out of sight.

An hour after sundown, Martinillo could not lie still another minute. The airplane had flown away. The pelones and hooded men had gone inside their bunkhouse. Rafa and the man with no face had gone down the canyon with rifles. Ibrahim and Abdullah had gone into the cookhouse with the women. That cookhouse was against the wall of the ravine, and the wall had a deep chute in it. Martinillo could see that someone might go out the back door of the cookhouse and lose himself in the chute. If that someone knew a way to climb out of the ravine through the chute, Martinillo was in trouble.

Martinillo picked up his belongings, struck out for Canela feeling stiff and heavy as a bee laden with honey, and did not look back. For a half minute after he first left his lair he was in view of the camp, but he put his head down and moved out as surely as he could. He found a game trail on a line toward Canela. He watched for the sentry on horseback, but did not worry about the sentries on foot. He thought he had them all located.

He was about to top the last ridge that would put him completely out of sight of the ravine when a bullet knocked him down. At first he did not realize he had been shot, only that he had been knocked down and could not breathe. He then knew that he had been hit high between his right shoulder and his spine, and his neck and right arm were shocked numb. His breath finally returned and with it a lot of pain.

He had to move to live. He would be dead in five minutes if he did not find a place to hide. He could not take time to stop the bleeding. The blood filled his shirt, front and back. He hoped his clothing would sop it so he would not leave a trail. He hoped he could find a place to hide before he fainted. His legs worked well enough. He saw a canyon a hundred meters away and hurried toward the edge. A solid apron of granite covered the brink. He would leave no trail on that granite. From the edge of the cliff he looked down at a narrow ledge of rock. If he could drop the fifteen feet to that ledge and not bounce into the bottom of the canyon five hundred feet below, he could get out of sight immediately and might find a permanent place to hide. He let himself fall.

He landed solidly on both feet on the ledge. Pain shot from his feet clear into his back teeth, but he stuck to the ledge. He saw a crack in the cliff where he might hide if he could squeeze through the opening. He squeezed through and found room to let himself down through a chimney. He found another ledge that could not be seen from the crack above. He stretched out on the ledge and fainted.

He soon awoke and cut up his blanket to stop the bleeding on both sides of his shoulder. The bullet that struck him had pierced him through and through without exploding, but the bleeding was bad on his breast where it came out. He stopped that up with *hierba el pasimo*, an herb hunters and vaqueros carried to heal wounds. After his wound stopped bleeding, he would bandage it with the sticky leaves of green *chicura*.

He carried that too. Hunters and vaqueros carried their own means of first aid in the Sierra, or knew where they could find it quickly.

Martinillo heard his searchers' voices on top the cliff. He saw the beams of their flashlights light the canyon below him. He saw their glow through the crack above his chimney, but none of them touched him. He heard the helicopter pass overhead and its spotlight shined on the canyon below, then hovered right above him and illuminated most of his hideout with a bright, white light. He felt the wash of its blades too, but it went on without him. He fainted into a long spell of unconsciousness before he knew for certain that his enemies would not find him.

Eight

—⟋⟍⟋— Dolly Ann and Cody Joe returned to El Trigo with Kane after the spring roundup at the 7X. Marco Antonio met them at the airstrip with Gato, Paseador, and Negrito and finally got to see Dolly Ann. His first sight of her when she stepped out of the airplane struck him dumb. He could not move or speak until she smiled at him, waved, and called his name. Then he ducked his head, turned and busied himself with the horse and mules, and only murmured an answer.

"Here's La Muñeca, Marco Antonio," Kane called. He knew how bashful the boy was, and he could not help but rub it in. The bloodless streaks appeared again on his cheeks.

Dolly Ann walked up to him with her hand outstretched. He took it, but did not know what to do with it, so she pumped his hand up and down, then smiled into his face. Cody Joe stepped up to give him an abrazo and he remembered how to do that, so he looked at the tops of the pine trees and patted his friend on both shoulders.

As they rode away from the airstrip toward Guazaremos, Kane asked Marco Antonio about his grandfather Martinillo.

"While he was home we killed four of the wolves, or whatever they were," Marco Antonio said.

"You killed them how?" Dolly Ann asked.

Marco Antonio told them about the wolves' raid on the Martinillo stock at Las Animas and how they were received by the family.

"Good," Cody Joe said. "That's just right for them."

"Nooo," Dolly Ann said. "Don't wolves have a right to live?"

"Wolves do," Kane said. "Not those fake things that have been raised on beef and kept close to people. They need killing. You killed four, Marco Antonio? What happened to the other one?"

"A female got away."

"She'll have a litter."

"She might."

"So, where did your grandfather go? To hunt the female?"

"He went to hunt Lupinos. He was angry at them for turning the wolves out in our country. He said he also wanted to find out why don Nesib did not want us to spy on his racehorse."

"*Ay caray*! I promised don Nesib we wouldn't spy on him," Kane said. "Did your grandfather go to La Golondrina?"

"I think so."

"How could he do that? He knew I promised we wouldn't spy on their horse."

"My grandfather said that you made that promise, but he didn't."

"*Carajo*. Well, he has a right to find out more about people that turn wolves out to prey on his livestock. When will he be back?"

"He said he would return for the roundup."

"He's probably at Guazaremos waiting for us."

The conversation between Marco Antonio and Dolly Ann livened up, and it seemed to Kane that Marco Antonio made the girl laugh a lot. He sure did not make Kane and Cody Joe laugh, but then Kane could not see his expressions and it took a whole lot to even make Cody Joe smile.

Kane usually rode in silence, because he liked the stillness of big country. That day with Marco Antonio and Dolly Ann laughing and talking and even singing along, he felt that he was part of a darned cavalcade.

They stopped at El Trigo Pass to have a look at the country before they started down the long mountain trail to Guazaremos. The view quieted them. This was the driest time of the year. The forest was green but wore a burden of dryness that dulled its color. The country wore a coat of dust, but the view north from El Trigo Pass was a feast for the three Kanes' eyes.

The riders stood a mile higher than the Mayo River that they could see underneath the horizon twenty miles away. They could see Guazaremos, their destination, on the south side of the river. They could see the trail that began at their feet and dropped to sea level over twenty miles of rocky ground, deep canyons, and spiny thickets.

"You see Guazaremos?" Kane asked his youngsters.

"I see El Limón there below us," Cody Joe said.

"Then Teguaraco and Gilaremos, a little farther," Dolly Ann said.

"Then the white ravine below Guazaremos," Kane said.

"And we're there," Marco Antonio said, and laughed. "It's only eight hours away."

"We can see almost the whole ranch right here at our feet," Kane said. "It's all in this bowl below us that is bordered by the cordon of mountains of Guasisaco on the west, the mountains of Canela on the east, and the Mayo River on the north. It can't get away, and we can't get lost. The peaks of those blue mountains of the high Sierra north of Canela are fifty miles from here."

"Where's La Golondrina?" Cody Joe asked.

"On this side of those blue mountains," Marco Antonio said, and pointed to them. "My grandfather is up above in that high Sierra, somewhere."

The Kanes and Marco Antonio rode into the yard of the Guazaremos hacienda an hour before sundown. Juan Vogel stepped out into the yard with a glass of mezcal in his hand and his hat on the back of his head. The El Trigo roundup crew was having a feast at the end of the first day of branding. Miguelito, a Guarijia Indian who lived with his family at Guazaremos, had a mezcal distillery, which gurgled only fifty feet from the front door of the main house. The crew was enjoying a banquet of mezcal and *criadillas*, calf nuts, that they had harvested in the corral with their ropes and knives that day.

The roundup of the four El Trigo divisions had become a vacation time for these vaqueros who had been raised on the El Trigo ranch. They would split up and return to their homes after the Guazaremos roundup. They had already gathered the El Limón, Teguaraco, and Gilaremos divisions.

Only Miguelito and Che Che Salazar, who cared for the El Trigo hacienda on top of the mountain, stayed on the ranch when cattle were not being worked. The other vaqueros had more lucrative ways to make a living. They helped Kane and Vogel gather and work their cattle in the spring and fall, but they ran their own ranches and transported their crops to market the rest of the time. They helped on El Trigo purely out of loyalty. The partners could only pay them twelve dollars a day. They made two hundred times more than that in their other enterprise—called la mota.

These vaqueros were all either godsons of Kane and Vogel, or compadres, fathers of the godsons, or uncles of the godsons. This stock of vaqueros had helped on El Trigo for 120 years. One benefit the present generation received by returning to El Trigo for the roundup was the pure joy and fun of *la vaquereada*, the cowboy work, for which they had been born. The other joy of it came with the annual look they were given at each other's faces, the faces of new youngsters who joined the crew and the faces of Kane and Vogel. Cody Joe and Dolly Ann had begun to help on the roundup of the Guazaremos division five years before, but had stayed home with Kane after he was injured.

Kane began to worry the next morning when he went to the kitchen for coffee with Vogel and found that Martinillo had not returned. He did not worry about himself and the crew being short Martinillo's reata, or that Martinillo was not tending to business, but he did worry about the safety of his carcass. Kane knew that wherever he was, he would look out for Kane and Vogel. He was their mayordomo. Whatever he had found to do on La Golondrina must have turned out to be more important than the Guazaremos roundup, but he would only fail to show up for a roundup because of trouble. Martinillo was not on a friendly mission, was there without being invited, and was no friend of the Lupinos. He had not made them his enemies, but they did not know him well.

Cody Joe and Marco Antonio were ready to leave with Gato to start his training for the race in Rio Alamos, so Kane made himself stop worrying about Martinillo. If anyone could take care of himself in the Sierra Madre, even surrounded by people who would do him harm, Adan Martinillo was the man.

Cody Joe and Marco Antonio stood in front of their mounts Negrito and Paseador. Marco Antonio held Gato's lead rope.

"Aren't you taking a pack mule?" Vogel asked Marco Antonio.

"No, if we leave now we'll be in San Bernardo early this evening," Marco Antonio said. "My father and uncle will meet us there with their truck to take us and the animals to Rio Alamos tonight."

"You ought to take it easier than that," Kane said. "I don't think you can make it to San Bernardo before midnight."

"*A lo mejor*," Cody Joe said. "You're probably right, Pappy."

"Nooo, we can make it to San Bernardo by eight o'clock unless both our mules step in the same hole. These are the best saddle mules in the Sierra," Marco Antonio said.

"Don't kill our mules," Vogel said. "You young people think you can run mules the way my daughter Mari runs her car—a hundred and fifty kilometers an hour. You think you have to go as fast as you can over bad trails and good. Take it slow. We would rather you made it to Rio Alamos tomorrow night. Better for you and better for our race-horse. I want him to make us rich. Go at an even pace, even though it pulls your mouths down at the corners and seems a much too ponderous way to go."

"We'll not turn a hair on these animals," Marco Antonio said. "But we have to go now."

With that the two boys mounted their mules and led Gato up the trail. Kane and Dolly Ann watched them go. Just before the trail led them into Arroyo de Guazaremos out of sight, Marco Antonio turned and waved. Dolly Ann waved back.

The crew had been branding, vaccinating, and castrating two hours when Jacobo and Rafa Lupino showed up for a visit. They had heard that Kane's grandchildren were there and wanted to meet them. Kane was on his good horse, Lagarto, Lizard, roping and dragging calves to the branding fire, and he did not go near them. Vogel dismounted to receive them, and that was fine with Kane. He did not care if he ever spoke to either of them again.

After Rafa shot off his mouth about being an enemy of Americans and their women, then insulted Dolly Ann, how could he be considered a friend? Two hundred families had lost their homes and ranches in the region because of the Lupinos' opinions and activities, so how could they be his friends?

Kane and Vogel had not lost anything of their own except the real friends who had been dispossessed by the Lupinos. How nice to be so privileged. But the Lupinos' bid for El Trigo might indicate that Kane and Vogel would not be so privileged anymore.

Kane was busy in the middle of the work in the corral when he saw Vogel call Dolly Ann over to meet the Lupino brothers. She marched up to them and smiled into their faces and shook their hands. After the criticism Rafa had spouted about American women, Kane felt defensive about his granddaughter's looks. The girl wore tight jeans and a tailored, snap-button shirt. Her figure was plenty evident, but how could she hide it any better unless she wore a rebozo on her head, a floor-length robe, and a veil? She wore her old hat pulled down over her eyes so that she had to tilt her head back to talk to the Lupinos, but it did not hide her pretty face. She wore bright red lipstick, her complexion was clear as a cloudless sky, and her blonde hair shined like placer gold. She was darned good looking, and any shittin' Arab who would say she was a whore for the way she dressed had a twisted mind.

Kane worried when Dolly Ann returned to her duties at the branding fire with a flushed and serious face. Mexican men like to praise young-sters to their faces in a gentlemanly way and the Lupinos might only have done that, but the look on Dolly Ann's face made him think she had been insulted, even though Juan Vogel had been there to referee.

Dolly Ann's job that day was to be the doctor and the tarbaby. She daubed medicinal tar on the fresh brands and the bleeding scrotums of the calves and wielded a syringe to vaccinate against disease. Vogel mounted his horse to help Kane rope the Lupino yearlings they had bought. The Lupinos moved over to sit near Dolly Ann's station. The kind of attention Rafa began to give her did not suit Kane at all.

Jacobo tried to keep his brother in check. Rafa leered and said things to Dolly Ann and Jacobo tried to shut him up. Kane could not hear any of it, but he could read the smirk on Rafa's face and Dolly Ann's reaction to what he said. She kept blushing with her eyes downcast.

The crew broke at noon and Dolly Ann took the bucket of criadillas to the kitchen. She and Miguelito's wife Neli cleaned them, rolled them in cornmeal, fried them in deep fat, and prepared to serve them to the crew on hot corn tortillas.

♾

Kane, Vogel, and the vaqueros washed their faces and hands and rested in the shade while Dolly Ann and Neli prepared the lunch. Rafa Lupino was not dumb enough to insult Dolly Ann in front of the crew. He did not want to get his throat cut. The crew adored La Muñeca. These vaqueros were not the kind to fight with their fists. They filled their hands with weapons to kill when a fool made them angry. Each of them carried a fine El Arbolito blade, a gift from their *patrón* Jim Kane.

Dolly Ann served the crew their criadillas wrapped in tortillas. She poured coffee in the vaqueros' and guests' cups with one hand and held the sugar bowl for them with the other. She attended to each of them as though one of them had not spent the past hour insulting her.

The crew settled down and dozed in the shade after lunch. Kane and Vogel went into the dining room of the hacienda to tally their cattle. Jacobo went away to make sure his and Rafa's horses were still in the shade. Dolly Ann and Neli washed dishes and pans and straightened the kitchen.

During the lull, Rafa went into the kitchen after Dolly Ann. Anyone could slip up on anything in that old kitchen, because the lumber floor had long since rotted out and only a dirt floor remained.

Rafa asked for more coffee. Dolly Ann filled his cup without looking at him, turned her back to him, and went on with her business. She and Neli kept up a quiet conversation and ignored him. Dolly Ann had already forgotten what he looked like, because she always forgot the features of the people she disliked.

What Rafa did next to Dolly Ann did not come to light until later that day, after what came to be known as Rafa Lupino's Skinning. After a while, when it seemed to Dolly Ann and Neli that Rafa had only come into the kitchen to grin and stare at them, Neli went out to see to her babies and left Dolly Ann alone with him.

That was when the earthen floor and Dolly Ann's contempt for him came in handy for Rafa. He set his cup down and walked up behind her without a sound, reached under her arms, clamped a hand over her mouth, and grabbed her breast. He rubbed himself against her butt while he mauled both breasts and punished her, pinching her breasts so hard he bruised them. She kicked up her heel between his legs and came so close to his private parts that she scared him and he let go. She spun to face him and slammed four straight-armed blows into his mouth and nose and only stopped when he fell out the door onto his back. Rafa jumped up and looked around to see if anyone had seen him spill out the door, then turned and walked away toward the tree where his horse was tied.

Dolly Ann leaned into the wall and suffered the pain in her breasts.

She stayed in the kitchen until she heard the vaqueros head back to the corral. She straightened up and prepared to go back to her job at the branding fire. She was not sure she had inflicted any damage on Rafa when she knocked him down, but she intended to make sure he at least went home with a bloody nose that day. She did not want to tell her grandfather what he had done, because the old man would murder him.

She could still taste the palm of Rafa's hand in her mouth, but she would not scream that she had been violated or whine to the men. She wanted to go back to work, and she wanted Rafa to try to insult her again so she could land a precise combination of jabs, crosses, and hooks on his doltish head for her edification and for the entire Sierra Madre to see and include in its storied history. She could be darned sure that before sunrise tomorrow everybody within fifty miles would know about the lumps she put on Mr. Rafa's head.

To scream accusations at Rafa was also the wrong thing to do. After all, she did not feel that she had a complete right to work with these vaqueros. Their women never went near a corral. Men wanted to cuss when a calf kicked them, wanted to step away from the fire to relieve themselves when they had to. The women respected this and stayed away from the corral when their men worked cattle.

The crew was always so polite and respectful to her—she did not want to cause them trouble. They did not carry on and banter with her, but they watched her back in the way that they thought they were supposed to. She would not call them out to defend her honor. She was there because she wanted to be there, not because she was needed. They were quietly protective of her, watching out for her safety, but modestly.

Dolly Ann saw that her Pappy watched her with concern. He did not have a good poker face. She had sent him distress signals without meaning to, and she was sorry, but maybe that was only right. She needed to resolve the outrage that she felt and Pappy could help her do that. He could keep Rafa from getting away while she savaged the coward with a combination or two.

That gave her an idea for an alternative way to get even with Rafa. What would happen if she went to her Pappy and pantomimed her accusation of Rafa without uttering a word? Rafa used the weapons of a coward. That meant he was probably afraid of what she would do next, so he might not let her get close enough to punch him out. Well, what if she only made a mad face and pointed a finger at him. She bet he would run like a coyote. She would only mouth the accusations silently and express it on her face. She could get even with him that way without anyone else knowing the reason.

The crew was weaning big calves off their mothers and putting them in a separate pen. One hundred and sixty healthy calves and their mothers bawled their hearts out for each other. The crew had to shout into each other's ears to be heard.

During a lull in the work, but not in the din of the bawling cattle, Dolly Ann left her post and walked across the corral toward her grandfather, as though she needed to talk to him. She stopped by her Pappy's horse, mouthed words that made him bend down from his saddle so he could hear them, then pointed at Rafa and showed her distress.

Kane did not understand a word of it, but Rafa must have been sure that his atrocity was being discovered. When Dolly Ann pointed at him, Kane looked at him from under his hat brim. That made Rafa think that Jim Kane had just been sicked on him and his life was not worth a nickel.

Rafa climbed down off the fence. Dolly Ann mouthed something like, "Stop him, Pappy, he'll get away."

Rafa ran for his horse, but he was not under the tree where he had left him. Jacobo had led the Lupino horses away to new shade. In a panic, Rafa turned back toward Kane and Dolly Ann. "I didn't mean to do it," he shouted, and then he hit the trail at a run for La Golondrina and his mama. Before he went out of sight, he lost his hat and his hair stood on end.

Jacobo watched as though he thought his brother had gone crazy.

"What's wrong with him?" Kane asked.

"I wonder why he's acting like that?" Dolly Ann said.

Jacobo mounted his horse and trotted after him. Dolly Ann did not think the Lupinos would be back, so she told her Pappy what Rafa had done.

This poisoned Kane against Rafa Lupino for good. He dismounted, led Lagarto out of the corral, went to his bedroom, got his rifle, and carried it outside. Che Che had overheard what Dolly Ann told her grandfather and he told Juan Vogel. Juan Vogel tried to dissuade Kane from going after Rafa with the rifle. They could expect Jacobo to bring the state and federal law and probably the Sierra's military patrol down on Kane if he even scratched Rafa's skin. Kane said that in that case it might be a good idea if he eliminated Jacobo too. That way he would make sure no Lupino returned to La Golondrina to accuse him of being half-assed.

Vogel took the rifle away from Kane as Jacobo and Rafa reappeared on the trail.

"Let them get all the way back before you do anything," Vogel said. "Look, I'll smile at them for you." He smiled and waved to the Lupinos. Kane watched them come on and did not smile.

"Give me the rifle," Kane said.

"No. I don't care what you do to him with your bare hands, but I don't want you to kill him. Think of Fatima and the old man. Let them handle him. In the meantime, let him come all the way into the yard. You're so old and slow that he can outrun you, so I'll get ready to cut him off if he tries to get away. Just talk to him a minute before you do anything."

Kane mounted Lagarto. He could do what he now planned to do a whole lot better horseback.

Rafa hailed Kane with a wide grin. Vogel sat his horse beside Kane's as the Lupinos approached. Kane unfastened his eight-strand, sixty-foot reata and built a three-foot loop in the end. The hand that held it rested on the swell of his saddle. The loop hung along his leg on the side away from Rafa.

Rafa untied his horse, mounted, rode over, and stopped in front of Kane.

"I thought the female said something that made you angry with me, *meestair*," he said.

"She said nothing to me. You ran because you're a coward and she knows it. The girl discovered your cowardice only by pointing a finger at you. That's all she had to do to make you run, cowardly dog that you are."

The vaqueros gathered around to listen.

"Isn't that the lowest kind of filth any Arab like you can become, a cowardly dog?" Kane asked.

Rafa's grin faded and his eyes glowered at Kane. "You're wrong, *meestair*, and so is the female. All I did was tell her that I could get a lot of money for a female like her. It's a pity she's no businesswoman, for she must know that she would be better off if she spent her time in a perfumed bath waiting to be serviced than in a dirty corral collecting bull testicles in front of a crew of men."

"What did you say?" Kane asked.

"You mean about the perfumed bath, or the bull testicles?"

"No, before that. You said something about being able to get a lot of money. For what? Tell me again. I'm old and don't hear well anymore."

"Open your waxy ears to reason, *meestair*, and consider what I told you when you were in my father's house. I'll gladly cut you in. I guarantee you, I can get a fortune for your female, and you can have her out of your hair, out of your corral, and far away where she won't cause trouble with your neighbors again like she did today."

"That's what I thought you said," Kane said. "That's the third time one of you sons of filthy bitches have said you can get a lot of money for my granddaughter. You son of a bitch, the third time's the charm."

Kane rammed Lagarto into Rafa's lighter horse and knocked him down. Rafa spilled out from under the horse onto his back. Kane rode over the top of him and lashed his ears with the reata. Rafa howled and ducked his head under his arms. Kane lashed his hands, then lashed at his eyes, then lashed his hands away from them.

Kane dismounted, but only to get his breath. He positioned the hard, thick, rawhide honda on the down side of the loop and brought it down on the top of Rafa's head. It bounced off his head and spattered blood every time it struck. Rafa's head turned bloody and Kane's reata bathed itself in it and became more efficient as a weapon. Blood flew into Kane's face. When he thought he had blinded the coward, he stopped.

"Please don't beat my brother any more, Jim," Jacobo said.

"You're next, you son of a bitch," Kane said. "If you want to carry this piece of filth home after I kill him, don't get close to me."

"I'm pleading for his life, and for mine. He won't bother you again. Please don't hurt him any more."

"To show you I'm merciful, I'll let you have him back now." Kane measured the bloody head, growled, "*Yyyyyyy, vámonos,*" swung the honda down one more time, and split Rafa's nose. He walked away, coiled the reata, tied it on his saddle, led his horse to the shade of the veranda, and took a drink of water from the tin cup in the olla.

That evening Lucrecia and Luci Martinillo rode in to Guazaremos to see Dolly Ann and Adan and found out that he had not returned to the roundup. Kane and Vogel sat down with Lucrecia to examine the situation. They believed that Martinillo had found something that the Lupinos wanted to hide, and it was not a racehorse. He had probably decided to skulk around and watch their opium operation for a while. The partners did not believe the Lupinos or their vaqueros were quick enough to catch Martinillo. As long as he did not want them to see him, they would not even dream he was there.

After Lucrecia and Luci went to bed, however, Kane told Vogel that he hoped Martinillo had not disappeared the way all other uninvited visitors to La Golondrina did.

"He's not disappeared, because he never appeared to anyone at La Golondrina," Vogel said. "I'm not worried. When he hunts, he's a ghost. He's there for his own reasons, and he'll return when he's satisfied. Don't worry about him."

The next day Dolly Ann begged Kane to let her go home with Lucrecia and Luci. She had never seen him act the way he had the day before. She knew of his reputation for settling differences with his fists man to man, but that meant clean hands, empty hands, not with weapons. She would never have believed that any cowboy's tool could inflict the pain and damage, the humiliation that her Pappy's reata had done to Rafa. The sight of Rafa being sliced up by Kane had been outrageous. The sight of Kane's anger had been worse. She did not want to stay and help brand at Guazaremos anymore.

Kane was glad to let her go. He did not like having her in the middle of the work any more than the crew did. He was old-fashioned about having women around the work. His mother, grandmother, and aunts had always stayed away from the corrals when cattle were being worked. They had never even worn trousers.

The first female of his family who had ever come into the corral to work as a doctor had been his sister Maudy, although she had not handled the nuts. Kane's mother would not have a mess of nuts in her kitchen. Testicles were for the dogs to eat, not for her daughter to clean and roll in cornmeal and fry in deep fat, and Kane's mother was a tenth-generation cattlewoman. Some families messed with calf nuts, and some families did not.

Kane had not ever eaten them at home, but in cow camp with other cowboys and vaqueros, he chowed down on them. His mother did not mind that, only she did not want them in the vicinity of her kitchen. The same went for the *menudos* of a beef: the brains, tongue, marrow gut, paunch, kidneys, heart, and blood. The men could have all the menudos they wanted, but they were not for her, or her daughter, or any of the other women in her family.

The next morning, Lucrecia awakened Luci and Dolly Ann early, and they made ready to leave as soon as the crew saddled their mules. No one in the crew said anything about Dolly Ann leaving. They liked the sight of her pretty face and figure, and they liked the way she attended to them, but they were relieved that she would not work with them anymore. They could spit. They could pee in plain sight. They could cuss and make bawdy jokes. They could lash nasty Arabs and animals with their reatas, latigos, and ropes. Ribaldry would return to the Guazaremos corral, and with it glee when the crew recalled the sight of Rafa Lupino as he attempted to find his head with both hands and looked around to be sure that he did not leave any of his parts on the bloody ground when he left the area.

Dolly Ann was relieved to leave the crew. She realized now that she made the men uncomfortable. She had not thought about that before yesterday. The men had shown no sign of it either, but then Rafa made her aware of it and embarrassed her. The blush that Kane noticed had been caused by the realization that she brought discomfort to the crew, not because Rafa's insults hurt so much.

She also felt responsible for her Pappy's awful, bestial anger and the beating he gave Rafa. She realized that none of it would have happened if she had stayed out of the corral. In the Sierra Madre, her place was not in the corral with the men and the dust, blood, snot, manure, and bull nuts. Lucrecia and Luci could use her a whole lot better at Las Animas. Her Pappy had never told her that. Neither had her brother. Her godfather Vogel had never even intimated that she was out of place. It had taken a coward like Rafa to make her aware of it. Maybe it was all right in a crew that included other women, all right inside her own family at the 7x, but it darned sure was not all right in a crew of serranos in the Sierra Madre where no woman *ever* worked in the corral.

At Las Animas everything turned sunny for Dolly Ann. She and Luci and Lucrecia worked hard, and she did not have to worry that someone would be offended, tempted, or embarrassed by her presence. The three women all climbed aboard El Toro Buey's broad back and rode out to clear and burn the brush of a *mauguechi*, a new field. They used axes and machetes to clear brush and trees off virgin ground. With the bull they dragged the brush into a pile and burned it. They would plant corn and beans on the clearing before the rains began in July.

Dolly Ann helped sew, churn for butter, and turn sides of fresh jerky to the sun. She helped haul water in a *bota*, a canvas container that hung on the sides of a burro and carried five gallons on each side. She helped gather the cottontail rabbits they caught in snares on game trails.

Dolly Ann loved it at Las Animas and forgot about boxing and school in buildings of concrete, glass, and steel. The youngsters who studied with her were lost without their eyeglasses, their ball-points, their combs, their cell phones, their laptops. They thought themselves mature and in control of all aspects of politics, religion, business, entertainment, and work in their lives. Luci and Lucrecia redefined the term "expertise" for Dolly Ann.

She wondered if any of her fellow students would believe the story of the raid of the wolves on Las Animas. She had thought some of them were close friends. Now, nobody could be a friend unless she was a Lucrecia, a Luci, or a Marco Antonio. How could she ever fit in with that Tucson crowd of students again? Who among them had ever had to fight off a wolf, ride ten hours from a place like Las Animas to a place like Guazaremos in one uninterrupted journey, back home the next day, then up on the mountain to cut down brush and trees and drag the slash with a big old bull to be burned in a pile? Who among them had a grandfather who had whipped a man nearly blind because he insulted and manhandled his granddaughter?

"Tell me about your friends, Muñeca," Luci said on the second evening after they arrived at Las Animas. "How do they dress? Do you go dancing? Tell my mama and me what you do for fun."

Dolly Ann told them about her school and friends. Lucrecia was interested, but Luci was enthralled and wanted to know everything about Dolly Ann's life. She kept Dolly Ann up long after Lucrecia went to bed. She wanted Dolly Ann to take her to the "United."

Dolly Ann asked Lucrecia about Luci's desire to leave home. Lucrecia did not want Luci to spend her life at Las Animas. She did not want to stay there anymore herself. She had grown too old to live alone in the Sierra without Martinillo. Since the drug wars, she had no neighbors. She had been happy at Las Animas with her children before the wars, but that time was over and her children were gone. Her husband stayed away at work with other men. She wanted to live in town near her remaining sons and their families and her former neighbors. No one could blame Luci for wanting a civilized life. Lucrecia asked Dolly Ann to take Luci home to the 7X. Dolly Ann promised that her Pappy would take her after the horse race.

Nine

⎯∿⎯ The thugs from the camp in Culebra Canyon and their helicopter searched for Martinillo four days. He stayed at the bottom of his chimney and hoped the searchers would not climb down to the ledge and investigate. He could stand and he could sit and rest his head on a bulge in the rock in front of him, and he could lie on his left side with his legs doubled. He slept that way because he could not lie on his back and stretch out.

The searchers stopped on the edge of the cliff above him more than once to speculate about how to find him. After listening to them for four days, he did not think they had identified him, for he never heard his name called. They called him "the spy." Abdullah had been the one who shot him. Some of the thugs believed the spy had been hit, as Abdullah said. Others did not believe Abdullah had shot anyone, because no sign of a wounded spy could be found. Three footprints were found at the place where Abdullah indicated that the spy had been hit, but no blood.

Martinillo's clothes sopped up the blood of his wound, and his own fastidiousness more than anything else made him decide to leave his hiding place and try to make it back to Canela. He wished he had brought more food. He drank from a pool of rainwater in the bottom of the chimney. Before he left he washed most of the blood out of his clothes with the remainder of it.

He took an hour to climb out of the chimney, a climb that would have only taken him a few minutes when he was healthy. He did not worry about the pain, because he had searched the wound carefully with his fingers and decided it was not serious unless it got infected. The bullet had missed an artery where it went in and had torn a ragged hole where it came out, but it probably had not been a hollow point.

He was sure Abdullah had been the one who discovered him in his lair and shot him. Bad luck, to look up and lock eyes with a hawk. Bad luck that the only one with hawk eyes in Culebra Canyon, against hundred to one odds, looked up and saw him. The hawk was a good shot. One more step and Martinillo would have made it over the ridge and out of sight. The man had taken the shot as Martinillo's head disappeared under the ridge. Martinillo bet that his head and shoulders were all that Abdullah could see when he took the shot. Six inches to the left and the bullet would have hit him in the neck. Martinillo decided he would settle for the shot the man had taken. He was alive. For quite a while he would be worthless, so he had to distance himself from La Culebra while he could.

He used another hour to climb out of the fissure. He wondered how he ever made it through before. For a while his head and shoulders hung out in the open and the rest of himself remained stuck in the fissure. His weakness and pain kept him half in and half out. When he finally squeezed out, he lay on the ledge awhile and looked at the next climb to the top of the cliff. That climb took him another hour. He started home at a rate of about ten steps a minute.

He stayed off the trail to Canela, but kept it in sight. He walked on rock and pine needles wherever he could. He went slow and kept himself hidden.

Later in the evening, as he moved through a forest of big trees where he most lacked concealment, he heard a voice, then hoofbeats and the rattle of equipment. He lay flat on the ground against the base of a large pine, in the open for most of the world to see.

Horses came on and he began to feel good about it. That many horses might mean that Captain Emilio Kosterlinsky and his troop of twenty-five cavalrymen were on their patrol through the region. If this was the captain, Martinillo would be given food and water. His wounds would be examined and treated. He would be given a horse to ride and the protection of Mexican cavalry.

Captain Kosterlinsky rode behind the soldier who carried the troop's banner on a lance. Martinillo was about to stand up and wave when the captain saw something up the trail on Martinillo's right, raised his arm, and ordered the troop to halt.

Martinillo could not turn his head because of his wound. He wished he could fashion a splint to keep his head in place, because if he moved his chin a fraction to the right or left, up or down, the pain almost felled him.

He watched Kosterlinsky's face and decided he better wait to show himself until he saw what had made him stop.

"Hello, illustrious sentry," Kosterlinsky called, then smiled. Kosterlinsky always used elegant language.

"*Hola*, my captain," someone said from the trail behind Martinillo's right shoulder. Martinillo let his forehead rest on the ground and listened. Hoofbeats sounded on the trail behind him. He lay stretched out in plain sight of that rider.

"Have you found your spy?" Kosterlinsky asked.

"Nooo, when will we find him in this wilderness?" The rider spoke from Martinillo's right front now.

Martinillo raised his head. A tattooed pelón in camouflage utilities with an M-16 rifle slung across his back stopped his horse in front of the troop. He rode a corriente mare, not a Lupino Arab, but that did not surprise Martinillo. Lupino was so particular about his Arabian pets, he would probably weep if he ever saw one of these thugs astride one. Martinillo bet that old Nesib did not have much to do with these hoodlums at La Culebra.

"How is the commando training coming?" Kosterlinsky asked.

"Difficult," the sentry said.

"Where is the other sentry that rides with you?"

"We separated at the last fork in the trail, but we'll meet up ahead."

Thank you, Emilio, Martinillo thought. *You just told me which trail to take to Canela. I guess I better not ask for your help. I won't get a can of pork*

*and beans from your knapsack, and I won't get a shot of antibiotic or a dress-
ing for my wound. However, you've shown me that my government knows
about this training operation of Lupino's. You are plenty free about patrolling
the high Sierra of La Golondrina now. I bet Lupino doesn't even pay you extra
to do it. La Culebra is part of a government patrol. You and your troop protect
an enemy of Mexico.*

"Your spy disappeared, did he?" Kosterlinsky asked.

"He disappeared, or he never appeared at all," the sentry said.

"We'll bivouac at La Brava Spring tonight. Bring your partner and
have supper with us."

"We'll do that, man, thank you."

"Fine. We'll see you at the spring."

The troop filed past Martinillo's right and continued on. After a
while the sounds of loose chains on the pack mules died, and he sat up
with his back against the trunk of the tree.

Lucrecia was sitting under the shade of the ramada in her yard and
kneading clay for a new pot when Che Che Salazar rode in that afternoon. He sat his mule until Lucrecia asked him to dismount. He told
Lucrecia that he had come to get Dolly Ann so she could fly with her
grandfather to Rio Alamos the next day for the horse race. She and Luci
were also invited to go.

Lucrecia rinsed her hands, wiped them on her apron, and shook
hands with Che Che. He took off his hat for her, hobbled his mule's
front feet, and sat in the shade of her porch. She went in to put coffee
on the stove to warm. She came back out with a swallow of mezcal in a
coffee cup for him and a measure of corn for his mule.

"My nino Jim would like you to fly to Rio Alamos with him early
tomorrow," Che Che said. "You should spend the night at El Trigo."

"Here come the girls," Lucrecia said. "You can tell them."

Dolly Ann and Luci came to the porch with two young cottontail rabbits that had been caught in Lucrecia's snares. Each girl carried one and
they petted and crooned to them while they showed them to Che Che.

"Give them to me and visit with Che Che," Lucrecia said.

With great care the girls handed the rabbits to her, then shook hands with the man.

Lucrecia went into the kitchen and put the rabbits into a small wooden box. She carried coffee to Che Che, then went out the back door with the rabbits, rapped them behind the ears one at a time with a horseshoe hammer, cut off their heads, skinned them, gutted them, dismembered them, salt and peppered them, rolled them in cornmeal, and put them in a skillet on her stove to fry.

Lucrecia had decided to send Luci with Dolly Ann to Rancho Quemado with Che Che. She would pack the tan suitcase for her and let her go as far as she could go with Dolly Ann and Jim Kane, if her compadre Jim would take her. She took the valise down from its shelf and filled it with Luci's clothes.

Luci and Dolly Ann rode away with Che Che that afternoon. Lucrecia stayed at Las Animas in case Martinillo came home. The look on Luci's face haunted her all night. Luci had wanted to go to the "United," but did not want to be rushed off at a moment's notice and turned loose in the outside world without her *abuelita*, grandmother. Dolly Ann's look had been as woebegone as Luci's when they rode away.

Faced with the reality of achieving Luci's dream, they had not been sure they should take the first step. They did not say anything about their worry to Lucrecia, because it was nothing to fly with Jim Kane to Rio Alamos for a horse race. Luci could stop there and wait for her grandparents to come and get her, or to send for her. Lucrecia knew that while Martinillo was away and unable to object, this might be the only chance Luci would have to go to the United States with Dolly Ann. The good-byes they had said would probably be for a long time.

That night Dolly Ann and Luci waited in the kitchen of the El Trigo hacienda for Kane and Vogel. Everyone at El Trigo went to bed early. Sundown usually killed everything dead at El Trigo, but Che Che stayed up with the girls to wait for Kane. The girls discussed the situation with him, so he gave them his opinion that Luci should not leave home. He did not want to see a product of the Sierra corrupted. The values she learned in the Sierra would be good anywhere she went. The values she would learn from the girls in the United would not last. After about a half hour of that discussion, because he had stayed up an hour and a half past his bedtime, Che Che went to sleep in his chair with his face to the girls.

At ten o'clock the girls thought they heard someone mumble a word outside, then heard nothing, then they heard a rustle, then the soft scuff of a boot, and the door opened and Kane and Vogel walked in. Che Che woke up and took his employers into the kitchen to show them their supper on the stove, saw the girls serve their plates, then excused himself and went to bed with his family in the recently finished commissary.

"And your grandfather?" Vogel asked Luci. "Has he returned to Las Animas? We've not seen him."

"I hoped you'd have news of him," Luci said.

"He's on another big hunt. I hope he brings home a valuable pelt of some kind, a king of a buck deer, the fang of a wolf, or the claws of a jaguar."

That was all the conversation Vogel could entertain. He ate and went to bed. Kane still felt high from the ride in bare moonlight through pine forest. He and Vogel had watched faraway lightning in the north, but had not smelled rain or heard thunder. Although it happened far away, the sight had refreshed them.

Now, he wanted to sit in the light of the kerosene lamp and watch the flame and look at the faces of the girls. He thanked them for waiting up.

"Pappy, I have a problem," Dolly Ann said in Spanish.

"Oh, hell."

"It concerns Luci."

"What's wrong? What's happened to Luci?"

"She's growing up, Pappy."

"Oh, no. She's not going to have a baby, is she?"

Luci and Dolly Ann laughed merrily at that.

"No, nothing like that. She wants to have a life, Pappy. She's almost grown and wants to leave Las Animas."

"Life at Las Animas is good, granddaughter. She belongs to the most exciting family I know. Who do you know in Arizona that runs jaguars and wolf packs out of their front yards? The Martinillos do that every day, practically as a drill."

"That's it, Pappy. She has wolves, drunk drug growers with Uzis, rapists, killers, and plain old hardship every day for drill too. Lucrecia wants her to go home with us and start her own life. Luci wants to go to school."

"She does?"

"Yes, Pappy."

"We have to think about this. Maybe the easiest way to cross her would be to enroll her in a school so she can get a student visa."

"Her grandmother wants her to go before her grandfather gets back. She wants her out of the Sierra before the same thing happens to her that has happened to other girls her age. Nobody courts up here anymore. Some Sinaloa jackass will see her, want her, steal her away, get her with child, and ruin her life. It happens to every girl who stays here."

"I won't smuggle her across. I smuggle a lot of contraband down here, but I've never taken anything illegal to the States. The guys on the line in customs and immigration trust me."

"I only want to help Lucrecia and Luci."

"I'll have to think about it. Maybe I can get her a seventy-two-hour permit from my friends in immigration at the airport. We might get her a provisional permit, then you can get her a student visa."

"Good, Pappy. I knew you'd think of something."

"We'll see. Call the immigration service in Nogales from Rio Alamos tomorrow and tell them we want to bring Luci, a minor, across the border, so they can tell us what papers she needs. Tell them we'll go through the airport customs and immigration about noon. We'll radio from thirty minutes out."

"Hear that, Luci?" Dolly Ann said.

"Yes, thank you," Luci said.

"Don't be giving me any wet kisses for that," Kane said. "Don't get mushy. Just a little dry one will be all right."

"You'll get nothing from me," Dolly Ann said. "It's only right that you do this for Luci. You don't need to be rewarded for doing right, do you?"

"Just a little."

"A little what?"

"Neck sugar."

"Oh, I can do that." Dolly Ann laughed and hugged and kissed his dusty neck.

"Bath time, Pappy," she said. "Che Che heated a whole tank of water."

Kane could see that the whipping he had given Rafa did not bother Dolly Ann anymore. She would probably turn out to be the same as all the Kane women. They took the men the way they were, because they could see themselves in them and knew they would have to get over the atrocities they committed.

Kane loaded Vogel, Dolly Ann, and Luci in Little Buck a half hour before sunup the next morning and took off. He ran Little Buck off the end of the runway, stuck its nose down into the canyon to gain airspeed, followed Arroyo Hondo south, then Arroyo de los Mezcales west, and down the Mayo River to Rio Alamos.

The horse race would be run the next day. Vogel's daughter Mari picked them up at the airport and took them to Vogel's home, then took the girls shopping so they could gussy up.

That afternoon Kane and Vogel withdrew $90,000 in cash from their bank accounts in Sonora and Arizona to put down in side bets on the race. They put down $10,000 in each of five bars so that bettors could match all or parts of it. The bartenders had done this before—took bets and held the stakes until after the race.

The partners kept $40,000 to bet against special adversaries who hungered to beat them out of money any way they could. They would only be able to get even money on the $50,000 they left in the bars. However, some of their adversaries would bet any amount of money they wanted and give them odds on who could pee the farthest, if that happened to be the only contest the partners proposed. By race time tomorrow, they expected some of those adversaries would practically run the partners down to give them odds against their horse.

The partners drove across the Mayo River to the Escondida ranch that Kane used to own near the Mayo Indian community of Chihuahuita. The Escondida had been Kane's first ranch in that region. Vicenta Solano, the present owner, had been Kane's mistress before he met and married Adelita Pesquiera. After Vicenta gave him a dose of strychnine to celebrate the news of his betrothal to Adelita, she had calmed herself and begun to like him again. Killing him would have made her happy at the time, but she was also happy later when the strychnine only swelled him up and split him open. She tried to kill him other times, then had been happy that he lived through it, so she thought it was probably best that she let him live. When they finally parted, Kane gave her the Escondida.

The fifty hectares of the Escondida lay on the north bank of the Mayo River and in the center of a Mayo Indian *ejido*, five thousand hectares of brush pasture that was shared by the Mayo community. Kane had acquired a long-term lease on the pasture for fencing it with five strands of barbed wire.

Kane and Vogel found the dirt road to Escondida crowded with Mayo Indians who celebrated Gato as their champion. The whole community of Chihuahuita had guarded Gato's training since he arrived.

Ursulo Valenzuela, a chief of the tribe, met Vogel's truck at the entrance to the ranch. Since all trucks looked the same to him, he walked up to show his authority and inquire as to the business of its occupants. When he recognized Kane and Vogel, he grinned, climbed into the pickup with them, and guided them to Gato's stall, as though he had taken total charge of the training.

Ursulo had taken a crew of fifty men and cleared a *brecha*, a right of way, through the brush to serve as Gato's training track. Its sandy loam protected the horse from strain and conditioned his legs, heart, and lungs.

Mayo Indians crowded around the stable to watch Gato rest. They had brought him a billy goat so he would have a friend other than the mules Paseador and Negrito and to ward off sickness. The billy goat, Gato, and the mules gazed at the partners from their stalls with expressions that said, "Ah, more public. We have so much admiring public."

Marco Antonio braided a rawhide halter as he and Cody Joe lounged on their cots in another stall. Cody Joe whittled a stick with a new pocketknife. Both their hats were cocked jauntily on their heads.

After six weeks of careful, gentle training, Gato looked as though he could outrun the wind. Daily workouts, baths, rubdowns, and good grass hay and grain had made him bloom. Every lustrous hair on him seemed to vibrate. His eyes were clear as mezcal and showed an antagonistic gleam that came straight out of his stallion's heart. He was ready to run a race, or fight a battle, and his look said that he hoped it would start soon.

"I've never seen a horse in such good shape," Kane said to Marco Antonio and Cody Joe. "What's you boys' secret?"

"We've had everything right," Cody Joe said. "Doña Vicenta came and got us and made us move here from the racetrack the day after we arrived. Since then, we've just stayed with the horse. She gave us her roof, her kitchen, her truck, has watched over us, and fed us way too much."

Ulp, Kane swallowed, and thought, *More for me to feel guilty about.*

Vogel saw Kane's big swallow of consternation. "Vicenta's my compadre Jim's best friend." He laughed.

"She's been a mother to us," Cody Joe said. "The Mayos have been our family. We're happy here. Even Lupino is happy."

"Lupino?" Kane asked.

"The goat." Cody Joe laughed. "We think he might be related to the Lupinos, with those chin whiskers."

A tall, handsome young man came to the stables and stood in the shade while the partners and the boys discussed Gato's training. Kane thought he might be a youngster from Chihuahuita who had grown up while he was gone. Vogel introduced him to Kane as Miguel, "Vicenta's man."

"Handyman? Maintenance man? Engineer?" Kane shook Miguel's hand.

"He's Vicenta's all-around man. Her day and night man," Vogel said.

Miguel smiled.

"Ah," Kane said.

"La señora would like you to come to supper. I'll stay with the horse," Miguel said.

"I'll stay with the horse too," Ursulo said.

"I'll stay," Cody Joe said.

The partners and Marco Antonio went to the house that Kane had built. He loved that house. He had built it square with each side a hundred feet long. Every room opened to a cobblestoned patio inside the square. Livestock, wagons, trucks, and cars could be parked or corralled in the patio. The two rooms on each corner shared the same fireplace. Vicenta had built a long bar in the kitchen with heavy wooden stools and the partners and Marco Antonio sat there while Vicenta gave them drinks.

The woman was trim as the day Kane had left her forty years ago, eighty pounds and no fat. The little brown girl with the big smile, the little Zapotec from Jalisco, had lived with Kane during his first eight years in Rio Alamos. No woman in the world had more heart, more perseverance, more integrity. No one was more jealous-hearted of her property and loved ones either. The young Jim Kane had been a tomcat. He still carried a .22 long rifle bullet with the rim crimped by her pistol's firing pin. He had come home after a week of tomcatting and she had opened the door, stuck her pistol in his brisket, and pulled the trigger. The pistol said, *"Click."* Kane took it away so she would not try to shoot him again, and she fainted. When she returned to herself, she was glad again that she had not killed him.

Now, she sat on a stool across the bar and smiled at him. Kane might as well have been an old friend of her brother's, which he was, or the godfather of her son, which he was, or an old drunk whose hangovers she had cured many times, which he also was.

"How does your horse's conditioning go?" she asked Vogel.

"Not mine, my compadre Kane's," Vogel said.

She gave Kane a tolerant, and patronizing, look. "You look good, Jim, for a man who almost died . . . for a man who might as well have died, because he stayed away from us for a year and a half and did not bother to send us any word."

"I meant to, but I was too busy recovering." Kane laughed.

"Yes, it must be hard for an old jade to try to recover his stature after a half ton of horse smashes him into the bottom of a canyon. I bet it finally thinned out your girlfriends. How many you got left now?"

"None. How many boyfriends have you got?"

"Only one. I try always to keep one."

"You've always been good that way. You were good to me."

"Well, I am good. And men make me happy. Anyway, what kind of horse is Lupino's horse? How good are my chances of winning money?"

"My compadre Juan and I drew all the money we could scrape out of our accounts to bet on our horse, so we will win."

"All your money?"

"All of it."

"How can you do that? Your horse could drop dead."

"He'll have to drop dead to lose. He can't lose any other way."

"Still, that's too much a gamble."

"It's no worse than the gamble on cattle," Vogel said. "No worse than the gamble with livestock on the weather, sickness, or the market. Those are bigger gambles that a cattleman takes longer to win or lose. This gamble is also on our livestock and will be resolved tomorrow. It's the best thing we could do with our money. We don't have to wait for a good rain or worry that our stock will starve, or get sick, or that the market will go bad."

"There are other things that could happen to your horse, you know," Vicenta said. "That's why I brought him here. He's safer here than in his own home now that the Indians from Chihuahuita surround him."

"Thank you, Vicenta. We appreciate it," Kane said.

"I mean it. Your horse is in danger. If he had stayed at the racetrack, he would have been harmed. It still might happen."

"What do you mean?" Kane said.

"I was going to tell you," Marco Antonio said. "Somebody told doña Vicenta that Gato would be shot."

"Who would do that?"

"The Lupinos, probably," Vicenta said.

"Old Lupino wants the race. It's his idea."

"Did you make him put up a hundred thousand dollars and his horse against your horse alone?"

"Nobody was supposed to know about the terms of the wager except me and Juan Vogel. We told Adan Martinillo. Not even Marco Antonio and Cody Joe knew about it. Did you Marco Antonio?"

"No."

"Everybody here knows about it. The Lupino brothers know," Vicenta said.

"They must," Kane said.

"What did you expect from them? They don't want to lose that money. It comes out of their pockets too, doesn't it?"

"Of course. They're Lupino's heirs."

"They handle his money. Everybody knows it."

"Well, what of it?" Kane said. "A bet is a bet. Lupino made the race to see which horse is best. He doesn't care about the money."

"The grandsons care about it plenty. They plan to kill your horse. The word is that they will kill him as publicly and sensationally as possible, probably while the race is run, so you won't decide which is the best horse, and you won't take home a hundred thousand of Lupino's big dollars."

"Vicenta, how do you know all this?"

"From the Molino Rojo. I still have friends there. Why wouldn't I? I've never been without friends in that place, and there is no better place to hear the truth."

The Molino Rojo was the main establishment in the zone of tolerance, the red light district of Rio Alamos.

"If it comes from there, it's true." Vogel laughed.

"It not only comes from there, it comes from Rafa Lupino's favorite whore, Carmelita, the granddaughter of Carmela, one of your favorite whores, Jim Kane."

"Carmela's granddaughter is there?" Kane asked.

"Of course. Her mother was born there. Your Carmela gave birth to Carmelita's mother in the Molino Rojo. You knew that. Her mother might even be related to you, Jim."

"Oh, no. I didn't leave any bastards in whorehouses, or anywhere."

"Still, Carmela was your friend, still is."

"That's right. How is she?"

"Don't ask me. I've never been her friend. She had eyes and a pair of buttocks for you when you belonged to me. How could she be my friend?"

"You had much in common."

"Yes, and she did what we whores used to do. She got you in bed as soon as she could."

"No, Vicenta. She was a good friend to both of us."

"Well, the granddaughter of your friend is a favorite companion of Rafa Lupino's and word came from her that they plan to shoot your horse. The word they used is *venadear*. They're going to venadear your horse, whatever that means."

"That means they'll lay for him and sniper him from seclusion, the way a hunter shoots a deer."

"As soon as the girl told me about Rafa Lupino's plan, I got your horse over here where our friends the Mayos could protect him. He's safe here. Who knows what will happen when you take him to the racetrack."

"You still visit the Molino Rojo? I thought we agreed to put that behind you."

"Why not? That's where I came from. That's where I met you, Jim. My being there got me here where I am now, a happy woman. Those women are still my friends. I'm still their kind of woman. I've never been accepted by the 'decent' ones, except one or two like Alicia Vogel and your Adelita. I was only your mistress, but that got me out of there. Besides that, you were the best man any of these women in Rio Alamos had ever seen. For eight years I was the envy of every woman in this region."

"Seven years," Kane said.

"Eight years. Count them again."

"I took you away from there because I wanted you. Not to save you from anything."

"Best of all, you showed me I could go. Before I met you I thought I would never have a better life than the one in the bordello. Thank you, Jim." Vicenta walked around the end of the bar, stood on tiptoes, and kissed Kane on the lips. "That's in case the next time you fall off your horse, you get finally killed."

"I didn't fall off—he fell on me."

"Whatever. I didn't want you to go away and die on us again without having thanked you for being good to me."

"You were a lot better to me. Who wouldn't have been good to you?"

"Anyway, one hundred Indian families on the Mayo River are watching out for your horse Gato, and everybody's on the lookout for Muslims."

"What? Now, how in the world will they identify a Muslim?"

"Aren't they the tattooed baldies who have been swaggering through the town?"

Kane and Vogel laughed.

"That's right," Vogel said. "The enemy has been identified. There's no mistaking how he looks and acts. Tell everybody not to go near those Muslims and to watch for them at the racetrack."

Ten

Vicenta brought out a bottle of Presidente brandy and poured large measures for Vogel and Marco Antonio. Kane went out to sit with Gato for a while. He found him alone. Cody Joe and Miguel had stepped away, but he could hear them talking. Ursulo was trying to pry Cody Joe loose from his new pocketknife.

That made Kane think of his own knife, Abdullah's gift. He did not think he could call it a new knife, for all the material in its makeup was probably aged. Certainly its maker was aged, if not ancient. Kane carried it in a new sheath in his belt, under his shirt, the way Abdullah carried his knife. He did not want to put it away. He thought it to be the kind of gift Abdullah meant for him to keep handy.

He unsheathed the knife and let the soft light from Vicenta's kitchen play on it. He liked to feel the blade. The steel was not soft, but it felt soft, like a big tooth. To him, a tooth was not soft, but felt soft under the tongue, or the touch. He ran his fingers along both sides of the blade in the dark and found a rough line on one side. He brought it closer to his face and ran his fingers carefully along the rough line, just below its backbone. He shined the boys' high-powered lantern on the blade. Abdullah had carved an inscription on it in tiny letters that Kane had missed. It said, *"Yo soy el colmillo de Jim Kane."* I am Jim Kane's fang. *Colmillo*, also eye tooth, or canine, has another connotation. To have colmillo also means to be sagacious, farsighted, not easily imposed upon or fooled, not easily bullied, because the person with colmillo has a big, dangerous tooth to support his sagacity. Kane was sure that only the sight of his blade would stop any bully, but he did not intend to threaten anybody with it. If he showed it, it would be to cut some flesh. It would bring awful unhappiness to anyone to whom it grinned. Right then enemies who needed to be grinned at were revealing themselves in every part of his world.

Kane admired the orderly way Cody Joe and Marco Antonio kept their camp. Marco Antonio crossed Vicenta's yard and joined Cody Joe, Ursulo, and a group from Chihuahuita at a fire they had built behind Gato's stable. Kane felt proud of the admiration and respect his grandson and godson gave him. They were still young and shy but had taken all the responsibility for the horse race upon themselves. Now that Vicenta had alerted him to the danger of the post to which the boys had been assigned, he felt grateful to them for handling it so well. Without realizing it, he had placed all the responsibility of the race on them and given them no advice or guidance. This would be their first race as trainer and rider, and Kane and Vogel had been so busy with their own business that they had not helped at all. He hoped they had done a good job, because he and Vogel had bet their last dime on them.

At that moment the young men returned to their stall and were surprised to find Kane there. "I brought you some beer," he said. "It's on the front floorboard of your nino Juan's pickup."

He noticed that the boys had bathed and shaved. Their clothes were clean and unwrinkled. Kane knew they must have washed them in the canal and hung them in a mesquite to dry. That was the cowboy way, to carry everything they owned in their bedrolls and warbags to a job. When these two boys had only been buttons on their first sashays with Kane, he had shown them how to wash their change of clothes, dry them in a tree, and roll them in their bedrolls to press them. Cowboys could always keep a clean change of clothes if they had a canal handy, as these boys did. Cody Joe brought back six cans of beer in a bucket of ice. He offered Kane the first can he opened, but Kane refused it. "I thought you might want to take the evening off, if you can get some-body to look after your animals," he said.

"Ursulo said he'd do it," Cody Joe said. "Marco Antonio wants to go to town this evening."

"And you, Grandson?"

"Me, too, Pappy," Cody Joe said shyly.

"You got girlfriends lined up or something?"

"No, we thought we'd eat a steak and then cruise around awhile."

Marco Antonio looked down and smiled.

"You want to ride into town with Nino Juan and me?" Kane asked.

"No, doña Vicenta loaned us her pickup," Cody said.

"You won't get drunk and stay out all night, will you? Tomorrow's a big day for all of us. Godson?" Kane stared at Marco Antonio until he looked up.

"We want music tonight," Marco Antonio said.

"My partner wants to impress girls." Cody Joe laughed.

"And you?"

"*También*. Me too."

"*¡Eso!* I approve. A serenade for a girl at her window is the surest way I know to get her to like you," Kane said.

At two o'clock in the morning, El Trio de Sonora, the classiest three musicians in Rio Alamos, unloaded with the boys from a taxi in front of Vogel's house at Hidalgo #308 and began to tune their guitars on the sidewalk. Dolly Ann awoke, looked out her window and saw Cody Joe and Marco Antonio, awakened Luci, and they put on their robes.

"Begin when you're ready, Manuel," Marco Antonio said to the trio's leader. "Play 'Two Little Trees' first."

"Quietly," Cody Joe said. "Softly."

With wide smiles, the three mariachis stepped back from the window and put their hearts into the song. The two partners took hold of the iron bars that protected the window and pressed their cheeks against them to see inside. They grinned and the girls laughed, because the girls' faces were already there, side by side, only inches away, and each faced the person he or she most wanted to see.

On the morning the race was to be run, Juan Vogel went to see Gerardo Cepeda, the chief of the traffic division of Rio Alamos, and asked him to protect Gato. The chief said he would double his usual guard of cops at the racetrack and assign two patrolmen as bodyguards for the horse before he left La Escondida.

The international highway ran north and south along the west side of the racetrack. A row of alamo trees, an *alameda*, lined the road on the track's east side. Bleachers were set up on both sides of the finish line. A pasture on the west side of the highway was choked with a monte, a jungle of spiny brush.

Kane thought the best place for a sniper would be in that brush. A sniper could hide there and be close enough for an easy, hundred-meter shot at the racetrack.

The Mayo community of El Datil lay along the north side of the thicket. Placido Ruiz, another of Kane's compadres, lived there and pastured his daughter's cows in the thicket. Kane had been trying to get Placido to come and live with him on the 7X. The man had worked for Kane since Kane first came to Rio Alamos. He still worked for him when he was needed, but he would not work for Juan Vogel. He liked Vogel, but he worked for no one except Kane.

He had been out of work while Kane was laid up. First, he could not work because of the worry when Kane lay near death. Then he could not work because he got on the Viva Villa mezcal. Vogel told Kane that Placido had been on the Viva Villa since Kane's accident. The Viva Villa was tough stuff and only cost two bits American per liter. Kane knew that when Placido was on it, he required at least two quarts a day to function. He always ran out before he went to bed at night and suffered when he woke up in the morning until he could walk a league hung over to buy another two quarts.

On the morning of the race, Kane went to an *expendio*, bought two quarts of Viva Villa, and drove Alicia's sedan to El Datil to look for Placido. He found his compadre sitting in the shade of the same ramada where Kane had last seen him. An empty Viva Villa bottle lay on its side beside him. He stood and embraced Kane and began to weep. Kane sat on a cot and cracked open a new bottle, handed it to him, and stopped the weeping.

"I knew you were here, compadre," Placido said. "I've known about the race and that your grandson Cody Joe came here with the horse. I saw them the evening they arrived. I went over there with all the rest of the common folk to look at your horse. He's a nice horse, even prettier than Pajaro, but I bet he's no Pajaro."

Placido had been Pajaro's personal bodyguard until Kane put the horse down at the age of thirty-three. Pajaro and Placido had been as close as any two persons could be.

"He's still young," Kane said. "He might be as good a cowhorse as Pajaro, but he will probably never have the life that our old horse did. No animal will ever be the horse to us that Pajaro was."

"*De veras*, that's true," Placido said. "If we talk about this horse, we should not talk about Pajaro. Pajaro should not be mentioned in the same breath with any other horse."

"For a long time, I thought no horse could love a man the way he loved another horse, but I was mistaken," Kane said. "I've known one horse who loved one man. Pajaro loved you. I knew that when you cared for him and I know it now. However, I never thought of you two as man and horse. I thought of you as *único*, as one. You had more than a love. You had a oneness."

"Ah, thank you. I miss him." Placido's face started to break up again.

Kane pushed the hand that held the bottle toward his mouth. "Have another swallow and don't break down on me, compadre."

"*Sí.*" He curved his lips to meet the mouth of the bottle exactly and took five big swallows of Viva Villa. The stuff that stayed in the bottle roiled like the surface of the sea in a typhoon, the way the sea acts when a typhoon sucks at its waves, takes big swallows, and spits them back.

"Viva Villa," Kane said quietly, then gave Placido time to allow the mezcal to have its way and bring him back to his responsibilities. When he saw that he felt better, he said, "What do you hear about a plan to shoot my horse, compadre?"

"There's been some drunken talk, but I haven't paid attention, compadre."

"Have you seen any strangers in El Datil?"

"Some of those shaved heads who call themselves Los Lobos have cruised through here in their car."

"Your comadre Vicenta got word that someone will try to shoot our Gato horse during the race."

"How does she know, compadre?"

"Some of her cronies in the bawdy house told her. One of them is the favorite woman of Rafa Lupino. You know this race is against a Lupino horse, don't you?"

"Ooo, everybody from Sinaloa to Chicago knows, I think."

Kane laughed. "Why Chicago?"

"Isn't that where all the Mexicans have gone?"

"What do you mean? Have only Mexicans gone there, no Mayo Indians like you?"

"Yes, only Mexicans. They've left Mexico to us poor brutes."

"We have to keep our horse safe. What can you do to help me? I think if a sniper wants to shoot him during the race, he'll have to hide in the brush along the west side of the highway."

"That would be indicated, for that is the only place by the racetrack where anyone can hide with a rifle."

"I haven't been in that thicket for a long time, but you have."

"I go in there every evening after my daughter Concha's milk cows. That's what I'm good for. I cut and carry in the forage for the cows in the afternoon, go find them and bring them in and feed them at night, milk them and drive them out to pasture in the morning. I pasture them there, because it's so brushy nobody minds. They're safe in there. Nobody bothers them and nobody can find them in there but me."

"I need you to do something for me now, compadre."

"*Ya sabes*. All you have to do is tell me what it is."

"I need you to lead me unseen into that brush to watch for the sniper. Can anybody find a place in there to shoot my horse without our knowing it?"

"That is one thing no one can put over on me. I know every trail, every hiding place in that thicket. Nobody can shoot a horse from in there if I don't want him to."

"We need to go into that brush."

"I heard that you bet a million pesos on this race, compadre. How will you spend it if the sniper shoots you?"

"If somebody doesn't shoot our horse, we'll win, and no gun can keep me from spending that money. No gun can fill me with enough holes to stop me from collecting it and spending it the way I want to."

"So, you finally admit that you want money? You always told me that you run horse races to see who has the best horse. Now you're doing it for the money? How come?"

"By God, to have some fun again. Remember how much fun we had when we were young? We had fun fixing a wagon wheel out in hundred-and-twenty-degree heat. Remember that? I want to have plain old fun with my friends and compadres like you, and to afford to have the music."

"Not me, compadre. I don't enjoy my life anymore. Each swallow of mezcal puts another spot of poison on my liver. I am damned. I've come so low that I'm condemned to suffer hell before I die. My wife is gone. My self-respect is gone. How can I even call myself your friend? I honestly am not sure that I can take you into that brush and do what needs to be done."

"You want to know why I call you my friend, compadre? You've always been good to me. You've loved me with a generous heart."

"I'm a *borracho*, compadre."

"So what? For you, *la borrachera* is no worse than a pair of dirty socks. All you have to do is take them off and wash them and you'll be all right. Haven't we been brothers for sixty years? Who knows you better than I?"

"No one."

"Then believe me. You're the man to help me stop a coward from shooting my horse."

"I guess we'll see."

"Are you ready to try?"

"Of course. *Yo no me rajo*. I might fail, but I won't back out."

"All right then. Wait here for me and keep watch. I'll be back after we've taken the horse to the track."

∽

Kane and Vogel drove along in the pickup with a host of mounted Mayo Indians from Chihuahuita as Cody Joe and Marco Antonio led Gato to the racetrack. Chief Cepeda posted motorcycle cops at both ends of the cavalcade, and it marched down the center of the highway.

Gato traipsed along as though all this attention was only his due. The walk to the racetrack from La Escondida was only a good stretch of the legs for him. He glided along, looked all around, and enjoyed every step, as though he knew he had been born a prince and soon would be a king.

As Gato neared the racetrack, the entourage grew. By the time he reached the track, a horde of people accompanied him afoot and horseback. He arrived at the track at 4:00 p.m., but Auda had not arrived. Kane asked Marco Antonio and Cody Joe to keep him away from the press of people. What better way to get near enough to hurt a horse with a knife or a pistol than to sidle up to him inside the press of a crowd? With $100,000 and his father's best stallion at stake, Rafa Lupino certainly did not want the race to be run.

On the track Gato began to realize that he had become the center of attention. He enjoyed the sights and sounds of the promenade of people, the cars, a band of mariachis, and the other horses. Kane had never seen a horse with more grace and good looks. The curve of his neck when he turned his head could stop a horseman's heart.

Kane went to the top of the grandstand on the highway side and looked into the thicket. More people arrived and took seats. He worried that his horse might be the cause of a bullet finding someone in the grandstand. He walked away from the racetrack, crossed the highway, and walked up the road that was lined with the date palms of El Datil. He found Placido resting in the shade on the side of the road.

"We won't get to see the race, will we?" Placido said.

"We will if we do what we have to do and catch the sniper before it starts," Kane said.

The thicket lay on five hundred hectares of land between El Datil and the edge of town. Kane and Placido slipped into the brush and out of sight. Placido led the way on a trail that tunneled through the thicket. Used all the time by cows and horses, it was the only way into the thicket. Short, dim trails branched off to dead ends, but the two men followed the main one toward the highway. A sniper would have to use another trail that paralleled the highway and racetrack. He would have to stay on the edge of the highway, because if he moved more than six feet inside the brush, he would be unable to have a clear field of fire to the track. When he settled in his spot to shoot, he would not be able to see more than twenty feet behind him either.

Placido led Kane off the trail. They crouched and sidled and pushed their way through the brush, but kept in sight of the trail that the sniper would have to use. They moved slowly, watched and listened. Now and then they could see through the brush to the racetrack and hear the voice of an announcer. Auda arrived and the grandstands filled.

Kane suddenly realized that Gato had never been so close to so many noisy people. That might do more to determine the winner of the race than the fleetness of the horses. The horse least distracted by the crowd might win. Crowds had been known to scare a racehorse right off the track. Kane knew better than to try to run a race with a green horse that had never been near a crowd. He could only hope that the Mayos of Chihuahuita who attended Gato's training sessions had been many and loud.

Placido froze and motioned Kane to move back, then turned and hurried him to a hiding place that happened to be on the tiny bed-ground of Concha's cows. When Kane and Placido dropped into their boudoir, the cows only looked up in surprise, then continued to chew their cuds comfortably and did not stand. The men knelt among them in total concealment, smelled their cud, and waited.

A man dressed in a T-shirt and khaki trousers appeared on the trail that paralleled the highway. A faded red baseball cap and dark glasses concealed his features so well that he was almost faceless. He stopped only twenty yards away. He could not see Kane and Placido, and he did not seem worried about anybody else being in the thicket. He positioned himself directly across the highway from the starting line of the racetrack.

If he was the sniper, he had a clear field of fire all the way to the finish line, except for the cars that passed in front of him on the highway.

The man carried a scuffed leather case. He looked around, knelt and opened it, and took out a bolt-action Springfield rifle with a scope, the piece that Marine Corps snipers preferred to use in Kane's time. The varnished stock gleamed with the care the man had given it. He loaded it with cartridges that also gleamed.

Gawkers slowed their cars to watch the goings-on of the racetrack and began to clog the highway between the sniper and the track. The sniper was calm and relaxed. He watched the police hurry the traffic along. A motorcycle cop ran by him and could have seen him if he turned his head, but he was intent on moving ahead to stop traffic during the race.

Kane drew his colmillo and started toward the sniper on his hands and knees. The bedground did not have one inch of spare room for two men and two cows. Kane moved a cow's head aside so he could get beyond her. He kept his eyes on the sniper. The sniper turned and looked right at him. Surprised at Kane's sudden familiarity with her horns, the cow stood up, saw that everything was all right, then stretched. The sniper turned away, unconcerned.

The announcer ordered the horses to the starting line. The cops stopped all traffic on the highway. Kane left his hat behind and began to move his old bones along the ground. He would have to make it all the way to the sniper on his belly. He hoped he did not encounter a snake, or a centipede, or a man-eating scorpion. If he tried to make a run at the man, he would fail. He could not outrun a fat woman. He could crawl a lot more efficiently. The sniper could shoot at any moment. Now was the time to shoot Gato, as he slowed and was contained with the business at the starting line. The eyes of at least five thousand people were on the horse. The man would never have a better opportunity for a sensational hit.

The sniper seemed to read Kane's mind. He wrapped the sling of the rifle on his arm, assumed a target shooter's sitting position with elbows squeezed between his knees, then put his eye to the telescopic sight. Kane scurried the last five yards, grabbed the end of the rifle barrel, and jerked it up as it fired. He jerked the rifle so hard that he almost lifted the sniper off the ground as he dragged him into the concealment of the brush. The sniper's hands were still on the rifle above his head. Kane sliced through his upper arms with the colmillo and lifted the rifle free. The man wailed, rolled on his side, and kicked and cried in pain. Blood sprayed from the big smiles in both the severed triceps that Kane's comillo had cut to the bone. The sniper could not even lift them to look at them. Kane emptied the rifle, threw the bolt away, and dropped it out of the man's reach but in plain sight.

Traffic poured by as the police released a stream of cars. The sniper's eyes were masked by his dark glasses. Kane took them off and gently backhanded the baseball cap off his head so he could see his face. Shock and bleeding had blanched out all its color. A moment ago the man had thought himself to be the consummate assassin. Now he was only a skinny cripple, probably maimed for life. For the rest of his life, he would have a tough time pulling on his boots, if he ever got to put them on again. He might bleed to death in the next few minutes.

Kane took hold of the sniper's hair and forced his head back, put the point of his blade under an eye and twirled it there until the sharp edge touched the nose, then sliced off the end of the nose. "That's so you'll have a face for me to recognize, if I ever see you again," he said. "This too," he said and notched a two-inch swallow fork in the man's left ear.

"Don't kill him, compadre," Placido said.

"I'm through with him now, compadre," Kane said. He started to cross the highway toward the racetrack.

"No, compadre," Placido said. "They'll see you. This way." He turned Kane around, handed him his hat, and headed him down the trail to El Datil. "Wait, the rifle."

"Leave it," Kane said. "It's against the law for him to have it, so the traffic cops will have good reason to arrest him if they find him in time."

Kane and Placido hurried back past empty homes to Placido's ramada. Everybody in the Rio Alamos region seemed to be at the horse race. Placido washed the blood off Kane with cold water, then they hurried to the racetrack. As they arrived, Kane saw Dolly Ann, Luci, and Alicia and Mari Vogel in the grandstand together, their attention on the horses at the starting line.

Lupino and Kane had agreed on a lap and tap start. Vogel stood on the starting line and directed the two jockeys to ride off the end of the track. Side by side they rode away from the line. On Vogel's signal they were to turn back head to head and run at the starting line. If the starter saw daylight between the horses when they crossed the line, he would call them back to start again. If he could not see daylight between them, he would shout "Santiago" and the race would be on.

The horses had made several runs at the starting line, but Vogel had called them back. He ordered the jockeys to ride away from the line again, then ordered them to turn back. The horses ran at the starting line. Kane saw Cody Joe hold Gato back before he crossed the line so that Auda caught up and passed him. Vogel shouted "Santiago" and Auda jumped out four lengths ahead. Cody Joe leaned over and shouted into Gato's ears. Gato exploded, caught Auda quickly, and came on. "Go, Cody, go," screamed Dolly Ann above the crowd's roar.

The rest of the race was a gift for Kane as he was given three of his favorite sounds in all the world: the jockey's shouts of encouragement into the ears of his horse; the furious blast of his horse's lungs and nostrils with each stride; and the pound of his horse's hooves as they sounded the doom of his rival. Gato outran Auda that day as far as big, husky Rafa Lupino could throw a rock, but the race was all over in less than twenty-five seconds. Up in the grandstand, Dolly Ann, Luci, and the Vogel women engaged themselves in a joyful cluster hug.

Someone began to yell for help on the highway. *"Auxiliooo!"* a woman yelled. "A man over here has been hit by a car. Both arms are broken. *Policiaaa, socorrooo.* Call the Red Cross. A man is bleeding here with broken arms."

People hurried toward the woman who had stepped out of her car and was anxiously waving her arms. A motorcycle cop turned on his siren and threaded his way through the crowd. Kane and Placido tried to see the unfortunate victim but already knew the manner of hit and run that had befallen him. But they could not see him, so they went on to congratulate Cody Joe and Gato.

The crowd of spectators stopped both horses on the track. Kane found Chief Cepeda and asked that his officers clear the press of people away from Gato. He did not want his enemies to knife his horse. If they would hire a coward to shoot him, they would hire someone to sneak up in the crowd and gut him for winning the race.

Chief Cepeda moved the crowd away from the horses so the jockeys could walk them and cool them down. Marco Antonio rode up beside Gato on Paseador and put a halter on him so Cody Joe could switch to Negrito. Kane asked the group of Mayos to stay close to Gato on their horses so the crowd could not get close, and more riders joined the escort.

Kane found Vogel and was surprised to see that Nesib Lupino and Abdullah were with him. Kane shook hands with them. Lupino's eyes brimmed with tears, but he looked Kane in the eye. "You beat me in a good race, Jim. A fair one too," he said.

"My horse won, but nobody beat you, don Nesib," Kane said. "You're a gentleman and so is your horse. Neither one of these horses was used to the crowd."

"No crowd nor absence of a crowd could have changed the outcome of the contest," Abdullah said. "The race has been run, the race has been won. Your horse is the best of the two. Maybe better than any other horse in this country."

"We only brought Auda down from the Sierra day before yesterday," Lupino said. "We didn't want him to be here until today, because we were afraid for his safety. We weren't afraid of the loudness of the crowd, because we have run him here before. We heard that gamblers intended to harm him."

Rafa Lupino rode up on Auda, his head a mass of scabs with a seam of black stitches along the bridge of his nose. His legs flopped on the horse's sides. His trousers crept above the tops of his jodhpurs to show his hairy legs. The stirrups on the jockey saddle were too short. He had strapped a heavy pair of sharp-roweled spurs on his heels. Kane saw that he must be full of the chemical. He slouched on his tailbone and wallowed on Auda's kidneys.

"Eh, *meestair, meestair*! Where's your horse? Get your horse. We'll run another one. This time for one million dollars, but you ride yours and I ride mine."

Kane ignored him and turned back to Vogel and the two old men.

"*Meestair . . . meestair.*" When Kane ignored Rafa again, he jerked

Auda around and jabbed him in the flanks with the spurs. The little horse almost jumped out from under him, but Rafa hung on and held him down to a trot that bounced him on his butt. He jerked Auda around and jabbed him again, but this time held him on such a tight rein that his mouth gaped open. He jabbed the spurs into the horse's flanks at the same time that he held tight on the rein. In effect, he signaled the horse to hurry away at a run, and at the same time held him up. The horse did not know whether to stop or to go, so he began to prance in place and dance. That was what Rafa wanted, to make Auda dance while he bled from spur wounds, bled from Rafa's heavy hand on his bit, bathed in a nervous sweat, and his eye showed the abuse.

Kane could not stand it. "Your Rafa makes an obscene fool of himself again, don Nesib," he said. "You don't deserve it, and the little horse doesn't deserve it."

Lupino did not look at Kane or at Rafa. "He does as he pleases. I don't have a say in what he does," he said.

Abdullah met Kane's gaze.

"He has the horse so hot, he'll founder him, Abdullah," Kane said. "He hasn't been cooled down and watered."

"We have nothing to do with the horse anymore," Abdullah said. "Auda's care is out of our hands. You own the horse now, Jim. Didn't you bet your horse against don Nesib's horse and money?"

"Of course," Lupino said. "That was our bet: my horse and one hundred thousand dollars against your horse. Pay the man his winnings, Abdullah." Abdullah pulled a fat envelope out of an inside pocket of his vest and handed it to Kane.

Kane took the envelope and looked inside at a sheaf of one-thousand-dollar bills.

"Where did you get thousand-dollar bills, Nesib? I thought the American Treasury Department recalled these bills years ago."

"Nevertheless, they're real and must be honored as legal tender, do they not?" Lupino said.

"I think they've been out of circulation for at least ten years." Kane laughed. "You've been hoarding this money all that time? How many more have you got like this?"

"If you don't want them, give them back and I'll pay your winnings in hundred-dollar bills."

"No, these are fine. As far as I know, my bank has to honor them."

"If it doesn't, bring them back. I'll honor them. And you can take charge of Auda any time you want to now," Lupino said.

"Then, with your permission," Kane said, "I'll go get my horse."

"I'll help, if you wish," Abdullah said.

"Do you want me to come with you?" Vogel asked.

"No need," Kane said. "I have enough colmillo to take charge of the horse." As he walked toward Rafa and Auda, he caught Marco Antonio's eye and motioned for him to stand by.

Rafa made Auda dance up the track toward Kane. A group of townsmen from Rio Alamos had hired a band of mariachis to accompany them. As the mariachis played, the townsmen strolled toward Rafa with grins on their faces to show him how much they enjoyed kissing his ass. Rivulets of sweat ran down Auda's legs and washed over his hooves. Blood ran from his flanks and bloody froth from his mouth.

Kane drew his colmillo and stepped out in front of the horse. Rafa gave Auda his head and spurred him to run Kane down, but did not give him rein enough to let him go. Kane grabbed both reins under the horse's neck, sliced them in two just behind the bridle, and turned everything loose.

With the sudden release of Rafa's grip on his mouth, Auda shook his head with relief and spun back toward Gato and the Mayo horses and stood Rafa on his head on the racetrack. He sat up and looked at the loose reins in his hands.

Auda stopped when he reached Marco Antonio, Cody Joe, and the Mayos. Cody Joe took hold of Auda's headstall and helped Marco Antonio catch him in the loop of his reata.

The townsmen surrounded Rafa as he stood up and looked around for the horse. Kane asked the Mayo horsemen to escort Gato and Auda and the boys to La Escondida. He told the boys to walk home slow and cool the stallions down before they watered them and put them away. He told them to be sure the stallions did not fight and to stay with them until he and Vogel arrived. Both horses might be in danger now.

Kane watched his grandson dismount and hand Negrito's reins to

Marco Antonio. Placido mounted Negrito and helped Marco Antonio lead the racehorses away from the press of people afoot. Another half dozen horsemen joined the escort. Kane wondered why Cody Joe wanted to stay behind.

"*Meestair . . . Meestair Sonumabeech.*" Rafa had found his voice. Don Nesib and Abdullah were gone. Juan Vogel joined Kane.

"Are you ready to go, compadre?" Vogel asked.

"Whenever you are, compadre," Kane said.

"*Meestair Sonumabeech,*" Rafa shouted again. Kane walked toward him. All the color drained out of Rafa's face. He skipped behind one of the townsmen and made a threatening move, as though to kick Kane from thirty feet away. Two townsmen grabbed his shoulders to hold him back. He wanted that, but Kane was about to get close enough to break open the stitches on his sore nose. He made a last lunge at Kane and broke away from his handlers, but this time turned away to leave Kane behind and ran into Cody Joe. The boy was only trying to reach his Pappy's side. Rafa thrust out his arms with all his weight behind them, caught Cody Joe in the chest, and shoved him aside. Cody Joe kept his feet, dropped his chin between his shoulders, and measured the range to his target. He landed a straight right hand to Rafa's ribs that made him arch his back, then stepped in and landed a right hook that split open the stitches on his nose and straightened his back. A left hook on the side of the nose sent Rafa's head toward the ground, then a right shovel hook lifted him over on his back, spread-eagled on the ground. Kane decided that the hook to the nose had been the best of the combination. Rafa would wake up tomorrow and find that his septum no longer separated his nostrils on the end of his nose, but lay all in a lump inside one nostril.

Cody Joe stood over Rafa and waited for him to get up. Rafa rolled dazedly over to his hands and knees, let his head hang, and watched the blood pour from his nose. Kane wrapped his arms around his grandson from behind and turned him away. "He's done, Grandson," he said. "Let's go."

Vogel stepped up to watch Kane's back and to hold back Rafa's townsmen friends, but they were no threat. They had scattered backward and been struck dumb when they saw the boy step up and land his machinelike combination of blows on their hero.

"If you're Rafa's friends, take him away from here, before he brings more hurt on himself," Vogel said and to the townsmen. "I mean it. He should not be out here drunk. Take him away and help him get sober."

Musicians and townsmen turned and walked away.

Only one of Rafa's friends stayed. He helped Rafa to a sitting position and pressed a clean handkerchief to his nose. Vogel stayed to make sure Rafa was helped off the ground.

"That boy hit me from behind," Rafa said through his bloody lips. "I didn't expect the blow."

"What do you mean, Rafa? You looked him right in the eye and pushed him before he hit you," Vogel said. "You insulted his grandfather and almost ran over him with the horse. You still want to make something of it? Don't act stupid anymore. Get up from there and go home and take care of yourself."

"For you, I'll go, Juan," Rafa said. "You're my father's friend. But that boy hit me with brass knuckles, or a pipe, or something that made me bleed like this. I'm not even sure he didn't have a knife. Under Mexican law he spilled my blood and he will have to go to jail for it." He looked away at Kane and Cody Joe and called to them. "Yes, *Meestair Gringo*, you will rue the day you spilled Lupino blood. You can't do that in my Mexico and get away with it."

"Get him out of here before I unleash both my gringos on him," Vogel said to Rafa's friend.

Kane saw that Marco Antonio and Placido and their Mayo escort were riding back toward him on the racetrack. More than a hundred people from the grandstand and the alameda had stayed to watch Rafa's spectacle. He saw Alicia and the girls had been watching from the grandstand. Kane caught Alicia's eye over all that distance and motioned for her to take the girls and go. She gathered them up, walked off the bleachers, and headed away to their car. Dolly Ann turned a wan, worried face back to look at her brother once. Cody Joe walked out and met Marco Antonio's cavalcade and swung up on Gato's bare back. Marco Antonio stopped long enough to see for himself that Kane and Vogel were not in trouble, then turned his mule and led the escort back toward La Escondida.

Kane and Vogel boarded their pickup and drove up the alameda toward Rio Alamos. Rafa's shouts followed them all the way to town. Kane looked back and saw that he stood alone on the darkening track like a scarecrow that had finally chased all the blackbirds away.

"How did that one get all the poison, cowardice, and foolishness of his family?" Kane asked. "He's all dopehead and braggart. He can't have exclusive ownership over everything that's bad in that family, can he? I would think that Ibrahim, Jacobo, and Ali would have some of it, but if they do, they don't show it. He never shows that he's anything but an evil fool. Never has."

"Some people just have it all." Vogel laughed. "He's got all of what you say and money too."

"I don't understand how he could have every trait that other men dislike and be absolutely unable to hide any of it."

"Speaking of having it all, you have money now. How does that feel, compadre? How does it feel to come away this day with all the money in Rio Alamos?"

"Not only me. We, you and I, came away with all the money. We go fifty-fifty, as always. I told you that at the start."

"Let's see how much of the fifty thousand dollars the bartenders were able to bet. Alicia and the Montenegro brothers bet all of the forty thousand we brought to the track. They were given odds on a lot of it too."

"That is wonderful. Where is it?"

"Alicia took it home."

The partners drove around to the cantinas and picked up their winnings. The reputation of the Lupino horses was so great that the bartenders had only failed to bet 3,000 of the $50,000 the partners laid down. That night at Vogel's house they counted out $210,000 in cash winnings and an Arab stud worth another $50,000. They figured that was not bad for livestock that usually never made money unless it rained a lot and the market got hot.

Kane and Vogel drove out to La Escondida to see what they could do for Marco Antonio's and Cody Joe's diversion. When they arrived, Vogel handed each of them a fat bonus of Mexican currency that he said he wanted them to spend that evening in celebration.

Before he turned them loose to have some fun, Kane asked Cody Joe a question. "Grandson, just as you rode up to the finish line the last time for your lap and tap start, I saw you pull up and stop Gato. In other words, you ran him at the line, but you didn't let him go, you pulled up. Why did you do that? That gave Auda a four-length lead at the start. If he had been a little faster, you would not have caught him."

"I know what you mean, Pappy, but I had to pull up at the starting line, or my nino would have called us back again. Auda's rider kept holding back, lagging back at the start, so that Nino Juan couldn't start us. So I thought to outsmart him. I held Gato at the line and let Auda run by me and Nino had to shout 'Santiago' and let us go."

"You mean he outsmarted you, Godson," Juan Vogel said. "The reason he kept hanging back and making me call you back was because he wanted you to get impatient and stop your horse and wait for him. That way he got a running start and left you standing still. That's called jockeying for position. He out-jockeyed you, but in the end he couldn't outrun you. You had the most horse."

"Now do you understand what happened?" Kane asked.

"I got hoodwinked, didn't I?"

"That's all right. Gato made up for it."

"Lupino's jockey cheated."

"No, he didn't cheat, son. He did his job and out-jockeyed you."

"What could I have done to beat him at the start, then? He kept hanging back."

"When you rode away from the starting line and then turned together to make your run at the line, you should have held Gato neck and neck with Auda until you crossed the line. That way you would have outrun him by ten lengths instead of four."

"Boy, I sure am I dumb."

"No, you're not, son. I should have coached you on how to jockey at the start. We all had too much on our minds and didn't get a chance to talk during the training. To tell the truth, I never worried about it either. We had a whole lot better horse. He would have won that race if they'd shot him anyplace but through the heart."

"Well, it worries me about myself."

"Don't worry. You won. Now you and Marco Antonio go and have fun. Your nino and I will look after the animals."

As the boys drove away in Vicenta's pickup, Miguel came down and invited the partners for brandy and supper at Vicenta's table. Ursulo and a dozen Mayos stayed with the horses and celebrated.

Vicenta spread a million pesos in cash out on the kitchen counter for them to see. She had taken five hundred thousand pesos to the Molino Rojo and the two other bawdy houses in the zone of tolerance for her friends to bet on Gato.

After the partners congratulated her, Vicenta said, "Listen, when I heard everybody's high opinion of Lupino's horse, I got scared that I'd made a bad bet."

"You mean people praised Lupino's horse that much to you?" Vogel asked.

"Absolutely. Lupino's horses are famous in Mexico and yours are not," Vicenta said. "Ask Rafa."

"Yes, he knows famous stuff," Kane said. "However, anybody who knows horses could look at Auda and Gato and tell who would win."

"*Valgame.* Who is talking about people who know horses?" Vicenta said. "I'm talking about people who spend everything they own in the whorehouses. Those are the ones most susceptible to big talk from people like Rafa Lupino. He had all the whores convinced that Auda would win. My friends all tried to talk me out of betting on Gato. Auda is known as the best stallion in Mexico, isn't he?"

"He might be known to have the finest mane and tail hair and the prettiest little feet," Kane said. "But he's not known as a quarter-mile racer."

After supper, the partners sat on Vicenta's front porch, listened to the music from the celebration in Chihuahuita, and drank brandy with Vicenta. Gato and Auda were in adjoining stalls. Even though they were two young studs, they got along so well that after they ate their grain and hay, they slept nose to nose.

Kane and Vogel were discussing what to do with Auda when they saw a truck career off the highway and race down the ditchbank toward them. When it stopped in Vicenta's yard, they saw that it was a Montenegro truck. Adancito Martinillo, Martinillo's oldest son, left the motor running, stepped into the lights of the truck, and walked to the house.

"Godfather, is Jim with you?" he called when he recognized Vogel.

"Yes, Adancito, what is it?"

"You both better come with me."

"What is it, son?"

"Marco Antonio, Cody Joe, and my brother Memin have been shot."

Eleven

⎯⎯ᴠᴠ⎯ Kane and Vogel hurried to Sanatorio Lourdes, a small hospital run by Catholic nuns in Rio Alamos. Placido met them on the street in front of the hospital. He had been with the boys when they were shot. He told the partners that Marco Antonio and his uncle Memin were gravely wounded. He knew nothing about Cody Joe's injuries.

The partners went inside. Traffic policemen stood guard on both ends of the corridor where Memin and the boys were being treated. Two were posted at each of the four entrances of the hospital. The partners found Chief Cepeda in the front office. Kane asked him how the shooting happened.

"The boys were with Marco Antonio's uncle Memin and the Montenegro brothers celebrating in El Retiro restaurant near the racetrack," the chief said. He took off his barracks hat and wiped his brow with a clean handkerchief. "I had assigned a patrol car for their protection, because I was afraid this might happen."

"What did happen?" Vogel asked.

"The boys sent beer out to the patrol car, but thank God the officers sent it back. Then they sent them sodas and a plate of grilled marrow gut and tortillas, and they accepted that."

"Nothing wrong with that, Gerardo, but what happened?"

"You know El Retiro is a drive-in and a lot of families had come to park outside to drink beer and eat meat. There were so many that the Montenegros and Martinillos went inside and sat at a table by a door. The band Los Ciegos, three blind brothers, played music for them while they ate and drank."

"For God's sake, tell us what happened, Gerardo," Kane said.

"My officers in the patrol car watched a carload of men cruise around the restaurant twice, stop in front of the open door by the boys, and pour automatic fire into the restaurant. At the same time, the shooters fired on our patrol car and caused my men to fall out onto the ground to save themselves. Before they could recover, the shooters raced away. My men pursued them, but never saw them again. They gave me a description of the car and its occupants, but could not identify any of the individuals. Their description fits members of the border gang that calls itself Los Lobos. They have been seen in Rio Alamos a lot these past weeks.

"We have other evidence that the shooters were members of the Lobos gangsters," Chief Cepeda continued. "They left the same unusual signature at El Retiro that they have at border shootings. They rub garlic on their bullets to make them more deadly. Have you heard of this practice?"

"I never heard of such a thing," Vogel said.

"I have," Kane said. "American gangsters in the nineteen twenties and thirties did that to make their bullets poisonous. Are you telling us that the bullets that hit our kids had been rubbed in garlic? How do you know?"

"Their empty cartridge cases smell of garlic."

"Lord almighty," Kane said.

"Another thing, Jim. Probably it's completely unrelated, but right after the race yesterday, we found an American by the highway with both arms crippled. We arrested him because we think he hid in that thicket across from the racetrack to shoot your horse. Someone caught him there, maimed him, and left him for dead. He had a sniper's rifle with him that bears his fingerprints, although someone had certainly incapacitated him as a sniper."

"Imagine that," Kane said. "Someone did us a big favor, didn't he? How was he incapacitated?"

"Someone almost cut off both his arms. We might not be able to jail this man for attempting to shoot your horse, but we will put him in prison for possession of a loaded rifle near a crowd. It's against the law to carry a firearm in Mexico any place, any time."

Marco Antonio and his uncle Memin lay close to death. Cody Joe had been hit by two bullets. One nicked the side of his neck and his chin and another drilled the calf of his leg. The partners went in to see him. The doctor in attendance was Vogel's brother Oscar, an experienced surgeon who had been educated in Tucson. Oscar was one of the few doctors in the region who had been educated in the United States, and he was all too aware of the lack of medical facilities in Rio Alamos. He told Kane and Vogel that he hoped that Cody Joe, Memin, and Marco Antonio would recover enough to be flown to Tucson for better treatment. A bullet had exposed Cody Joe's jugular vein and missed killing him by a fraction of an inch. His calf would heal quickly, but the danger of infection would be extreme. After he gave the partners this brief account, Oscar hurried away to his duties.

The three bachelor Lupino brothers owned a house in Rio Alamos where they stayed when they were in the region to oversee their produce and cotton businesses. They also owned a house in Huatabampo that they used to oversee their resort hotel, fishing, and freight business in that seaport, only thirty miles away on the Sea of Cortez. Ali Lupino was at the hospital and he gave the partners a more thorough account of Marco Antonio's and Memin's injuries. Marco Antonio had been shot through the throat, the lung, and the abdomen. Memin had been shot near the heart and in the groin. The Montenegros and Adancito Martinillo had hurried them to the hospital and donated the first blood that kept them alive. Kane and Vogel were directed into an examining room where they lay down and gave a pint of blood apiece. Adancito had gone in search of more blood donors. Donors began to arrive and line up in the corridor outside the room where the nuns attended to Kane and Vogel.

Ali Lupino joined the partners out in the hallway after they gave blood. Ali had something more to tell Kane. "Cody Joe can be released in the morning, if you want to take him home, Jim. This hospital is small and needs the room. Be careful that his wounds do not become infected. Bring him to me at my hospital in Tucson for treatment day after tomorrow. I'll be back there then."

"What's this about garlic on the bullets, Ali?" Kane asked. "Does it really make them more poisonous?"

"Garlic on bullets? I never heard of that. If the garlic houses bacteria, I guess it would make bullets infectious."

"Chief Cepeda says the bullets that hit our boys had been rubbed in garlic."

"I'll look into it, Jim. I also urge you to take your compadre Vogel to Tucson so I can examine his lungs with the proper equipment." He went back into the hospital.

Just then Oscar Vogel came out of Memin Martinillo's room. He walked past Kane and Vogel to the room where Memin's wife and other Martinillo relatives waited. Kane and Vogel were so engrossed in their own business that they had not noticed the quiet huddle of Martinillo relatives in the waiting room. Oscar told them that Memin had died. Memin's wife walked past Kane and Vogel to his room without a word or a whimper.

"I thought Adancito and Memin were raising their families in the states," Kane said. "What are they doing back here where they can get shot? I thought they were happy in California."

"They came back to work for the Montenegros," Vogel said.

"The Montenegros must pay well. I didn't think there was enough money in Mexico to lure those boys back."

"The Montenegros have made them rich, Jim. Besides that, they missed Mexico."

"They didn't make Memin rich."

"No. But that's the game they play to get rich."

"Where's our compadre Adan? What's happened to him? He knows we worry about him, yet he stays away."

"He's gone to the high Sierra because he wanted to, not because we asked him to. You still must not realize that we're at war here and have been for thirty years. Where have you been?"

"I've been here, but not like you. You've stood between me and the war. I can ride in the Sierra without a guard, because I go with you and Martinillo. If you were not my partners, I might not be able to do that."

"Yes you would. You have as many friends in the Sierra as we do, but keep in mind what's going on. We have enemies, and enemies kill each other. By the way, wasn't it surprising that Chief Cepeda caught the man who tried to shoot your horse?"

"Surprising," Kane said.

"Don't tell me you found nothing when you searched the monte across the highway. Who broke that man's arms?"

"What man?"

"The man Chief Cepeda found in the brush. The man who had the rifle he couldn't shoot, because his arms were broken. What do you know about that?"

"The man was about to shoot the rifle when Placido and I caught up to him."

Vogel stared at him.

"We separated him from the rifle so he wouldn't shoot."

"And broke his arms."

"No, but I cut them with the colmillo to get the rifle away from him."

"Valgame." Vogel shook his head.

"Where did they take the man?"

"He's being treated in the social security hospital under arrest. He's not under restraint, though. You fixed him so he might never even scratch his own ass again."

"Well, he was about to shoot our horse."

"I take it back. I guess, you haven't forgotten that we're at war."

Oscar Vogel appeared again. "Are the parents of the Martinillo boy here?" he asked.

"His mother is in the waiting room, his father is dead, and his uncle Adancito is out looking for blood," Vogel said. "How is the boy?"

"He just died," Oscar said.

The Vogels and Kanes made arrangements for Memin's and Marco Antonio's funeral the next day. In accordance with Mexican law, they were buried within twenty-four hours of their deaths. The *velorio*, the wake, for both men was held at Vogel's house. Alicia, Mari, and Dolly Ann arranged the flowers and cooked most of the food. As Luci mourned with her family, Dolly Ann's tears for her friend Marco Antonio would not stop, but she kept working. She believed that friends had no right to collapse in grief and look for solace with the dead one's family, but she would have liked to close herself up in a windowless room away from everybody for life.

The partners did not stay to mourn with the family. In a war they had no time for that. The dead were buried and the combatants needed to prepare to engage the enemy. The women took the time to weep, the men to arm themselves.

Marco Antonio and Memin went to their graves well attended. Luci's mother gave Kane permission to take her to the 7X. Since her husband's death, the mother had not gone near the Martinillos. She had divorced herself from them because her husband had been killed in the drug war, and she wanted nothing to do with anyone who lived in the middle of it. She had returned to her own family. She appeared at the wake with her mother and a sister, wept silently, and left early. No one blamed her. Martinillos were being machine-gunned down.

Adancito left for the Sierra to tell his mother and father that their son Memin and their grandson Marco Antonio were dead.

Kane called the immigration inspectors at Nogales Airport and arranged for a seventy-two-hour pass for Luci. If he brought the necessary documents, they would let her cross in his custody as a special favor. Kane's years of flying across the border without trying to fool anyone in customs and immigration paid off again.

Kane loved the simple, uncomplicated life of the Sierra Madre so much that he was not sure he would do Luci a great favor by taking her home to the 7X. The 7X had its own trouble with dangerous people. Cody Joe and Dolly Ann were not totally aware of it yet. In fact, nobody else knew the trouble Kane and the Lion had seen on the 7X lately. He and the Lion agreed that they would be the only ones who dealt with thugs when they came to the 7X. They believed that border trouble should not happen to any other kind of American except cowmen. At least two cowmen, Kane and the Lion, had proved they could handle it. That's why they had allowed the four thugs they caught in the Ruby pasture to go home. The thugs would tell their mamas that horses ran over people and old grandfathers would drag them by the neck if they trespassed on the 7X.

Kane almost overloaded Little Buck with Vogel, Cody Joe, Dolly Ann, and Luci Martinillo, and flew to Nogales the morning after the funeral. After the customs and immigration inspection at the airport, they flew on to the 7X and landed before dark.

The Kanes would be busy with cattle for a few days because La Golondrina steers were scheduled to cross at Nogales the next day. The cattle would be trucked from the border to the 7X to be fed and rested until a buyer came for them.

Güero Rodriguez did not know Kane's schedule, but he considered himself to be a patient man. He had returned to the 7X after being told to stay away because he intended to snatch Kane's granddaughter. He and his four bodyguards crossed some rich illegals on Buster trail early on the morning after the Kanes returned to the 7X and saw Kane's airplane parked on the strip. After he delivered his customers to the Hummer at the mine, Güero returned to his lookout on Buster trail and trained his binoculars on the 7X headquarters. Kane was not there, but the grandson was, and so were the blonde and another pretty Mexican girl about her age. Now he might snatch two virgins instead of one. He watched the youngsters all day. His cohorts in Rio Alamos had told him the grandson had been shot, so he was not surprised to see the kid's throat wrapped in bandages and his leg propped up on a chair in the screened Arizona room of the main house.

He liked it that Kane was gone all day. This was a bonanza. He knew people who would pay a lot of money for two sixteen-year-old virgins. The grandson would be no problem, wounded as he was. If Kane and the Lion went away from headquarters again tomorrow, he might make the snatch.

That evening he watched truckloads of cattle stream in and unload at headquarters. Kane and the Lion arrived with Juan Vogel, Güero's own uncle. In Mexico, the first cousins of a person's parents were called that person's aunt and uncle, not his second cousin. Some uncle. Vogel had never claimed him.

Güero and his bodyguards stayed the night at Buster cabin. The next morning, from his lookout on Buster trail, Güero watched the family drive La Golondrina yearlings away to a pasture. Six hours later, they returned to headquarters and stayed there the rest of the day.

Güero and his bodyguards again stayed the night in the cabin at Buster camp and went back to their lookout the next day. Kane's pickup was gone, so Güero sent the four bodyguards down the Manzanita trail to wait in ambush, in case the youngsters rode out that way as they had before. He moved down the mountain to a closer lookout where he could see into the main house. Kane, Juan Vogel, and the grandson were gone. He watched old Cañez saddle his horse. He knew from weeks of spying that the Lion never returned from his circle until after three in the afternoon. The girls would be alone.

Güero climbed back to Buster trail and from that vantage watched the Lion for a solid hour. Then he went down to spy on the girls again. If they went out horseback on the Manzanita trail, they would be his.

The chattering girls came out of the main house carrying their do-gooder gunnysacks. To Güero's surprise and utter glee, they caught and saddled their horses and rode out in exactly the direction he wanted, chattering every step.

His good luck did not surprise him, because it only proved his genius. He had prepared for this exact eventuality, because he had been sure the girls would ride out with sandwiches and water for the poor Mexican immigrants. This would seem like such a good deed for young, empty-headed girls to do that he had set the trap before they even prepared the sandwiches. Now, he set fire to a young cedar tree, the signal to his bodyguards that the girls were on the way.

Güero stayed well behind the girls as he followed, but he did not have trouble keeping up. They did not make steady headway, because they stopped often to talk and laugh. The blonde enjoyed telling the Mexican girl the names of the trails, the springs, and the mountains.

At the narrowest, highest, most dangerous place on the mountain above a deep ravine, a place where their horses could not step off the trail without killing themselves, the girls dismounted to rest and chatter. One of Güero's bodyguards stepped out of hiding and grabbed the horses' bridles. The girls were so surprised, they did not even whimper.

Armando, the lead bodyguard, the stocky thug whose head still showed the scabs of the reata lashes that Kane had put there, pushed Dolly Ann against the rocky bank beside the trail. "I'm going to have this one right now," he growled, then reached out with both hands to grab the front of Dolly Ann's shirt.

That made him vulnerable to a boxer's right cross, so Dolly Ann fell on his nose behind the straightened shaft of her right arm. The man was big and heavy enough that he stayed on his feet. Only his head snapped back on the thick neck, but his eyes crossed. As Dolly Ann's weight fell on her target, her trunk cocked to the left, and she landed on her feet closer to the target. She snapped her trunk back to the right and brought her left fist from her belt to the man's jaw. Her fist ended over her right shoulder with her trunk cocked to launch a right hook. The thug's head started toward the ground and the girl snapped her trunk back to the left and landed the three outside knuckles of her right hand in a classic hook to the man's chin. The fist bounced through the target, ended over her left shoulder, and dropped the thug into the chasm beside the trail. His big carcass slithered off the trail, toes up, but a boulder saved him from going into the ravine.

Dolly Ann spun to face the other three thugs. Her exhibition of the sweet science had stunned them. The one who held Luci from behind gathered her closer to his breast, stepped back, and offered her as a shield against Dolly Ann. Dolly Ann made a fist and showed off the bicep muscle of the right arm that had incapacitated the biggest thug, and said, "Next?"

"Does that one even have a womb?" asked the thug who held Luci. "Is she even a she? If it is a she, it fights as though the very hole between her legs has fangs."

Güero had arrived in time to see the elimination of his thug. He snuck up beside Dolly Ann's horse on the cliff side, smothered her with a tackle, and brought her down.

The bodyguards came alive and forced the girls down on their faces, covered their heads with black sacks, and tied their hands behind their backs. They noosed their throats with choke ropes, loaded them on their horses, and tied their feet together underneath the horses' bellies.

Güero went to the edge of the trail and stared down at Armando. The thug had recovered enough to sit up with his back to the boulder and to hold the front of his sweatshirt to his bloody nose. Güero sighed with new exasperation. He had thought that the paramilitary training that was being given the Lobos gangsters made them capable commando raiders. He had armed them for this raid with cuernos de chivo, Uzi submachine guns that made them look just like guerilla warriors. They had walked and talked the role well enough. Now he reevaluated them. If a little yellow-haired, hundred-pound girl could, with bare hands, disarm and incapacitate the leader of his "commandos," the leader of grown men who had been trained by Arab terrorists to be robbers, smugglers, killers, and kidnappers, he and the Lobos gang were in awful trouble.

Armando climbed back to the trail and took Dolly Ann's choke rope from Güero without a word. Dolly Ann found her voice and demanded to be released. One jerk by Armando on the noose that encircled her throat shut her voice down in mid-sentence, but he did not seem to enjoy it. He did not even look at the girl again.

"Be careful you don't allow hate to cloud your judgment, hombre," Güero told Armando in an even tone. "We can't scar the merchandise. We don't want to have to give our buyer a discount. This is handsome stuff, so think of the dollars we'll get. Don't tarnish them with abuse just because they're stupid. They evidently thought those choke ropes were for adornment."

Cody Joe was running a fever when Kane and Vogel got him to the hospital in Tucson.

"The boy does have an infection, and I would like to put him to bed and begin his treatment here and now," Ali said.

"Do it," Kane said.

"As for you, Juan," Ali said to Vogel, "now that you're here, let's look at your lungs."

Vogel followed Ali down the corridor to submit to treatment and soon returned to sit with Kane and wait for the results. When they became available, Ali examined them quickly and brought them to the waiting room to show Vogel a suspicious spot on one lung.

"That's only a scar," Vogel said.

"It might be a scar, and it might be a tumor," Ali said.

"I know it's a scar. A heifer gored me there when I was sixteen."

"Still, I want a biopsy done. It's early and we have all day, so we can do it right now."

"Today?"

"Why wait? You want to know if it's cancer, don't you?"

"It's not cancer."

"Maybe not, but let's allay all doubts and fears, Juan."

"Juan, why not just go ahead and do it?" Kane said. "What have you got to lose?"

"All right, but do it quick," Vogel said.

The required staff was quickly prepared. In half an hour Ali and a pathologist performed the procedure. In another forty-five minutes Vogel returned to Kane's side fully dressed.

The partners wanted to visit with Cody Joe before they returned to the ranch, but nurses still attended him, so they sat in a waiting room. Ali introduced Kane to another of his patients in the room, a man named Silverio Garcia, the *ministerio público*, public prosecutor, of Rio Alamos. He had been appointed to the post while Kane was laid up in Arizona with his injuries.

Garcia's wife and children were with him. He was an old friend of Vogel's and was at the hospital to receive the first radiation treatments for a spot on his lung. He acted friendly to Ali, but Kane wondered how they could be friends. Garcia had recently received widespread newspaper and television publicity in Mexico and the United States for his prosecution of drug lords.

Vogel asked Garcia if cancer had been found in his lungs. Garcia said that the biopsy of his spot had proven to be negative for cancer. However, *por las dudas*, to allay all doubts and fears, and for his family's sake, he was submitting to the radiation treatments.

"That's also the only reason I'm here, por las dudas," Vogel said. He then told Garcia the history of the fears that had been invented for him by a little cough.

"He X-rayed you and also did the biopsy today?" Garcia asked. "I waited six weeks between the X-ray and the biopsy."

"Yes, and this is the first and last day for me," Vogel said. "I know the spot is only a scar. Por las dudas is not enough reason for me to have radiation, and I won't have it."

"I don't want it either," Garcia said. "My family does. Your family will too. Everybody says it's the best way to make sure there's no cancer."

"If it's not found to be cancer in the biopsy, it's not cancer, as far as I'm concerned," Vogel said.

❧

The partners sat by Cody Joe's bed for a while. The nurses were loading him with antibiotics.

Captain Cunningham, the commanding officer of Tucson's Marine Corps Reserve unit, came to see Cody Joe after Kane called him. By telephone from Cody Joe's bedside, the captain notified his commanding officer at Camp Pendleton, California, that the boy was laid up so he would not be listed as AWOL.

Ali found the partners again and promised that he would have the result of Vogel's biopsy in two or three days. Still, regardless of the results of the biopsy and por las dudas, he wanted Vogel's permission to order radiology treatments. Vogel said that he would think about it, and he and Kane left for the 7X.

❧

The Lobos bodyguards and Güero Rodriguez led Dolly Ann's and Luci's horses to a Hummer on the Mexican side of the border. With black sacks over their heads, trussed hands and feet, and ropes around their necks, the girls gave the Lobos no trouble. If they tried to speak, someone jerked on the choke rope. Holes in the sacks allowed them to breathe, but not to see. The sacks kept the choke ropes from chafing their necks, unless someone jerked on them, so they kept quiet. They were helpless as cargo on packhorses. They were Güero Rodriguez's payload of a lifetime.

Luci cried, but Dolly Ann did not. Dolly Ann knew that worse treatment probably awaited her, so she counted herself lucky for the time being. This was what her Pappy referred to as "The Plight." You do wrong, you find yourself in a plight. Disobey orders and you become an unfortunate person. Every time Dolly Ann got herself in a plight of some kind, her Pappy said, "How unfortunate you are."

A plight is a misfortune a kid suffers that is all her own fault. She just had to take Luci for a ride on the Manzanita Mountain trail, even though her Pappy had forbidden it. What had she found on the ride? She found the very kind of plight her Pappy had foreseen. It most certainly would get worse, but it still was not too bad, so she did not cry.

Dolly Ann knew when they rode through the wire gate into Mexico. They rode another fifteen minutes and stopped and her choke rope tightened. "Now I'm going to get even for being whipped and trampled by this one's old man," Armando the thug said.

"Don't jerk on that choke rope again," Güero shouted. "It's counter-productive. Whose idea is it to use the choke ropes anyway?"

"My idea," Armando said. "It's the way I lead a slave."

"You can't vent your anger on the merchandise. The girl's grandfather ran his horse over you? Get even in other ways. You have Kane's whole family where you want them now. Act in a professional manner and forget your anger. Help me get the packages to market. Look at them. They're packaged whole and healthy. This is merchandise we handle here. Don't jerk them off their horses onto their heads, and don't put rope burns on their necks. Help them down, load them in the car, and let's get going before a posse of sheriffs catches up to us."

"When do we get to screw them?" another captor giggled. "Packages of this quality should be unwrapped upon receipt."

"Yes, unwrapped naked," another captor said.

"Don't think about that now," Güero said. "Untie their feet. Get them off the horses and into the vehicle. Let's move. I don't know how far ahead of pursuit we are."

"Will they pursue us?" the fourth captor asked plaintively. "Are they close?"

"No use taking chances," Güero said. "You don't want the *viejo* to lay more *latigazos* on top your head, do you?"

"He didn't lash my head," the plaintive captor said. "He knocked me down and ran over me with his horse."

"Ah, Armando was the one he whipped upon the head and shoulders?" Güero laughed. "I've been admiring the tracks of the latigazos on his head. Look, we don't want the two viejos to catch up to us, but you have your Uzis and have my permission to kill them if they do."

"They find the girls gone, they might arm themselves too," the plaintive captor said.

Güero helped Dolly Ann off her mare. The horse stood a moment, as good servants do, and when the people paid her no mind, lowered her head and began to graze toward home.

"I'm ready for the gringo viejo, this time," Armando said. "I hope he comes, because I crave him. I'm going to kill him and rape his females." He brandished his Uzi. "This time I'm armed."

Güero chuckled. "Can you hit anything with that? Are you sure you can get close enough to the target? Don't you think it would be better if you carried a banana? A banana will be easier to swallow when the gringo viejo shoves it down your throat." He put his hands around Luci's waist and helped her off the horse. He raised his voice. "All right, let's move now. Let's go."

They sat Dolly Ann in the backseat with three captors. Armando and Güero sat in the front seat with Luci between them. Armando drove the Hummer.

When they were underway, Güero said, "Armando, what happened to the other Lobo who went with you the day the viejo gave you your latigazos?"

"The big Mexican viejo must have chased him away," Armando said. "We didn't see what happened to him."

"We didn't see anything, only the big horse of the gringo viejo when he ran over us," the plaintive captor said, but he knew what had happened. The comatose Lobo they had carried back to Mexico had expired. The other three Lobos had buried him under the bank of a wash. The two old cowboys had given them that idea.

"I wasn't acquainted with your other partner. What do you think happened to him?" Güero said.

"*Saaabe*," Armando said. "Who knows? He peeled off and ran away in the high grass. We didn't see."

"If the gringo viejo didn't impress you enough, and you feel that you can someday get even with him with that cuerno de chivo weapon with which you are no expert, think about that other viejo who rides with him. They call that one the Lion. Now, that is one big man you better be ready for. I've studied those people many hours at their home with my binoculars. Let me tell you, the gringo viejo loves these girls, but the Lion adores them. You don't want either of those old men on your trail. That's why the farther we get away from them right now, the better off we'll be."

The Hummer was crowded and the five men and two girls sat close together. Güero knew his thugs would try to give him trouble over the use of the girls, because they believed it was their God-given right to commit rape. They were in Mexico where they had little respect for the law and were fast leaving behind all possible pursuit. What would be the use of having pretty girls under their power if they could not screw them until they quit breathing and their hearts stopped? Güero did not intend to allow that. He intended to sell two whole and healthy girls. He would make an example of the first thug that tried to rape them. He did not care when they decided to do it, or how bad they wanted it. He would not allow it.

Güero's word was good. When he told a trader that he had two sixteen-year-old virgins for sale, it was because he had guarded their virginity as he would his own sister's, if he had a sister, Lord forbid. Traders paid a lot more money for virgins than for sixteen-year-olds with black eyes and holes poked in them. The thugs might roar their discontent, but this was business.

Güero's thugs did not believe they had become criminals to serve Güero and make him rich. They had become criminals so they could have all the sex and drugs they wanted. They were not businessmen or merchants. They were hoodlums with the appetites of animals. That was the reason they called themselves Los Lobos, The Wolves, and the unfortunate reason, the only reason, Güero used them.

Just then the Hummer reached the bottom of the mountain and Armando looked at Güero and said, "You think we helped you pick these posies so you can sell them as virgins?"

"Yes, and I expect you to obey my orders. These 'posies' are not for you to play with, or even to smell. You can have your fun elsewhere. Right now, business. Get me and these females down the road. We can't be late for our meeting with the other Hummer that will take us on to Rio Alamos."

"That's what you think, Güerito," Armando said. "I'm going to screw this one right now." He stopped in the middle of a sandy wash, grabbed Luci by the wrist, and dragged her out of the car.

Güero walked around the back of the car, drew a .22 Beretta, switched off the safety, and prepared to put its tiny ball of lead through Armando's skull. Now was a good time to show the Lobos that they had no say in the fate of these girls. Armando had acted as a leader of the bodyguards and now believed he was Güero's leader too. Güero would not tolerate bullies who thought they were smart. He stopped at the back of the Hummer and waited for Armando to forget about everything except rape. He took a cigar from a handful in his shirt pocket and lighted it.

"I warn you, Armando. You won't like what happens if you try to rape this girl," Güero said in an even tone. "I can't sell damaged goods for the kind of money I want. This day's work has been good business until now. You have a lot of money coming. Don't ruin it for yourself."

"I don't see how I can damage the goods. The things women carry for our use are indestructible. I'll show you. After I get through with her, she'll be healthier and much more satisfied with her situation."

"Don't tear her clothes, either," Güero said.

"Don't tear her clothes? All right." Armando stepped away from Luci, but held her by the choke rope. "Take them off," he ordered. He tugged on the rope. "Get naked."

Luci unbuttoned her shirt and dropped it on the sand, then unbuttoned her jeans, let them fall, and stepped out of them.

"Naked," Armando ordered.

Luci pulled on the choke rope for slack. Armando gave it all to her and dropped the rope. After all, she could not run far with a sack over her head.

Luci stepped out of her panties and sat on the sand. Then, while a grin spread over Armando's face, she spread her legs. Armando began to unbutton his pants. Then, to everyone's disbelief, Luci filled both hands with sand, raked up a pile between her legs, and carefully began to put it inside herself.

"What are you *doing*?" Armando shouted as he tried to bat her hands out of the sand.

Güero howled with laughter and relief that he did not have to kill the man. The girl had come up with a much better solution to the problem. Armando's ardor extinguished. The bodyguards could get back to business and forget about rape, maybe even get on the way to becoming an efficient unit. He helped Luci back to her feet and stood by while she tidied herself, then climbed into the Hummer behind her and ordered Armando to drive on.

⌒

At a ranch called El Molino in the Altar Valley, Armando delivered Güero and the girls to another Hummer manned by two more Lobos bodyguards. He then turned around and took his partners back the way they had come.

Güero took the girls to see a doctor that night in Altar. He posted his new bodyguards at the front and back doors, then sat down to wait.

After a while the doctor came out of his examination room. "You brought fine specimens this time," he said. "I see the little one fitted herself with a special devise for the repulse of rapists."

"She told you what she did?" Güero asked.

"She had to submit to my examination. Her little thing looked like a bat cave."

"She's not damaged is she?"

"Not a bit. They are both in excellent condition."

Güero waited for more. "And?"

"Yes, their hymens are intact. They're both virgins."

"Isn't that unusual for girls who ride horseback a lot?"

"Not in my experience."

"I thought horseback riding ruptured hymens. That's what everybody says. The blonde rides more than any girl I know."

"In my experience it's not true that girls who ride horseback have to lose their hymens. I believe it depends a lot on the kind of animal a girl rides. As far as I know, the animal that walks on two hairy legs is responsible for most ruptured hymens."

Twelve

As Kane and Vogel neared the 7X in the pickup on the way home from the hospital, they saw the smoke from the cedar tree that Güero had set on fire and picked up the pace. When they arrived, they saw that the Lion and two U.S. Forest Service rangers had contained the fire, but there was no sign of Dolly Ann or Luci.

Before Kane lifted a tool to help snuff out the last of the smoke, he asked the Lion where the girls were. The Lion told him their horses' tracks in the yard pointed toward the Manzanita trail.

Ranchers sometimes set small trees on fire as emergency signals. Kane examined the ground around the burned tree and found Güero Rodriguez's tracks. He already knew those tracks. He told the rangers the reasons the tracks worried him and since only an hour of evening light remained, he wanted to take the Lion and Vogel and search for the girls. The rangers understood and said they had the fire under control and the partners should go on.

Kane's and the Lion's encounter with Güero and the illegal Arabs had fixed the look of Güero's boot track in their memories. The girls were in danger. The partners armed themselves with pistols and rifles and ammunition, saddled horses, rode out on the trail, and found Güero's track following the girls'. The tracks were contained on the trail and easy to follow, so the partners spurred into a high lope and soon arrived at the place where the girls had been ambushed.

The partners still had light enough to read the trail, so they ran the rest of the way to the Mexican line. The girls' horses nickered and came to them on the Mexican side of the fence. The partners led the horses through the gate, tied them, and followed the tracks to the spot where the girls had been loaded into a vehicle that used thick, cleated tire treads. They did not know the tracks belonged to a Hummer, but they knew Los Lobos used Hummers on both sides of the border. They had seen them parked in that spot more than once, and the Lion had seen a Hummer that left the same track pick up the Arabs at the abandoned Vincent mine on the north end of the 7X. They hurried south on the vehicle's tracks until they saw that it had turned west and gone down off the mountain. They could see twenty miles into the Altar Valley and the car was long gone.

As Kane and his partners sat their horses and watched the light fade in the valley, he felt a constriction in his throat. It spread to his jaws and ears, then into the top of his chest. *What is this*, he thought. *Anxiety from the loss of my little granddaughter. Will I be able to stand it?* He looked into the empty valley and knew she was gone. How could he quit and ride home? He wanted to keep his blood up for the chase. He began to feel lightheaded and the tightness in his chest started to hurt.

"*¿Qué tienes?*" Vogel asked. "What's the matter, compadre?"

"Why do you ask? You already know," Kane said.

"You look like you just lost half your blood. You want to get down and rest a minute?"

"I don't feel that bad. Nobody could look good, the way I feel."

"We'll get the girls back, compadre."

"Not today, though."

"Bueno," Vogel said. "We'll just have to find another way to run them down."

Kane felt his friend's gaze, but did not meet it. The chest pain spread to his back and his left arm began to ache. A pain in the little finger of his left hand became an agony. He thought, *Well, I'm having the heart attack my doctor warned me about.* He would not turn toward his partners, because he knew his trouble would show. It scared him and he did not know what to do about it. He did not want to have to worry about it right then. He took a deep breath and made himself relax. He was on his horse. That had always been a remedy for his ills. He would sit his horse and wait and see what happened with the pain. The tightness in his chest began slowly to recede. The constriction in his jaws, ears, and throat let go. His arm still ached, but the pain in his finger eased to a tingle, and he knew the spell would probably pass.

A vehicle's headlights appeared at the foot of the mountain. Its engine growled as it crawled toward the partners. Vogel said that he hoped it was the car that had taken the girls. Nothing in the world would move the partners from that spot until they found out if that car was a Hummer. It came on, and when it turned broadside to them after it rounded a switchback, they saw it was a Hummer.

The partners put their horses away where they would be safe from gunfire and took cover behind thick boulders beside the road. They chose a place where the Hummer would have to go slow because of big humps of bedrock in the track. The Lion and Vogel made ready to ambush the right side of the car. Kane hid on the driver's side. They agreed not to wait to be sure the Hummer contained Lobos. As soon as it came in range, they would shoot the tires out on both sides and stop it on the bedrock.

The partners still had time to wait. Kane still felt tightness in his chest and thought, *I might die of a heart attack any minute. If I get Dolly Ann back and Cody Joe gets well, how can I leave them to deal with these border thugs? After me, they'll only have the Lion and he's even more ancient than me. If this Hummer carries the sonsabitches who stole my little granddaughter, after they tell me what they did with her, I can't let them live. I could die within the next few minutes, so this is my last stand, whether I get shot or my heart quits. The Lord knows, my compadre Juan won't be able to stop thugs on this border. He has his Sierra to look after. He's brave, but not mean enough. He's tough, but he's the gentle husbandman of his ranches. That's why I put him over there with the Lion and not here by me. The Lion will pull the chain on these sonsabitches, if they're the ones who took our kids, the same as he'd pull the chain to flush a pot-full of turds. My compadre Juan is a lot different. He'll first have to make sure that he doesn't know the sonsabitches, then make sure he doesn't like their faces.*

The Hummer crawled over the brow of the mountain toward the ambush and lurched along in time with rock music from its radio. Kane turned away so the headlights would not blind him, then rose up when they had passed, and shot the front and rear tires flat. Then he jerked open the driver's door. The explosions of Vogel's and the Lion's rifles made both doors fly open on their side. The Hummer could not negotiate the humps of bedrock on its rims, so it settled into deep cracks between them and stopped. The door light illumined the faces of two men in the front seats for Kane.

"*Bajense secuestradores, hijos de la chingada,*" Kane shouted into the car. "You kidnapping sons of fornication, get out of the car."

"*¡Viejo cabrón!* Old cuckold!" the driver shouted and stared up at Kane's face. The passenger in the front seat raised his Uzi. Kane stuck a .32 automatic into the driver's ear and blew the side of his head into the passenger's face. The passenger dropped onto the floorboard on top of his weapon. Kane stepped back and emptied the automatic's magazine into the backseat. Vogel and the Lion poured fire into the car from their side. Kane stuck the empty pistol into his back pocket and stooped to pick up a .30-30 carbine.

"*Whoosh,*" said the wind from the muzzle blast of an Uzi as a burst rushed by his ear. He stepped out into the headlights and levered .30-30 bullets into the windshield.

A thug fell out of the backseat at Vogel's feet. "Don't shoot me, I'm not a Muslim," he cried.

"Good, you can go straight to hell then," Vogel said, but he hesitated to shoot the man. Kane walked up and shot him in the head.

The Lion dragged a bloody Lobo off the floorboard in the back and dumped him on the ground. "I think I killed this *sawnawmahbeechi,*" he said.

The thug looked bloody enough to be killed, but he sat up. Kane raised the rifle to his head. "No, no, no, no," the thug said. He scurried away from the rifle on his knees and tried to hug Vogel's legs. Vogel stepped back, disgusted. "We didn't do anything," the thug wailed. "We didn't harm anybody."

"Tell us what you did," Kane said.

"We didn't harm your girls."

"Never mind what you harmed. Tell us where they are, or you're going to die."

"No, no, no, no."

"That's not the right answer." Kane shot that one in the head too. He turned back to question the passenger in the front seat and reached for the door, but it flew open in his hand. The thug scampered clear of the car on his hands and knees, then raised his hands in supplication. "Please don't kill me, Mr. Kane," he said in English. He wailed like the other one. "We didn't hurt the girls. They're all right."

The man found himself in a plight and his upturned face was covered with blood, tears, and slobber. Kane liked that.

"Wipe the blithering slobber off your chin," Kane said. "I can't look at you."

"Just don't kill me, patrón. I have the information you want. I can tell you about the little girls. I beg you, *no me mates*."

"Calm down. We won't kill you. Where did you take them?"

"To El Molino ranch on the road to Altar. I'll tell you everything you want to know."

"You mean the Caballero family at El Molino has a part in this?"

"No, no, no. We don't know anybody at El Molino. We only met the other car there, because it is a landmark. Our boss took the girls away in another Hummer."

"Away where?"

"*¿Cómo?*"

"Where did they go, man?"

"To the Wolf Cave in Huatabampo."

"The Wolf Cave? What's that?"

"It's a nightclub at the harbor of Huatabampo where Los Lobos meet."

"And from there, where?"

"Only there. That's as far as they have to go."

"You're sure?"

"Sí, patrón. I won't lie to you. I don't want to die."

"Who's your boss?"

"What?"

"You said your boss took the girls away in the other Hummer. Who is he? What's his name? Don't lie to me. Tell the truth and I'll let you live."

"Who else but Güero Rodriguez."

"The truth?"

"He's our boss. We have no other. I've never given that man's name to anybody, and I only give it now to save my life."

Kane shot him in the forehead.

The partners searched the pockets of the dead men. Kane opened the driver's wallet and found his license. His name was Armando Mendez, his address, #10 Calle Embarcadero, Nogales, Sonora. Kane kept the card to count coup.

The partners laid the four Lobos on their backs side by side by the Hummer with their arms crossed on their chests, their pockets turned inside out, and their cards and papers scattered on the ground. They took their money, gold chains, and watches, because the Lion insisted that booty should never be left behind. Kane gathered what he could and laid it on the hood of the Hummer for the Lion. He saw no reason the old bandit should not have his plunder. Kane had known all his life that he was an old pirate.

The partners took their time and pulled the shoes off their horses, wiped out all the shod tracks on the Mexican side, then rode their bare-foot horses three miles down the road toward the valley. They rode back to the Hummer on a different track in the road so anyone might think the killers of the thugs had come up from the valley and returned the same way. They put their horses back across the line and wiped out all their tracks between themselves and the Hummer.

The partners tied the girls' shod horses head to tail. The Lion would lead them behind Kane and Vogel so their tracks would obliterate all other tracks on the Manzanita trail, including the tracks Los Lobos had left. The last touch they added before they mounted their horses to leave was to bless themselves and set the Hummer on fire so the corpses would have a vigil light.

When the partners led the girls' horses away from the border fence toward home, their tracks said that an undetermined number of riders on shod horses had stopped at the fence on the American side and turned back. The tracks on the Mexican side said that the four Lobos had climbed the mountain from the Altar Valley in the Hummer, had paused at the border for too long a time, and had been overtaken by three men on horseback and murdered. At least that was the way the partners hoped they would be read. They would feel a whole lot better if a good rain came along and wiped everything out.

Kane felt a chill as soon as he started his horse on the trail toward home. By the time he and his partners reached the corrals at the 7X, his teeth chattered. Before he unsaddled, he put on a lined jacket that he kept in the saddlehouse. After the horses had been fed and he and his partners were on their way to the house, he put his hands in the jacket pockets to warm them and felt Dolly Ann's rubber boxing mouthpiece. He had taken Dolly Ann to a dentist to have it custom fitted to her mouth. He remembered that he had taken it out of her mouth at the end of the last sparring match with Cody Joe. She had not been out of breath after out-boxing her big old brother. The mouthpiece had been real wet when he put it away in his jacket, a sign that his granddaughter had no fear or anxiety in a fight, a sign of her poise. He squeezed the mouthpiece with fondness, as he would a good friend. His little granddaughter had been all over the thing and had depended on it to keep her safe. He squeezed it again and put it in the pocket of his Levi's. He would carry it, squeeze it, and appreciate its presence until he could put it back in her mouth.

Lightning had begun to strike at the partners' heels on the trail. Now, a high wind bashed a cloudburst into their faces before they reached the house and they ran for the front door. Inside, Vogel slapped his wet hat against his leg, grinned, and said, "There comes the water we asked for."

To find someone who could run interference for him in Huatabampo, Kane phoned Beto Montenegro in Rio Alamos. Beto knew the Huatabampo underworld. He came wide awake when Kane told him what had happened to Dolly Ann and Luci and asked for his help.

"You know I'm with you, Jim," Beto said. "Those poor little girls. What's your plan?"

"First, recruit ten men and arm them."

"I'll have my brother Manuelito and ten more men ready to go by ten o'clock tomorrow morning. Then what?"

"Get them to Huatabampo tomorrow, get rooms at the hotel nearest the airport, post a man or two at the airport, and wait for us. We'll be there before dark tomorrow night, or before noon the next day. If you have friends or people you trust in the underground, get in touch with them. The girls might be at La Cueva del Lobo, a nightclub."

"I know the place. I know that the Lobos gang hangs out there, and I know a man who can help us, Jim. He used to own the Wolf Cave and might still have friends among the employees. I take it we're dealing with Los Lobos gangsters?"

"That's right. Güero Rodriguez and Los Lobos kidnapped our girls."

"I wonder how that bastard thought he could get away with it. We'll be in Huatabampo early tomorrow afternoon and we'll be well armed. Then, I'll go nightclubbing with my brother Manuelito." Beto hung up.

The three partners held council while they ate breakfast. Kane felt like leaving for Huatabampo that minute, as did Vogel, but nobody could fly at night in Mexico. The law prohibited it. He called the Tucson hospital and was told by the night nurse that Cody Joe was still being treated for dangerous infection.

No matter how much the partners were in a hurry to overtake Güero Rodriguez, they would have to plan an operation. They needed to find out how much help the Rio Alamos and Huatabampo police would give them. Huatabampo was under the jurisdiction of the municipality of Rio Alamos.

"There's a way to find out about the Huatabampo police, Jim," Vogel said.

"How, compadre?"

"Silverio Garcia is the municipality's prosecutor. Remember? You met him at the hospital in Tucson."

"De veras. You're right, compadre."

"If we stop and think from time to time, more solutions will show themselves."

"You know you have to stay here and take care of the ranch, don't you, Andres?" Kane said to the Lion.

"It goes without saying," the Lion said. "We can't all run away and leave the gate open."

"We don't want anyone to know what we're doing."

"That also goes without saying."

The three partners decided to take one careful step at a time. When they were young, all their horses had been bronco and all the cattle wild. As they grew older they were amazed to find how much horses and cattle had gentled down. When they were young they tested everything to see if it would come apart, a bronco horse, a downhill run, a bull on the end of a rope. Now, they found that they did very well when they worked within the limits of their old tools and old carcasses, and they did not need to put stress on everything to see if it would come apart. They would think this problem through, gather all the help they needed, and do what had to be done. They would not weep and wring their hands, or worry about the way they felt. They would try to bring devastation to the kidnappers and not get any of their blood, tears, or slobber on the little girls.

The next morning Kane and Vogel went to see Cody Joe. The boy was having an awful fight of his own. Ali said that in a cattleman's terms, his wounds were septic. His system fought a strain of septicemia, a germ like the one that caused shipping fever in cattle, the same infection that killed bullfighters when they were gored by the bulls.

"The garlic," Kane said to Ali. "Do you suppose that the garlic on the bullets caused the trouble?"

"It could, I guess. I don't know enough about it. I'll do a study."

A priest named Paul Garcia walked in to see Cody Joe. Kane was happy to see him. Spiritual medicine might help the boy. Ali's hospital medicine did not seem to work. Ali took one look at the priest and fled the room as though the owls were after him, as though he was the devil and Father Garcia the Archangel Michael.

After Kane and Vogel shook Garcia's hand, Kane said, "What got into Ali Lupino? He left here like a coyote leaves a chicken house. Doesn't he know you?"

"Oh, yes," Father Garcia said.

"Well, why did he leave without even an *adios*?"

He smiled. "He doesn't like me."

"Why not?"

"Maybe he's a Philistine." He laughed.

"That's for sure. Historically, he comes from Philistine stock, doesn't he?"

"Sure. You know what else? I only tell you this because it's a belief that's not well known. I've read that in Biblical times the people of the Arab countries, the countries that were known as Egypt, Babylon, and the land of the Philistines, were all called Egyptians. Have you heard that?"

"No," the partners said.

"Well, somewhere in the Bible, I think in the story of Joseph who took his cattle to Egypt in search of pasture, it says that to the Egyptian, the cattleman is an abomination. You two men and I are the sons of cattlemen. Besides that, we're Christians. So, from what I've read, we can expect that most Arabs probably don't like our kind."

"Ali's from cattle people and he's always been friendly to us. Do you count him among the ones who don't like Christians, Father?" Vogel asked.

"When Ali and I first met, we had many interesting conversations, until he made it clear that he could not be my friend because of my faith. To him, I'm a Christian devil, an infidel. I suspect he and his brothers have no Christian friends. In business, Christians are free game to them. Business is war to them, no holds barred."

"We would like to talk to you about Huatabampo, Father," Kane said.

"I was born and raised there."

"Do you know anything about a gang of criminals called Los Lobos?"

"Everyone from Mazatlan to Nogales knows about them."

Kane steered the priest outside to a bench where the three men could speak privately. Kane and Vogel had known Father Garcia for twenty years, ever since he had been assistant pastor of Sacred Heart Church in Rio Alamos and had served as chaplain to the Charro Association of which Kane and Vogel were officers. The priest was a good horseman and an artist with a lariat. He liked music and wine too. Now he served as pastor of a congregation in the tough Embarcadero barrio of Nogales, Sonora. He had been there seven years and knew everybody in Nogales from the mayor to the shoeshine boys. Kane had walked down the main Calle Obregon in Nogales with Paul Garcia and seen his popularity. Anyone would have thought he was Cantinflas, the popular Mexican movie star, by the attention, smiles, and cheery greetings people gave him.

"You probably can't tell us a whole lot about Los Lobos, but we need to find out all we can," Kane said.

"Why would you think that I can't tell you about Los Lobos? My brother Silverio knows more about them, but I can tell you a lot."

"I thought you might not be able to tell us anything because of your vow to guard the secrets of the confessional."

"Valgame. What secrets? I know a hundred Lobos and not one has ever come to me to confess his sins, or for anything else. They're worse than any godless pagan. They're mercenary devils who cause more fear, suffering, and violence in my barrio than the VD."

Kane told the priest the details of the kidnapping, but left out the partners' ambush of the kidnappers.

"This is nothing new," Father Garcia said. "Rodriguez and his Lobos have raided on both sides of the border for over a year. Simply put, they catch young girls and boys and sell them. Any child, from a toddler to a teenager, can be sold to an illegal adoption agency, a chain of whorehouses, or into abject slavery. Los Lobos have also found a worldwide market for young people who are used as subjects for rape and snuff movies. One of the main clearinghouses for the market is rumored to be in Huatabampo, and the Lobos gangsters are its main providers of subjects, or victims."

"What's a snuff movie?" Vogel asked.

"A film in which the subject is raped or put through some other act of torture. His or her life is slowly snuffed out for the pleasure of the audience."

"But who would buy such a film?" Vogel asked.

"My brother Silverio tells me that a lucrative market exists for them. The Lobos have also found a black market for human organs. It is said that some of the young people they kidnap are sacrificed to provide organs for transplant."

Father Garcia told Kane and Vogel that Los Lobos also killed for hire. They kidnapped for ransom. They were burglars. They had taken over Nogales's world-renowned pickpocket school. They cruised the border to mug and rob families who tried to cross illegally in search of jobs. The families seldom reported the crimes. Los Lobos also preyed on these vulnerable people for training and practice.

This news astounded Kane and Vogel. Until the kidnapping of the girls, they had thought the gang was made up of bungling, teenaged cattle rustlers who aspired to be big-time gangsters.

"I would never have believed they were so competent or ambitious," Kane said. "The Lion and I jump some of them from time to time and handle them easily." He decided again that he better not tell the priest that he, Vogel, and the Lion had just slaughtered a whole pack of Lobos who had taken their girls.

"The Lobos who rustle cattle are apprentices. They rustle and mug cattle and people for drill, for practice. Rustling entails stealth to catch the animal, efficient killing ability, and intelligence, strength, and stamina enough to transport a heavy product to the market. To rustle, Los Lobos go out on the ranches barehanded and afoot. They are given a few bullets and a small caliber weapon so they can stun a beef enough to cut its throat. On a kidnapping run, or to kill, they have sniper rifles and Uzis and all the ammunition they need. Rumor has it that they are given commando training in hidden camps in the Sierra Madre and in the heavy brush country of the coastal desert."

Silverio Garcia, the ministerio público of Rio Alamos, walked out of the hospital with his wife while the partners and his brother were talking. The priest went to greet them and bring them to Kane and Vogel.

Silverio must have sensed that Kane and Vogel wanted to talk about something he did not want his spouse to hear, because he took her back inside and returned alone. The four men strolled on the hospital grounds while Kane told Silverio about the trouble.

Silverio had changed a lot since the day Ali had introduced him to Kane, before his first radiology treatment. His face was drawn and wasted, his skin much darker. He had black circles under his eyes. His movements were aged and slow.

"How do you feel, sir?" Kane asked.

"Not good. But I was warned that the radiology would sap my strength," Silverio said.

"How many more treatments?"

"Many more during the next month."

"I hope they're successful."

"Thank you. Now, I have to tell you that I can't help you much."

Silverio told the partners that they could not count on help from the Huatabampo police. The entire Huatabampo force was suspected of collusion with crime lords. He verified that Los Lobos met regularly at the Wolf Cave nightclub, but he did not believe the girls would be kept there. Güero Rodriguez would hide them in a more secluded place, use them to entertain special clients only a day or two, then sell them. During the short while that he kept them, he would sell only their virginity. After that, he would sell their bodies to the highest bidder and be rid of them.

"Where would the Lupinos keep the girls, if they were the kidnappers?" Vogel asked.

"You think the Lupinos have something to do with this?" Silverio asked.

"We don't know, but everything bad that happens to us nowadays seems to come from them. I think they could be connected to this kidnapping. Güero Rodriguez is a half brother to the Lupino brothers. They were all sired by my cousin Eliazer. Old man Nesib made his daughter's sons use the Lupino name instead of Vogel. Güero was educated in the same schools with them and is Rafa's best pal. His mother is Maria Ester Rodriguez, a Lupino maid who helped Fatima raise his half brothers."

"Ah, we didn't know that."

"The Lobos hit our kids in a drive-by shooting after we beat the Lupinos in a matched horse race. Rafa Lupino went into a murderous rage after the race. It's not unreasonable to believe that he hired Los Lobos to hit my godson Cody, who jockeyed our horse, and my godsons Marco Antonio and Memin Martinillo, our trainer and his uncle."

"I heard about the race and the hit," Silverio said.

"I think you're right about the Lupinos," Father Garcia said. "They have long been suspected of being the brains and money behind every criminal endeavor in Huatabampo. They own an inordinate percentage of the ships and airplanes that come in and go out of the port, and lately they've employed Los Lobos gangsters in their warehouses."

"I think we can assume they're holding our girls," Kane said. "Where would they hide them?"

"Grab a Lobo out of the Wolf Cave, take him out by the canals, and make him tell you where the girls are," Silverio said. "If I mount a search by my police force, it will alert the kidnappers that we know the girls are in Huatabampo. Every one of my officers and every inspector of customs and immigration at the harbor are on the Lupino payroll."

"What do they do for them?" Kane asked.

"The ones in immigration look the other way when unidentified people debark from ships and airplanes that arrive from foreign countries. The ones in customs overlook Lupino cargo that arrives on the ships. Nobody knows what the Lupinos load on the ships and airplanes they send out of the country."

"How many warehouses do they have?" Kane asked.

"About twenty big ones. Each one covers about one hectare."

"What will you do when you find the girls?" Father Garcia asked.

"We don't have a plan. I want to land on the kidnappers and kill them without hurting the girls."

"What weapons do you have?" Silverio asked.

"They'll be supplied by the Montenegros. This isn't their first rodeo."

"Then you intend to assault the place with firearms?"

"What else can we do?"

"Guns will start a firefight, and every city, state, federal, and security policeman in the harbor will be on you in five minutes. Start shooting and a horde of Lobos and policemen will come at you with a legal right to kill you. As you know, possession of firearms is prohibited, and your gunfire will be a call to arms for every bully cop in the city."

"Our reatas worked well up to now. But I don't think they'll work against Uzis."

"No, they won't. Every Lobo in Huatabampo carries an Uzi to work. Count on them to be ready for you."

"I wish we had Martinillo, the hunter," Kane said.

"What would he do?"

"Take our enemies by stealth."

"That's what you have to do," Silverio said. "I'm sorry I can't go with you. I belong in the first assault on those cutthroats."

Back at the 7X that night, Kane called Beto Montenegro and told him to meet Little Buck on a dirt strip on Vogel's Cibolibampo ranch north of Rio Alamos, instead of at the Huatabampo airport.

Before he turned out the light so they could sleep, Kane wanted to ask Vogel about one more idea he had. Vogel was already under the covers and composed for slumber with his face to the wall.

"Juan, let me pose a solution to the gunfire problem to you," Kane said. "How are good men to defend their families against bad men with machine guns without making noise? What if we use pellet guns? They're quiet enough, but do they hit hard enough? Would that work, or is it too damned law abiding? Pellet guns are used more as toys than as weapons in this country."

Vogel yawned. "Not law abiding enough if we miss, but totally law abiding if we hit every one of the *cabrones* in the eye," he said.

Thirteen

Kane loaded Vogel and took off in Little Buck at dawn the next morning. Beto Montenegro and his brother Manuelito met them with a five-ton bobtail truck at Vogel's Cibolibampo ranch airstrip outside Rio Alamos at midmorning. The brothers brought, aviation gasoline to top Little Buck's tanks.

In Huatabampo, Beto left Manuelito and the truck at the hotel with the ten men who would help them retrieve the girls. Then he and the partners boarded a sedan and drove outside town to see Rodolfo Almada, the former owner of the Wolf Cave. Almada, a dark man with curly black hair, came down from his veranda to welcome them. His smile made a white slash across his face.

"Did Beto tell you about our trouble?" Kane asked, after Beto introduced them.

"Yes, he did, and I feel for you. I have three teenaged daughters."

"One of the girls they kidnapped is my only granddaughter, and the other is my goddaughter. We need to find them quickly."

"I know you do. I've already taken steps to do it, though I can't go near the club. I've been feuding with the Lupinos since I sold it to Rafa, but Urbano, my old bartender, still works there. After he leaves the club tonight, he'll be able to tell us if the girls are there."

"What time will that be?" Kane asked.

"He closes the club at three a.m."

Kane looked at his watch, then at Vogel. "Lord almighty," he said. "Do all the Lupinos own the Wolf Cave?"

"Man, they do everything together, don't they?"

"We pursue Lobos, find them, and uncover a Lupino. Tell us about the bartender."

"I talked to Urbano this morning. He told me that he had not seen or heard anything about two young girls. Rafa's office suite is the only place where they could be without his knowledge. He'll find out if they're there during his shift tonight and call me after he leaves the club."

Kane, Vogel, and Beto waited by the telephone in Almada's front room all night and slept in their chairs. Urbano called soon after 3:00 a.m. and Kane picked up the phone. "This is Jim Kane, Urbano," he said.

"They're not at the club, Mr. Kane," Urbano said.

"Are you sure?"

"A lot of new girls pass through the club. It happens all the time and nobody tries to hide them."

"I don't understand," Kane said.

"The Lobos don't bother to hide the people they bring to the club, so they must be holding your girls somewhere else. None of the girls who come here stay more than a few hours, anyway. There's no sign that your girls have been here."

"OK. I appreciate your help and won't forget it."

"Don Rodolfo told me about your trouble, sir. I went to your fights at the Mutualista all those years ago when you boxed. I apologize that I haven't been more help to you. If I find out anything, I'll call don Rodolfo."

Kane hung up the phone, and looked at his watch and at Vogel. Vogel never carried a watch and never asked for the time. He had worn huaraches and strapped spurs on his naked heels until he was twenty-one. Why did he need a watch? He kept a slow and patient pace. No matter how Kane hurried him along, he always kept sight of their partnership goals and prizes.

"I don't know what to do next, compadre," Kane said. "We're as close to the girls as I can get us. I guess we could catch one of those pelones who wears his trousers on his hips, pull them down, take his parts in the jaws of a pair of pliers, and squeeze until he tells us where the girls are."

"If he knows," Vogel said. "If he doesn't know, you'll have to get another pelón. You might squeeze the parts of ten or twenty and not find anything but a way to get your hands dirty and cause a lot of howling. Try to imagine how far away from the girls that will get us."

"What then?"

"Who are our friends here? I think we should go to them for help."

"We haven't got friends here, have we?"

"You have a very good old friend here. She doesn't know where the girls are, but she'll know where Rafa is. Rafa is almost sure to know. If he doesn't, he'll know where Güero is. Squeeze Rafa's little finger and he'll tell us everything."

"Fatima," Kane said. "Is she here, or at La Golondrina?"

"When we were at La Golondrina, she told me she spends most of her time here to be near Jacobo and Rafa because most of their business is here. They haven't married, so she thinks she has to take care of them."

"You think she's here?"

"Let's go knock on her door."

"At four a.m.?"

"Why not? She's our friend and won't care about the time when she knows the reason we woke her up."

The Lupinos' home was three blocks away in the same elegant sector of Huatabampo. Beto drove to the house in five minutes.

Kane stepped out of the car and waited for Vogel, but he stayed inside.

"I'm not going in, Jim," Vogel said. "You should go alone."

"Why? She likes you better."

"Maybe so, but she loves you. To get what you want, you'll have to woo her as you would a sweetheart who's been angry with you. If the Lupinos are in on the kidnapping, you'll have to coax her away from her family as though you want to marry her."

"How can I do that?"

"You can do it, because it's what she wants."

Kane went up to the front door and rang the bell, then looked at his watch. Four a.m., a helluva time of day to try to woo somebody.

He did not have to wait long before he saw a small figure move toward him down a long corridor of the big house. She turned on the porch light, looked him over through a side window, and opened the door. "Jim," Fatima said. "What brings you here?"

"An emergency, Fatima."

"What emergency? Come in. I'm making coffee."

Kane stepped inside, embraced her, and kissed her on the lips. She stepped away from him. He did not try to hold her, but he stayed close.

"What's wrong, Jim?" she asked.

"I'm scared to death and I need you. Güero Rodriguez kidnapped my granddaughter and her little friend Luci Martinillo."

She reached up and cupped his cheek in her hand.

"I have to find them before they're taken out of the country, and I think you can help," he said.

"Come to the kitchen," she said

Kane followed the tiny person down the corridor. From behind, she could be a quick, limber little child. His old bones were still stiff from being caged in Little Buck.

Fatima offered him a chair at the kitchen table. He sat and watched her prepare the coffee. He was so anxious he caught himself gripping the seat of the chair with the cheeks of his butt. He knew he would not find out the information he needed any sooner if he let anxiety take him over, but it was all he could do to sit still. He was surrounded by patient people and did not think he would be able to stand it another minute. Vogel and Fatima could have been Bible characters, because a wait through a deluge of forty days and forty nights would have only been a good time for them to rest and cogitate.

He found that he had also been gritting his teeth. "I like your coffeepot. I have one just like it," he made himself say.

"Why did you kiss me like that?"

"That's the way I kiss hello. I've always kissed you like that, haven't I?" They both knew it was a lie.

"You never kissed me like that."

"I need you."

"That's what you said. So have you come to give me an ulcer again?"

"Again?"

"Ah, I should bring you up to date. In the life I lived after you dumped me, I suffered a chronic ulcer from loneliness and raised four sons for a man I didn't love in a house without love. I waited through a lot of misery for you to come and kiss me like you did a moment ago, but you didn't want me."

"Don't tell me that, Fatima."

"One thing about the early, early morning. Two people alone can speak the truth."

Fatima was unsophisticated, but foxy. He could expect the truth from her most of the time, but she could be a good liar when it suited her. He should have come to her before this, when he first recognized that the Lupinos meant everybody so much harm. That way, he would have known by now if he could trust her.

"You're right. The truth is, I'm in trouble." Kane watched the dark eyes. The woman did not have the careworn face that a sixty-five-year-old mother of kidnappers should have. She needed to be as good as she looked, if she were to give him the help he needed.

"Tell me what happened," she said.

"Fatima, I already told you, my granddaughter Dolly Ann and her friend Luci Martinillo have been kidnapped. Vogel and I traced them here. That's all there is to tell, except that if I don't find them in the next few hours, they'll lose their lives, and if that happens, I'll lose mine." The statement made him recognize the helpless dread he felt for the girls. Day before yesterday that dread had made him a merciless killer, today a beggar. What would he be in another hour?

"Are you going to weep?" she asked.

"No."

"Wouldn't that be awful? Weep if you want to, man."

"I don't need to weep. I need to find Güero Rodriguez."

"You suspect that my Rafa has a part in the kidnapping, don't you?"

"I don't suspect anyone and I suspect everyone. I'm distracted and in an awful hurry. I'm only certain that Güero and Los Lobos are the cowards who abducted my girls."

"Why do you suspect my son?"

"Fatima, don't mistake the reason I'm here. It's not to castigate Rafa, or to blame him for anything. I need help. You've been my friend a long time. You're close to your son and everybody knows he is close to Güero. Güero and his gang of pelones hang out at Rafa's nightclub."

"I don't want you to suspect my son. He wouldn't harm your granddaughter."

"That's good, but I bet he can tell me where Güero is. That's all I want from him. Where is he?"

"He sleeps in his apartment when he works at night. He concentrates better at night and in the early hours of the morning."

Kane thought of a thing or two he could say about that but did not have time. "Where?"

"In the old warehouse district. I can show you the way, if you want. If you don't want me to go with you, I'll call Jacobo and he can go."

"No need for you to go, Fatima. Beto Montenegro is with us, and I bet he can find it."

"Nevertheless, I'll call Jacobo. I'll feel better if someone goes with you who knows the district." She went into another room.

Kane thought, *If Rafa is connected with the kidnapping, it will be good to take Fatima along.* Then, something dawned on him that had not occurred to him since the day he practically whipped Rafa's teeth out of his head at Guazaremos: a statement about Dolly Ann that Güero had made on the Manzanita trail when Kane and the Lion confronted him had been the same as Rafa's statement at La Golondrina and again at Guazaremos. The half brothers were so much of one mind about Dolly Ann that they both had said, "I can get a lot of money for that female." Now, Güero's flight was leading Kane straight to Rafa. If he found Lobos guarding Rafa's warehouse, Güero and the girls would not be far away. In that case, nothing would be better than to have Fatima along as a ticket past the guard. Fatima might be his way to get hold of Rafa and Güero without waking the town with a firefight.

Kane had been pacing slowly around the kitchen. He stopped at the door of each room he passed and looked inside. The light of the overhead chandelier was on in the dining room. A pile of account ledgers lay on the table. Three ledgers were open and an old-fashioned quill pen and an open bottle of ink sat beside them, ready for use. Also open on the table was a popular magazine that featured stories and pictures of American and Mexican movie stars. He thought, *Now that's lonesome, if reading that magazine is all the poor woman does for fun when she's on her own.*

When Fatima rejoined Kane in the kitchen, she told him no one had answered Jacobo's telephone. She thought it strange because Ibrahim and his family had flown in from the Sierra that day, and she thought they had spent the night with Jacobo.

She handed Kane a slip of paper with the address of Rafa's warehouse on it. Kane took it and kissed her again, this time like Judas. "You've probably saved the girls' lives with this," he said. "You know what? I think I'll take you up on your offer to guide me to Rafa's warehouse, if you still want to do it."

"I'm glad. You might never find it on your own. The alleys and streets of the old district have been changed, barricaded, and rerouted so many times that only someone who has been there knows how to find anything."

Now Kane had become a Judas. Killer, beggar, and Judas. He intended to betray Fatima to get at her son. If he found that Rafa had bossed the kidnapping, the poor woman was about to watch Kane cut off his ears. If he had not, she might still have to watch it happen, because whether he was party to the kidnapping or not, Kane would hurt him to find Güero. Kane hoped for her sake that Rafa was not part of it, but she was Kane's insurance. With Fatima along he would be able to go straight into that warehouse, even if he had to take her by the nape of the neck as a hostage.

"Why don't Rafa and Jacobo stay with you in this big house?" Kane asked. "You like to be alone here?"

"Oh, I'm not alone. I have them as much as I want. They come every day to bring their dirty clothes and eat. I'm not surprised that Ibrahim and his family didn't come to see me yesterday. His wife probably made him take her to the resort. She prefers to stay at our beach hotel. She stays there to relax, but never leaves her children with me."

"Why not?"

"She doesn't like my influence on them, and she knows I don't like the company she keeps when she's here. I don't like the way she dresses the children, or the religious training she gives them either."

Kane acted interested but did not give a cowboy damn about Fatima's daughter-in-law problems. As she talked, he herded her out the front door and into the car with Vogel and Beto.

A half hour later, Beto stopped the car in an unlighted alley beside Rafa's warehouse. The truck full of Montenegro men stopped behind them.

Under glaring lights in an apartment inside the warehouse, and wearing nothing but a g-string that barely covered her nakedness, Luci fought a naked man as he tried to handcuff one of her hands to a bedpost. Two burly Lobos gangsters stood off camera on each side of Luci to keep her on the bed. Her struggles were filmed by two cameras and directed by Rafa Lupino. A crew for camera, light, and sound were in attendance. As assistant director, Güero Rodriguez stood off camera and coached the leading man.

Adolfo, the tired and woebegone naked man, was ready to beg for a break, because he could not handle the girl. Rafa did not have to give Luci any direction at all, because she was not acting. Her well-aimed fists and kicks at Adolfo's groin really hurt, and she scored more than she missed. Rafa would not allow anyone to help Adolfo subdue her. For Rafa, the more spontaneous the conflict, the better the sequence, and he could see that his leading lady had overtaxed his poor, bare-assed leading man.

Luci growled and wept with anger and everybody on the set could see what the camera captured. She actually seemed to crave more conflict, because she was winning. The tall, gangly Adolfo could not keep hold of her and could not stay on camera if he moved out of range of her kicks and fists. She did not even try to get away from him. The heavy handcuffs that he held in one hand handicapped him, because they knocked on his bones when he used the hand to defend himself. To follow Rafa's direction and stay on camera, he fended away another kick at his groin with his free hand. As he dodged the kick, he threw up the other hand and struck himself on the forehead with the open jaws of the handcuffs. With this new setback, the man stumbled backward off camera, rubbed his sore head, and looked down at himself. The crew followed his gaze and began to laugh. Luci's ferocity had unmanned her rapist. His thing had gone limp.

Adolfo's hairdresser had spent an hour on his hairdo and Luci had already snatched it apart like a cobweb. He could not stay on camera and keep his poor, beaten member out of range, but Rafa ordered him to climb onto the bed. He dropped his hands and looked around for help.

"She can't kick you if you get on top of her, you fool!" Rafa shouted. "Get those handcuffs on her, because if you can't handcuff a little girl, you can't play the part."

Rafa stumbled around the side of the bed.

"Kick him, kick him, Luci," Rafa directed. "Disable him and you go free. You are our brave Luci. Defend your Martinillo honor. Kick him in the eggs."

Adolfo threw his weight on top of the girl's legs, straddled her, and grabbed her hair with both hands. Luci clamped her jaws on a nipple and hung on. Adolfo howled and pulled her head back, but her jaws held fast and his howl climbed up three octaves.

"Good. Stay on camera, Adolfito," Rafa shouted, laughing. "This is too good to waste. Do anything you have to do, but don't leave the bed."

Adolfo slapped Luci weakly on the ear. When that did not loosen her, with the very last of his strength, he struck her on the temple with his fist. Luci lost her mouthful of flesh, but scored a bull's-eye with a knee to the groin. Adolfo turned loose all holds and fell off the bed.

Rafa signaled the Lobos by the bed and they stepped in, grabbed Luci's arms and legs, and held her down. She stopped resisting, lay still, and rested, and the thugs stepped back off camera again.

Dolly Ann had been stripped, cuffed hand and foot to the wall at the head of the bed, and gagged. She could make almost no sound at all, but she began to weep. Rafa directed the camera to her face, then slowly along her body. When she twisted away to hide her nakedness from the camera, Rafa directed it back to Luci.

Luci's face was composed now. She waited and gathered her strength. Her legs, arms, teeth, and hard little head were her only weapons. She had not been taught any science of self-defense, but she had the temperament of a Mayo warrior.

Dolly Ann stared at Rafa and caught his gaze. He stared back at her, walked up close to her, reached on camera, and tore the tape off the gag. With only his hands on camera, he untied the cloth that had been tied in her mouth so tight it held her jaws apart. He grabbed her by the hair and tried to stroke her cheek with the back of his hand, but she turned her face away.

"Someday, everybody gets what he gives, Rafa," Dolly Ann growled. "You'll have to kill us before we lie still for·you. Your stud can't rape us, because we've got more balls than he does. It's going to give me great pleasure to watch my Pappy cook you in a stew of pig dung and scatter your parts all over the state of Sonora. After that, he'll get your grandfather, your brothers, your mother, and all your gangsters."

Rafa ordered, "Cut," then turned to the sound man. "Be sure to delete 'Rafa' from that line."

"Understood," the sound man said.

"All right, somebody help Adolfo," Güero ordered. "Let's see if we can recoup our losses. We can't allow our victim to blunt the edge of our swordsman's blade any more than she already has, can we?" Rafa and Güero looked at each other and laughed. A pelón helped Adolfo to his feet and the hairdresser and makeup man worked on his looks.

"All right, Adolfito," Rafa said. "As soon as you're ready, you will handcuff Luci to the bedposts. The camera will be on your and Luci's hands and then on her feet. While you handcuff each limb, our stagehands will hold the other three, so she won't destroy you before we finish filming the movie. All right? Can you handle that?"

"I still think we should save the virginity of these girls awhile longer," Güero said. "Rafa, think of the money."

"What is a virgin?" Rafa shouted. "Prove to me they are virgins. Who is going to know that one is a virgin and one is not? Let's see how the scene plays out. When we finish here tonight we might still have two whole virgins. If we don't, who will know? Let's shoot it. Play it out. Let's be creative and see what happens. I like the way the scene is going, don't you?"

"I understand." Güero turned to the crew. "Stand by," he said.

"Action!" Rafa said. Adolfo shackled Luci's hands and feet to the bedposts one at a time as the cameras rolled. "Aaaand, cut!" Rafa said. "Print. How you like that? All in one take. Adolfo, stay on your mark."

A crewman brought up a ten-inch, narrow-bladed knife that was curved like a half moon, demonstrated its razor edge by slicing a sheet of paper, and handed it to Adolfo. For the next scene, Rafa instructed him to climb on Luci and draw blood with the knife from a spot on her throat under her ear.

"Be careful, because you have to draw the blood in only one take," Rafa said. "Then, while you hold the knife to her throat, you will enter her. Now, Adolfo, even though the female seems helpless, we must have a struggle. The knife may scare her so bad that it paralyzes her, so you have to animate her. If she does not respond properly by showing fear and does not writhe to avoid your probe, use the point of the knife to make her struggle. Begin by drawing blood from her throat. You've heard the expression, 'her throat was cut from ear to ear'? Now you can see what that means. You start to slice just below the ear lobe."

"Isn't that spot too vulnerable?" Adolfo asked. "I might cut too deep. This is a very sharp knife. She could bleed to death."

Rafa grinned. "Don't stall, Adolfo. This isn't your first movie."

"Don't worry about it," Güero said. "If it happens, it happens. That's what we're here for: to film a real movie. Even if you nick the artery, she won't bleed fast enough to hurt us. We'll get the whole scene and still probably have time to stop the bleeding. If you cut the artery, the blood will start to pump out, but whatever you do, continue with the sequence, penetrate, and finish the scene. If she dies before we get another shot, she dies. We'll go slow with the torture and rape of the other female for the rest of the movie."

Dolly Ann began to cry. Adolfo stood on his mark, but showed no sign that he was ready to start the scene.

"All right, everybody quiet," Güero announced. "Stand by . . ."

"Action!" Rafa shouted.

"Wait, please," Adolfo said.

"What do you mean?" Rafa demanded.

"I can't perform yet."

"Well, you will when you get up there and rub on the female, you fool. That's the first part of the sequence. Do you have to be shown how it's done?"

Adolfo climbed on top of Luci with the knife in his hand.

"No, no, no, no. Get back on your mark," Rafa screamed.

Suddenly, the door banged open and Ibrahim and Jacobo barged into the room with baseball bats. Ibrahim batted aside two Lobos who tried to stand in his way, kicked the legs of Rafa's director's chair out from under him, bashed the lens of a camera, and knocked down a light stand. Rafa came to his feet in a runner's crouch, dodged his way through the room, and scurried out the back door.

Jacobo grabbed Güero and made him unlock Dolly Ann's shackles. He jerked him backward out of the way and hugged Dolly Ann. "You're safe, girl," he said. "I'm sorry this happened."

Kane and Vogel roared into the room with the Montenegro men and Fatima right behind them. Ibrahim had taken Güero by the front of the shirt and was backing him toward the door. Vogel picked up a chair and brought it down on Güero's head. He cocked it again to bash Ibrahim, but Ibrahim stepped back and held up his hands. "No, Juan," he shouted. "Jacobo and I came here to stop this, like you."

Adolfo looked over his shoulder from atop Luci, saw Kane coming at him, screamed at Kane, and brandished the knife over Luci's head. Kane drew his colmillo and pointed it, blade up, at his butt. Adolfo threw the knife away, fell off the bed, covered his head with his arms, and assumed the fetal position on the floor.

Kane saw Dolly Ann in Jacobo's grasp and started for him to cut off his head. Dolly Ann shouted, "No, Pappy! Don't hurt him! He rescued us!"

Kane lowered the knife. Jacobo's blank, white face stared back at him.

"Jacobo stopped Rafa, Pappy," Dolly Ann said. "Don't hurt him."

"Where's Rafa?" Kane said. He looked around and did not see him. He had caught Güero, but he was not being allowed his revenge. Ibrahim and Vogel were watching him. Güero stared up at him from the floor, did not like what he saw, and backed into a corner on the seat of his pants. The Montenegros' men had bunched the movie crew into a corner and in another corner were methodically using their clubs and boots on five Lobos they had caught.

Kane looked for Fatima and found her smoking a cigarette out by Beto's car. "Fatima, don't you want to come back in and see what your son was doing when we arrived? Didn't you say that this is the place where he concentrates best on his serious work?"

"I already saw all I want to see," she said.

"What do you think I should do to Rafa for kidnapping my girls and using them to film a pornographic movie?"

"I didn't see Rafa in there."

"Dolly Ann told me Rafa was there, but ran away."

"You only want to punish Rafa? What about my other two sons you caught in there?"

"Your other two are honorable men, Fatima. They had already rescued the girls when we arrived."

"Yes, and do you know how they came to get here on time to put a stop to this awful thing?"

"Tell me."

"I called them when I left you in my kitchen."

"Why did you lie to me about that?"

"I wanted them to beat you to Rafa's office to warn him so you wouldn't give him another beating."

"Then you knew he was doing something to deserve a beating."

"No, I didn't, but I knew you would give him one, regardless of what he was doing. Where is Rafa?"

"You can believe I will find that out."

"Go find him, then. I'll wait here."

"Will you please come in and see to the girls?"

"Yes, I'll do that."

Fatima followed Kane into the apartment, sat on a bench between Dolly Ann and Luci, and put her arms around their shoulders. Someone had wrapped them in bed sheets. The five Lobos lay flat on the floor. Güero sat in his corner. Adolfo had put on his pants and now stood against the wall by himself between the crew and Güero.

"Has anyone called the police?" Kane asked.

"I called Silverio Garcia's special police," Vogel said. "But I don't know what good it will do."

Kane headed toward Güero's corner. "Fatima, take the girls out to the car," he said. Ibrahim stepped aside to make way for him.

Kane took hold of Güero's ear to help him to his feet. Güero wailed with such fear that it angered Kane and he sliced half the ear off. Güero collapsed on the floor and covered the bloody remainder of it with both hands. Kane sliced the hair off his head and threw it back in his face, handful by handful. "You're a lucky coward, as usual, but you ought to at least look more like your gang," he said. "If Fatima and my girls were not here, I'd cut off your chile and eggs too, then your throat. Fatima doesn't deserve the grief you and your brother have caused her. Stand up, before I cut off your other ear." He stood up and Kane cut it off. When Güero shrieked and covered the wound with his hand, Kane grabbed the end of his nose and sliced it off. He stuffed the two halves of the ears in Güero's shirt pocket. The end of the nose was stuck on his blade, so he wiped it off in the same pocket. "If you hurry, you can probably get somebody to reattach all that," he said. "Just remember who gave it to you as a present. But then, you also still have your life, don't you, you little bastard?"

Güero did not answer.

"Don't you?" Kane said.

Güero nodded.

Kane walked away, saw the evil knife Adolfo had thrown away, and picked it up. He examined it and saw that it was like his colmillo in material and workmanship, but thinner and wicked looking. He turned it over and found an inscription in the same lettering as the one on his knife. It said, "I am the gay blade."

Fourteen

At 5:00 a.m., Huatabampo chief of police Ramon Guevara was notified at home by his lieutenant that blood had been spilled at a Lupino warehouse. He reached his office in the *comandancia* only a few minutes before the five Lobos gangsters, Adolfo, and seven movie crewmen were brought into the station by Manuelito Montenegro and his companions. The lieutenant informed Chief Guevara that Kane and Vogel were on the way to issue a complaint against the actor, the gangsters, and the crew.

Kane, Vogel, and Fatima had stayed awhile at the warehouse so the girls could wash and dress. They left Fatima at her door before they went on to the police station. At the station, Kane and Vogel and the girls headed for the chief's office to swear out a *demanda*, a formal complaint against Rafa Lupino and his employees, that could not be ignored. Even if Chief Guevara proved to be crooked, their formal complaint would have to be recognized by the public prosecutor.

Before the partners reached the door to Guevara's office, he brushed past them, sought out the gangsters and their cohorts, and sat down for an extremely polite and solicitous conversation with them. When he was through with them, he ordered his lieutenant to take written statements from every person who had been bruised or bloodied at the movie set. Not one of the Montenegro men had been hurt and none were questioned.

After the chief briefly questioned Jacobo and Ibrahim, he called Dolly Ann and Luci into his office. Kane and Vogel went with them. The girls showed every sign that they had just come away from a fight for their lives. They stared as though every image they saw bounced away before it could be understood. Kane had considered taking them straight to Rio Alamos and putting them in the hospital under the care of Oscar Vogel, but he needed them to be with him when he swore out the complaint. He needed to stay on the heels of the culprits before the police allowed them to scatter. The enemy had been stayed, but the war had not been won.

The chief questioned Luci first.

"Your name, child?"

"Lucrecia Martinillo Montenegro."

"Why are you in Huatabampo?"

"Because a man brought us against our will."

"Where is this man?"

"One of your officers took him to the hospital," Kane said. The chief ignored him.

"Were you harmed?" the chief asked Luci.

"Yes."

"Were you beaten?"

"Yes, señor."

"Raped?"

"No."

"You say that you were brought here against your will?"

"Yes, we were tied and they put sacks over our heads and brought us here from my friend's ranch in the United States."

"All this way? Do you have wounds or cuts and bruises, proof that you were forced to come here?"

"I was struck on my ear and temple." Luci turned her head so the chief could see where Adolfo had struck her.

The blows had made no mark that showed yet.

The chief turned to Dolly Ann.

"Your name?"

"Dolly Ann Kane."

"Why are you here?"

"I was kidnapped with Luci."

"And brought here against your will?"

"Yes."

"Do you have proof?"

"I'm not a liar."

"Very well. We'll have you examined by a doctor and you can give us a written statement of what happened."

The chief turned to Kane and Vogel and told them that they were in worse trouble than the people against whom they wanted to issue the complaint. He could find no reason to justify the beatings and knifings that he understood had been done to Güero Rodriguez and the others at the Lupino warehouse. He awaited a report on Rodriguez's condition from the doctors at the hospital.

The chief said that he saw no evidence of a kidnapping either. By their own admission, the girls had not been harmed. Blood had been spilled among the accused, but none among the accusers. The accusers could not prove that the accused had done anything wrong. To the chief, everything pointed to the fact that Kane and Vogel and company, and especially Jim Kane, were the wrongdoers in this affair.

Kane looked at Vogel.

"These people kidnapped our girls," Vogel said. "We broke in just as they were about to cut their throats."

"Perhaps, but look at it from my point of view, Señor Vogel," the chief said. "There's no proof that these girls were taken by force, no proof that they were made to submit to anything illegal. What am I to do? If the ministerio público were here, he would have to bring charges against you and Señor Kane."

"If the ministerio wants to take over this affair, we're all for it," Kane said.

"Alas, he's in Tucson for cancer treatment. No, this is up to me. I'll release you now, but I order you to remain in town. Leave the name of your hotel, so we'll know where to contact you."

"Is that it, then?" Kane asked. "You're placing us under house arrest? What may I ask will you do with the kidnappers and pornographers we caught in the act of trying to snuff our girls? You want proof of a crime? Look at their film."

"I will, but won't that only prove or disprove your girls' ability as actresses? For now I have to release the people you accuse for lack of evidence. I have to keep you where I can find you while I wait for the persons you injured to bring charges or not bring charges against you."

"Are we free to go?"

"Yes, but stay in Huatabampo and stay away from the people you injured. I don't want any more blood spilled on my watch."

Kane and Vogel turned to leave the office with the girls.

"One more thing," the chief said. "I understand that you have a ranch on the border, Señor Kane."

"I do."

"What do you know about the murder of four young men that took place on the border near Nogales only a day or so ago?"

"I haven't been home for a day or so."

"Well, someone ambushed, murdered, and robbed four young men near your ranch a night or two ago. I wonder if you know anything about it. I understand that horse tracks were followed from the spot of the massacre on the Mexican side and across the line to your ranch on the American side."

"Really?" Kane knew the man was as much a liar as he was now. Kane and his partners had left no tracks.

"Don't you own a ranch called the 7X, the one that its Mexican neighbors call Rancho la Manzanita?" the chief asked.

"Of course. Everybody from Rio Alamos to Tucson knows I do."

"It seems that the killers of the young men escaped onto your ranch."

"Yes? Well, tell me something new. All kinds of murderers, smugglers, terrorists, and thieves, not to mention thousands and thousands of honest men and women who seek work, use my ranch as their thoroughfare."

"Isn't it your contention that your girls were abducted on your ranch, Señor Kane?" the chief asked. "Because if they were, I will have to call in your FBI, as well as the Mexican Federal Judicial Police, in order to determine jurisdiction in my investigation of your charges, if and when they are ever filed. Boundaries must be clarified. This so-called kidnapping may be linked to the murders of our four young Mexicans."

"Yes, so why don't you also link them to the crimes all the rest of the Mexicans are committing on the border at this time? Your Los Lobos kidnapped my girls and we followed them here. Jot that down in the notes of your investigation. Our girls will attest to it. That's all you need to know."

"Duly noted, Señor Kane."

"Is that all?" Kane asked. "We've been up since yesterday at this time and need to rest." He wanted to get himself and his people out of there before the chief decided to question every individual involved. To hell with issuing the girls' complaint. He would wait until Silverio Garcia came home.

As Kane and company filed out of the police station alongside Rafa's gang, Kane turned to speak to Adolfo. The coward was going awfully free for someone who had been stopped only inches before he committed rape and murder. "When I see you again, you can say good-bye to your chile and eggs, coward," Kane said softly.

"What happened to your kidnapping charges, *meestair*?" Adolfo sneered. "Did the female Kane finally admit that she only came to Huatabampo to have some fun?"

Before Kane could answer, Ibrahim and Jacobo shouted him down and made him duck his head and scurry inside the protection of his companions.

Vogel and the Montenegros took the girls to the hotel to rest. Kane caught a taxi to the hospital to have a talk with Güero. Half the morning was gone. He found Güero's doctor and asked to see him.

"You'll be happy to know that his ears and the end of his nose have been reattached, Mr. Kane," the doctor said.

"Good," Kane said. "Maybe he'll thank his God and not lose them again."

"Tell me, sir, do you know how the ears and nose were removed? The patient won't say, but it appears to be the work of a skilled surgeon. Both ears were cut in the same angle and exactly in half."

"I have no idea," Kane said, as though the idea should be given a lot of thought. "Imagine. The skill that an operation like that must involve."

He found Güero in bed in a private room. When he felt Kane's presence his eyes opened, then widened, and he tried to sit up. Kane put his hand on his chest and held him down.

"*Ay, nooo*," Güero moaned.

"Yes, bastard, your nightmare has returned," Kane said. "But I'm not here to hurt you if you listen to me, and I won't be long."

Güero looked wildly around and squirmed under Kane's hand. "Be still," Kane said in English. "Keep squirming and I'll cut your whole nose off flush with your face right now and leave you for dead. For your own good, lie still and listen."

Güero quit squirming and tears filled his eyes.

"Aw, don't cry. You're a goddamned kidnapper who makes snuff movies. You don't have any right to cry to try to move my heart. You terrorized my granddaughter. Your life is mine, now, so pay attention. Are you listening?"

Güero nodded.

"Good, here's what I have to say. This can end here. If you want to make more of it, and that means if you bring charges against me, or any of my people, or try to take revenge on me, I won't rest until I kick your rotting corpse to make sure you're dead. I caught and killed Armando and the other three kidnappers on their way back to Nogales. I didn't kill you at the warehouse, because my granddaughter, Luci, and Fatima were there. I held back because of them. However, you and I both know you deserve to die, because you took my granddaughter and her little friend away from me, and when I caught up you were only one click from snuffing them out. Don't make me regret that I didn't kill you.

"You still have to cope with Adan Martinillo. I don't think he will let you live. You're lucky I gave you back your ears and you were able to have them reattached. Enjoy them, because I don't think Martinillo will want to send you to your grave without cutting them off again.

"Up to now, you have been very, very lucky, but you do understand that I can change your luck again, don't you?"

Güero looked Kane in the eye and said, "It's over. I won't cause you any more trouble. I swear."

"That's good, bastard, because next time you raise a hand against me or mine in any manner, you die."

Kane found himself without wheels when he left the hospital. He was about to call a taxi when Fatima drove up. Kane got in beside her and told her he would buy breakfast. Fatima stopped at a restaurant that belonged to a widow friend of hers. The lady sat them at a table by her kitchen stove where fresh steam rose from a three-gallon kettle of menudo, a large skillet of eggs fried sunny-side up, a pile of beans fried in a pan, a kettle of beans boiled, and jerky fried in another skillet. A young girl gave tortillas their pats and laid them out on a large, clean expanse of the stovetop to cook. With that and Fatima's company and the widow's cheerful hospitality, Kane's blood slowed to a normal pace. The widow brought them *café con leche*, and after a while, freshly squeezed orange juice.

Over the meal Fatima wanted to know everything that had happened in the police station and the hospital. Now that she knew her son to be a pornographer, she wanted to know everything else he had been doing so she could give him the remedies he needed. She intended to find out everything that had been going on in that warehouse and how the Lupinos were involved.

"Jacobo and Ibrahim put a stop to Rafa's movie before anyone got seriously hurt, so you don't have to worry about their morals, courage, or principles," Kane said. "Be proud of them."

"They told me that Rafa directed a man to rape Luci Martinillo. Is that true?"

"You saw what he was doing."

"I saw something that I have not yet sorted out."

"Did you see a naked man on top of Luci with a knife in his hand?" Kane said.

"That was sick," Fatima said. "An awful, sinful thing."

"Well, we got there in time," Kane said. "Thanks to you, Fatima."

"This is a catastrophe for my family. My father will be harder on Rafa than you were on Güero Rodriguez. He'll probably want to castrate him."

"I don't know, the old man is inordinately tolerant of Rafa."

"He loves his grandson. What can I say? He's my son and we have to tolerate him. Will Dolly Ann be all right? I want to pay her medical expenses."

"She's a little hard-twist, but we'll have to see how she recovers. I'm very proud of the way she's handled herself."

"It's good that you can still be proud of her. I've always wished I could be proud of my son, but he's never been right about his values. It could be that he has no principles at all."

"What do you mean, 'still be proud of her'? Nothing could take away my pride in that girl."

"I mean, if she'd been raped, how could you have coped with the shame? She'd have been better off dead. Your family would be disgraced forever."

Kane heard the words and understood them to be a reflection of the differences in their beliefs, but thought, *Right there, that's the reason I could never team up with this lady as her husband. Everybody else in the world can love their girls unconditionally, except a Muslim mother. Her girls will go to hell if they sing and dance, or show a leg, and she'll go to a place that's just as awful if somebody rapes her, or her daughter, and so will her whole family.*

After a long moment in which he decided not to go into his and Fatima's separate criteria for shame, Kane said, "I'm glad I don't have to cope with the girl's rape and death. How will you cope with Rafa's depravity?"

"But he's not depraved, Jim. He only has the powerful, dangerous urges of every man. Certainly the way he takes his pleasure behind closed doors is not abnormal for a man, is it?"

"You mean it's only normal that he likes to take young girls by force, torture them, then snuff out their lives on film?"

"I don't believe Rafa kidnapped those girls, or ordered Güero to do it. Have you considered that the girls might have *wanted* to play those parts in Rafa's movie, and the entire scene was only an act? These days, movies like that with stars as pretty as Dolly Ann and Luci make a lot of money. Your granddaughter and her friend might just be very good, enterprising little actresses. No one will ever make me believe that my son intended to take the girls' lives. I know him better than anyone, and he's not a murderer."

Fatima's statement that the girls could make a lot of money surprised

Kane. He did not want to distrust Fatima. He liked her. Even now in his old age he was attracted to her, but that was the fourth time in a very short period that he had heard a Lupino and their cohort say that Dolly Ann was worth a lot of money. However, he put it out of his mind. He wanted to trust Fatima and be good to her. Without her, he would still be looking for the girls. He would stop being suspicious of every Lupino. Rafa was the only Lupino who had done anything wrong.

Kane asked Fatima to take him to the hotel. He wanted to think this over. The war was not over.

The next morning the chief called Kane and Vogel at the hotel and told them that no charges would be filed against them by Güero Rodriguez, Rafa Lupino, or any of their associates. He told Kane he was a lucky man, because Rafa was willing to write the incident off as nothing more than a misunderstanding.

Kane and Vogel and company returned to Rio Alamos that morning. The girls stayed at Vogel's house and were asked not to go out. Kane told Alicia that they should be locked in their room.

Oscar Vogel examined them within one hour of their arrival. Afterward, he stood outside the door to their bedroom and quietly proclaimed that their bodies had not been harmed, but their minds were probably still in shock. He was confident they would recover, but could not predict how soon.

As he sat in Alicia Vogel's front room and listened to Oscar's diagnosis and his answers to the questions of the women, Kane's throat constricted again. The tightness spread to his jaws and ears, then down into his upper chest, and became painful as it spread to his left arm and down into his little finger, where it became an agony again. The doctor caught his eye just as he unconsciously pressed his fingers to his throat to ease the discomfort in his jaws. Kane looked away quickly.

Oscar needed to return to his office. The family escorted him to the door, but Kane kept his seat on Alicia's divan. Oscar turned at the door and looked over the heads of the Vogel women at Kane, excused himself, and returned to the front room. He offered his hand and Kane looked up at him and shook it.

"You just turned pale as a ghost and took hold of your throat, Jim. Do you deny that you're having some sort of spell?"

"No, but I've had it before and it will pass in a few minutes."

"Has it spread to your arm?"

"All the way down into my little finger, and it hurts like hell down there."

"At the very least, you're having an angina attack. At the worst, for your information, it's a heart attack."

"No, because it will go away in a little while."

"How do you know?"

"I told you. It's happened before."

"How many times before?"

"Once."

"Ah, well, then you know all about it. You're an old veteran."

"No, but it's not all that painful and will go away."

"Would it do any good if I asked you to come to my office for an examination?"

"Not now."

"I want you in my office in one hour."

"Not now."

"No, not one hour. *Within* the hour."

"He'll be there." Juan Vogel spoke up from the kitchen door behind the divan. He had been talking on the kitchen telephone.

That afternoon, armed with a tiny jar of nitroglycerine pills, Kane returned with his compadre Juan to the house, and Vogel announced the results of Oscar's examination to the women. Kane had the blood pressure and pulse of a seventeen-year-old athlete, but he needed more tests. Kane would not say a word about any of it.

Kane and Vogel flew in Little Buck to the Sierra the next day to look for Martinillo. They buzzed the El Trigo hacienda, circled until Che Che came out and waved to them, then landed on the strip. Che Che came to the strip with Lagarto and Colorado, their saddle horses.

They penned Little Buck at the head of the strip, then rode down to Las Animas. They found Lucrecia all alone. Adancito had already sent her a messenger from San Bernardo with word of the deaths of Memin and Marco Antonio. Kane and Vogel hugged her, patted her shoulder, and gave their condolences. She knew the girls had been taken, but did not know they had been recovered. When the partners told her they were safe with Alicia Vogel, she wept with relief.

The partners headed for Canela. They hoped to find Martinillo's tracks there, follow them to the high Sierra of La Golondrina, and find him. This time, they did not care that they were not invited to La Golondrina by Lupino.

Four hours later, the partners stopped on a switchback beside a cliff and looked down into the Pool of the Duck and the Hawk at Tepochici. Kane enjoyed the sight of the pool of blue water inside the maze of hot, dry rock canyons. Martinillo had told Kane and Vogel that once, when he was a young man, he had stopped on the edge of that cliff and watched a grandfather jaguar stop and speculate over his chance for a meal as he watched a duck in the pool. The duck kept diving under the surface to avoid being snatched out of the water by a hawk that hovered over his head. Finally, the jaguar turned to look at Martinillo, snarled gently at the sight, and went on about his business. Martinillo had been as busy as the jaguar and had gone home without finding out if the hawk caught the duck. The place had been called the Pool of the Duck and the Hawk since then.

Kane thought about Tepochici often. He had missed it as he recovered from his injuries. He knew his favorite spots in the Sierra never changed, but he often thought about them as he did people. He never stayed at Tepochici longer than to have a drink of water, but he was always thirsty and ready to get off his horse when he first looked down at the blue water from the cliff. He always enjoyed the beauty of the place for only a few minutes, then moved on and did not look back. However, when he found himself hundreds of miles away from his favorite places like Tepochici, he wondered if he would ever return. He hoped they would be unchanged if he did.

He found the pool unchanged this time, except that a man lay on his belly beside it and carefully drank from his cupped hands.

"*¿Qué hubole?* What have we here?" Vogel spoke under his breath, as though he did not want to startle the man. "It's himself."

The man heard him and raised his face. He was Martinillo. He smiled, sat up, and crossed his legs to wait for them.

They rode across the stream and dismounted at his side. He stood, but did not offer his hand, and when Kane reached out to embrace him, he stepped back. "No," he said. "I have a hole in my shoulder."

Martinillo pointed to a brown tear above the right breast pocket of his shirt. The shirt had been washed, but a brown bloodstain surrounded the tear.

Kane and Vogel placed both hands gently on his shoulders in token embraces.

"What happened, Adan?" Kane asked. "Where are you hurt?"

Martinillo sat again, filled a slim, long-necked, pint amphora with water to drink, and began the story of his adventure in the high Sierra. The three partners tried to figure how much time had elapsed since they were last together and decided it had been four to six weeks. Martinillo admitted that he was the least qualified to know the time. He had lain delirious at Canela for many lost days. He did not think he would have survived, except that an Indian happened along and helped him through his fever and delirium. He had been so sick that he only saw the man's dark form, never his face. Martinillo had spoken to him, but he seldom replied, except when he heard the names of Kane and Vogel. Martinillo awoke one morning much improved and called to him, but he was gone.

"Who is this Indian?" Vogel asked. "I know every *tegueco* in the country."

"He knows you, compadre, and he knows my compadre Jim," Martinillo said. "He referred to you both as his compadres, as though you had baptized or confirmed his children. He seldom spoke. He only nodded when I asked him to go find you. I thought he went to look for you when he left me."

"No," Vogel said.

"How strange. He had the touch of a saint. From the minute he arrived, I began to improve. He could take away my pain by touching me."

The partners made Martinillo take off his shirt and show the wound. The purple scar on his back resembled an imploded star and the place where the bullet had erupted from his upper breast was the shape and size of an exploded silver peso.

The partners stood away and looked at the scars.

"You're almost healed," Kane said. "You know? Maybe your guardian angel came to you in the form of that Indian."

"The Indian," Vogel said. "Who could he have been? Was he a complete stranger, or did his face seem familiar?"

"His movements were familiar. I only saw parts of his face in the light from time to time. He always stood between me and the light, but the way he moved reminded me of someone I knew well. I have been near him and touched by him before. I remember him as I do my grandfather who died when I was only three or four. I would have known him if he had ever given me a good look at his face, or if he would have told me who he was."

"Your guardian angel," Kane said. "That was him."

"You ought to know, compadre," Vogel said. "If anybody's seen his guardian angel, it's you. Nobody's come back from the dead more times than you."

"Believe it, compadre," Kane said.

"I'll believe it when I come back from the dead as you have from plane wrecks, pneumonia, horse wrecks, stabbings, shootings, and car wrecks. My guardian angel hasn't shown himself to me yet, but I'll know him when I see him."

Kane changed the subject. "Compadre Adan, we have to give you bad news," he said, then looked to Vogel for help.

"What is it?" Martinillo said. "Tell me."

Vogel put his hand on his shoulder. "Marco Antonio and Memin are dead."

"No! How?" Martinillo said.

"Los Lobos shot them down as they ate supper at El Retiro after the race."

"How can that be?" Martinillo asked. He turned away and lifted a hand to his brow. Vogel started to give him details, but Martinillo told him not to say any more for a while. The compadres unsaddled their horses to cool their backs and led them to the pool to drink. Kane gave Martinillo a drink from his amphora of mezcal.

"You know that Los Lobos did it?" Martinillo asked.

"No mistake," Vogel said. "Several people saw the shooters, among them your son Adancito and Beto and Manuelito Montenegro. A carload of Lobos with Uzis drove by and sprayed their table in El Retiro with gunfire."

"What's been done to them?"

"They haven't been caught."

Martinillo thought awhile. His face had turned pale, his eyes hard. "It's the Lupinos," he said. "The Lupinos train them to kill at La Culebra. La Culebra, the snake. Cut down the Lupinos and behead the snake."

"We know that Rafa Lupino is behind the killing," Kane said.

"The dirty sons of their fornicating, whoring mothers are all to blame, Lobos and Lupinos alike," Martinillo said. "For my mother and father, from this day, I am going to hunt them down one by one and kill them all."

Kane and Vogel remained silent. Kane regretted that he had not voiced his anger the same way. He wanted too much to return to the peace that his old bones enjoyed before he and Vogel went to La Golondrina to receive the Lupino cattle. Now, as he looked into the diamond glitter of anger in the eyes of his compadre he felt shame. He should have run Rafa down and cut out his gizzards while his trail was hot. What did he think a seventy-five-year-old Kane carcass was worth, anyway? It certainly was not worth saving for a peaceful Old Geezer retirement.

After a while, Martinillo said, "Vámonos. I better get home." He mounted Lagarto behind Kane.

On the way to El Trigo, Kane and Vogel gave him the details of the killings of his grandson and son and the kidnapping of the girls. With no emotion at all, he told them what he had seen and endured in the high Sierra.

"How well does your arm work, compadre?" Kane asked. "We have a lot more to do."

"I have soreness and numbness, but it is better than it was. The numbness recedes as I use it."

"When will you be fit again?"

"Someday, if I use the shoulder and give it rest."

After a while, he said, "Who won the horse race?"

The compadres stopped at El Trigo to saddle a mule for Martinillo and went on. They reached Las Animas two hours after dark. Martinillo's dogs barked, came out to meet them on the trail, and accompanied them into the yard. Lucrecia come around the corner of the house and climbed the steps into the lamplight of the veranda. Her movement showed her sixty years. Kane looked at Vogel and Martinillo ahead of him in the dark and saw how old they were too. Any time that sixty-five and seventy-five-year-old men rode into camp three hours after sundown, they felt their age, and so did the people who waited for them. He felt stronger than he had when he returned to the Sierra, but the miles and hours of anxiety that he and his compadres had recently endured bore down on their old bones that evening.

Kane did not feel tired in his purpose. He could do the work that must be done, but he would not be able wait another hour to rest. When he had been young, he liked to say that he had never been drunk, sick, or tired. Well, now he knew the tired and sick parts. He had found out about the drunk part a long time ago.

Kane and Vogel had served as godfathers for Marco Antonio and Memin Martinillo and were close to them in their upbringing. They felt it their responsibility to hold a new wake for them when they sat down for supper at Lucrecia's table. They happily recalled good times they had enjoyed with the young men. They told the stories of the horse race between Gato and Auda, the recovery of the girls, and the money they had won. Without having consulted Kane, Vogel promised to give the Martinillos a third of his race winnings. Kane followed his example and did the same.

Even though the compadres were now convinced that the Lupinos had always been their enemy, they did not feel required to immediately go to war with them. They could return to their cattle business tomorrow, or they could do something about the Lupinos, and not feel guilty about either decision. The Lupinos would be at La Golondrina like a wide, untouched, bull's-eye target for as long as the compadres allowed it. Of one fact they were certain: they had the courage and the purpose to attack that target and leave it in tatters any time they saw fit. They could live with the Lupinos as before and everybody could mind their own business and be allowed to do as they pleased, or they could finally make the Lupinos pay for the ruin of their community.

Kane proposed that the compadres castigate the Lupinos without starting a war. He wanted to hurt them as he and his compadres had been hurt, but secretly. He believed that if the compadres hit the secret place at La Culebra, the Lupinos would keep it a secret.

Kane told Vogel and Martinillo that he would not blame them if they did not join the brawl he planned. They patiently and firmly stated that they would join him in anything he wanted to do. They could not allow a rabid dog to prowl their yard, and they could not allow two-legged predators to take their young. Every wolf in the pack might not have tasted the blood of Dolly Ann and Luci, but that did not mean the pack was not to blame.

What good were three old compadres unless they used their principles and experience to rid their country of predators? They could at least wipe out the foreign pack of Lobos at La Culebra. If they sat on their geezerhood and did nothing, they would only prove to their neighbors that the three old codgers of El Trigo begged to live out their old age in peace. Instead, they would hit the Lupinos with every weapon they could muster and a purpose that was neither young nor old, but as effective as their old talents could make it. It remained for them to decide on the method.

"This time we have to agree on a plan," Kane said. "My leadership in the recovery of the girls almost got us put in jail. We only got away with it because Rafa and Güero are afraid of what we might do to them next and did not bring charges. Nesib, Ibrahim, and Jacobo are not like them."

"Compadre," Vogel addressed Martinillo. "Can you describe the weapons they have at La Culebra?"

Martinillo brought out his drawings of the weapons the pelones had unpacked and studied in front of the bunkhouse at La Culebra.

"You think Abdullah was the one who shot you?"

"I'm almost sure, although I didn't see him do it. I'm sure our eyes locked over the top of that horse, so he must have been the first to come after me."

"Do you think he recognized you?"

"I don't think he knows me, and no one who came near my hiding place during the search said my name."

The compadres agreed that Rafa was not their main adversary among the Lupinos. Fools were not in charge of Lupino business. Rafa was only a minion. The Lupinos let him do as he pleased on the fringe of their projects, but he acted only as an unruly court jester. The other Lupinos, the hard workers, the polite professionals, were the dangerous ones.

These conclusions alarmed Kane. He had botched the recovery of the girls, made his partners look like criminals, and had come away without his revenge. Every Lupino except Rafa had emerged from the fracas as law-abiding, just-minded, even-tempered, gentlemanly heroes.

"This time, we have to use our weapons better," Kane said. "The Lupinos are smart as the devil. We caught them about to rape and murder our girls, but came away with our tails between our legs. Their holdings include a high-dollar war machine with new weapons and equipment, a battalion of Mexican cavalry and gang members, and a lot of money. We can't start an open war against them, so how can we hurt them?"

"They can't hurt us unless they know us as their adversary," Vogel said. "If we can wipe out everything at La Culebra, we'll stunt their growth and shrink their bank account. They're dedicated to the accumulation of goods and money. We don't care whether the purpose of their paramilitary camp at La Culebra is for protection against rivals, war against political and religious enemies, or to make a profit out of the training of criminal manpower. La Golondrina is the headquarters for billions of pesos worth of goods and property. If we can destroy everything at La Culebra now, while they harvest their opium gum, we might break their eggs. While we wipe out their men and machines, we'll destroy their billion-peso crop. If we succeed, they'll know that an enemy as mean as they are has found them out, can hurt them bad, and will probably keep doing it. That will be our best blow of all.

"Pancho Villa and Zapata hit their enemies hardest where they were fattest and then ran, often without even being seen. Their enemies were never sure who had hit them. A broadcast would report that Villa's army had been seen at Parral one day and the next day in Durango. Only a fleet of airplanes could have hit and run with that much range. Before he made a name for himself and invited news reporters and film crews on his raids, Villa was a phantom who not only leveled his enemies when he attacked, but demoralized them, because they could not find him.

"We need to use the same stealth and deceit that Villa and Zapata used before they became generals. We're horse and mule men and know the horseshoe trails of this region better than anyone. With my compadre Jim's airplane, we're also airmen. If we maintain secrecy and equip ourselves properly, we might not destroy the entire Lupino barony, but we can cut off one leg and cripple the other. *Then* we take aim at the head and heart."

"Am I the only one who wants to kill every Lobo pelón, but not any Lupino except Rafa?" Kane asked.

"I don't want to kill the Lupinos, either," Vogel said. "I leave Rafa to you. The girls came away from the ordeal without a serious bruise or a cut. They didn't even get dirty. I think Jacobo and Ibrahim were responsible for that. Maybe we should thank Nesib and Fatima for the way they raised those two."

"Yes, and maybe we ought to cut out their livers for the way they raised Rafa," Kane said. "As wolves go, every single pack has a good mother and grandfather."

"Do you say that we should spare the Lupinos, compadre Juan?" Martinillo asked Vogel. "How will that help us?"

"Don't spare any of them. Blow them all up," Lucrecia said.

Kane and Vogel laughed.

"Let's realize our limitations," Kane said. "We can't blow up their warehouses, resort hotel, airplanes, and fishing boats in town because we might hurt a customer, or a child, a cook, or a neighbor. We can blow up their heroin factory and warehouse at La Culebra, and burn their opium crop and the airships we catch at the camp. We can kill that bunkhouse full of Arabs and pelones, and probably get away without being identified.

"I don't want to kill the Lupinos, Abdullah, or their horses, but I sure want to kill all their help. Anyway, what's the use of burning their goods if we kill the Lupinos? Who would wail over their losses? You know they'll raise a great lament, because no one has ever done them any hurt. I may not want to kill them, but I want to hear them howl. I bet nobody ever beat them out of even a spoilt tortilla. However, if one Lupino shoots at me, I'll shoot out all their gizzards."

"What about old Nesib and Fatima? Will you shoot them too?" Lucrecia asked.

"No matter what happens, they'll be hurt," Kane said. "Nesib is the one who profits most from all the businesses. The family would not have that camp at La Culebra without his full consent. That ravine stores the deepest well of his conceit. If he'll allow enemies of his country to have a guerilla war school on his place, he'll do anything."

"What about Fatima?"

"She's always enjoyed don Nesib's confidence," Vogel said. "She keeps the family books and writes all the checks and collects all the cash, at least for La Golondrina. Nesib can't go to the bathroom without her knowledge and consent. As far as I know, neither can her sons. She's probably the smartest of them all. She has to know the extent of the family's criminal business."

The compadres agreed that old man Lupino and Fatima must be the bosses, because somebody made sure that Ibrahim, Jacobo, and Ali kept their savoir faire, minded their good manners, and knew what to say and how to act among decent people. That was what grandfathers and mothers did. The dangerous Lupinos did not brandish weapons, curse, or shout obscenities. Abdullah was their mentor and had instilled his principles in them. They seemed to be as chivalrous as the Arab opponents of the Crusaders had been. They might even be called honorable, but they certainly must have criteria for evil that was a whole lot different from their Christian one.

The compadres agreed that the Lupinos would not break their word, if they gave it, but they would not give their word to an enemy. They deceived people into thinking they were good, because they made a show of being honorable and kept their real business secret.

The compadres then agreed that they should destroy everything in

Culebra Canyon, except the horses. They laughed about that. They would not destroy the horses, because they were indebted to their kind.

Kane and Vogel proposed that they spare none of the Lupino pelones or the Arabs, except Abdullah. Abdullah was also their own kind. They understood his loyalty to Lupino, and he had been a friend to Kane and Vogel.

"You want to spare Abdullah too?" Lucrecia asked.

"I won't spare him," Martinillo said. "If he's at La Culebra, I'll kill him. Wherever I see him, if I meet him on the trail, I'll kill him, because I know he won't spare me. You, my compadres, know him better than I do, but I know he'll ask no quarter and give none, no matter who you are, and he'll be hard to kill. If anybody gets away from La Culebra, it will be him. If we spare him, he'll be the one who gets back at us for his masters, and he is the most efficient killer of them all."

The faraway moan of a wolf interrupted the conversation for a long moment.

"Ay, malhaya. Meanness," Vogel said.

"Sweet mother of God," Kane said as a chill swept over his skin.

Martinillo laughed. "That's the she-wolf we spared when we sent her pack to hell. I wonder if her loneliness will make her as mean and smart as the old, lone black wolves that used to terrorize everybody in the Sierra. They say that loneliness in wolves makes them more savage and bold."

"That reminds me of a thought that nags me," Kane said. "Do you know the word lupino means wolflike in English? Wolfish. That has to be the reason the thugs who work for the Lupinos call themselves Los Lobos, the Wolves. That's why we're surrounded by wolves that howl in our mountains at night, that prey on our border on two legs, that train as terrorists and shoot us. The Lupinos turned them loose on us."

"You, Lucrecia, do you think that we should give the pelones and the Arabs at La Culebra a fair trial before we blow them up?" Vogel asked. "Should we capture them, march them to town, and turn them over to the government?"

"I told you, the government already guards the Lupino business in the high Sierra," Adan said. "Kosterlinski and his troop serve as their personal guards."

"Lucrecia, what do you say?" Kane asked.

"Kill them all any way you can, as we did the wolves that raided us here," Lucrecia said, her eyes hot. She had been roaming the room as she served the supper. She stopped and hugged Martinillo's neck from behind. "They're not brutes, but they have no God. They're worse than wolves, because the wolves are innocent brutes. Why spare their leaders? Kill that Arab Abdullah first, for he shot my Adan."

Lucrecia kissed the top of Martinillo's head. He rolled his eyes at his compadres, but not so she could see it.

Fifteen

Che Che was summoned by radio and charged with the care of Las Animas and the three compadres and Lucrecia flew to Rio Alamos the next day. Dr. Oscar Vogel came to Alicia's house to examine Martinillo's wound. The *hierba el pasimo* had healed it. Oscar was happy that Martinillo used the herb and gave it credit for the healing. Martinillo needed to rest the shoulder and exercise it lightly for the next six weeks. Alicia Vogel insisted that the Martinillos stay at her house during his recuperation. Luci decided to stay and help her godmother Alicia with her grandparents and not go home with Dolly Ann. Kane hired his friend Chamaco Ortiz, a veteran Bantamweight boxer, to supervise a daily training schedule for Martinillo. In only five weeks, Martinillo would need to be a healthy, stealthy hunter-marksman again.

The next morning Kane, Dolly Ann, and Vogel flew to the 7X. Dolly Ann did not want to communicate with Kane and was evasive, even dismissive, when he and Vogel tried to draw her into their conversations. After they landed at the 7X and carried their bags and duffel to the house, Vogel went outside to take a walk, and Kane and Dolly Ann were left alone. Kane decided not to push the girl to talk, but he kept watch for the chance that she would open up. From his office, he saw her go into the kitchen, then heard the Lion's rumbling voice as he gave her a hug. Kane went in to say hello and his old friend stood up from the table and gave him an abrazo at arm's length with pats on the back. Dolly Ann had found a few dishes to wash.

"Did you see Juan?" Kane asked him.

"No," the Lion said. "Is he here?"

"I don't know how you missed him. He just went outside."

"The Doll looks like she's been played with too much, doesn't she?"

"She's had a bad time, all right."

"Well, she can forget it and start feeling better now," the Lion said to her back. He stood up to his full six feet four inches and put on his hat. Kane knew him to be at least eighty-five years old, but he stood as straight as he had when he was seventeen, was still cowboy lean from riding circle on his cattle every day, and was brighter than any man that Kane knew of any age. He was the Lion, and always listo, always ready, always figuring which way to go next, even if he needed to connive. Here was one like Kane and Vogel who did not care what sort of misfortune had befallen the girl—it could not affect his love for her. He had never let misfortune weigh him down and neither should anyone he loved. Kane knew the Lion could see that the girl carried a new burden and he did not like it. Naturally, he worried about how the kidnapping affected her, so he was sensitive to this evasive attitude that she had brought home.

Now he spoke to the girl's back again as she worked at the sink. "You must be tired from that airplane, Muñeca," he said. "You can't spend the rest of the day in the house. Come with me."

She turned to Kane for his opinion of the Lion's order, because it had been an order, not an invitation.

"You ought to go," Kane said.

She went out the back door ahead of the Lion, and Kane watched them walk across the yard toward the corrals. Vogel came out of the saddle house and shook the Lion's hand and gave him an abrazo, and all three went back into the saddle house. Kane sat at the desk in his office to count the cash and checks of the winnings from the race and prepare the bank deposits he would have to make. After a while, he heard the Lion's hammer on the anvil behind the saddle house and knew he would be shoeing a horse. He knew what Dolly Ann would be doing too, because she had been the Lion's favorite helper since she was big enough to keep up with him. She had horseshoe nails in her mouth, sweat was running off her brow and the end of her nose, and she was tacking shoes on the horse's hoof while the Lion or Vogel held it up. Kane had never been able to convert the Lion and Vogel away from the vaquero way of shoeing. One vaquero had to hold the hoof up while the other trimmed it and nailed on the shoes. Cowboys shoed horses all by themselves. Vogel would spell the Lion from time to time, and then sit back, watch, and smoke while Dolly Ann nailed on the shoes.

Kane finished his figures and put all the money into one envelope for pesos and another for dollars, then leaned back in his comfortable desk chair, listened to the sounds of the horseshoers, and fell asleep. Much later, Dolly Ann woke him up when she came through the back door. Before he could get out of the chair, she came and kissed him and knelt beside the chair with her head on his breast.

"You still worried?" Kane asked.

She nodded vigorously so he would be sure to know she nodded.

"No use asking what about, because I know, but tell me anyway."

"Am I grounded for life? You said I'd be grounded for life if I rode out alone again, like Cody and I did."

"I have taken that into consideration."

"I shouldn't be allowed to saddle a horse again, let alone ride."

"I've been trying to think what else I could find for you to do."

"What else do you think I could?"

"You're getting to be a good cook and housekeeper."

"Yes."

"And you're a pretty good horseshoer."

"I can tack them on a hoof, but I'm not too good at holding them up yet."

"I guess you need to build a lot more muscle on yourself."

"A whole lot more."

"Then, too, you're a pretty good boxer. You might be able to do that, but it's like riding on this ranch. You can't do it alone, even when you're alone in the ring. A grownup has to be with you all the time."

"I forgot I could still do boxing."

"I didn't." Kane brought the mouthpiece out of his shirt pocket. "I've been carrying this since you ran off and got kidnapped."

Dolly raised her head and took it. "My mouthpiece. Where did you get it?"

"It was in my jacket pocket from the last time you and Cody Joe sparred."

"You've been carrying this dirty old thing around in your pocket all this time?"

"Why not? I had to carry something of yours and it's had you all over it all its life."

"Oh, Pappy, I love you so much."

"Me too you."

"I'll take being grounded, if you'll forget all the problems I've caused."

"You know you can't stay grounded. We have too much to do."

"Yes."

"And most of the problems you caused, you caused the kidnappers, don't you know? They had to pay me a lot of money before I'd take you back."

"Oh, Pappy."

"You think I'm kidding? You want to see the money the kidnappers had to pay me before I would take you back? Look in those two envelopes. One's for pesos and one's for dollars. I bet you've never seen so much money in your life."

The next afternoon Kane and Vogel drove to Tucson Hospital to see Cody Joe. As they walked down the hospital corridor, they looked into a room, saw Father Garcia with a patient, and stopped to say hello.

At first they recognized only the priest and thought he was there to minister to some old man who looked as though he was about to die. When the patient sat up and offered his hand, they recognized Silverio. He was supposed to be an outpatient while he received the radiology treatments, but he lay on the bed in a hospital gown. His grip was brittle and weak. His body had been destroyed. He had lost at least fifty pounds. To Kane, he looked like a burnt kitchen match. Most of his hair had fallen out and only unhealthy wisps remained. His eyes were dull and his breathing shallow and labored.

The partners did not stay long. Outside Silverio's room, Kane said, "Our friend looks bad."

"They're burning him alive," Vogel said.

"I don't think you need that radiology treatment."

Vogel laughed at Kane's expression. "No, compadre, I don't. However, por las dudas, I think I should have it, don't you?"

"I think Ali Lupino has been assigned the chore of incinerating his family's adversaries. Silverio campaigned against the drug lords in his jurisdiction, so he's probably uncovered some Lupino dirt. Even if he hasn't, what would it cost them to eliminate him in this manner, to allay their criminal doubts and fears? As an honest lawman, he's their enemy."

"We better tell Silverio to stop the treatment and find himself another doctor. It might already be too late," Vogel said.

"When Father Garcia hears our story, he'll convince his brother to stop it. By the way, how's your little cough, compadre?"

"What cough? It went away when I quit smoking."

"You're smoking again, though."

"Why not? I'm rid of the cough."

Dolly Ann and Marine Captain Fitzgerald were in the room with Cody Joe when the partners walked in. The captain respectfully stood for the two older men.

"The lad is not doing well, Mr. Kane," Fitzgerald said. "About the time the doctors quell the infection in one spot, it flares up in another. He has a cyst in his hip from the infection on his heel."

Cody Joe's handshake and color were not good, but when his godfather Vogel fanned his face with his big hat, he smiled big. Dolly Ann had just finished telling Captain Fitzgerald about the kidnapping and her recovery by her marine grandfather. Fitzgerald shook hands with Kane and Vogel, then turned and made a big show of asking Dolly Ann if she would consider joining the marines. Kane saw in her face that she was starting to put the ordeal behind her and felt no shame over it.

The captain's visits to Cody Joe had made them good friends. He told Kane and Vogel that the Marine Corps had decided that it would be better if Cody Joe was cared for by doctors who knew more about bullet wounds and garlic. He would be transferred the next day by army helicopter to the hospital at Fort Huachuca.

"Be warned, Private First Class Kane," the captain said with a straight face. "Fort Huachuca is an army base. The army has been known to use marines for experimentation when it could get its hands on sick ones. It needs to find out what makes us tough. Its doctors might cut out your brain, lay it under a big light, and pick it apart with tweezers."

Cody Joe only grinned at him uncertainly and tried to decide if he was serious.

When he read the young man's look, the captain laughed. "Don't believe it, Cody," he said. "The Marine Corps decided that you belong in a service hospital and the fort will be your new station until you get well. If you have any trouble with the dogfaces, I'll send ten marines on bicycles with .410 shotguns and capture the base. We can call it Fort Chesty Puller after we take it over."

Dolly Ann wanted to stay and visit with her brother for the rest of the afternoon. The following day she intended to register at the Tucson YWCA for a class in physical fitness and begin her own boxing regime. She planned to stay in town at the home of a girlfriend who had also enrolled in the class. Kane told her it was a fine idea. He did not tell her of the plan to get even with the Lupinos.

Before they left the hospital, the partners took Father Garcia outside, sat him down, and told him about their recovery of Dolly Ann, about the Lupinos' involvement, and about their fears for Silverio.

"My brother is disintegrating," Father Garcia said. "He was a healthy man when he began these treatments."

"Get him out of here," Kane said. "Take him home. Don't even say good-bye. Radiology treatments might be good when administered by the right hands, but your brother is in the wrong hands."

"What will you do about your treatment, don Juan?" the priest asked Vogel.

"My compadre Jim and I are on our way back to the Sierra. I'm not going to say good-bye to anyone here and I'm never coming back. I won't even *look* back."

"What will you say to Ali Lupino?"

"I doubt I'll see him, but if I do, I'll tell him the truth. We need to get back to our cattle."

"I understand." Father Garcia looked puzzled to hear that the partners could turn away from their trouble with the Lupinos and return to ranch work. "Maybe that's the best way to do it, the Christian way," he said. "I guess it's always best to steer away from trouble with your neighbors."

When the partners returned to their pickup, Kane said, "Well, we deceived our friend the priest. It remains for us to deceive our enemies. If a single outsider to this project finds out what we intend to do, we lose. We are too few to engage in open war with Los Lobos, the Arabs, government cavalry troops, and the Lupinos."

The partners began to blueprint their raid on La Golondrina at Kane's office in the Montezuma Hotel in Nogales. Kane knew two expert government agents who could help with advice, guidance, and technical expertise, so he telephoned them. His friend Jackie Lee Brennan's son Joe was an agent for the Bureau of Alcohol, Tobacco, and Firearms. Jack and Kane had grown up together in boarding school and served in the Marine Corps together. Jack still enjoyed a successful fifty-year career as a movie actor.

Kane called Jack to get Joe's telephone number. When he called Joe, the young man listened for a few minutes and said that he would not only give Kane the advice he needed, he would take thirty days leave and help him in person.

Kane then called Billy Buck, a cowboy who had worked for Kane and Vogel in Arizona and Sonora during his teens, then served in Special Forces in Vietnam and Cambodia, and later in Afghanistan. Now a civilian, he still disappeared from time to time on contract missions for his government. He told Kane that he did not need to sit and talk about a raid on the telephone. He would never have anything better to do than to help his two old mentors.

With these professionals, the partners would have all the help they needed. These men knew every legal and clandestine way to obtain arms and explosives, knew the laws and how to dodge them, and would lend their youth to a project dangerously peopled by oldsters. As an agent for ATF, Joe Brennan welcomed the chance to see an unknown region of the Sierra Madre with two cattlemen who knew the people and the trails. Billy Buck wanted to help because he did not give a damn about doing anything else. Brennan lived in Phoenix and Buck lived in Flagstaff, and they both promised to be on their way to Nogales that day.

Kane's office in the Montezuma Hotel was comfortable, with leather easy chairs, a sloppy leather sofa, and a sprawling old desk that had been scarred by fifty years of boots, spurs, spilled ink, and whiskey. A bookcase full of books in English and in Spanish about cattle, horses, and cowboys covered one wall. Kane registered Brennan and Buck in the hotel, and he and Vogel began to plot the raid against the Lupinos.

Five horseback raiders would hit La Culebra. Their staging area would be in a clearing near Cerro Prieto, at the foot of the Sierra. The place had been named after a mountain of black rock that stuck up out of thick brush on the coastal desert northwest of La Golondrina hacienda. In bygone times, the partners had cleared and scraped out an airstrip there to land contraband Johnny Walker Black Label whiskey that they flew into the country. They had also cleared a narrow road through miles of impenetrable thicket to the strip. As far as they knew, cattle and horses still used it for a trail and kept it open. Kane often flew over it on his way between Nogales and Rio Alamos. People did not use it now, because it was on Lupino property and inside their strong fence. The area was so hidden, lonesome, and hard to traverse that not even the Lupinos went near it.

In one night of full darkness the partners could truck their animals, equipment, and people to Cerro Prieto, pack in to La Culebra on horses and mules, burn everything there, and return. The run from La Culebra to Cerro Prieto would be all downhill and their tracks would lead any pursuit away from El Trigo. After they loaded their trucks and fled Cerro Prieto, the brush would hide them during the hour-long run to the paved international highway. Once on the highway, their tracks would be lost.

The partners would know what they needed in explosives and arms after Martinillo took Buck on a surveillance of La Culebra. The horses and mules would be trained and conditioned for a fast raid of forty miles. The raiders would try to hit La Culebra at about three o'clock in the morning.

Billy Buck showed up at the Montezuma at nine o'clock that night. Two Brennans instead of one arrived an hour later. Jack Brennan had hired a plane from Palm Springs to Tucson and intercepted his son after he decided that he would never get another chance to go on a commando raid. How could Kane, his oldest buddy, let him sit at home while he took his son on high adventure?

While the partners sat with drinks in the office, Kane called Jack's wife Apache to complain. Her real name was Mona, but Jack had called her Apache since the day they met while on location for a picture he filmed in her hometown. When asked why he called her Apache, he always answered, "Apaches are wild people, aren't they? So, what better name for a wild woman?"

"You sent this man to me because you're tired of him and want him to die, didn't you, Apache?" Kane said on the phone. "Don't you know he's too old and slow for this?"

"That's why I told him I had to go too," Apache said. "I don't think it's fair. If I don't look out for you two old geezers, I'll probably have to live another forty years a widow. Go without me and neither of you will come back."

"If Jack gives you permission to go, I'll come and get you," Kane said.

"He already told me I couldn't go, so don't tease me about it. You probably really believe you're going to do it."

"He's in good shape for an old geezer, isn't he?"

"He plays a lot of golf, so he's in good enough shape to go out and get his ass shot off. He can probably dodge a bullet, because he hustles these gamblers around our golf course and has to be ready for the day they'll get mad and try to shoot him."

"Nobody's going to shoot him, Mona."

"You too. You're too old to go on raids. You're just old geezers. When will you realize that?"

"Aw, us old geezers know everything and everybody else don't know nothing. Nobody'll even see us. We get up too early."

"Well, you'll have to get up real early, slow and crippled as you are."

"We're not crippled anymore. I've got a new titanium knee and Jackie Lee told me he has a new fused backbone."

Kane explained the situation to Buck and the Brennans, and before he began to outline the plans for the raid, Billy and Joe excused them-selves and stepped out of the room to talk. After a while they returned to say that if they were to help the partners, they would have to follow an established protocol with their colleagues and counterparts in the Mexican government. Billy and Joe would have to notify the Mexicans with whom they had worked before that the raid was planned. Besides that, all arms and explosives for the raid would have to be procured through their Mexican counterparts.

"Is there a chance your colleagues will leak our plan to the Lupinos?" Kane asked. "Because if there is, I'm not telling them a damned thing. I can buy the weapons and smuggle them in myself."

"This will not be the first time a secret, clandestine raid has suc-ceeded in Mexico, nor will it be the last," Billy said. "A lot of Mexican and U.S. government people are connected with the drug lords, people who would warn the Lupinos to put up a barricade and give us a big surprise, but our contacts are not among them. This will be about the twentieth raid of its kind, except that this time it will be done by private entrepre-neurs, instead of agents like Joe and me and our Mexican friends. If we do right by our Mexican counterparts, the raid will be kept secret. Joe and I have both engaged in this kind of action in Mexico before."

"This raid has to be kept secret," Kane said. "We have to use equip-ment and ammunition that can't be traced to us, and we have to get it in time to make the raid during the dark of the moon. Today is the first of July. We'll go on a night in early August."

"We'll get Russian arms and explosives," Joe said.

"We can do that?"

"Hell, yes. We can get anything we want from Brazilian dealers who furnish it to drug traffickers. We'll have to furnish our own communications equipment, but that's the only gear we're allowed by protocol to bring into the country. We can also get damned good American equipment from our Mexican friends that can't be traced to us."

"We have money from a horse race we just won, but we're not rich. We need to know how much it's going to cost."

"The weapons, ammunition, and explosives won't cost anything. The communications gear we bring from the U.S. might not, either."

"How can that be?"

"Just leave the acquisition of the gear to us," Billy said. He looked to Joe for confirmation and was given the nod. "You give us the chore? Then let us do it our way and stay out of it."

Billy and Joe insisted that they needed a spy inside Lupino's camp. They felt that no operation of this kind should be attempted without one.

"What do you think, compadre?" Kane asked Vogel.

"Someone like Martinillo might take a radio and spy, if we absolutely need that," Vogel said. "But why do we need it? Martinillo gave us a good report. We'll never get anyone at La Golondrina to spy for us. The Lupinos have enjoyed sixty years of rock-hard security. Every person who works for them has been there all his life."

"I don't think we need anyone inside," Kane said. "We'll go as a tight unit in the middle of the night, scout as we go, hit them, and take flight."

"If we go by the book, we need to have a man inside. Nobody inside, no raid," Joe said.

"Well, none of their workers or family would betray them, and we don't know anybody on our side who has their confidence," Kane said.

"How did you match your horse race?" Joe asked. "Did you call the Lupinos by telephone? Did you send them a letter? Did you meet them someplace? Do you ever go there, or is that out of the question?"

"It would not be out of the question for my compadre Vogel to go, but they'd be suspicious if I did. After all, I whipped one of the sons until he peed his pants and cut off his bastard half brother's nose and ears."

"How about if we go to don Nesib with a gift to show that we don't suspect him of having any part in the kidnapping?" Vogel said. "What if I go kiss his ass and make him think we still want to be his friends?

I bet he'll like that right about now. He's always liked us. He's probably worried that his grandsons caused him to lose our friendship. After all, he's lived up there for sixty some years with no other friends except the Vogels and Kanes."

"That's true," Kane said. "But I have an idea that will make us look stupid and forgetful that we have been wronged by the Lupinos and also get us back in their good graces. We hold a ticket that opens almost any door in the world."

"You want to give him Gato so he can breed him to his donkeys and raise hinnys," Vogel said.

"Compadre Juan, we have Jack Brennan, the world famous movie star. Let's tell Lupino we want to make a movie about his horses. If that doesn't disarm Ibrahim and the old man, because they seldom go to town and haven't been influenced by the movies, it'll get the attention of Fatima, Jacobo, Rafa, and Ali. We'll have a good reason to visit their ranch, and they'll have a good reason to let us. Fatima has probably hoped for something like this all her life. Almost everybody has a weak spot for the movies. I know Fatima reads movie magazines and if that doesn't show a weakness for them, nothing does. If the old man won't let us on his place to film his horses and make them famous, Fatima might welcome us with all her heart and soul. Rafa's supposed to be a moviemaker, so we ought to be able to hook him with Jack as our bait. Jacobo must know about the money that movies generate, so we'll make him the producer. The prospects of fame for their horses and the movie money it will generate, combined with their having Jack Brennan as a guest on their place, might get you and Jack inside the enemy camp."

"I can't imagine the old man allowing a movie to be made on his ranch. It's been a fortress of secrecy for sixty years," Vogel said.

"What's his weakness, compadre?" Kane asked. "How do we get in? If we make him a gift of one of our horses, he'll take it and say thank you and good-bye. His weakness lies in what he wants for his daughter, his grandkids, and his horses. He's seen to it that they've never wanted for anything. Let's see if we can fix it so his daughter and her kids invite you and Jack to La Golondrina at the time we hit La Culebra. Another thing, if you and Jack are with Lupino when we make the raid, how can he suspect us?"

"A movie project would certainly be a good reason for some of us to be at La Golondrina at the time of the raid," Joe said. "Lupino is not likely to believe that Vogel's associates would raid his property if Vogel and my dad are his guests when it happens. The raiders ought to be able to communicate with Vogel and my dad, though."

"Why is that necessary?" Kane asked.

"Just in case something goes wrong," Joe and Billy said in unison.

"That's up to you guys who know spy technology," Kane said. "Right now, I want to call Fatima and tell her that a moviemaker friend of ours wants to make a picture about the purebred Arabian cow-horses on exotic La Golondrina ranch. I'll ask if we can bring him there to discuss it. What do you think Jack? If she doesn't drop her drawers and melt all over the floor at the prospect of meeting and working with you, my name ain't Jim Kane."

"It's a good idea," Jack said. "I've never known a son of a gun in this world who wouldn't like to see a movie made about his life, his family, or his business."

"Flatter Lupino's horses and he forgets he's the patriarch of the dirty deal," Kane said. "Everything gets pure, innocent, and true for him when somebody brags on his ranch and horses. What do you think, compadre?"

"It might be the only way to get inside and stay awhile," Vogel said. "He might not let us take pictures of his ranch and livestock, but he'll want to listen to praise for his horses. By his own rule of hospitality, he almost has to take us in and give us all his attention while we're there. We won't have to be there long, and we don't even have to spy on him, but we can be a hindrance if he finds out about the raid and tries to stop it."

"You'll be his hostage instead of his guest if he finds us out."

"If that happens, we can make it so hard on him, he'll pay you to take us back," Vogel said.

Jack laughed and rubbed his hands together in anticipation.

"Shall I call Fatima and make the proposal?" Kane asked.

The partners all nodded their heads.

Kane telephoned Fatima in Huatabampo and switched the receiver to a loudspeaker.

"Hello, dear," he said, the Judas. "I just called because Vogel and I have been worried about you."

"I'm as well as can be expected. How is your grandson?"

"He still has a bad infection."

"And you? Have you calmed down?"

"I'm at work again. We have to find vaqueros and move cattle off the ranches. Is it ever going to rain?"

"When will I see you again? Come to Huatabampo. Bring your grandchildren and stay as my guests at the resort. All young people love the beach. Let's be friends again, like we used to be."

"I'm your friend, Fatima. That hasn't changed." He looked up and saw Vogel roll his eyes and the other partners grin. Even so, everybody was soldier enough to keep quiet.

"That's good, but friends should pay each other frequent visits, not just once or twice during their lifetimes, as you and I have."

"Well, that's the reason I'm calling. My compadre Vogel and I wondered if we could visit La Golondrina in the next few days. A boyhood friend of mine wants me to take him and his son to Mexico to make a documentary film about Arabian horses. I could think of no better *parada* of Arabians in this hemisphere than your father's. I know La Golondrina is a private place, but I thought my friend should see your animals and interview don Nesib and Abdullah. I know you'll love this man."

"Your friend is a filmmaker? Do you know that film is my hobby? What's his name?"

"Well, he hasn't made a name for himself as a filmmaker, but he has as an actor. He's Jack Brennan."

"You mean *my* Jack Brennan? *The* Jack Brennan?"

"Yes, the famous Jack Brennan. The one who starred in *The Outfit*."

"Jim, I love that man. I've seen every one of his movies. Where is he?"

"He's right here. Want to say hello to him?"

"Wonderful."

Kane handed the phone to Jack. "Say hello to Fatima," he said. The man put on such a dazzling smile that Kane was sure that it warmed Fatima's loins straight through the telephone wire all the way to Huatabampo.

"Ay, compadre Jim. *No tienes perdón.* This time God will not pardon you," Vogel said.

⌇

Fatima called back the next day to tell Kane that she had arranged for Jack Brennan's visit to La Golondrina. Billy Buck took an airliner south to inform his contact in the Mexican government about the raid and to obtain weapons and explosives.

Kane and Vogel and the Brennans flew to El Trigo and were met at the airstrip by Che Che with saddle horses and mules. He brought Gato for Kane. Jack Brennan had been raised in Oklahoma by a cowboy uncle. Because of his prowess as a horseman, his first television role as a young-ster had been as the second lead in a western series. During that era of the popular Hollywood Western, actors were required to know how to ride. Directors and producers were not patient with actors who did not look good on a horse.

Joe Brennan knew little about a horse. He was athlete enough to get along with his mule Paseador, but he suffered as he learned to ride. The ride from the airstrip to La Golondrina was a hard one for anyone, and Kane imagined that Joe underwent absolute torture. However, even though every step of the trail was rocky, steep, and uneven, the young man made no complaint. Kane and Vogel stopped often to rest the tender butts, so they arrived at La Golondrina late in the evening.

When they topped La Golondrina Pass they saw that every room in the hacienda was lit up. Two lighted oil lanterns hung for the visitors from the roof of Toribio's ramada at the promontory entrance. Generator-powered electric light flooded the yard. When his guests reached the cornfield, don Nesib signaled for the ranch's band of musicians to play and sing "La Golondrina," the song of the swallow.

"Dammit, it's too bad this old man's outfit kidnapped my grand-daughter, because he's a chivalrous son of a bitch," Kane said under his breath.

"Just remember how the girls looked when we broke into that studio," Vogel said.

Kane was in the lead with Vogel. He stopped to speak to his partners before he could be heard by the Lupinos. "Whatever we do, we can't say anything to each other in privacy that we don't want the Lupinos to know. Eavesdropping is their favorite pastime. They'll listen to what you do in the bathroom. If they hear you talking in your bedroom, they'll plaster themselves against the other side of your door to listen. They'll spy on you. They figure you belong to them while you're here. They live out here in isolation for months at a time with no guests or visitors. They figure it's their right to find out everything they can about you and no rule of etiquette inhibits them. They'll come into your room while you're asleep and listen to you snore if they want to."

The visitors rode up to the front of the hacienda and were formally invited to dismount by don Nesib. He took hold of Gato while Kane dismounted. This surprised Kane. He had expected at least some petulance from the old man for the way he had savaged Rafa, but he shook Kane's hand, then Vogel's, then turned toward the Brennans to be introduced. Fatima came forward, embraced Kane and kissed him on the cheek, did the same with Vogel, walked up to Joe Brennan and introduced herself in Spanish, then smiled close enough into Jack Brennan's face to kiss him. She took charge of Jack and went arm in arm with him into the house ahead of everybody else. She spoke good English, although with a nice, thick Mexican accent, and she looked beautiful.

Don Nesib led them into his living room and gave them drinks. Kane saw no signs of fatigue or pain in the Brennans. Jackie Lee Brennan might look and act as fancy as any actor in Hollywood, but he was tough and brave as a wood hauler. He and Kane had spent their boarding school childhood together laughing one minute and bawling the next. The bawling had been for real hurt, because a boy did not cry frivolously in that place. Somebody had to hurt his heart or his carcass a lot to make him cry. Laughter came easy and filled every other minute. Boxing, football, and bare-knuckle fights behind the gym made them tough. They watched each other when they made tackles in football and jumped all over each other when they missed. They remained friends through every kind of adversity. If they got mad at each other, they knew that sooner or later they would be thrust together in the ring, the place where all differences were resolved. Every bout in the ring was a formal event, an all-out contest, and no place for frivolity. No quarter was asked or given, but all differences were resolved once and for all.

Kane was glad to see that Joe Brennan was another Jack, as tough and smart, as full of the blarney, as ready to laugh after twelve hours on a mountain-climbing mule, and too proud and dignified to admit that he was sore. In the warmth of fellowship and comfort of don Nesib's front room, Kane felt contented. His friends were with him and even his enemy was acting like a friend. What better enemy could a man have than one who feasted and serenaded him?

Kane felt that this first phase of the raid on the Lupinos could not have gone better. Kane and Vogel had breached the fortress with four men and the enemy was glad to see them.

Without Rafa to disgrace them, the Lupinos might not be any more evil than anybody else. Kane and Vogel were not angels. They certainly were not easy on people who did them wrong. In business they did their own kind of pirating. They just thought they had more style than other pirates. In their minds they sometimes did business that might be called bad, but they didn't think they ever did anything that was evil. A rapist cannot show any style, but a pirate has a chance to show a lot of a kind that people admire. The partners' kind of pirate could be chivalrous, generous, and gracious as they took daring risks to rob a rich man of his goods, cattle, horses, and crops. He could be generous with his gains and look good as the devil. The devil at least knows how to show the right amount of style, when he needs to. When he does not, he looks like Rafa.

Two big swallows of mezcal on top of a twelve-hour ride landed inside Kane's gizzards with the right kick. Now he would be graciously given a feast and a serenade by his enemies and looked upon with affection. Awful nice for a pirate to have everything his own way. Nice to be comfortable and content while he cut off the ears of evil bastards who deserved it.

Ali was the only Lupino grandson not present at the supper table. Nesib explained that Ali's patients demanded his dutiful presence at Tucson Hospital. Rafa wore a docile smile and a closed mouth. Kane kept his mouth closed too. He did not want to listen to himself that evening, because he did not like the sound of a hypocrite.

As usual, Vogel spoke as the friendly neighbor, always saying the truth and never being a hypocrite. The Lupinos had become so ingrained with success that they were sure no ax of retribution would ever fall on their necks. Juan Vogel was the one person who could drop the ax on them in a style they liked.

Vogel was used to being called on as an executioner. Anytime someone in his family found a viper under an armload of stove wood, they ran and got Vogel to chop off its head. Anyone who knew him could be certain that the blade he used would be sharp and he would be brave. Vogel was adept at chopping off heads with kind efficiency, and he hardly ever scared his victims. When Kane needed a horse castrated, he called on Vogel. When he needed a beef's throat cut, he called on him. Anytime the community needed a sharp knife or an ax for an execution, it called on him. He executed with style and compassion and always soothed his victim before he applied the blade with verve and awful force.

After supper Jack Brennan poured on the blarney about the beauty of the Sierra Madre and especially La Golondrina hacienda with its quiet, hospitable aura of peace. He could not wait to see don Nesib's horses. The Lupinos marveled at his every move and sound, as his fans had marveled at his performances for fifty years. Kane marveled too. The man sure knew how to do his job with style.

Kane and Joe were assigned a room together. Vogel and Jack were given another room. The hacienda's windows had no curtains. A lot of ranches did not use curtains, the excuse being that nothing but an owl or a coyote would ever look in a window. Kane knew the Lupinos did not put curtains on the windows because they wanted to see what went on in the rooms. Lupinos did not think it was wrong for them to spy on their guests, but had shot Adan Martinillo for spying on them, so they were dangerously serious about surveillance.

Joe set a gym bag with his personal belongings on the floor between their beds. Kane had carried it to La Golondrina on his saddle horn so that Joe would not be bothered with it. Mindful of the open windows, Joe began to unload the contents at his feet. He took out his toothbrush and toothpaste, a bar of soap, and a comb and laid them on the bed. He laid other small, technologically advanced contraptions on the floor between Kane's feet.

When Kane looked down to see what he was doing, Joe pointed to the contraptions and then turned up his empty palms, as if to ask, "What can I do with my spy tools?"

Kane knew they were bugs that Joe intended to distribute around the hacienda so Kane could eavesdrop on the Lupinos during the raid. Out loud, Kane said, "These people will clean every single corner of this room as soon as we leave it. Can you imagine? They'll brush and scrub it clean for our next night of rest. Even when the room has been empty for months, the maids come in every single day to see if a cobweb has accumulated in a corner, or if an ant or a bug has found its way in here. Let's take all our wrappers and any bugs we might discover out with us when we go. I've seen Fatima catch flies and other bugs in the house and turn them loose outside the minute I left the room. We ought to do that with any bugs we find and save her the trouble." He laughed.

Joe put his contraptions back in the handbag. They might be three hundred miles from nowhere, but Kane wanted him to know that they would not have as much privacy as they would in the rest room of a gas station.

The next day Nesib introduced the Brennans to Abdullah and his Arabian horses. Kane and Vogel were not given a private moment with Abdullah. All the talk was about movies, and Jack made himself the leader of the project right away and Fatima translated.

Kane saw that the establishment of a beachhead at La Golondrina had been accomplished. Nesib agreed to allow Jack to film the daily schedule of his horses, so a time for the start of the filming needed to be established. Kane said that he and Vogel would not be able to bring Jack back for another month because of other business. Jack quickly said that he would not be free for another month, either. Kane, Jack, and Vogel looked at a calendar together and without a word or a glance to each other placed their forefingers on the date of the darkest night of the month as the day to begin filming. All three nodded that they could be at La Golondrina on that date. Rafa would furnish the crew, cameras, light, and sound, and serve as assistant director and producer. Jack would be brought back in time to begin filming on August third. With that, the partners also established that the date of the raid on La Culebra would be in the dark of the moon.

Sixteen

—〰— Dolly Ann had stayed late with Cody Joe in the hospital after Kane and Vogel left for the 7X and had begun to read Will James's *Smokey the Cowhorse* to him. He did not read enough to suit her. She thought that he would find the fun of reading if she made him more aware of good stories. All he wanted to do was play sports. Now, as she read him James's great story, he only yawned and looked way off at infinity like an old Longhorn steer that wanted out of the corral.

Ali Lupino bustled into the room in fresh, starched white coat and khaki slacks, his swarthy face clean-shaven and every hair on his head in place. At first he busied himself at the foot of the bed with Cody Joe's chart and did not say anything. Cody Joe and Dolly Ann fell silent and Dolly Ann found herself studying Ali's hands. They were slender and fragile, the fingers long and delicate, the nails flawlessly manicured. The thumbs were long and thin and more like fingers. Dolly Ann thought, *If the son of a gun ever had to do a day's work in a corral with those hands, he'd cripple himself for a year. A layer of dirt and the heat of a day's sun would shrivel them up like prunes.*

After Ali satisfied himself with the information on the chart, he looked down his nose at Dolly Ann. "Well, well, what have we here?" he announced. "Who are you, young lady? Where has my favorite patient been hiding you?"

"Who're you?" Dolly Ann asked.

"This is Ali Lupino, Sister," Cody Joe said.

Dolly Ann turned away, closed the book, and placed it on the bed table.

"You know, I heard that you were a little beauty and now I see you really are," Ali cooed. "I knew that someday we'd meet, but I always wondered when. I was afraid your brother would be transferred out of my care before it happened."

Dolly Ann turned and looked him in the eye. "Imagine that," she said. "I never thought of you at all. In fact, I would have liked it if every one of you Lupinos had been wiped off the face of the earth before I ever heard the name." She turned away and did not look at him again.

"You're not serious, are you, girl? Can you be so stupid that you blame me for the pranks my brother played on you? I'm not anything like Rafa."

"Oh, and your brother Güero isn't like you either, I suppose. He's your bastard brother too, isn't he?"

"Güero's just another prankster. That's all. A clown. I've been told that he is solely to blame for any harm that might have been done, but as I understand it, you came away totally unharmed. Haven't you heard? All the problems have been solved between your family and mine. My mother and grandfather intend to make everything right with you in every way possible."

"Pranksters, are they?" Cody Joe said. He sat up and eased his legs out of bed. "You call stripping two girls naked and ordering a man to rape them and cut their throats in front of a room full of people only a prank?"

"I don't know what kind of joke my brother or Güero tried to pull, but I know that no real harm was done, or intended. Even so, I've served as your physician and friend since your grandfather brought you to this hospital. As your doctor, I'm here to see to all your injuries."

"Let me tell you something, Lupino," Cody Joe said quietly. "You have no business of any kind here in this room. You're not my doctor and you're not our friend. I've put up with you while I've been under this hospital's care, because my grandfather has, but stay away from me and my sister when he's not with us, because we don't like you. You might think your kinfolk made peace with my grandfather, but none of you can ever make peace with us."

"But I'm not here to make peace with you, boy. I have no quarrel with you and never have. I'm your physician."

"No, you're not. I'm a United States Marine and you're my enemy, and so is all the rest of your bastard family."

"Let's please start over, here. Remember me? I've been at your side since the Montenegros carried you into the Sanatorio Lourdes in Rio Alamos. To be friends is in the best interests of our families. At least, the three of us here in this room can make a new start, because we've never had a quarrel. Look, let me take you both to dinner. I'm sure I can get Cody released to my care for the evening."

"Go look in the mirror," Dolly Ann growled. "You have the same look in your eye as your bastard brothers did when they tied me and Luci Martinillo naked to a bedpost, and you let off the same stink. You might talk nice and wear cologne, but the look in your eye is black as a hellhole and you stink like a dead carcass. Get out and take your Lupino stench with you."

"If I'm discharged as Cody's physician, I'll need it in writing."

"You wormy joke," Cody Joe said. "Get out of here."

Ali finally got it and showed that he did. "I won't be dismissed by you, you pitiful dog," he said quietly. "Keep this in mind, then. I *am* your enemy, and I'll always be nearby. Watch for me, because I might hire someone to step out of your bedroom closet with a butcher knife for your throat. You want to be rid of me, you fool? I want everything my brothers want and more. You can't just declare your enmity and make me go away. The same way I might have healed you, I shall make you sick. Before I'm through with you, I'll cause the flesh to rot off your bones. And for a starter, I'll do this." He drew a scalpel from a sheath in his breast pocket, grabbed a handful of Dolly Ann's ponytail, and cut it off. Before either of the youngsters could move, he fled the room.

Cody Joe shut the door and began to put on his street clothes.

"What do you think you're doing, Brother?" Dolly Ann asked. Calmly, she went to the basin mirror and showed herself the back of her hair.

"You don't plan to stay here tonight, do you?" Cody Joe said.

"No. You got any scissors? I need to trim a little more of my hair off the back. I've been thinking I'd cut off my ponytail, but kept postponing it. Maybe we ought to run Little Farfel down and thank him."

"I'll run him down when I can, but first let's get out of here. I can't stay in this hospital one more minute. I'd like to have at least one night out before I check in at Fort Huachuca. Little Farfel, as you call him, had a good idea when he asked us out to eat. Let's go have a steak, then I'll take you home so nobody'll get you."

⌐⌐

The youngsters got into Cody Joe's pickup and drove to the Santa Rita Hotel. Its restaurant was a favorite place for the Kanes to eat and meet with business associates and friends. Cody Joe's pockets were full of the money the partners had given him for riding Gato in the race. He and Dolly Ann sat down at a corner table that was already set up with a clean tablecloth and napkins, a pitcher of ice water, crystal glasses, and silver place settings. They ordered T-bone steaks.

The hour was late and the youngsters were the only customers in the place. Even their waiter had gone away when Ali walked up to the table. This time his arrogant look exactly resembled Rafa's. His black, unblinking eyes fixed on them. Cody Joe had only seen the man dart and dash about on doctor's errands in the hospital, his eyes focused on his business. At work, his eyes never showed care or compassion for people, only that he was intent on the quick dispatch of his chores. Now they showed that he cared a lot. They showed his hate for the Kanes. They had turned so black and hard they glittered and their pupils had disappeared.

"I followed you out of the hospital, then followed your shabby little truck here," Ali said. "When you leave here, I'll follow you to the place where you hope to sleep. When you sleep, I'll send someone to get you. You won't know when. It will be a surprise."

Cody Joe tried to shove his chair away from the table, but the infected leg failed him and he almost upset the chair.

Ali's mouth grinned and he dropped a hand on Cody Joe's shoulder to hold him down. "Steady, Kane," he said. "It won't do you any good to get excited every time you see me. I won't harm you. It's your sister I want. How do you think she will look with only one ear? Jim Kane likes to earmark people, does he? Soon he will be able to identify the pick of the Kane litter by the *Lupino* earmark."

He reached to lift Dolly Ann's chin with a forefinger and she let him, then doused his face with a full glass of ice water. He stumbled backward as though he had been clubbed and his mouth opened wide so he could take the big breath that the ice water had shocked away. Dolly Ann's aim had been so good that not much of the water missed his face. He reached for a folded napkin on the table and Cody Joe grabbed his wrist, jerked him toward himself, pounded the outside of the elbow of the outstretched arm with the heel of his hand, and heard the joint pop. The overextension of everything that held the elbow together shocked Ali's mouth as wide open as the ice water had done.

Cody Joe pulled down on the arm and brought Ali's face close to his. Ali struggled to lift his chest off the table.

"I don't have my knife, so I can't earmark you, Lupino," Cody Joe said. "I wouldn't want your blood to mess up our nice tablecloth, anyway. I don't think I'm strong enough to break your bones right now, but I can be hell on your joints." He grabbed the thumb of the hand he held and twisted it until it snapped. When the fingers on the hand splayed out and stiffened with the pain, Cody Joe pounded the heel of his hand on their ends and jammed all the knuckles. He stood and jerked up on the shoulder socket to stand Ali off the table. "You want to follow us around?" he asked. "Follow this." He jerked Ali toward him and stomped his boot heel down on the outside of his knee, pulled him so he had to stand on it again, then stomped it again to make sure the joint came undone. When Ali howled and raised his free hand in supplication, or agony, or surprise, Cody Joe pounded the ends of his fingers and jammed them too, then bent them back until they broke, grabbed that wrist, jerked the arm straight, and disjointed the other elbow. The pain sent Ali into shock and he slumped to the floor, stiffened under the table, and mewed. Cody Joe stomped him heavily on both his slender little ankles.

Alarmed by what she had seen her marine brother do, Dolly Ann tried to pull him toward the door. He still had a good hold on one of Ali's wrists, so he twisted that thumb until it popped, then dropped the arm and went with her.

Outside, Dolly Ann looked Cody Joe in the eye, shook her head, and said, "Us Kanes. I wonder when our plight will be over."

Cody Joe examined the calm look on his sister's face. "I know how you feel, Sister," he said. "I guess war's always just hell until it's over, so we'll just have to be ready."

⌒

Billy Buck and Martinillo returned to El Trigo from their reconnaissance of La Culebra Canyon a day after Kane, Vogel, and the Brennans returned from La Golondrina. The next morning Che Che and his wife made them breakfast, then cleared away the table so they could sit with coffee and plan the assault. Each phase of the raid and every bit of conversation, even the trivial, was first laid out in Spanish, then Kane translated it into English word for word for the Americans.

Vogel and Jack would train with the raiders that month, but they needed to be at work on the film at La Golondrina at the time of the raid on August third. They would not risk communication with the raiders while they were at La Golondrina.

The reconnaissance gave the partners the information they needed on the sentries at La Culebra, the armament and explosives required for the raid, and the number of people who would go on it. They planned to destroy a hundred hectares of ripe opium poppies, the bunkhouse where thirty Arabs and Los Lobos thugs slept, a plant where opium was cooked, and a warehouse big as a hay barn stored with fuel and armament. By the time of the raid, it would probably also be stocked with part of the harvest of opium gum.

Each raider would carry a Russian AK-47 rifle. The partners calculated the weight of the explosives and armament that would be taken on the raid and decided they needed three pack mules and five saddle horses and mules. Kane, Martinillo, Che Che, Billy Buck, and Joe Brennan were to go on the raid. The march on the target from the Cerro Prieto staging area would take seven hours. The flight back to staging would take four hours or less. The assault phase was all uphill to the target. The flight back to staging was so straight downhill it would practically be an airborne operation.

The men were given their assignments that morning. Che Che would lead the file as scout, because he knew the trails as well by night as Lupino's sentries knew them by day. Kane would follow him and lead a pack mule. Joe would follow Kane and lead a pack mule, and Billy would follow Joe with the third pack mule. Martinillo would guard their back trail as the last man in the file. Che Che and Martinillo were to carry halogen lanterns for emergency use on that darkest of nights.

As the unit began to climb the first mountain of the high Sierra, the men would unsling their rifles and carry them at the ready. At the ravine, the team would dismount on the cliff edge 150 yards above the target buildings, tie the animals head to tail without changing their order in the string, and unload the weapons.

Martinillo and Joe would man RPG-7 antitank weapons, the Russian equivalent of the American Bazooka, and fire phosphorous rockets. The bunkhouse was to be their first target. Three rockets were to be launched into each building. Che Che would help load the rockets, attend to the needs of the shooters, and light the canyon with a halogen lantern. The rockets would pierce the adobe walls of the buildings and explode inside. The first rocket would probably light up the whole canyon. After that, the raiders hoped that the burning buildings would provide all the light they needed.

During his first reconnaissance of the ravine, Martinillo had seen that kerosene, avgas, and explosive armament were among the most volatile supplies stored inside the warehouse. He knew that kerosene was stored there because he recognized the black *barricas*, twenty-liter barrels that were used to transport it by mule and by airplane to mercantile stores in the Sierra. The avgas was in blue barricas. Billy warned the partners to expect a lot of shrapnel, flying debris, and flame when the fuel barrels, rockets, grenades, and ammunition went off in the warehouse. He also knew from his experience in Afghanistan that the five-pound clods of opium gum would make a beautiful, multicolored, gushing flame.

Billy Buck would fire American M-79 incendiary rifle grenades into the poppy field from the rim of the ravine. From experience he knew that an opium crop was as flammable as lighter fluid. The poppy bulb was fat with sap, or resin, that gushed with a torchlike flame when ignited. He asked the partners to each say a rosary for a breeze to come along and spread the flames. He loved the lightweight M-79 launcher that resembled a sawed-off shotgun with a large bore. The grenades only made a *poof* sound when they left the muzzle, and they armed themselves to explode on contact after they were thirty-five feet away from the shooter.

After Martinillo, Joe, and Che Che filled the buildings and any aircraft that was there with white hot phosphorous, they would direct automatic rifle fire on the people who ran out of the buildings. Kane's assignment was to hold the horses and protect the gunners' backs. La Culebra's sentries could be expected to come running when the shooting started.

The horses and mules would be conditioned to the small arms fire during the next month of training. They could not be conditioned to the brightness of the phosphorous, the explosions of the rockets, grenades, and barrels of fuel that would cause a rain of shrapnel and metal debris. Kane could expect that the animals would try to break away during the fireworks.

Each man was responsible for the placement of the saddles and the tightness of the cinches on his animals at all times. All weapons and ammunition would be returned to the same pack animals. Nothing but empty cartridge cases would be left behind. Every round of small arms ammunition would be smeared with garlic.

The partners would set up a hidden camp in a stand of pines on the rim of El Carrizal, a box canyon that branched off Arroyo Hondo. No trails led to that campsite. The seven men would eat and sleep on a spot where they could see fifty miles in every direction: to the Sea of Cortez in the west, to La Golondrina in the north, to the village of Guadalupe Victoria in the east, and to the Camino Real, the main trail for horseshoe traffic between Sonora and Chihuahua, to the south. A brush corral for the horses and mules would be built in El Carrizal Canyon below the camp.

The horses and mules were to undergo severe training. El Carrizal was at the same altitude as the high Sierra of La Golondrina and the animals would be ridden hard for the next month. Three days before the raid, they would be ridden and packed to San Bernardo and trucked from there to Vogel's ranch at Cibolibampo.

Little Buck would not be used in the raid. The bobtail truck that would be used could not be traced to the partners. Any animal crippled on the raid would be destroyed by incendiary grenade to prevent identification. No dead or wounded raiders would be left behind.

All the necessary weapons, ammunition, and explosives had been delivered by Billy Buck's Mexican counterparts by Mexican Navy cutter to a remote beach on the Sea of Cortez and stored in a safe house.

During the four weeks that remained before the raid, all seven partners would study the maintenance and care of the AK-47s and RPG-7s. Every hand would snap in and take rifle practice with live ammunition, and their animals would stand close by to become accustomed to the noise. Che Che, Martinillo, and Billy Buck would design a sandbox that would show the topography of the terrain between Cerro Prieto and La Culebra and would include every trail, mountain, canyon, building, and aircraft that the raiders would traverse and target.

The box canyon of El Carrizal was four miles from El Trigo and the most secluded area in the region for their camp and activities. Their rifle fire in the canyon could not be heard a mile away. The closest other ranch, except Martinillo's Las Animas, was more than ten miles away, so the hideout would be their own secret sound stage.

Every man on the team would be trained to do every other man's job. All would undergo daily physical training.

Kane asked Martinillo again where the Arabs and pelones stored their weapons.

"The bearded teacher made the pupils stack them in the big warehouse every evening before supper, and he always locked the door and pocketed the key," Martinillo said.

"They must be awful sure that nobody will give them trouble," Kane said. "Did they keep any weapons close at hand in case of attack?"

"Only the sentries on the rim of the canyon kept their weapons."

"Are you sure the Arab locks the door?"

"He did when I was there."

"I wonder who he thought would steal from him?"

"I thought they might have kept their weapons in the bunkhouse after they caught me spying on them, but no, when Billy and I were there they locked everything up as before."

"Good. That will make it easier for us to cull that bunch of trained pests away from humankind," Kane said. "I only wish we could catch a whole convention of them up there."

The raiders would wear black from head to toe, including black hoods. They would charcoal their light-colored boots. Dark colored animals would be used. White marks on their horses and mules would be blackened with charcoal. One phosphorous grenade was to be assigned to each animal and fastened to his saddle, in case it had to be destroyed.

Kane asked Martinillo if he could get Lucrecia to make the black coveralls and masks. Martinillo said he thought she would be glad to do it.

"Let's talk about Kosterlinsky," Vogel said. "What if he bivouacs within the sound of our gunfire and bombs?"

"No matter where he is, when the raid starts, we should have the advantage of surprise," Kane said. "We'll certainly try to have him located before we fire the first shot. If he bivouacs too close to La Culebra, we might decide to turn around and try again some other night. Remember, we ought to complete our destruction of the camp in only a few minutes. If he rushes toward the sounds of the assault, he'll meet black riders on dark mounts head-on. His troop will be in single file on the trail as we are. He will not recognize what we are, and he'll have little time to organize his troop to spread out and open fire. There are no straight and level stretches on that trail between La Culebra and Cerro Prieto, so if we encounter him it will be with a suddenness that will astound him. We'll have our rifles ready and hope he does not. We can't predict what will happen after that, but we'll drill for every possibility we can imagine."

"One more thing," Vogel said. "We haven't said enough about the sentries."

"Only two sentries patrol our side of the ravine," Billy said. "Martinillo and I were at La Culebra two nights. On both nights the sentries slept in bivouac with the cavalry troop. If the troop is in bivouac at its usual campsite on top the mountain when the assault begins, the sentries will probably be with it. If the cavalry is not in the vicinity, we have no idea from this reconnaissance where the sentries will be. We'll have to slip in and blow up targets to attract them so we can kill them, because we'll never find them in that darkness before the first phosphorous rocket goes off."

"I thought about that too," Kane said. "I'll have to head off the sentries when they come running."

"How about the sentries who are posted on the other side of the ravine? What kind of trouble will they give you?" Vogel asked.

"None," Billy said. "They're a quarter mile away. Their Uzis don't have the range to bother us, and they'll never make it across the ravine in time to do us harm. The canyon will be so lit up with phosphorous that we'll be able to pick them off if they try to cross it anyway."

Everybody was assigned his mount for the raid. Vogel and Jack Brennan would ride a pair of well-built, dog-gentle, El Trigo mules to La Golondrina. Che Che would ride Vogel's Colorado, a dark bay horse with no white marks on him. Martinillo would ride the dark brown Paseador mule, because they knew each other so well. Joe Brennan would ride the black Negrito mule, because the animal was smooth, surefooted, and wise enough for both rider and mount. Billy Buck would ride Kane's horse Lagarto, a dark roan with a round white spot on his forehead. That spot and several tiny white spots on his hips would have to be blackened. His sides also had white spots on them, but they would be under the saddle. A few swatches of wet charcoal would make him invisible in the dark.

Che Che would furnish three dark brown mules to carry the cargo. Kane had seen them at the hacienda. They were so perfectly matched, they could have been triplets. They were so stocky and well muscled that Kane had already remarked to Vogel that they must be half quarter horse. Che Che could not have taken them from the partners' mares, so they must have been sired by one of their studs. Kane asked Vogel about that.

"What would you do if it was your job to take care of good horses that belonged to owners who lived hundreds of kilometers away and you wanted your donkey mares bred to their studs?" Vogel asked.

Kane grinned.

"You'd invite one of your bosses' studs to a party every time one of your *burritas* came in heat, and you would keep inviting studs until you found one who liked a little strange stuff. After all, with your bosses far away, what would be the problem? Ownership is established by the dam, not the stud, anyway."

"Ay, compadre. Why did I even ask?" Kane said. "We taught the youngster well, did we not? Otherwise who could have furnished us with better pack mules for this sashay?"

Kane gave Che Che a token scowl, and Che Che looked down at his hands and said, "I have nothing to say."

"What youngster? Che Che's fifty-five years old, compadre," Vogel said.

"That old and we've yet to give him a good stud?"

"I guess that's right, but I don't think he wants a horse. He has no use for one. He's learned how to furnish himself with everything he wants up here in this Sierra where nothing is ever given to him."

"That's good, then," Kane said.

Kane decided to ride Gato. When he announced this, not one of his partners objected, although he suspected that they thought the horse might be too young and green for magnified, grownup, nighttime fireworks on the edges of cliffs.

"He's a youngster," Kane said. "But I could ask for no better partner on this raid. He'll probably be my last top horse, and I want him to do this with me. No one will see how dashing a figure of a man on a horse we will make in the dark, but I want to make it anyway.

"This could be the old geezer's last sashay, and how could anything be better for a man who has spent his life in search of one good mount after another? I've owned a lot of good horses, but only two that I called my top horse, and young Gato is the second. I won't ever look for another. Young as he is, I already know he's a marvelous horse and evidently so do you. None of you has been so fearful that he asked if I thought we ought to wear steel helmets on this sashay, so I don't think I'm imposing on you by riding a green horse. We'll all sacrifice enough style by wearing black masks and coveralls, and we'll have to think about leaving our hats at home. I'm too old and set in my ways to ride a safe, foolproof horse for my last raid. I have to do as I always have, risk it all on my best, high-powered animal. To do that, I'll go on one that might be unpredictable and make a mistake, but ay caray, how I will go."

Kane translated what he had said for the Americans and they laughed.

"Before you felt you had to make this speech about the mount you intend to ride, I had made up my mind to speak for Jack and tell you that you and Joe should be the ones to go to La Golondrina and make the movie," Vogel said. "Jack and I should go on the raid, because we are better raiders, and I want to ride Gato."

"Next time." Kane laughed. "This time, you be the moviemakers and we'll be the brigands."

"OK," Jack said. "We don't mind furnishing the diversion this time, but next time we go on the raid."

"We'll have to find somebody else to raid then, Jack," Kane said. "The Lupinos will never get over this. Even if the financial loss and the wipeout of their thugs don't cripple them, their sensibilities will fall into a funk. They're going to think their asses have been laid bare for all of Mexico to see. They'll probably get in bed and cover up their heads until the Muslims take over the world."

"You hope," Jack said. "I hope so too."

"Don't anyone get caught, that's all," Vogel said. "Stay on your horses and stay together. You'll have to stay close to one another in that darkness, or you won't all come home together."

"Let's hope we can shoot everybody so there'll be no pursuit," Billy said. "If we destroy them all, they can't come out of the ravine after us, no, Martinillo?"

Martinillo smiled gently and extended his hand for one of Vogel's cigarettes.

That afternoon, Kane flew to Camauiroa with Billy to get the first load of armament. The next morning he went alone and brought back the second load, provisions for their camp at El Carrizal, and bolts of thin, black, cotton material. The other partners caught up the horses and mules and set up the camp.

Che Che met Kane at the airstrip with Gato, Colorado, and the triplet black mules at sundown and helped him unload the cargo and pack it to El Carrizal. They saw a glimmer of the Carrizal campfire from high on the Arroyo Hondo trail beneath the airstrip, then did not see it again until it warmed their hearts as they rode into camp.

Billy and Martinillo gave them a swallow of mezcal and served them a campfire supper of fried beef jerky, eggs, and coffee that Lucrecia had brought from Las Animas. She had come to see Martinillo and had already gone home. She had been too long alone without her husband and family, so he had been obliged to tell her that he would only be an hour away from her at El Carrizal. When Kane heard that, he told Martinillo to saddle Paseador and go home. He could commute every day from Las Animas.

Kane asked Martinillo to take the bolts of black cloth for the coveralls and masks to Lucrecia. This brought a laugh out of his partners, but he reminded them that they had agreed to wear black, and now they would have to be fitted for it. Martinillo said he would bring Lucrecia to camp the next day to take their measurements.

Kane and Jack unrolled their beds on the ground outside their tent beside each other because the night was clear. Kane would have liked to groan as he unraveled himself in bed, as a grandfather would do when he lay down near somebody who cared. He gritted his teeth instead. He might be old and sore, but he got stronger every day, and brigands did not groan. He had not heard one complaint from his friend Jackie Lee Brennan. He did not think Jack had uttered a complaint since he first met him in 1942 at Saint Michaels, when Kane was eleven and Jack was nine. Jack's mother worked as a Harvey Girl in the Alvarado Restaurant at the Albuquerque train depot. His father had died on the USS *Arizona* at Pearl Harbor on December 7, 1941. The day they met, Jack and Kane had chosen each other as lifelong friends. When one had something, so did the other, and they had never groaned or complained to each other.

"Thanks for letting me in on this," Jack said when he settled in his bedroll.

"Thanks for throwing in with me again. We're awful lucky to have you and Joe," Kane said. "When was the last time you spent a night outside like this?"

"I can't remember the last time I even looked at the stars. That's why I thanked you. Before I came down here, I was getting old. I'm not old enough to get as old as I was getting."

"You're in good shape. I had been on my ass for eighteen months and had gone soft, myself."

"Well, you won't get any softer now, but you might get your ass shot off."

"Who could ever imagine such a thing?"

"This is a good idea, for me to hide in this timber and train on these trails to get ready for the raid, even if Vogel and I aren't going."

"You never know when you need to be in shape. My granny used to say that her church was the great outdoors, and when you sleep on the ground and cover yourself with the stars, you'll be in a lot better shape than people who don't. I figured we'd even get smarter if we did this."

They slept.

Kane made another trip to Camauiroa for the last of the armament the next morning. The rest of the partners finished cutting brush to fence a pasture of grass and browse for their animals.

The training routine for the raid began the morning after that. Che Che was the first man up to build the fire and put on the coffee. Martinillo and Joe wrangled the horses and Billy helped Che Che cook breakfast. The three oldsters hung morrals full of grain and alfalfa pellets on the horses and mules and took responsibility for their care and for the maintenance of the tack and pack gear. They brought in spare saddle horses and pack mules in case any broke down in training. Kane did the shoeing, not because he liked to do it, but because nobody else in the world did it to suit him.

All seven partners did a half hour of calisthenics before breakfast, supervised by Joe or Billy. After breakfast Billy gave them school on weapons. Each of the raiders was constantly reminded of his place in the order of march on the trail. The order was strictly observed in every drill. Vogel and Jack brought up the rear on every sashay and led the spare horses tied head to tail to condition them.

Every day the raiders saddled their horses and packed their mules with all the gear they would carry on the raid, and then struck out on the trail uphill for two hours of conditioning. At the end of the second hour, they dismounted and set up for a dry run with the RPG-7 antitank weapons.

After they rehearsed the unpacking and manning of the weapons in a dry run, and repacked and remounted in proper order, they rode another conditioning hour downhill back to camp. They pushed their animals hard, but paced themselves and stayed together in a tight group. They walked and cooled their animals another half hour before they grained them, then turned them out into the brush-fenced pasture to rest. In the afternoon they studied their weapons and rehearsed each step each man would take in the raid. Each partner stood up and recited his role, from the time he packed his mule with the gear he would carry and saddled his horse at the Cerro Prieto staging area, until he repacked his mule and left the ravine after the assault.

Vogel gave Joe riding lessons, and he soon found his seat on Negrito. Problems such as an encounter with government cavalry or the crippling of a horse were discussed and resolved and a practice drill devised for each contingency. They used pine logs as dummy animals, then blindfolded themselves and saddled the logs with riding saddles and pack saddles, then packed the same gear in the same places on the pack saddles, then unpacked the gear and set up for the assault, then repacked it, as they would on the night of the assault in the dark of the moon. They practiced their knots, especially the sheet bend they would use to string their animals together head to tail. Blindfolded, they led their animals up and tied them head to tail, then untied them, then tied them again.

The partners used their time around the fire for school, discussion, rehearsal, and planning. During the first week they snapped in every day with their AK-47s. That meant they wound their slings on their arms to hold their rifles still and practiced firing from the standing, sitting, kneeling, and prone positions. They carried their rifles at the ready when they moved horseback. They carried them during the conditioning rides and when they packed and unpacked the mules and manned the other weapons. They kept their rifles with them in camp. Like soldiers and marines, they made constant companions of their rifles.

Vogel and Jack Brennan participated in the routine as though they would go on the raid. They trained in case the raid would have to go without the movie diversion at La Golondrina.

During the second week the partners practiced daily two-hour sessions of live fire. They used black bull's-eye and silhouette targets that came with the armament, and Kane was satisfied that every raider finished that week a marksman. They practiced firing a half hour every afternoon with the sun in their eyes, because they expected to fire their rifles with the white light of the phosphorous rockets and grenades in their eyes on the night of the raid.

On conditioning rides during the final week, the seven partners rode with loaded rifles. Kane pointed out targets and ordered different raiders to take snap shots at them from atop their horses. They trained the entire third week at night, did all their saddling and loading, all their unloading, set ups, snapping-in with aimed rifles, and conditioning rides after dark. They found their gear and set it up with only the light of the moon and stars, mindful that on the night of the raid, they would have no moonlight. Che Che and Martinillo would be equipped with the most powerful, portable halogen lanterns manufactured by man, lanterns that shined brighter than daylight.

Lucrecia was the only person outside the seven raiders whose aid Kane had enlisted. She brought the black coveralls and hoods to the camp on a burro. She had made the masks with evenly sewn, oblong eyeholes. The comments the raiders made when they saw how their partners looked in raider suits made her giggle. She had made them for Vogel and Jack Brennan too. She asked everyone to put them on so she could see how they fit. She made each of them parade past her and pirouette. As a *pilón*, an extra boon to her work, she gave each man a pair of gloves of the same material.

Kane looked around at his partners in their raider suits and black hoods, and then looked for the old black hat he had resurrected for the raid, put it on, and found that it no longer fit. "If I wear the hood, I won't be able to keep my hat on," he said. "My head will be too big. If I loose my hat, I won't be able to stop and go back for it. People know me by the shape of my hat. Why didn't I think of that, before? We can't wear our hats."

"Can you go naked into battle?" Vogel laughed.

"Who cares?" Joe said. "I know you don't like to go anywhere without your hat, Jim, but who's going to see you in the night? You don't want to be seen, anyway."

"I care. I'll see myself. I can't feel right without my hat, can I, compadre? You wouldn't either, would you?"

"No, but you're the one who wanted the hoods and it's a good idea. Unless someone can identify you by your saddles and your mounts, you'll be unidentifiable with the hoods on. And you're right, even when people can't see our faces, they know us by our hats."

"How in the chingado can I swashbuckle without my hat? What's the use of even going on a raid if I can't wear my hat?"

"Why not wear them?" Martinillo said. "I'm wearing mine. I've never considered not wearing it. The Lupinos won't find my hat, because I won't lose it. And if they do and come after me, they'll be sorry."

"*Vale madre*. I'm wearing it," Kane said. "I'm too old to go anywhere without my hat."

"Eso." Vogel laughed. "Do it. Put the hoods in your pockets in case you need them."

"What if you lose a hat on the trail?" Joe asked. "Think about it. Won't it lead the Lupinos to our door?"

"Vaqueros don't lose their hats," Martinillo said. "My compadres Jim and Juan and have kept them on in the wind and brush for seventy-five years. I have done so for sixty-five. That's practice enough to keep them on for one more night."

"If my compadre Jim loses his hat, he has to buy breakfast for everybody." Vogel laughed

Three days before the raid, Kane flew alone to Rio Alamos. That night, he drove back to San Bernardo in an undocumented bobtail truck supplied by Beto Montenegro. Martinillo, Che Che, Billy, and Joe rode down from El Carrizal with the animals and equipment and waited for him at San Bernardo. Kane hauled them in the bobtail to Vogel's Cibolibampo ranch before first light. Vogel and Jack packed the El Carrizal camp to El Trigo on the extra animals and hit the trail for La Golondrina the next morning.

Seventeen

〜〜〜 Vogel and Jack Brennan arrived at La Golondrina early in the afternoon on the day before the raid. Fatima ushered them into the house for coffee and a swallow of mezcal, but then Rafa hustled them outside to the stables where he had assembled the crew and the camera, light, and sound equipment for the documentary. His crew consisted of the hacienda's household, stable, farm, and vaquero workers.

Jack had written a script while at El Carrizal, so he was ready to begin. Fatima would translate his interview with the elder Lupino for the first scene. The script called for don Nesib to lead the camera through the stable to an interview with the ageless Abdullah in his living quarters. With Fatima acting as interpreter, Jack intended to tell about the Arabian traditions of horsemanship that Abdullah had brought to the Sierra Madre from his home in the Arabian desert. The first day also called for don Nesib to show off his stallions, broodmares, and cow horses.

That was what Jack's script called for. However, when they arrived at the stables, they found Abdullah and Ibrahim had packed three mules with their beds and tools and were prepared to leave for La Culebra. Vogel and Jack knew that this would not be good for the raiders who planned to hit the ravine the following night, right after Abdullah and Ibrahim arrived in the bull's-eye of the target. The seven partners had agreed not to target the Lupinos, Abdullah, the hacienda at La

Golondrina, or its help. Besides that, they did not want to be found by the rifle sights of Ibrahim and Abdullah and not be able to shoot back.

Jack shook hands with Ibrahim and Abdullah, took great pleasure as a filmmaker in their hawk-like faces and carriage, and asked Rafa to take his picture with them. He then asked Rafa to ready his crew and equipment to film Abdullah and Ibrahim as they prepared the horses and mules for a trip, because he needed that kind of footage for his film.

When Ibrahim told Fatima that he and Abdullah intended to leave La Golondrina within the next fifteen minutes, Jack acted flabbergasted. "Why do they have to leave today?" he asked "We need them here all week. We're trying to make a movie, for God's sake." He put on his astounded director's face.

"They're needed in the high Sierra for the corn harvest," Fatima said.

Vogel realized that Abdullah and Ibrahim were going to La Culebra to harvest opium gum, not corn. He wondered how Jack would hold them at La Golondrina.

"These two are the most colorful characters on the ranch," Jack told Fatima. "We have to have them. We can't leave them out of the film any more than we can leave out the horses. They have to stay."

Fatima drew her father aside to explain Jack's need for Abdullah and Ibrahim. Don Nesib bowed his head and listened but did not comment. Fatima called Jack over and asked him to explain his need to don Nesib. Abdullah and Ibrahim finished packing their mules, tied personal items on their saddles, slung rifles over their backs, mounted, and rode away on the trail toward the high Sierra.

Jack looked up and saw that the two hawks were about to disappear around a high bend in the trail. "Fatima," he said, "they're leaving. Where are they going, and when will they be back?" He put on his devastated director's look that said, "There goes my movie."

Jack looked at Vogel, then at his hosts. Nobody was paying any attention to him. No one looked up to see where Abdullah and Ibrahim had gone, either. The hawks of La Golondrina had taken flight and might never come back, because they were headed for an aerie that was about to blow up.

At that moment Kosterlinsky and his troop appeared at the gateway to the hacienda and Toribio, the lookout, announced them. The troop came on in a rush with chains and accoutrements rattling in cadence. Captain Kosterlinsky raised his arm to the sky and called a halt in the front yard.

Jack had listened to talk about this troop for the past four weeks and now studied it closely with a marine's good eye. The troopers carried their rifles in saddle scabbards. Only Kosterlinsky and the carrier of the unit banner carried side arms. Both their pistol holsters were covered by hoods that folded over the grips.

Jack announced that he would use the cavalry troop in his movie. When he found out that Kosterlinsky spoke English, he told him that he needed his troop for two days. Kosterlinsky graciously answered that it could be available that day and the morning of the next, but he would have to take it back on patrol the next afternoon. Jack decided to work the troop so hard it would be too tired to do anything but stay in bivouac at La Golondrina until the morning of the third day. He did not want Kosterlinsky and Jim Kane to come face to face in the high Sierra.

Jack saw that Kosterlinsky was in love with the idea of being in a movie. That first afternoon, he worked the captain, his troop, and his horses until the sweat rolled off them, then worked them until it dried, then worked them until it rolled off again. He filmed an interview about horses with Kosterlinsky until deep in the night. He asked how they were obtained, what the Army's criteria was for cavalry animals, and the names of the colors and breeds it preferred. Kosterlinsky's commentary was mediocre, and he told such long, sonorous stories that Jack began to feel abused. He had thought he could tire the man enough so that he would want to lie down on the ground and sleep, as a true combat soldier would do after a battle. Instead, before Kosterlinsky finished with him, he was so desperate for sleep himself, he had to turn his head away and pry his eyes open with his fingers.

The raiders rested at Vogel's camp in the thicket of Cibolibampo on the coastal desert. They cleaned their weapons and wrote letters, as soldiers do when they are about to go into combat. They came together periodically to plan and review their roles again. They smeared garlic on their rifle ammunition. The next morning they made their final preparations, then slept through the afternoon and ate a supper of broiled beefsteak and beans boiled in their own soup at sundown. Before they loaded themselves and their animals in the bobtail and the pickup, they blackened their faces with mesquite charcoal.

Under cover of the first hour of darkness, the raiders hauled their animals and equipment to Cerro Prieto, unloaded, saddled their mounts and packed their mules, and struck out for La Culebra. They advanced the first seven miles on a trail through heavy brush. The climb to the high Sierra began north of the hacienda at La Golondrina and for about five minutes they were given a good look at the whitewashed buildings in the floodlights a league away. The night was so still, they heard a snatch of the trumpet melody of the mariachis. They saw the bivouac of Kosterlinsky's soldiers and the picket line of their horses outside the light of the hacienda yard.

No one said anything, because the team had agreed to keep strict silence. They did not worry about what they might encounter, because they had rehearsed for every contingency. They moved on, moved fast, and were ready to fight. Every man and animal felt good. Kane listened to the team for a wayward sound as it pressed on and heard none at all. All any of the raiders could hear was the breathing of his own animals, the nearest creak of leather and brush of canvas, and the nearest footfall. Every animal was so surefooted that a rock seldom rolled. The stars gave Kane all the light he needed to stay close to Che Che.

Gato acted no less sure of his step in the dark than he did in daylight, and he was strong, agile, and intensely alert, as though he knew the high stakes involved in this nighttime race on new ground. The horse performed his best, but controlled and saved his effort and kept his poise in the dark. Anyone in the world, horseman or hiker, would have been able to tell that his heart was full with this job that Kane had given him to do.

The night was so dark that only other men on the prowl would give the raiders trouble. Kane felt sure that the nearest other combat patrol was probably in Iraq. Kosterlinsky's troop and the wolves of La Culebra would soon be asleep.

When the raiders topped the last pitch of climb to the high Sierra, Che Che stopped the string to let the animals blow and to scout Koster-linksy's usual campsite at La Brava Spring. He dismounted and walked the quarter mile to the spring to see if any soldiers or sentries from La Culebra were there. The night was so dark that Kane wondered how Che Che could find the spring without stumbling and searching blindly, but he knew the place well. He had camped there many times at the risk of discovery by Lupino's sentries.

Che Che never discriminated against any place or any landowner when he wanted to use a place to grow his crops. He had grown his marijuana many years in this high Sierra and in tributaries of Lupino's La Culebra ravine without discovery. Kane did not see him when he left to scout the spring and did not know when he returned until he laid a hand on Kane's knee.

Che Che found no sentries or soldiers at La Brava that night. Now the raiders would have no way of neutralizing the sentries until they came to the fireworks of the raid. Maybe the sentries would be lucky and sleep through the raid and live to be grandfathers.

The raiders were able to move at a high trot through the pines on top of La Culebra mountain. Pine forests in most of the Sierra Madre did not have underbrush. Underbrush and the lower limbs of the timber had been burned off and the trunk of every tree was bald all the way to the top. Only the tops of the trees had foliage and the peaks of the trees were not sharp like Christmas trees, but round. This was the result of the mauguechis that the people cleared for their crops during the spring, the windiest and driest time of the year. New ground was cleared every year. The brush that the people cut down was set on fire and the wind carried the fire through all the underbrush it could find and burned the lower limbs off the trees. Fire left the ground bare and the trees bald on their trunks but crowned with heavy foliage.

So on the trail through that forest the raiders hit a high trot with no brush to impede them. The deep soil cushioned and muffled the footfalls of the animals. No saddle or load loosened, no rider voiced a sound.

The raiders stopped on the brink of the ravine above the build-ings at La Culebra. Kane stayed on his horse, but everybody else dis-mounted and tied their reins around their mounts' necks. Che Che tied

Colorado's lead rope to the tail of Kane's pack mule. Every other man tied his animals head to tail into the string in the order of march, then the team unloaded weapons and ammunition and carried them to the edge of the ravine. Billy carried his grenades and M-79 launcher to the place where he would begin to lob them into the poppy field. Kane led the string away from the ravine and off the trail. He dismounted and tied his pack mule to Gato's tail, tied Gato to a tree, and moved close to the trail to stand guard.

The reflection of the stars on light clothing showed him a man on the trail only ten yards away. The man's figure was so dark and quiet that Kane only became aware of him because he bobbed up and down, as though he squatted to see the outline of Kane's comrades on the skyline. When that did not work, he stood up straight again. He must have arrived only a moment after Kane dismounted. The sounds of his own movements must have covered the sounds that Kane had made. Three or four more steps and Kane would have bumped heads with him. Kane was not even sure the man was unaware of him. He could only be sure the man could not see him. Not even a cat could see him. Not even an owl.

Kane waited. If his partners fired their weapons before this sentry did, Kane would shoot the sentry. If the sentry discovered Kane's partners before the shooting began, Kane would have to shut him down quietly. The sentry would be the one to make the call, but he, or Kane, was about to die.

The man moved past Kane toward Kane's partners. Kane drew the colmillo. The fine blade sang a little ringing *snick* when it cleared the sheath. The man stopped and Kane wrapped his arm around his mouth from behind and cut his throat. The man's legs jerked and his feet and hands flopped, his rifle barrel banged against the side of Kane's head, his head came unhinged under Kane's arm, blood splashed on the ground, and he died. The dead weight of his body dropped out of Kane's grasp but continued to writhe and thrash. Kane dragged the carcass off the trail by the collar and went back to see if the high smell of the sentry's blood disturbed the animals. They stamped in place but kept their poise. Kane's hat remained in place.

The whole canyon lit up as Che Che's lantern illumined the bunkhouse target for the gunners. When the rockets fired up to leave, they singed ten square yards of brush and rock on the ground behind the launchers and left it smoking. Kane thought that the sound the first two rockets made as they left their launchers probably caused someone in the canyon to awaken and ask, "What's that?" He had been careful not to look into the backflash, because he did not want his night vision impaired, but now he had to look. The white light of the phosphorous explosions in the bunkhouse blanked out the frames of the windows. The windshields of the helicopter and the Twin Beach aircraft on the strip seemed to widen and stare into the light. They would be the next target for the rockets.

Kane looked away from his comrades. He was there to watch their backs. He heard people in the canyon bawl and scream. Two more rockets exploded on target, then two more exploded, another two, and one more. Both aircraft exploded off Kane's left shoulder and he saw the helicopter collapse around a ball of fire. The AK-47s began to pop in disciplined bursts of three, and Kane knew that his partners were satisfied with the work the rockets had done. They had carried plenty of extras in case the first ones missed.

The second sentry came over the last ridge on the trail at a run. Kane still held his knife in his hand. His rifle was slung over his shoulder. The sentry ran past him. Kane swung the rifle into its place, squeezed a burst into the sentry's back, and knocked him down. The sentry tried to crawl. Kane put another burst of three into his head, then sheathed the knife.

The buildings began to erupt with explosions of armament and fuel. Alarmed, the string of horses and mules wound behind Gato like a big snake and their wide eyes shone sightless with the light, but they did not panic. Kane walked in among them and talked to them.

The people in the canyon screamed and wailed in their hell but did not shoot back. Kane looked over the heads of his partners at the ruined buildings. The whole floor of the box canyon was on fire. Even the rocks seemed to burn. The ruined warehouse disintegrated with the explosions of fuel and ammunition it contained. The opium gum turned into a soft, running coal on the warehouse floor that gushed a multicolored fire and gave off a pleasant smell. Kane could not see one living person in the solid acre of fire where the buildings had been. Debris from the explosions flew sky high but did not reach the horses. Half the poppy field was already in flame from Billy's grenades.

Kane mounted his horse and led the string to his partners. They loaded their weapons and mounted, and Kane led them, still tied head to tail, to catch up to Billy. His throat began to constrict, and he knew his old heart announced that this much excitement might be too much for it, but he could not listen.

Kane sat his horse while the team unloaded more M-79 grenades and helped Billy fire the last of the poppies. He heard three distinct shots of rifle fire from the canyon that seemed directed at the nest where the RPG-7s had been set up. When the last square foot of poppies caught fire, the partners loosed their animals in the string, mounted, and headed for home with everybody in correct order of march.

As Che Che topped the last ridge to lead the string out of sight of the canyon, Kane turned for a last look at the hell of La Culebra. At that moment something startled his pack mule and he lunged forward and smashed Kane in the ribs with his head. Kane's right kidney and ribs felt pierced by an arrow. He grabbed Gato's mane to keep from falling off and slumped over his saddle horn in pain.

"Somebody's shooting at us," Martinillo shouted. "I'm going back."

Kane wanted to tell him to ignore it, but the pain overcame him. As he topped the ridge, he looked back and saw Martinillo fire bursts into the canyon from his seat on Paseador. He thought, *My compadre Martinillo is a valiant man and so can't help but make a valiant picture.* Martinillo lowered his rifle, turned Paseador toward home, and ran to catch up with the string. Kane could not see his face but would have bet a new hat that he smiled.

Fifteen minutes later they left the light of the burning canyon behind. The constriction enveloped Kane's jaws and ears and the pain in his right side did not recede, but he enjoyed a great sense of victory, much as he had enjoyed the victory of a hard, ten-round fight as a boxer. A man could get the heart almost beaten out of him for ten rounds, be beaten until even his psyche became one big bruise, but if the referee raised his hand in victory after the decision, or if he stopped his opponent in a late round, he totally disregarded the bruises and cuts. However, if his opponent's hand was raised after the same kind of fight, a man felt so beaten he might lay down his carcass and not raise his head for a week.

In the pines Che Che hit a lope and as the mounts and pack animals of the raiders warmed to it, he broke into a run. In the darkness and on the soft, loamy trail of the pine forest, the run seemed as real as winged flight. Kane always bragged that cowboys flew and here was the proof. He did not have to rein or spur Gato. All he needed to do was think where he wanted to be and the horse put him there. The youngster had not made one false step, not one nervous twitch, not one start at something scary, and a lot happened that was scary. Gato did not know fear that night, and Kane did not let the pain in his side, chest, and left arm scare him, either.

Che Che pulled up to a full stop at La Brava, where the trail began its descent to the foot of the Sierra. Kane rode up beside him and looked down on the north slope below them and saw only blackness, but heard a tiny, rhythmic sound of metal against metal. He whispered to Che Che and handed him his pack mule. Che Che led the raiders away off the trail so Kane could listen without the sounds of the animals to bother him.

A moment later he heard the more audible, multi-*click-click* of Kosterlinsky's accoutrements as the troop climbed the final, steepest pitch of the trail. The explosions at La Culebra had probably been heard as far away as Guazaremos, maybe even as far as El Trigo. They had surely been heard at La Golondrina and here came Kosterlinsky. The raiders could hide and let him go by, but Kane decided he did not want him alive on their back trail.

The raiders tied their animals off the trail and Kane told Che Che to hide near the place where the troop would reach the top of the climb. He sent Martinillo to hide fifty yards up the trail. Then he, Joe, and Billy took cover on the stretch between Che Che and Martinillo.

Kosterlinsky did not let his horses stop to blow when he topped the climb, but spurred on toward La Culebra. When all the troopers made it over the top and Che Che stood up behind them, Kane stepped out into the open and shouted, "*Alto*, cabrones!"

At the sound of his voice, Che Che and Martinillo turned on their lanterns, blinded the troop front and rear, and stopped it. Not one trooper carried his rifle at the ready.

Kosterlinsky drew his pistol. The man behind him spurred his horse and jerked his rifle out of its scabbard. Kane fired two bursts into the man and his horse. The horse flipped over backward and crushed his rider beneath the saddle when he landed. Kane targeted the horse, because he could not let him get away and cause the twenty-five-man troop to scatter. Kane and the four other raiders did not have the fire-power to stop them.

The sight of their comrade and his horse dead in their path froze Kosterlinsky and his troopers in place. Blood poured from the heads of the horse and rider. Kosterlinsky dropped his pistol so that it dangled on its lanyard and raised his hands over his head.

Kane used the falsetto voice that the *mascaritas,* masqueraders, use in the streets of Mexico during Mardi Gras so Kosterlinsky would not recognize it. "That's one dead trooper to your discredit, Captain," Kane shrilled. "Now, throw your pistol on the ground and tell the live ones to dismount."

Kosterlinsky and his troopers complied. The troopers' eyes were opened as wide as they would go but could not see one thing outside the halogen light.

Kane ordered them to take off their boots and tie them to their sad-dles and to lead their horses back to the top of the trail and turn them loose. When they had done that, he ordered them to walk up the trail toward La Culebra and keep going. Martinillo and Che Che kept the light on them and followed them a half mile, then came back.

Billy picked up the dead trooper's rifle and Kosterlinsky's pistol and threw them off the mountain. The raiders mounted their horses and drove the troopers' horses down the trail ahead of them. Kane was sure that the troop had not seen one raider or his horse. Dull pain in his chest and the sharp one in his side made him short of breath, but could not dampen the good feeling that soon he and his partners would have accomplished their mission to the letter and be gone from the high Sierra.

Dawn caught the raiders in sight of La Golondrina. They drove the troop-ers' horses to the bottom of the mountain, passed them and left them behind, and galloped on toward Cerro Prieto and their trucks. As they neared the trucks, Martinillo shouted for everyone to stop. Kane passed the word and Che Che raised his arm and brought the string to a halt.

"Abdullah and Ibrahim are right behind us," Martinillo said when he had ridden up to the front of the string.

"How far back?" Kane asked.

"Not real close. They're not dumb. I don't think they want to catch us. They're probably only following us to see what they can see."

"Can we outrun them to Cerro Prieto, load, and be gone before they catch up?"

"I don't think so. They can wait until we load, then come up and take a good look at us."

"All right." Kane ordered Che Che to lead everyone but Martinillo away to the trucks and make the dust that the two hawks needed to see. Kane and Martinillo rode off the trail and hid their horses inside a deep wash that ran through a dense thicket. They dropped their hats in the sand of the wash where their horses would not step on them. They grinned at each other and donned their black hoods.

Martinillo pointed to a puff of dust that rose above the brush close by. Abdullah and Ibrahim came in sight around a bend only fifty yards away with their rifles in their hands.

Abdullah was in the lead. Kane could see by the look on his face that he thought that he better pull up. Then he saw Martinillo and jerked hard on his horse to stop him. Martinillo let go a burst of fire as Abdullah's horse reared. The burst sent the horse over on his back, but thick brush cushioned the old man's fall.

Kane fired a burst over Ibrahim's head and the man threw his rifle on the ground, turned his horse's tail toward Kane, and left the country. Kane watched him race away as though the owls were after him, watched the dust mark his progress through the brush and guessed he would run all the way home. So much for the Lupino loyalty to Abdullah, the family's oldest retainer.

Kane kicked the rifle and saw that it was an M-16. He picked it up and dropped it in the brush to hide it from the road. He wanted to throw it farther off the trail, but the ribs that the mule had bashed were too stiff and sore.

Abdullah lay under his horse. The animal's blood poured out of its heart as it wallowed on the man in its death throes. The weight and bulk of the horse pressed the man deep into a tangle of brush. Blood from scratches and gouges of the spines and the hard wood of the thicket covered Abdullah's eyes, and he was too shocked to decide what to do. His rifle lay out of reach. Kane saw Martinillo check his rifle to see if he had a round in the chamber as he stepped purposefully toward Abdullah. Kane knew that he intended to walk up to the old man, look him in the eye, and kill him.

Kane stopped him and pushed him gently toward their horses. They mounted and galloped on to catch up with their partners. The trail widened enough for them to ride side by side. Martinillo galloped up beside Kane and looked at him. "*Lástima caballo,*" he said. "Too bad about the horse."

"Too bad I killed that trooper's horse too," Kane said.

"You know, compadre, at the exact moment he came in range, the minute he was able to see me, the old Arab's eyes locked with mine again, as I told you they did at La Culebra, just before he shot me."

"He's quite an old Arab," Kane said.

Kane rode in the pickup between Joe and Martinillo to Cibolibampo. He was the last of the three to step out of the truck. Martinillo held the door open for him, and when Kane walked by, he stopped him. "Where did all the blood come from, compadre?" he asked.

"What blood?" Kane asked.

"Your hip pocket is covered with blood." Martinillo lifted the back of Kane's jacket. "*Caray,* your shirt is sopping with blood."

"What's it from? Look and see, compadre," Kane said.

He looked back as Martinillo pulled his shirttail out of his belt and saw blood drops scatter on the ground. Martinillo helped Kane take off his jacket, shirt, and undershirt. The other raiders stopped unloading the horses and mules when they saw the bloody clothes. Martinillo found a small hole between Kane's ribs and kidney. "Who stuck you with an ice pick?" he asked.

"Nobody. The mule I was leading bashed me with his head," Kane said. "He must have had something sharp on his halter."

Che Che led up Kane's pack mule and no sharp object could be found on the halter.

"It looks like somebody stuck you," Martinillo said.

"Never mind," Kane said. "Let's throw hay to these animals and go to town for a steak and a beer."

Billy and Joe unloaded first-aid gear from Joe's mule to treat the wound. "It's deep," Billy said and powdered it with sulfa.

"I bet it's bled more inside than outside," Joe said.

Martinillo held up Kane's shirt so everybody could see the shirttail.

"Never mind," Kane said. "I'll give Oscar Vogel a look at it while you fools are getting drunk."

"I'll dunk the shirt and jacket in a bucket of cold water," Martinillo said. "Shall I throw the undershirt away?"

"Throw them all away," Kane said. "No, wait. I'll wear the jacket to town."

Martinillo searched the pockets of the shirt and pulled out a brand-new package of gum and a tiny jar. "You have some gum here, compadre," he said. "What's in this little jar?"

Kane held out his hand and Martinillo handed them over. "I forgot I had the gum. When did I have time for gum?" he said. He looked at the label on the jar and finally remembered Oscar Vogel's nitroglycerine for chest pain.

"What's in the little jar?" Martinillo asked again.

"Nitroglycerine tablets for his heart," Joe said in English.

"¿Cómo?" Martinillo asked.

"Only aspirin," Kane said. "I forgot I had it."

"Does the wound hurt?" Martinillo asked.

"Not much," Kane said.

"Liar," Martinillo said. "At least take an aspirin."

"I will. Let's unsaddle these animals and get going."

While the other raiders ate steak and drank beer that afternoon, Kane bathed and changed clothes in Alicia's empty house. He figured she had gone out for a card game or a visit to a relative. From Alicia's he went to Oscar Vogel's house and caught him home after his siesta. Oscar inserted a long needle beside the wound and removed several syringes full of blood, but this did not satisfy him. He told Kane that he would arrange for doctors at Tucson Hospital to insert a tube and use a pump to remove the blood. Kane said he would head for Tucson in the morning, thanked Oscar, and left his house. Outside, he said to himself, "Like hell, I will" and he went to join the raiders' party. However, the pain made him worry. Ibrahim had carried an M-16. The wound under Kane's ribs was about the right size for an M-16 bullet. What if he was carrying a slug somewhere in his gizzards?

Eighteen

⎯🌀⎯ Kane and Joe Brennan flew back to El Trigo at dawn the next morning. As Kane cut Little Buck's engine to descend toward the airstrip and soared close over the high pass of Las Parvas, they saw a pall of smoke on the horizon above La Golondrina. The phosphorous fires had spread.

The other raiders had left San Bernardo with the horses and mules at midnight so they could be at El Trigo by noon. Kane figured the raiders better make themselves available at El Trigo in case someone suspected them of the raid on La Culebra and came to look for them. El Trigo was straight south of La Golondrina, but the raiders had fled northwest.

Four of the raiders were at El Trigo and their animals had been turned out to pasture when Ibrahim Lupino showed up. Martinillo had gone home. Kane, Joe, Billy Buck, and Che Che were sitting on the veranda of the hacienda after a noon meal when they saw Ibrahim ride over the pass of El Trigo. Che Che opened the bars on the gate to the hacienda grounds for him. Kane stood and invited him to dismount and have coffee or a swallow of soyate or both. Che Che took his horse to the stable and unsaddled, fed, and watered him.

Ibrahim looked fifty pounds lighter than when Kane had last seen him at La Golondrina. Of course, the *very* last time he had seen him had been in the brush near Cerro Prieto the day before.

Ibrahim tiredly dragged his spurs across the cement of the veranda and Che Che's wife brought him coffee. While he sugared and stirred it, Kane contentedly studied his face. He was much disturbed. His mouth turned down at the corners and he dragged himself to a chair like a man in mourning. He moped, and this made Kane feel good.

"How goes the filmmaking?" Kane asked him. "Are you about finished?"

"Nooo," Ibrahim said. "They barely got started when a fire erupted in the high Sierra. We've had a terrible fire on our hands since early yesterday morning."

"I wondered about that. We saw the smoke, but didn't think the fire was close to La Golondrina."

"It's in the high Sierra."

"What's the problem? Don't your people clear new ground and burn the slag anymore? I didn't think a fire up there would find enough fuel to make that much smoke."

"This one destroyed a field of dry cornstalks that we needed as fodder for our horses, then spread to the buildings of a camp we have, *had*, at La Culebra. You know that camp?"

"I've never been to that part of La Golondrina," Kane lied, and he felt so good about it.

"Che Che must know that country. You've been to our camp at La Culebra, haven't you, Che Che?"

"Oooo, I've never been to that part of the high Sierra, either," Che Che said. "I have no business there and I've never been invited."

"We had a large camp down in a box canyon of La Culebra, but yesterday a fire took every stick of it and leveled every brick."

"Lástima," Che Che said. "A shame."

"Lástima," Kane said. "I know how you feel. Somebody burned down this hacienda of Vogel's five years ago, but that was arson. Someone started it with kerosene. How did the fire at La Culebra start?"

"We don't know. Maybe lightning. We don't think anyone's to blame."

"It's a terrible thing."

"Yes, well, that's why I rode over here. We need Che Che's oxen. You, Che Che, can you rent or sell us a yoke of oxen and a Fresno? We'll pay you well."

"What do you need them for?" Che Che asked. "I'm sure we can loan you the yoke, but it's not mine. The animals and Fresno belong to El Trigo hacienda."

"We need to widen some pools alongside La Culebra River. We have to move a lot of earth, and we can only get in there with oxen and a Fresno."

"You can have our oxen and Fresno for as long as you need them, but we can't charge you for them," Kane said.

"I can start out for La Golondrina with the oxen tomorrow, if you wish," Che Che said.

"Thank you. When the fire destroyed our buildings at La Culebra, we realized that we need to install a better water supply, and we want to rebuild as soon as possible. If you'll drive the oxen as far as La Golondrina, we'll take them on to La Culebra."

"That will be no trouble at all, though I've never been to La Golondrina, either," Che Che said.

"Can you bring them tomorrow?"

"I can start tomorrow, but I can't get there for at least three days, because I'll have to drag the Fresno."

"That will have to do, I guess."

"Don Ibrahim, my wife will attend to your place to sleep out here on the veranda with my nino Jim and our guests," Che Che said.

"That's fine," Ibrahim said.

"Joe and I will go with you to La Golondrina tomorrow, if it's all right," Kane said to Ibrahim. "I have to see my compadre Vogel and maybe bring him back with me. We need to return to our cattle as soon as we can. The Brennans did not intend to stay indefinitely, so maybe Jack is ready to come back too."

"Of course."

"Anyway, I don't think Jack needs Vogel's help to make the movie. Jack can continue filming with Rafa, if he wants to, but I need Vogel back here."

"It will probably be best to suspend the filming for a while," Ibrahim said.

That night, after everybody settled into their beds on the veranda, Kane allowed himself to gloat. He would bet his horse Gato again that the Lupinos needed oxen and a Fresno to bury their dead. *In a hurry to enlarge some pools? Bullshit. Arab and Los Lobos carcasses were making a pestilence of their hidden paradise pasture.*

Kane, Joe, and Ibrahim started at four the next morning and arrived at La Golondrina at noon. This time nobody but the old kitchen retainer met them when they rode up to the front yard. Ibrahim invited them to dismount and went inside ahead of them. After a while he came out with Fatima. Her eyes and nose were red and wet with weeping.

Kane was surprised. He would never have believed that she seriously cared about anything that went on at La Culebra. He could believe that she might be mildly concerned over the loss of an opium crop, but how could the millionaire bawl about it? He would have bet a new hat that she knew nothing about the Arab and Los Lobos paramilitary school.

Kane gave her a token abrazo and asked why her eyes were red.

"Ay, Jim. Abdullah has been killed and we have a terrible fire at one of our camps," she said.

"My goodness," Kane said mildly. "Ibrahim told us about the fire and we see the smoke, but nothing about Abdullah. How did he die? Ibrahim didn't tell us that anyone had been hurt in the fire."

"No, Jim. *Vandals* destroyed our buildings and corn warehouses at La Culebra, and when Ibrahim and Abdullah pursued them, they killed Abdullah. Abdullah is my other father. I love him as much as I do Nesib. He's so wise, so good to me."

"The loss of the buildings and crop is a *terrible* blow," Kane said with a straight face. "However, you can recoup the property. But our friend Abdullah was the only one of his kind."

"You don't understand. Our *security* has been violated. The property losses are nothing compared to the loss of our security. The fire was caused by an attack by enemies we knew nothing about. It means that the drug traffickers have finally singled us out as their enemy in this war that has affected so many other people in the Sierra. One of our own has been murdered. Explosives were used. Everything—crops, fields, buildings, and other expensive property were leveled by vandals, no, *terrorists.*"

"And only Abdullah was killed?"

"Didn't Ibrahim tell you anything? The terrorists also attacked Koster-linsky's cavalry and killed some troopers."

"Was Kosterlinsky hurt?"

"He and most of his troop escaped, but their horses were driven away and they even lost their guns." Fatima spoke in English so that Joe could understand and she could have his sympathy too.

Joe went with Ibrahim to look for Jack and Kane sat with Fatima on the veranda. He gave her all the sympathy he could simulate with a cold heart. The woman wailed out the story for him, and that only cooled his heart more and gave him more to gloat about.

"Where are your other sons?" he asked.

"Rafa and Jacobo are here. They went up to La Culebra to see what could be salvaged, but returned to report that we have nothing left."

"Who first told you that you had a fire?"

"Ibrahim."

"Maybe I should go up there and look around and see what I can find out about those terrorists. They might hit El Trigo next."

"Oh, no, there's nothing you can do," she said quickly. She must have felt that she had overdone her wrangle for sympathy, because she stood up. "You better come inside, my father will want to see you."

Fatima led Kane to Lupino's study. Kane had never been invited there. Thick curtains were drawn closed over the windows. The room with its thick adobe walls was as dark as any room could be at midday.

Lupino sat at a large desk. His chair was large, soft, and roomy, and he had let himself sink way down inside it. He looked mashed into the chair for good, but Kane found that he was not overjoyed to see it. He was sorry to hear that Abdullah had died, but how could the Lupinos know that? He had been alive when Ibrahim turned coward and ran away. He was alive the last time Kane saw him. Kane would believe the tough old Arab was dead when he saw his ten-day-old corpse, and not before. He was not happy to see that Lupino seemed to be in total decline, either. He had always respected the man, and still did.

After Kane sat down by the desk, the old man said, "Look how you found us, Jim. What do you think? Have they told you what happened? We're ruined."

"I'm sorry about Abdullah, don Nesib," Kane said. "We all loved him. He's been my friend for fifty years. Where's his body? Have you held his wake yet?"

"Ah, no, he was killed down in the brush this side of Cerro Prieto. With all the devastation caused by the terrorists, we have not had the time or the resources to bring back his body."

"Are you sure he's dead? You're not so devastated that you can't go find him and bring him home, are you? How can you allow worry over loss of property to keep you from bringing your old friend home? Fatima told me that no one but Abdullah was injured, no one burned in the fire. Sure, you lost some corn, but you can grow more. You're rich enough to buy all the corn in the Sierra, if you want. You would never miss the money. Be sorrowful for the loss of your old friend, as we all are, but you're not ruined. Where is Abdullah's body? Vogel and I will go get him."

"You don't understand." Lupino moaned like a spook in the darkness of his corner. Kane would have expected the man to be much more formidable when faced with disaster.

"The financial loss is terrible, but the worst part is that wicked people singled us out for attack," Lupino said. "In the nearly seventy years since I first settled here, no one ever attacked me. When I came here, President Plutarco Elías Calles was still at war with the Yaquis, but no one bothered me. Apache renegades were still a danger but caused me no trouble. Juan Vogel's father and I lived and worked in these mountains alone on our ranches while murder and robbery happened everywhere else. La Golondrina has been an island of peace these seventy years, because we never took sides and no one who ever sought safe haven on this ranch was ever turned away."

Kane thought, *Yes, and in a minute your lying ass will rise up and shit out your lying head, you've got it stuffed up there so far.*

"We have always been an example of good neighborliness and friendship for everyone in the Sierra. Now look at us, Jim. Yesterday someone destroyed a whole season's crop of our . . . corn. Why? Are they trying to run us out as they have all the other decent families?"

"I know how you feel, don Nesib," Kane said. "How can I help you?"

"You know, Abdullah and Ibrahim saw the gang that attacked us. They followed them down to Cerro Prieto."

"Ibrahim didn't tell us. You know who attacked you?"

"They wore masks. Ibrahim only escaped with his life when he and Abdullah were ambushed."

"That was lucky for Ibrahim, but tell me everything that happened. How did Abdullah die?"

"Ibrahim was in the lead when they rode into a trap. The attackers waited until he passed, then killed Abdullah and his horse. Ibrahim went back to help him, but saw that he was dead. Luckily he was well mounted and able to flee on the wind, or the attackers would have killed him too."

"My goodness," Kane said.

"They killed Abdullah first to assure themselves that he would block the trail and prevent Ibrahim's escape, but my son broke through a thicket and flew away."

"*Gracias a Dios*," Kane said quite formally.

"Have you been offered coffee or a swallow of mezcal, something to eat?"

"Oh, no," Kane said. "We only rode down to see if my compadre Vogel is ready to return to Guazaremos. We need him there, and I don't imagine he is much use to Jack and Rafa. We'll go back today. Don't worry about us. And don't get up. I'll go and see what Vogel has to say."

Kane broke outside into the fresh air. A shout from Toribio at the front gate made him step back onto the veranda to see over the top of the cornfield. A bareheaded man had arrived at the hacienda afoot and was opening the bars of the gate under Toribio's lookout. He let the top three bars fall to the ground, stepped over the bottom two, and shambled on toward the house. Fatima came out and shielded her eyes against the sun to look at the man. Vogel came around the corner of the house and stopped beside Kane and shook his hand.

"Jack and Rafa are about finished with their production," Vogel said.

"It's Abdullah," Toribio shouted from his post. The hacienda came alive and Kane felt the same emotion that his enemies felt. He was glad to see Abdullah. Not only was he back, but still tough enough to have walked eleven miles uphill after being mashed into the brush by his horse.

Kane and Vogel walked down the trail to meet him. No one else at La Golondrina seemed to want to walk a little way to give him a hug and shake his hand, but the partners embraced him and escorted him to the house. He had washed the blood off his face, but his shirt was covered with dried blood. He had a two-inch gash on his forehead, other smaller scratches and scrapes on his face, and his hands were skinned, but he seemed to have no other wounds or injuries. He stopped to tell Fatima he was all right, but she did not come down from the veranda to receive him, so he went on to his quarters with Kane and Vogel. Inside, he dipped a cup of water out of his bucket and drank it all, then another.

Kane and Vogel stood by because they liked the old man, although they knew he was their enemy, even if he did not. Kane wanted to find out if he had recognized any of the raiders' horses during the pursuit on the trail to Cerro Prieto. The man was a horseman with the eyes of a hawk and might have recognized Gato and the mules Paseador and Negrito. Lupino had given Kane and Vogel those mules, but Abdullah had picked them out. After he quenched his thirst, Kane searched his eyes for a sign that he knew that Kane had been one of the raiders who unhorsed him.

The old man looked Kane in the eye and said, "Where is Ibrahim? Did he get back?"

"Yes, he thought you were dead," Kane said.

"Yes, he left me for dead."

"What happened?"

"We ran into an ambush, like fools. I saw a hooded man, and when he raised a gun toward me, I brought my horse to such a sudden stop with such a heavy hand that I pulled him over backward. The horse's tender mouth and light rein saved my life, because when he reared, he shielded me from a volley of bullets that the hooded men fired at me. The good horse El Morito took the shock of the bullets and gave his life for me."

"I remember that blue horse," Kane said. "He turned out well, didn't he?"

"A valiant servant, maybe, but it was his tender mouth and total response to the rein plus my fear and heavy hand that saved my life."

"Ibrahim didn't tell us any of this," Kane said to rub in Ibrahim's cowardice. "What did he do when your horse went down?"

"I think he ran and left me for dead, but I'll wait to hear his story. I would never have thought that Ibrahim, whom I helped raise, would run away like that. You and your compadre Vogel would not leave me in a situation like that, would you?"

"I don't know what you mean," Vogel said.

"Do you know what I'm talking about, Jim?"

"Ibrahim didn't tell us anything," Kane said.

"Then I'll tell you. I know that neither of you would do what Ibrahim did, and that has always made me happy about you, but it makes me sad about Ibrahim."

Kane thought, *Isn't that exactly what I did? I left the old man for dead too. How am I any better than Ibrahim? Well, maybe I'm a little better, because I took Martinillo away from there. He would surely have killed him in the next minute. It's a war. Maybe I'll even be sorry someday that I didn't let Martinillo have him.*

Kane and Vogel stepped outside Abdullah's stall to give him privacy as Rafa, Ibrahim, and Jacobo walked into the barn with Jack and Joe behind them. "We're finished with all of you," Rafa announced. "And by that I don't mean the filming of a movie. You, Kane, have five minutes to get yourself and your dogs off this ranch. Take wing. Fly. That means, *get*, or I will loose the dogs on you."

Kane looked to Jack for an explanation. Jack only raised both eyes to the sky and then gave Kane a look of warning. Ibrahim would not look at Kane, and Jacobo stared at him as though he were a stranger. Nesib and Fatima walked into the barn, and she gave Kane a sorrowful look. Kane and Vogel moved closer together. Jack and Joe came on to stand by them. The Lupinos lined up side by side to face them.

"It looks like the whole family's here to see us off," Kane said. "Where's Ali? Are you sure you don't want to wait for him to help you run us off? The five of you are sure not capable of the kind of dogfight it would take to chase us off this ranch. If we are dogs, you are too, and we're bigger ones than you."

"We learned by radio a few minutes ago that Ali is in the hospital in Tucson," Jacobo said. "We're sure you know the reason."

"Well, he's a busy doctor, I guess," Kane said. He sat on a pile of grain sacks. He only wanted to get back on the trail to Guazaremos now and let the devil finally have the Lupinos. The pain in his side had become a constant agony, and he wanted to get the hell home where he could lie down.

"He's a patient in his own hospital now," Jacobo said.

"He was attacked and crippled by your grandson," Fatima said in a high, strained voice. "Your miserable grandchildren are probably responsible for the ruin of his career as a surgeon. Your bully of a soldier grandson broke all his fingers and both his arms."

"That can't be," Kane said. "My grandson is confined to a sickbed in the Army hospital at Fort Huachuca, miles away from Ali. Wherever he is, he's too sick to cripple anybody."

Jacobo told the Lupino version of Cody Joe's attack on Ali as received on the radio. Ali had encountered Kane's grandchildren in a restaurant and offered to pay for their dinner. The girl had reviled his family, and then her brother had viciously attacked him.

"Juan Vogel, I don't want you to take offense in this," Nesib said. "We hold no rancor for you or your guests, the Brennans. You are welcome to return to La Golondrina any time you wish to come without Kane. But for now, you need to take Kane away from here. As the sire of the brute who sired the whore and the bully who crippled one of my grandsons and defaced and humiliated another, I hold him responsible for unpardonable injury to my family."

"That's fine," Vogel said. "We'll saddle our animals and be gone in a few minutes." He turned to help Kane rise from his seat on the grain sacks. Kane knew that Vogel had been watching him and could see that he had thrown his last bucketful of energy into this final journey to La Golondrina.

Rafa sauntered away and took hold of a pitchfork that was leaning against a stall. Kane knew that he better get back on his feet, but did not think he had the strength. He had left his fight on the long, long trail that had brought him to that moment at La Golondrina. He certainly knew himself to be the seventy-five-year-old man who in the foolishness of geezerhood had brought himself a long way to the wrong place at the wrong time. Then he saw Rafa turn toward him with the pitchfork and decided that he could get up one more time.

With Vogel's help he regained his feet as Rafa charged him with the pitchfork. As a marine, Kane had spent many hours in bayonet drill. He waited and batted the pitchfork behind the prongs with the back of his hand and it passed him by a yard. He brought the heel of his other hand in an uppercut to Rafa's chin, but the big, young bulk of the man fell on Kane and draped him over the grain sacks. Rafa raised up and straddled him with the pitchfork in both hands. Both Kane's arms were pinned at his sides under Rafa's knees. Rafa raised the pitchfork overhead. Kane knew that he would not be able to deflect the next heavy, downward thrust, so he was a goner.

"Enough of this," Vogel roared. He took hold of the pitchfork, jerked Rafa down on his back, stomped on his chest, twisted the pitchfork out of his hands, and threw it aside. Rafa squealed with the strain on his doubled knees. Vogel lifted his foot and let him go. Rafa rolled off the sacks one way, and Kane wallowed off another and stumbled to his feet. Rafa came at him again. Vogel grabbed at his head as he went by and missed. Fatima stepped in with her hands up and shouted, "No, Rafa!" as Kane shoved her out of Rafa's path. The tiny woman flew away like a leaf. Rafa tripped on the edge of a grain sack and fell, stunned, at Kane's feet. Kane drew the colmillo, but he looked toward Fatima before he used it.

Fatima was on her feet facing Kane. Nesib was standing behind her holding the pitchfork. The shiny tines were lined up vertically and sticking out of the right front of Fatima's clothing. Every movement in the room had stopped and everyone stared at her face. Nesib had picked up the pitchfork and Fatima had been impaled on it when she fell away from Kane. Nesib stepped back and jerked the tines out of his daughter's side. She looked at the colmillo in Kane's hand, then looked into his eyes. "He's my son, Jim," she said. Kane threw the knife down in front of her and she collapsed.

Nesib threw the pitchfork away and began to weep. Rafa slumped on the grain sacks, wept, and rubbed his eyes with his knuckles. Ibrahim, Abdullah, and Jacobo had clustered together and moved toward the door. When they saw Kane and Vogel go to Fatima's side, they recovered and carried her into Abdullah's stall and laid her on his cot. She revived and refused to let them examine her. Kane felt better when she ordered them to send Rafa to the main house for a maid. Three maids came and ordered the men out of the barn so they could examine her, because Abdullah's stall did not have a door on it. After a while, the oldest came out and told everyone that the pitchfork had laid four long, deep scratches on Fatima's side, but the bleeding had been easily stopped.

Kane and Vogel went in to see her. She would not look at Kane, so he went out to saddle his horse. Abdullah came up to him with the colmillo. "Here, Jim. Take your knife," he said.

"Since I've had that extra tooth, I've discovered secrets about myself I don't like," Kane said.

"I understand."

"Leave these people and come with us, friend."

"No, I have the responsibility of the small Abdullah, my namesake. He's not mine, but he carries my name and I have no one else to do that."

"Then, if you stay with these people, I hope I never see you again."

Abdullah's eyes went cold. He stepped back, looked Kane in the eye, and buried the blade in the ground at Kane's feet.

Kane picked it up, sheathed it, and walked back to his horse.

An hour later Kane and Vogel and the Brennans stopped on La Golondrina Pass to let their animals blow and turned for a last look at the hacienda. Vogel did not often wave to people, but Kane liked to wave good-bye when he left a place. Toribio the one-armed watchman had always returned his wave, but this time he did not, so he turned his back and rode to catch up to Vogel. He and Vogel were in the lead and the trail was wide enough for them to ride side by side.

Right then a mocking bird sang her heart out nearby. Kane looked up and found him in a cottonwood tree. He smiled and murmured to himself, "Da boids in da trees."

"You're talking to yourself, old man," Vogel said. "Now, tell me what happened at La Culebra. I want to know everything."

Kane grinned at him, but had a tear in his eye. Ignoring Vogel's request, he said, "When Adelita was learning English, she became fascinated by the different American accents. She liked to mimic the ways that Americans from the eastern states talked. She loved to say, 'Ah, tis spring. Da boids are choiping and da woims are sticking der little noggins outta da doit.'" Kane then said it in correct English for Vogel, who had not understood one word, then he tried to make him understand by translating it into Spanish, then gave up and said, "The way she said it made my heart roll over. I loved it when she tried to speak English in a New York or New Jersey or Texas accent. Her Mexican accent always ruled whatever she said, and she laughed a lot about it. That made me happy and she knew it."

Vogel's face looked blank, but he smiled anyway.

"When I heard the mockingbird in the tree, I thought of Adelita, that's all," Kane said.

"That's a good thought," Vogel said.

"I think I need to see a doctor," Kane said.